SCIPIO RULES

BOOK FIVE OF THE
SCIPIO AFRICANUS SAGA

MARTIN TESSMER
Copyright © 2017

Dedication

To all my readers.

Thanks for pursuing Scipio's quest with me

ACKNOWLEDGMENTS

Among 20th and 21st century historians, I am primarily indebted to Professor Richard Gabriel for his informative and readable *Scipio Africanus: Rome's Greatest General*, and his *Ancient Arms and Armies of Antiquity*. H. Liddell Hart's *Scipio Africanus: Greater Than Napoleon* provided many valuable insights into Scipio the general and Scipio the man. Thanks to you both.

Among classic historians, I owe a deep debt of gratitude to Titus Livius (Livy) for *Hannibal's War: Books 31-45* (translated by Henry Bettenson) and Polybius for *The Histories* (translated by Robin Waterfield). Cassius Dio's *Roman History* provided additional details and confirmed some of Livy's and Polybius' assertions. Appian, Dodge, Scullard, and Mommsen, thanks to you all for the many tidbits your works provided.

Cato the Elder's *De Agri Cultura* and Plutarch's *Roman Lives* provided insight into Cato, the man who so influenced the course of Western History.

I must give a tip of the hat to Wikipedia. Wikimedia, and the scores of websites about the people and countries of 200 BCE. The Total War Center and Forum Romanum were excellent sources of information, commentary, and argument.

Susan Sernau provided invaluable copy editing. James Millington's assiduous proofreading lent a final polish to the manuscript. Thanks to you both.

Credits

- Cover design by pro_ebookcovers at Fiverr.com

- Roman Women at the Baths, provided by Wikimedia Commons courtesy of Lawrence Alma Tademadema.

- Antiochus III photo provided by Wikimedia Commons, courtesy of Carole Raddato

- Philip V photo provided by Wikimedia Commons, courtesy of World Imaging

- Scipio Africanus photo provided by Bode Museum.

- Amelia Tertia image provided by Wikimedia Commons, courtesy of the Promptuarii Iconum Insigniorum

- War Chariot image provided by Wikimedia Commons, courtesy of Clare

- Cato the Elder mage provided by Wikimedia Commons, courtesy of Carlo Brogi

- Hannibal Barca image provided by Wikimedia Commons, courtesy of Carole Raddato

- War Elephant image provided by Wikimedia Commons, courtesy of Helene Guerber

- Macedonian Phalanx image provided by Wikimedia Commons

- Gladiatrices photo provided by Wikimedia Commons, courtesy of Carole Raddato

- Gallic Chieftains image provided by Wikimedia Commons, courtesy of William Warde

- Thracian Peltast image provided by Wikimedia Commons, courtesy of Dariusz T. Wielec

- Cover photo by Andreas Praefcke, courtesy of Wikimedia Commons

A Note About Historical Accuracy

Scipio Rules is a dramatization of the events surrounding Publius Cornelius Scipio's military and political activities after his conquest of Carthage, as recorded by Livy, Polybius, Gabriel, Appian, Mommsen, Bagnall, and Beard.

This is a work of historical fiction. It is a story that weaves together elements of fiction and historical record. It is not a history textbook.

The book's major characters, places, events, battles, and timelines are matters of record, meaning they are noted by at least one of our acknowledged historians. You will see footnotes scattered throughout the text to document various aspects of the book. I have included several quotes of the character's actual words, as described by Livy and Polybius, with a source footnote at the end of the quote.

The Hellenic Party and Latin Party names were created to capture the recorded enmities between the faction favoring a more "decadent" Hellenic lifestyle and the agrarian traditionalists who disparaged them. Scipio and Cato were two notable examples of Hellenic and Latin attitudes, respectively.

"...Even before Scipio came back from Africa the question was, would the conqueror of Hannibal raise any constitutional issues and how would he meet the challenges of the hostile faction that had been intriguing against him during his absence."

Howard H. Scullard, *Scipio Africanus: Soldier and Politician*. Ithaca, NY: Cornell University Press, 1970.

"In trying to determine the place of Scipio Africanus in the military history of the West, one cannot ignore Basil Liddell-Hart's claim that Scipio was the greatest military commander in all antiquity, exceeding in military skill and ingenuity such luminaries as Hannibal, Caesar, and Alexander the Great.

For more than a decade after Scipio returned from Africa in 201 BCE, he was the "first man in Rome," the state's most famous and influential person. Although he did not win every political battle in which he became involved...Scipio was an important political player in all the major Roman policy decisions, and had some share in every important movement or event."

Richard Gabriel. *Scipio Africanus, Rome's Greatest General.* Washington, DC: Potomac Books, Inc. 2008.

TABLE OF CONTENTS

**Theater of Operations
201-194 BCE**

**Italia Theater
201-194 BCE**

North African and Iberian Theaters
201-194 BCE

**Macedonian and Seleucid Theaters
201-194 BCE**

Scipio Africanus

Cato the Elder

I. Three Wars Blooming

ROME, 201 BCE. "You think this is his blood?" Scipio asks, scraping the rim of the battered infantry helmet. "I don't want to remove it if it's his."

"Oh my gods, you fuss like an old woman! Here, let me see." Laelius grabs the helmet by its cheekpieces and turns it about, peering at the reddish-brown blotches that line its battered crown.

"I think the blood's from Korbis, that Balearic monster," Scipio says. "Marcus took a spear in the back, and he fell forward into the earth. He wouldn't have bled onto the top of his helmet."

Laelius sniffs the dome. He wrinkles his nose. "Phew! This is gut blood! It must have come from that Korbis, when Marcus slid under him and cut open his bowels." Laelius' mouth tightens. "Just before Marcus died."

"Just before he died protecting *me*," Scipio adds. His eyes moisten. The sun-washed atrium is quiet as Lucius, Laelius, and Scipio mull the carnage of that dread day at Zama.

"Blood from bowels?" Lucius suddenly blurts. "Get that thing away from me!"

"Don't be so prissy, brother," Scipio says. "You'd think you'd never been in a war. Here, give it to me."

Cradling the helmet in his arms, Scipio plops down on one of the atrium couches that border the Scipio manse's fishpond. He scrubs the helmet with a linen scrap, rubbing into every dent and crevice. Sweat trickles from his salt-and-pepper hair.

Satisfied, Scipio pitches the scrap onto the stone tile floor. He lays the gleaming helmet next to him. "There. It is free from taint, as ever he was." Scipio runs his fingers across the helmet's dents, his eyes distant.

"What are you going to do with it?" asks Lucius. "It's just an old piece of armor."

"It's the helmet of Rome's greatest warrior," Scipio snaps. "I'm going to keep it right here." He glares at his brother. "Forever!"

Scipio holds the helmet up and peers inside it, as if looking for its wearer. "Marcus will be with us at every military meeting. When we haggle over some issue, we have only to see it to wonder, 'What would Marcus say about this?' and gain his sage counsel."

"I already know what he would say to me," replies Laelius, his green eyes twinkling. "He would say, 'Laelius, you make overmuch of a simple thing, just like the way you dress.'" His smile wanes. "Jupiter's cock, I never thought I'd miss that dour little ape."

"He was the best of all of us," Scipio murmurs. "He never wavered in battle, or in his morality. Were he born a patrician, he would have ruled Rome."

Laelius nods. "He would have been a great Tribune of the Plebs, too. Those of us from the gutters worshipped him: the native citizens, the freedmen, even the slaves."

"Why do we need to have meetings, anyway?" Lucius asks. "The war is over. You defeated Hannibal, and Carthage has capitulated. What's left to do?"

"He's right, Scipio." Laelius says. "What's to do? The Senate has ratified the peace agreement. Are you afraid Hannibal will rouse Carthage against us?"

Scipio shakes his head. "From what my spies tell me, Hannibal is too busy fighting his own enemies in their Senate! They'd never grant him another army."

He strokes the red horsehair plume on Marcus' helmet. "No, our meetings will be about new enemies. Rome's conquest has brought her to the world's attention. We are a threat to nations that overlooked us before." He shrugs. "But I make overmuch of that. War is not my concern anymore."

Laelius shoves him. "That's right, and don't forget it. You have saved Rome enough times. Now you can rest on the laurels of your victor's crown. No more working at night, studying old scrolls and maps."

"Oh, I'll keep doing that!" Scipio says with a smile. "I'm never less at leisure than when at leisure, or less alone than when alone." [i]

"You had best stay home regardless, or the Carthaginians will not be your worst worry!" says a taunting voice from the entrance.

Amelia walks into the sunny atrium of the Scipio domus, towing three-year-old Cornelia and two-year-old Publius. Scipio's wife wears a floor-length emerald gown, the thick cotton flowing over her prominent stomach. "For once you will be here for the birth of your child."

Laelius and Lucius chuckle. Scipio raises his eyebrows in mock surprise. "Well, I may be called away. The Gauls have been rambunctious, and that cagey old Philip, his Macedonians might—"

Amelia flips back her auburn hair and raises her chin, her green eyes shining. "This time I will take no excuses. You will be standing right next to me when I sit on the birthing chair!"

Scipio bows his head and taps his forehead. "I hear and obey! I shall stray no farther from home than the nearest wine bar." He grins. "Or tavern."

Laelius throws up his hands. "I pray to Mars, you have just been elected Princeps Senatus,[ii] the first senator of Rome, yet you cannot rule your own home!"

"As the poets say, we must all serve somebody," Scipio replies. "My commander is certainly more beautiful than that new consul Publius Aelius. What is it they call him? 'Long nose'?"

"I have seen him. It is an appellation richly deserved," Laelius says, grinning. "He'd better watch out or the Gauls will chop it off when that pudgy old fluff is parading around up north, acting like a general."

"Well, at least Aelius picked a good time to campaign," Lucius says. "It's pretty quiet up there. He won't have to worry about a fight."

Scipio frowns at his brother. "I suppose avoiding conflict is desirable to some."

He stretches out upon the couch, watching the February rains pour down from the atrium's open roof, cascading into the marble-tiled impluvium in the center of the room. Two young slaves rush in and dip their pottery jugs into the pool, rushing off to fill the kitchen's cooking pots.

Scipio watches the boys fill their jugs. *By the gods, it has been ten years since I had the time to watch something this simple, without war plans buzzing about in my brain. I'd forgotten what it's like to pay full attention to nothing!*

Laelius notices Scipio's pensive expression. "Everything all right with you?"

Scipio stretches languorously. "Oh, everything is just fine—I guess. It's been two moons since I paraded through Rome, celebrating my triumph. The feasts and celebrations have finally died down, and I am no longer called to be at temple or Senate every night. I love the slower pace, but now I ask myself, 'What next?'"

Amelia hands her children to her slave nurse. She joins Scipio on his couch, toying with his tightly curled hair. "Now is the time for you to do something for the people, something that doesn't involve you going to war. You are the most famous man in Rome, Husband. The people adore you."

She digs her fingers into his curls. "You can do more good here than on a battlefield. Use your political power while you've still got it!"

"It's true," Laelius says. "Most of the Senate adores you." He shrugs.

4

"Then again, the rest hate your guts, especially the Latin Party! They think you'll turn us all into Greek-worshipping artists!"

Amelia glowers at Laelius. He sits down on a nearby couch, an ill-concealed smile on his face.

"I am saying you have power—more power than anyone in Rome," Amelia says. "You cannot waste your political capital by sitting idle."

"I have no intention of being idle. I can finally turn to tutoring, and scholarship. That's always been my dream, remember? You heard me say that thirty years ago, when I was but a child of six. I told it to our tutor Asclepius."

"There is time for that when you are old, Husband. Seize the day! You can set the future for Rome. You can build that public library you've been talking about, like that one in Alexandria." She pokes him. "That would be true scholarship, wouldn't it?"

"That would be a worthy pursuit," he says, nodding, "but I can't do it unless I'm a consul." He frowns. "Our stodgy laws say I can't run for ten more years, so I'd have to find another way to get it done."

Laelius snorts. "Consul! The two we've got can't find their ass with both hands! And they are out there trying to play general against the Gauls and Iberians. You should go help them. That's what you're good at. Use your genius to keep our children from becoming slaves."

"At least you have children," Lucius says, eyeing Cornelia and Publius.

Laelius pats Lucius on the back. "You will have dozens of them, I am sure. Enough that you'll regret ever having said that!"

Lucius eyes grow shiny. " I do not deserve children. Not after what I did at Orongis." [iii]

Scipio clasps his brother's shoulder. "Come on, you couldn't know there were children hiding under those shields. You did what any commander would do."

"Commit murder?" Lucius rasps, staring at his feet.

"Protect your men from being killed," Scipio says quietly. He hugs his brother. "You know, you should be the tutor and scholar in the family, not I. You have the sensitivity for it." *I should have never let him lead that Orongis mission, even with Marcus Silenus there to help him. I was a fool!*

Lucius glares at his brother. "You think I can't be a general? I have Father's blood in me, just like you. I can do anything you can!" He looks away. "I just need the chance," he mutters.

Scipio's face flushes. *Remember your promise to Mother. Help him make his way.* He takes a deep breath. "I am sure you will be a fine officer. I will help you get the opportunities I had. Now let me put Marcus to bed."

Scipio walks down the corridor to his and Amelia's sleeping room, cradling Marcus' helmet in his arms. He walks over to the stone shelf that looms above their sleeping platform and places the helmet in the middle of it, next to the thumb-worn figurine of Nike that Amelia gave him, flanked by his limestone statues of Mars and Minerva.

He shifts the helmet about. *There! It's perfectly straight. As Marcus would want,* Scipio thinks, smiling to himself. He taps the top of the helmet.

"Well, old friend, I may not need to consult you for a while. Peace is at last upon the land." He walks back to the entrance. He stops and turns back to the helmet.

"Do you think I should be out there helping consul Aelius? He is not a military man." Scipio stares at the helmet for several moments.

He shrugs. "Ah, I make too much of myself. Aelius has Italia's finest troops with him. He can handle a few fractious Gauls."

UMBRIA PROVINCE, NORTH ITALIA. "You want me to do what?" Gaius Campius splutters. The rangy Umbrian commander stomps around in front of consul Publius Aelius, his face reddening.

6

Three Wars Blooming

The plump little consul leans back into his padded tent couch. "You heard me. We need more food." He pops a chunk of roasted mouse into his mouth, staring placidly at the allied commander.

"You want me to use ten thousand of my veterans to gather grain and cattle?[iv] We came up here to fight!"

Campius pulls off his wolf's head cap and flings it onto the consul's thick carpet. "We don't need grain to get rid of the Boii, curse it! We can reach the Boii camp in three days. We could run them back over the Alps and go home!"

Publius Aelius stares coolly at the allied commander. "We will do that soon enough," he says, biting into an olive. "After all, it's part of my mission. Now that Scipio has vanquished Carthage, Rome has turned its eyes to Gaul. The Senate has designated the Po River Valley for Roman settlement. So I am here to, as you say, 'run them over the Alps.' But we need food for an extended campaign."

"Then you should have brought a legion of farmers with you," Campius grouses. "Umbrians are born to the sword. We want revenge on those raiders!"

Aelius closes his eyes. *Gods save me from Umbrians! Always wanting to prove they are as good as Romans.* "Yes, you are strong soldiers. As soldiers you take orders from your leader. You will harvest the fields, burn the land when you are done, and destroy any nearby towns that do not open their gates to you."

"What about the Boii's army?" Campius says. "Our scouts say they have twenty thousand men camped near Parma. They could come after us while we are working." He grips his dagger. "Let's go to Parma and destroy them. After that we can play farmer without danger. Jupiter's balls, then you can use Boii prisoners to do your slave work!"

Publius waves his hand. "Pish! The Boii are more interested in drinking and fornicating than fighting trained soldiers. They will be no trouble unless you attack them."

"If they're so untrained, why don't we go after them?" Campius

7

persists. "It would only take a day or two."

Aelius shakes his head. "That would only alarm the nearby Ligurians. They might rise up against us."

The consul smiles fatuously at the brawny Umbrian. "Look, I am meeting with the Ligurians' Inguani tribe. Let me make a treaty with them. That will keep them from attacking us. Then we can march on Parma. We'll take control of the entire Po Valley."

"And you will be accorded a triumph for it, eh?"

"You would benefit handsomely from such a conquest, too," Aelius says, picking a honey cake from his tray. "A quarter of the plunder would go to you and your men." Campius is silent.

He's as stubborn as a pig, Aelius thinks. "And you will get half the prisoners," he adds.

The Umbrian bites his lower lip. "I don't know. I still think you underestimate the Boii. They rampaged through northern Umbria, and overran the Roman garrison."

The consul pushes himself up from the couch, wiping the crumbs from his ample midriff. "Let me simplify the issue for you. The Latin Party wants Romans to own those lush growing fields here, and I intend to get them. And my triumph. And you will help me do that, or I'll get the Etruscans up here to replace you."

He grins deprecatingly. "I am not an unreasonable man. I'll lend you four cohorts of my best troops.[v] I certainly won't need them for a peace mission with the Inguani."

"I will command your Romans?" Campius says.

"Yes, yes. I will order the tribunes to follow all your orders." Aelius rises to his full five feet and two inches. He points toward the tent flaps.

"You leave the day after tomorrow. I suggest you make preparations."

The allied commander nods silently. He spins on his heel and stalks out the tent's exit flap. Aelius waves his slave over and plucks a roast canary from his tray. After one bite he flips the sesame-encrusted bird back onto the bronze platter. *That's the worst of being up here; camp cooks. Lousy mouse and worse canary. Should have brought my Nubian with me.*

The tent flap flies open. Campius steps inside. "Wait. Didn't those Ligurians fight with Carthage, as part of Hannibal's force?"

Aelius waves his hand dismissively. "Well, yes, several of their tribes joined Hannibal back then. But they've seen the futility of fighting Romans." He chuckles. "Gods above, Campius. Even these barbarians have heard about Scipio destroying Hannibal at Zama! My trip will be like a holiday in the mountains!"

"I certainly hope so, Consul," Campius replies uneasily. He raises his right hand, his fingers splayed out toward Aelius. "You will give me four Roman cohorts. Five thousand men, correct?"

"Good night, Commander," Aelius says, pointing to the exit.

Four days later Campius leads his army toward the town of Bononia, a garrison in the heart of Boii territory. Riding on his black war horse, Campius guides his Roman and allied columns through the Via Terrana, a twenty-foot roadway through the Po River valley.

As he jounces along the path, the Umbrian commander scans the horizon for enemy riders. *This road will be a lot more negotiable when we get some gravel on it. Maybe we'll capture enough Boii to do that, too.*

Fields of tall green wheat undulate into the distance on either side of the road, contrasting sharply with the smoldering wake of burned fields and rubbled towns that lie behind Campius' plundering legions. The Umbrians at the rear of the mile-long army train hasten their pace, anxious to escape the faint wailings from the wrecked town just behind them.

Campius chuckles. *Well, that gasbag Aelius was right. We have met with little serious resistance.* He looks back at the lines of stern legionnaires, their packs dangling from the tent poles slung over their shoulders. *Who could blame the Boii for hiding from us? We are their equals in numbers, and their superiors in battle.*

He grins to himself. *Perhaps I should just march on to Parma and take it myself. It's only two days out. Old Fatty can kiss my ass.*

Eighty miles to the northwest of Campius' army, Consul Aelius guides his two legions over a high mountain pass heading for the Inguani's encampment on the Alps' high plains.

Trotting along in the midst of his troops, the patrician general studies the cloud-clawing peaks that surround him, watching the wispy white clouds waft across their snow-cloaked pinnacles. He pulls his blood-red cape over his shoulders. *This would be beautiful if it weren't so miserably cold. No wonder Rome was in no hurry to settle this area. And I'm not staying up here to do it!*

A tribune rides up to Aelius. "General, look above you. Over to the right."

Aelius stares into the sun-dazzled crags. "What is it, Tiberius? Is another Ibex up there? They are magnificent beasts, don't you think?"

The tribune's mouth tightens into a line. *Patricians! Are you as blind as you are fat?* He pulls out his sword and points above his commander's head. "Up by that scraggly juniper."

Aelius cranes his neck. There, on a flat expanse of rock, a dozen Inguani warriors gaze down at him, their matted chests bared to the sharp, cutting winds.

A huge warrior steps out from the group. His gold neck rings glimmer brightly beneath his wild white beard. The bearlike man plants his feet at the edge of the precipice and stares down into Aelius' face.

Hope he doesn't spit on me, is all Aelius can think. He pulls his horse sideways, away from the looming barbarian.

The man raises a wrist-thick spear above his head and pumps it three times. His men follow his gesture. The barbarians resume their silent stance, watching the Roman train tramp past them.

Aelius scratches his oiled head. *What is that about? Do they want an answer?* He pulls out his sword and waves it thrice above his head. The Ligurians continue to stand still as statues.

Aelius shrugs. He rides on, looking over his shoulder at the motionless warriors. *Was that some type of Ligurian welcome? Hope so—this would be a nasty place for a fight!*

The little army tops the pass and wends its way down a narrow switch back trail to the valley floor. The clouds disappear and the late afternoon blazes down, glinting off the army's domed helmets. The army turns into a shimmering bronze snake, undulating its way down the snow-dappled slopes, its body rippling with every unisoned step.

Dusk arrives as the Roman van enters the mountain-ringed plain that sweeps out below them. In the distance, the town-sized Inguani camp sprawls in front of them. Hundreds of cooking fires stream upward from the camp's tents and wagons.

Charon take me, Aelius thinks. *This place is immense! How many men did their chief bring here?*

Following Roman custom, the army pitches camp close to water but far from any concealing trees, leaving an open line of sight in every direction.

The antlike marching army turns into a hive of bees. The legionnaires immediately start raising tents and harvesting trees for their palisade. Scores of soldiers dig a trench around the camp perimeter, while dozens under punishment plow out a latrine trench. The men swarm to finish their tasks, eager to pull out their porridge pots and cook dinner.

Aelius supervises the camp construction from atop his short gray mare. He rides about the center of camp. "Get my tent up first!" he yells to a tribune.

While his house sized tent is raised, Aelius dismounts and strolls out to the front of camp, his aide Tiberius following him. He passes a score of sweaty legionnaires who are erecting the palisade walls, unaware of their derisive glances.

The consul halts in alarm. In the distance, he sees a long line of tall warriors standing between him and the barbarian camp, thick-bodied men with bared axes and longswords. The white-bearded warrior is there, mounted on a white mare the size of a small elephant.

That must be Ambrix, their chief, Aelius thinks. *Why doesn't he come in and welcome me?*

Aelius looks nervously about him. "Tiberius, get me a turma of our equites. Quickly"

"Now?" Tiberius says. "Apologies, General, but what will you do with thirty-two cavalry?"

"I want them about me," Aelius replies peevishly. "They don't have to *do* anything but be here to protect me!"

The tribune is silent for several moments. He looks at the thousands of soldiers working around Aelius. *You need more security?* He stifles a sigh. "As you say, General."

Ambrix observes the Romans bustling about the plain, each one moving to complete his assigned task. *If we were going to attack them, this would be the time. Get them before they finish their camp. Forget about the treaty.*

The old chief's mouth pinches with distaste—and anxiety. *Those Romans work like demons, even after marching all day through the mountains! I bet those little bastards could fight from morning to night.*

He studies his own men. Most have plopped down to drink wine and watch the Romans. "Look at them, they run about like ants!" comments a burly warrior, scratching underneath his deerskin eye patch.

"Ha! Ants would at least stop to feed," chortles another. "Those runts are going to work until they drop in their tracks!"

Ambrix shakes his head. *The Roman leader is a sow, but his men are fit and organized. If we did not take his men in the first hours of battle, who knows what could happen?* He looks back at his camp. *If we lose too many men, the Cenomani could finally take us. Take our lands.*

He hears shouting behind him and turns. Two of his men grapple and roll about, engaging in a drunken wrestling match. The others blearily cheer them on, oblivious to the bustling Romans.

Ambrix sighs. *Oh, ox shit!*

"Osgar, get over here!" he bellows over his shoulder. A wiry young man trots up to Ambrix, shoving a stopper into his wineskin.

"What is it, Father?"

"You and I are going to the Roman camp tomorrow. But you are not coming back with me."

"What?"

"You will remain with them for now, as a hostage. It will demonstrate our sincerity in making peace with them."

"Peace? But last night you said we could…"

"I know what I said," Ambrix mutters angrily. "And I know what I must do. These crazy Romans, they will not be driven off. Ever. Go back to camp and tell your wife you will be gone."

The chief watches Osgar stalk away. *At least I will give them the worst of my lot. He talks too much.*

Two days later, Aelius leads his men back over the pass, heading east toward Parma. He carries a newly signed treaty in his saddle bag. A morose Osgar rides next to him, embarrassed at being devoid of any weaponry. Aelius glances at his captive and smiles. Osgar looks away.

Well, Ambrix proved to be a gracious host, after all. He raises his chin and smiles. *I'd wager he didn't want to get in a battle with me!*

Three Wars Blooming

"This is a disgrace," Osgar growls. "Kill me now."

"Oh cheer up, boy. You will be treated with the finest food and wine from my provisions."

Osgar spits onto the space between their two horses. "You had best pray to your gods you do not face me when I am chief," the young man growls. "I will be sacking Rome while my men sodomize you in front of me."

Aelius laughs. "You rabble did that once to our city, when we were but a group of farmers. But now we are much more organized. Soon we will rule the world!"

"And then your men will grow soft and fat." The Ligurian's eyes roll over Aelius' body. "Apparently it has already started."

"Do not be disrespectful, savage. I can have you on a cross by nightfall!" Aelius snaps, his face reddening.

He trots away from the glowering youth, struggling to regain his composure. *Irreverent dog! But who cares? I struck a treaty with the Ligurians, wait until the Senate hears about that!*

The stout little consul looks at the lush grain fields below him. *I hope Campius has done well on his little trip—we'll need the bread. Hmm. I'd like some fresh bread for dinner, maybe some Pecorino to go with it, and a nice red Rioja from Iberia, and...*

Ten miles south of the Boii fortress at Mutilum, Campius is organizing his men for their final foraging expedition. The allies and Romans are camped near a tree-lined branch of the winding Sapis River, preparing the wheat they have ravaged from the nearby fields and farms. Campius is intent on harvesting enough grain to fulfill Aelius' order, so he can return to waging war on the Boii.

The Umbrian soldiers pitch their wicker winnowing baskets into the air, tossing wheat to let the wind blow away the chaff. The Roman cohorts stand guard on the perimeter, having finished installing the camp gates and palisades. Acres of chest-high wheat stalks stretch as far as the eye can see.

Campius stands outside the camp gates, watching his scouting party return from their explorations. The six horsemen pull to a stop upwind from Campius, careful to prevent their dust from blowing upon him. Campius can be unforgiving about little mistakes.

A slim young equite dismounts and approaches the commander, pulling off his red-plumed helmet. He pauses before him and raises his right arm, palm out.

Campius grudgingly returns the salute. "What news do you bring, Sextus?"

"We have searched the lower mountains, and we detect no enemy presence. The Boii must be sequestered in Mutinum[vi]. Or Parma."

Campius summons the Umbrian senior tribune and relays the scout's news. "Postus, we now have enough food for Aelius and me to lay siege to Mutinum for a year, if it comes to that. Let's gather the rest of the wheat from these rich fields before we go back. It'll be easier to starve the Boii out."

Or I can just destroy them myself, right now. The Romans have to follow me into battle. But my men are angry about doing all the slave work. I have to placate them somehow. He grins slyly. *I know just the thing!*

Campius points toward the fields. "Sextus, I want you to take two turma of cavalry and ride through those fields tomorrow. Make sure there are no barbarians in them."

"It will be done." Sextus remounts and trots his horse toward the rear of camp, heading for the horse pens.

Campius hurries back to his command tent. "Summon my officers," he tells his attendant. "Tell them to be here after the second watch ends. We have new duty assignments for tomorrow. And get Claudus over here."

Minutes later, a sturdy old tribune hobbles into the tent, his wooden foot clomping on the fresh-packed earth. Campius waves him toward one of his camp stools. "Sit down, old friend. I have good news to give you."

"Which is what?" Claudus asks skeptically, as he eases himself onto the stool. Claudus is a veteran of twenty years of wars, and he knows a commander's version of 'good news' is oft otherwise for soldiers.

Campius smiles. "Ah, you were ever a man to get to the point. I know our men have been complaining that they do all the field work while the Romans stand around like a bunch of armored statues. Well, no more of that. Tomorrow we put *them* to work, and our Umbrians will stand guard over them!"

Claudus wrinkles his potato-shaped nose. "That will silence our men's complaining, but the Romans will not like it."

"Who cares what they like? Aelius told them that they must follow my orders." He grins. "Now they'll know what it's like to be treated like socii, as if we allies were a class beneath them."

Claudus nods, warming to the idea. "I can't wait to see the Romans' faces when you tell them!"

The next morning finds the allies and Romans again working the fields, but in entirely different circumstances. Four thousand Umbrians stand in cohort formation by the fields' front borders, guarding the five thousand Romans who will go out and gather grain. Wearing only a tunic and sword, the legionnaires stomp out into the waiting fields, glaring at the gleeful Umbrian guards.

Campius summons Sextus and three more of his scouts. "I know you have seen no Boii, but those Gauls can be stealthy, for all their size. I want you to make sure it's safe before our men go out there.

The allied commander grabs a straight-stemmed horn from a scout's side pack. "You four will ride around the upper perimeter of the fields, two on each side. Take your tubas with you. Blow one long note if all is clear. Like this." He blows a solitary, extended note.

"If you do see any enemies, you are to blow three short notes. Keep patrolling above the fields until you see the men returning to camp."

"I hear and obey," Sextus replies. He hurries away, his three compatriots following. When they come to the front of the field, the scouts separate to the left and right, each pair taking one of the foothill trails that borders the acres of wheatfields.

Sextus trots along a tree-covered trace trail, scrutinizing the heady waves of grain. He carefully scrutinizes the dense carpets of green and yellow, but he does not notice any movement, or glint of metal.

"Do you see anything out there, Glaucus?" he says to his fellow. Glaucus only shakes his head. "Nothing but a few deer."

Sextus slides his four-foot tuba from its saddle sleeve. He blows one long, plaintive note. Seconds later, he hears a similar note coming from the other side of the valley. *All is well*, he decides.

Sextus snaps the rope reins on his horse. "Let's get over to the end of the fields." Minutes later, the two see the walls of Mutina in the distance.

"Look there," Glaucus says, pointing below him. The fields near Mutina have already been harvested.

"The Boii must have cut the stalks down last night, under cover of darkness." Sextus says.

"They're probably storing food for a siege," Glaucus replies. Sextus nods. "Well, we're at the end of the route. Nothing out there in but burned land. Let's go back and check the fields near camp."

He takes out his horn and blows a single note. He hears an answering note from the other side. Sextus rides halfway back toward camp, pausing to watch the rest of the foraging expedition as it heads out of camp.

The Romans march into the edges of the fields, their mules dragging along the grain wagons they will load. The allied legion follows them, four, thousand Umbrians who are grateful not be chopping wheat stalks all day.

The Romans spread out along the width of the field. They chop off the tops of the wheat stalks and throw them into the wagons that follow them, grumbling and cursing about their ignominious task. The Romans inch farther into the field, their backs bent to their work.

Riding the foothills trail, Sextus watches the Romans hack their way into the middle of the field. He looks back toward camp and notes the hills of wheat that pile there, ready to be winnowed and bagged when the stubbled fields are burned. *Gods, I hope I am on a scouting mission tomorrow, so I don't have to do all that slave work!*

He watches the tall plants waving in the wind, their heads bowed toward the harvesting Romans. Sextus notices that the plants are bending contrary to the wind's direction, as if crawling away from it.

"Come on, Glaucus, there's something strange down there." Sextus eases his horse down the side of the foothill, closer to the field. He spies the glint of a bronze helmet in the field, its top sheathed with stalks. His stomach churns with shock. *The Gauls didn't harvest the grain, they harvested the stalks!*

"They're hiding down there!" he shouts to Glaucus. Sextus grabs his tuba and blows a short blast, then another.

The tuba flies from Sextus' spasming hand. He gapes at the spearhead jutting out from his throat, its three-pronged head dripping with gore. Sextus tumbles sideways from his horse, coughing out his lifeblood. He crashes to the ground and lies there, feebly fingering the cruel bronze shaft that protrudes from his neck.

Glaucus' decapitated head thumps to the ground in front of Sextus. It rolls over and faces him. Sextus stares into his friend's glassy, half-lidded green eyes. His mouth moves wordlessly. Then he sees no more.

Two deep, brassy notes sound out from the wheatfield beneath the two bodies. Then two more.

Thousands of Gauls rise up from the fields, throwing off their cloaks of woven wheat stalks. Clad only in their tribal blue plaid pants, the bare-chested giants charge forward, bellowing their battle cries as they raise their two-handed long swords. The stunned legionnaires have only time to raise their swords before the Gauls are upon them, hacking them down. The Boii dash from one victim to another, a vengeful bloodlust upon them.

The field echoes with screams of agony and rage, as hundreds of individual battles erupt. The tall stalks dance madly in every direction, battered by the bodies that lunge and roll beneath them.

Standing in front the camp gates, Campius hears Sextus' truncated warning. He sees the fields lurching madly in every direction, as if herds of wild boars were stampeding through them. He stares at the flash of Gallic swords arcing over the tops of the stalks, looping down to hew into Roman bodies and heads. He hears a tuba sound from his second scouting party. The blast begins, but it ends abruptly.

Campius' breath catches in his throat. *Gods save me, it's an ambush!*

"Get the Umbrians out there!" he shouts to no one in particular. But Claudus is already hobbling toward the fields, sword in hand. Thousands of Umbrians follow, rushing pell-mell toward the Gauls.

Campius waves over his cavalry commander. "Follow me into the fields!" Moments later, three hundred horsemen stampede into the wheat-shrouded melee, their lances at the ready.

The Umbrian cavalry swirl about in the fields. They shove their spears at the Gauls, who parry the thrusts with their five-foot swords. Scores of barbarians fall, pierced through their broad chests by Umbrian spears.

"Keep moving!" Campius bellows. "Strike and move on!"

Roaring in anger, the Boii attack the allied riders from all sides. Dozens of the Umbrian cavalry are struck from their mounts, with dozens more pulled down from behind. Every fallen rider is stabbed to death and decapitated. His gory head becomes a prized souvenir.

Campius darts into the center of the fields, galloping past mounds of butchered Romans. "Get the cavalry into line," he yells to Claudus. "We'll move through the fields together, with the infantry behind us."

Claudus replies, but his voice is drowned by the rumbling of hooves behind them. Campius turns his horse toward camp. His heart quivers.

Hundreds of Gallic horsemen are thundering toward him, tall warriors cloaked in ring mail tunics, their heavy lances leveled at the Umbrian infantry behind Campius. The charging Boii drive the Umbrians into the field, cutting them down as if they were harvesting their bodies.

Hordes of Boii infantry run out of the field and dash into the unprotected camp, pitching torches into the buildings. As flames leap about the camp, hundreds of Gauls ride in from each side of the foothills, completing the encirclement.

Campius watches in horror as the Gauls loop around the edges of the fields. *They were waiting for us to charge into here.* He slaps himself in the face. *I fell for their trap. I deserve to die.*

The commander looks over at Claudus, whose face mirrors his distress—and resignation. Their eyes meet, and an unspoken decision passes between them.

Campius smiles sadly. He drops his lance, draws his sword, and plunges toward the onrushing horde.

With a cry of desperate defiance, Claudus follows his friend. Hundreds of Umbrians charge in behind their leaders, heading into the teeth of the Gallic charge.

A half hour later, the remnants of Campius' army dashes for the mountains. They dodge and weave through the concealing grasses. The tall stalks that concealed their enemies now become their friends. The Gauls quit chasing their elusive enemy, content to plunder the seven thousand bodies that are strewn through the fields like death's own harvest. [vii]

A stout, one-armed Gaul rides into the wrecked Roman camp, his black bear robe draped down to the haunches of his snow-white horse. Scores of blood-spattered Boii cavalry flow past him, searching for movement among the Roman bodies strewn about them.

The Boii chief halts in the middle of the camp. He silently surveys the tents, armor, and wagons, nodding appreciatively. *We can use all of this. These Romans make good stuff.*

"Galdant!" the chief shouts. He waves at a rangy young cavalryman who is roping two Roman heads to his belt. Galdant trots over to the chief, the heads bouncing against his bloody thighs.

"Shall we burn the camp, Drustan?" Galdant says.

"Idiot!" Drustan snaps. "Take all the tents. All armor and weapons, too. Leave the walls. We can use this place for a livestock pen."

The young man slaps his right hand to his chest. "Done. Then what?"

Drustan stares south, down the dirt road that leads toward Rome. "Then we wait. They will come back for us, you can be sure of it."

Two days later, Aelius' army is marching up the mountain pass that leads down into the Po Valley—and Mutina. Aelius rides in front of his lead cohort, confident that no harm can befall him.

One of his lead scouts returns from the crest of the pass. He rides up to the consul, pointing back up the way he came. "General, there are men waiting for us up there."

"Are they Ligurians?"

The scout shakes his head. "Umbrians. And Romans." He swallows. "They say they are the last of Campius' men."[viii]

"*What?*" The stout little patrician puts heels to his horse and hurries to the top. He finds sixty-four soldiers waiting for him, half of them swathed in bandages.

"Thank the gods, you have finally come," says a young centurion, leaning on his tree-branch crutch.

"What are you men doing up here? Where's Campius? Where's my cohorts?"

The centurion limps forward. "We are what's left of the army. The Boii surprised us while we were gathering grain. Most of our men are dead. Some are hiding in the hills."

Aelius looks about him, his eyes dazed. "How could this happen?"

"I do not know," the weary soldier replies. He points below him. "But I know the result."

Aelius looks into the valley below, at the fields of naked dead—at the thousands of birds walking upon the bloated corpses, pecking away at them. The consul turns to his cavalry commander, his face slack with horror.

"They are gone, Tiberius. All my men are gone. What can I do?"

The aged officer rubs his eyes. "We can leave no man behind. Let's go to the camp site and reinforce it. The survivors come to us." He glances back at the fields. "The smoke from the pyres will attract their attention." He shakes his head. "The dead need us, too."

For the next two days, Aelius' men scramble to rebuild the walls and trenches. Soon thereafter, clouds of smoke billow into the sky, as the Roman dead receive an honorable burial.

The Romans remain at their new encampment for weeks. Every day, every hour, several men stagger into the camp. Some rush to the gates, weeping with relief. Others walk in as though they were under a spell, their eyes fixed with a distant stare. Dozens march in with bared sword in hand, tears running down their face as they scream for revenge.

Mounds of grain stand unmolested in front of the charnel field, rotting in the sun. Only a few birds attend to the pile, preferring to continue their feast on the field's grisly remains.

After recovering hundreds of survivors, Aelius marches his army back to Rome.

He finishes the remaining months of his consulship without achieving anything of note.[ix]

In the meantime, Drustan marches his Boii south into northern Umbria, ravaging the fields and towns of those allied to the Romans. He gathers men and food everywhere he goes, preparing for Rome's retaliation.

ROME. "In the Fourth Legion: two thousand, four hundred infantry. One hundred eighty-six equites. Twenty-three centurions. Six tribunes."

Standing in the center of the Senate floor, the Senate Elder slowly reads the tally of dead from Aelius' army. The senators sit in grim silence, their eyes avoiding the rotund little figure who slumps in a chair next to the Elder. For his part, Consul Publius Aelius stares fixedly at the floor.

Looking at the forlorn consul, Scipio feels a rush of guilt. *If I had been there to advise him, he wouldn't have sent Campius near the Boii. Amelia was right, I must use my newfound status—I must lead!*

After reading the totals, the Elder takes out a second, smaller scroll. He reads the name of every equite and tribune who died in the battle, all of them patricians. Each name elicits a gasp or groan from a senator who knew the deceased.

An eternity later, the Elder finishes his funerary chant. He hands the scrolls to the young patrician who serves as his assistant. "Have these read from the rostrum in the Forum. The people must know of Rome's loss." He looks up at the senators ringed around him.

"The Boii have destroyed our legions and invaded Umbria. We must decide what to do about it. The floor is open to discussion."

Flaccus rises from his privileged seat in the row. "This destruction cannot go unpunished. After the next consular election, one of our new consuls must march on the Boii immediately!" Scores of senators mutter their approval.

Sensing he has the moment, he just points his forefinger into the air. "In fact, I think we should send both consuls! We'll send two consular armies, and end the Gallic menace forever!" Dozens of Latin Party senators rise to their feet, shouting their agreement with their party leader.

Scipio rises from his seat in the front. He walks out and stands next to Flaccus, waiting for him to return to his seat. The stork-like senator stands silently, his lips pursed like a stubborn child.

"Scipio Africanus has the floor," the Elder intones. Flaccus stomps back to his place on the front bench and slumps onto it, arms crossed.

"It would be folly to send two armies to Gaul," Scipio says. "As the saying goes, 'we all cannot do everything.'[x] Yes, we must drive the Gauls out of Umbria. But I ask you: can we end their menace with one sweep of a massive army? Why, we have been fighting them for hundreds of years!"

"You are backing down from a fight," Flaccus growls, provoking muttered assent.

"If you recall, honored Senator, I was the one who led the fight in Iberia, when none would take it.[xi] And I took our legions to Carthage itself. The Gauls are a concern, but a larger menace looms to the east— King Philip of Macedonia. Just last month, the Aetolian league came to us for help, asking us to halt Philip's incursion into Greece!"

"We just signed a treaty with Philip four years ago,"[xii] an elder senator shouts from his seat. "He is not at war with us."

"No, he is not," Scipio replies. "Nor will he be, if we send an army near him. We need to send a consul to Macedonia, along with his army."

Cato rises from his seat, his face flushed. "Why dither with Philip by sitting idle in Macedonia? If he is the threat you say he is, let us march forth and destroy him!"

Scipio shakes his head. "Philip has his uses. He keeps other nations in check. Besides, the people will not approve another war. Many still mourn those we lost fighting Hannibal. But they do not have to approve us sending an army over there."

"Honored Scipio, I have a concern," says Horatius Julius, a fellow member of the Hellenic party. "We can't wait until a new consul is elected, Philip will take control of northeastern Greece. Didn't you hear the Greek delegates? As we speak, he is marching to take Abydus!"

Consul Aelius jumps from his chair. "The year grows late," he blurts, "but I am willing to take two legions to Macedonia right now, if you will assign them to me." He expectantly searches the senators' faces.

No one replies. The consul's recommendation is met with the thundering silence of disapprobation. Aelius' rounded shoulders slump. He realizes his power is forever gone. From now on, he will be a Man Who Sits in the Corner, a silent and ineffective senator.

"Gratitude for the offer," Scipio says softly. "But I think we should send an emissary to Philip. Let us warn him first, and see if he desists. Diplomacy before aggression, Horatius. The Gauls will always fight us, but they will always lose, eventually. Since Hannibal left Italia, they haven't had a leader to unify them, to train them as a single instrument of his will. They are not the true threat."

ABYDUS, HELLESPONT,[xiii] 201 BCE. "By Zeus' beard, this is turning into the most dreary battle ever," Philip moans. His manicured fingers pluck at the thin gold wreath that surrounds his brow.

The Macedonian king slumps down into the tall throne inside his tent, frowning with disgust. "I swear, Philocles. If you can't get over one little wall defended by a few hundred bumpkins, I shall have to get myself another general!"

"*Five* hundred bumpkins," the stocky old officer replies. "Their outer wall is very thick. Our catapults have had little effect on it, yet their own machines rain stones upon us. And their soldiers fight like demons. Our spies tell us the Abydans have taken a vow to kill themselves before they let you take them."[xiv]

"They'd kill themselves before surrendering to me, the king of kings? Gods above, what an impulsive lot!" He throws up his hands. "You'd think I was going to deny them sex or wine for the rest of their life! All I want is to make a garrison of their town. And loot their treasury, of course."

"Our spies say they're going to throw all their gold and silver into the sea," Philocles mutters.

"Throw away all my plunder? Now that is truly a barbarous act!" Philip points toward the tent entrance. "Go tell Admiral Heraclides to put some ships around their seawall. I want a hundred divers there, in case those fools start throwing jewels into the sea." He slaps his knee. "Fools with jewels, hahaha!"

Philocles rolls his eyes. "As you command. But the issue with their walls still remains to be solved. They have an inner one built around the heart of the town. If we get through the first barrier, they'll make a stand behind the second."

Philip steeples his spiderlike fingers and presses them to his mouth. "Hmm. Can't we do a full scale attack on that big first wall? Just swarm all over it?"

Philocles shakes his bald head. "We would incur heavy losses, my King. We need every man if we are to campaign across Greece."

"Details, details! I need solutions from you, not problems!" The leanly muscled king pushes up from his gilded seat. He paces about the tent, his black cape trailing along the ground.

Philocles patiently watches him. *He is a clever man, for all his frippery. He will think of something.*

For the third time this morning Philip fills his wine goblet. He walks back to his throne and plunks into it, sipping moodily at his drink. His sea-blue eyes stare at the battle tapestries hanging from his goatskin walls. The tapestries are laden with battle scenes of his two famous forebears, Alexander the Great and Philip II.

26

Philip's eyes wander over to a map table holding the bust of Alexander the Great. *What would Alexander do? They're always comparing me to him.*

He wrinkles his nose at the statue. *Well, you died young, and I have no intention of doing that! I'll be more cautious in my moves.*

"What about a seaside attack?" Philip asks. "We have dozens of catapults on the ships."

"The cliff is too sheer, and their outside wall goes all the way around it," rejoins Philocles. "It's impossible."

"Must you undermine every suggestion I make?" Philip fumes. Philocles takes a sudden interest in a tapestry over the tent entrance.

Hmm. 'Undermine.' Philip slaps his forehead and laughs. "I swear, I'm becoming as slow as a Roman. We will undermine them."

"Undermine?" asks a baffled Philocles. "You want our spies to spread rumors in town? About what?"

"No, nothing that devious. Well, actually it *is* that devious, but much more fun! Do we have those slaves we captured at Laurium, the ones who worked in the silver mines?"

Philocles nods. "We have hundreds of them."

"Have them at the camp gates tomorrow morning," Philip says, his voice rising with excitement. "And get me our head engineer. He has some engineering to do!"

In the weeks that follow, the mystified Abydans watch from their sturdy walls as the Macedonians scavenge their fields. They see no signs that the Macedonians are gathering into attack phalanxes but they can see there is a great furor in the enemy camp, with wagons coming and going out the rear gates.

Captain Vangelis is especially intrigued with the Macedonians' activity. The dark young militia commander watches from the top of the five-foot thick front wall, noting the flow of empty wagons that enter the rear gates in the morning. *Where did they come from? Were they out in the night? Why don't they have any food in the back? They've been foraging all day.*

"Get Spyro up here," Vangelis tells his watch commander. Minutes later, a wizened little man appears next to Vangelis, a dark green cloak pulled over his greasy stringlets of black hair.

"I need you inside their camp, Spyro. I hear strange noises, and I see fires burning all night by the front gates. They have stuck poles into the ground between our town and their camp. What do you think they're doing?"

Spyro shrugs. "I don't know. But I know how to find out."

Vangelis nods. "Then take some men and find out. Don't come back until you have something of worth."

Spyro bares his snaggled yellow teeth. "I will be back on the morrow's eve. By then I will know what hand Philip uses to wipe his ass!"

Two days pass, then three. Then four. Vangelis is on the walls at dawn, watching the palisaded camp as if it held his family.

Spyro appears at his side, his face covered with bruises.

"Where have you been? I was ready to send out another man."

"I just escaped last night," Spyro replies, grimacing as he rubs the back of his neck. "I got into the slave camp but I couldn't get out!"

"You should have tried," Vangelis says tonelessly.

Spyro touches the purpled bruises on his cheeks. "This is what I got when they found me wandering off one night. After that they put me to work at night."

"What work? You couldn't escape from their fields, or some dreary little kitchen?"

"They put me to work digging. Digging in their mine! We dug all night and hauled dirt out the rear gates." He stares at Vangelis. "They are digging straight toward us. Here, take a look."

Spyro pulls Vangelis to the edge of the parapet. He points to the line of short poles sticking out of the ground. "Those poles were not stuck in from the top of the ground, they were pushed up from below! They're marking their path toward Abydus, to make sure they're headed for the right spot."

Vangelis grimaces. "Curse their children, they're going to come up inside our walls!" He slaps Spyro on the back. "You did well, citizen. I imagine they'll try to come up at night and open the gates, like the Greeks did in the Trojan Horse story." He grins wolfishly. "We will be ready for them when they emerge."

Within the hour, Vangelis has assigned forty soldiers to stand guard inside the town square. Another forty patrols the space between the outer walls and the walls of the inner garrison. The guards pay particular attention to the areas aligned with the poles outside of Abydus.

Two days later, a guard shakes Vangelis from his bed. "The Macedonians are mustering!"

Vangelis is almost relieved at the words. *At last we will resolve this.* He rolls out from his bed mat. His sleepy wife watches him tug on his breastplate, helmet, and sword. "What is it?" she murmurs, rubbing her eyes.

"Our fate," he replies.

Vangelis dashes from his log house and rushes across the town square, scrambling up the stone block staircase to the wall. Peering over the rampart, he sees Philip riding a black charger in front of a phalanx of heavy infantry, his silver armor mirroring the rising sun rising in front of him.

The Abydan commander scratches his head. *He's coming at our walls with heavily armored soldiers? That's bizarre, they can't climb like*

29

that.

A horn sounds from the Macedonian ranks. Three thousand light infantry trot out in front of Philip and his phalanx, young men in black wool tunics and peaked bronze helmets. The unarmored youths form into squares of a hundred men. They slap their short curved swords against their wicker shields, summoning themselves for a charge at the forbidding Abydan walls. A score of laddermen trot out in front of the peltasts, each duo clutching a sturdy wooden ladder.

"Get the forks ready," Vangelis shouts. His soldiers grab the forked poles they will use to repel the ladders. "I want a pole and a spear on every ladder that hits the wall." The duos scramble to their stations.

Vangelis hears the Macedonian horns blare two long, mournful, blasts. He watches Philip wave his gold-hilted sword over his head, ordering his peltasts forward. The light infantry tramps toward the walls of Abydus, crouched beneath their shields. The phalanx lumbers in behind them, a forest of spears jutting over their heads.

Philip reins in his horse outside of spear range. His army halts. Long minutes pass; the Macedonians remain immobile.

What is he waiting for? Vangelis wonders. *Is he waiting for his men to pop out from that tunnel and surprise us? Are his ships' catapults going to fling stones?*

Vangelis calls over his watch commander. "Put sixty more men in the courtyard, in case they come up in there. I want every spear and stone we have up here on the ramparts. Bring statues and furniture. We're going to give them everything we've got."

He glares down at the Macedonian king. "Come on, Philip. Just try it."

Philip looks back toward his camp. He sees that Philocles is standing in the midst of its open gates, watching him. Philip nods. The king turns back and faces the towering walls of Abydus. He raises his sword and chops it down.

"Pull!" Philocles yells to the officers behind him. The cry is relayed to the teams of oxen waiting inside the camp gates.

The stout beasts start forward. They pull ropes as thick as a boy's forearm; ropes that disappear into the gaping tunnel inside the camp. The ropes tighten, thrumming with tension.

"Get on!" The drivers yell, lashing the beasts with thorny tree limbs. The oxen pull harder. A creaking sound echoes from the tunnel, then a splintering crash.

Vangelis feels the wall tremble beneath his feet. Blocks tumble from the rampart. The wall leans forward. His stomach churns with dread. *They're not coming up! We're going down!*

With a thundering rumble, the wall section to the left of him caves into the enormous hole underneath it. The wall's massive blocks topple down with its defenders, precipitating a torrent of anguished screams. Dozens of warriors speckle the landscape, their broken bodies writhing in agony.

King Philip claps his hands and chuckles merrily. *Hades take me, it worked! Listen to those poor bastards!*

"Into the breach!" the king yells. He trots forward, his two hundred cavalry at his back. The peltasts dash ahead of them, racing for the wall opening. They scramble over the rubble-filled hole and pour into Abydus' courtyard. The town's defenders rush straight at them.

The Macedonians fling their javelins into the charging Abydans. Scores of town militia fall, pierced by the enemy's rain of spears. "No surrender, no survivors!" the Macedonian captain shouts. His men take up the call.

The peltasts swarm over the defenders lying wounded among the avalanche. They stab their double-edged swords into every body they find, whether it moves or not, then turn their murderous attentions to the surviving militia. Soon there are none but corpses to oppose them.

Vangelis watches the slaughter from the top of the wall. "Spears and stones," he shouts, "give them all our spears and stones! Don't worry about hitting our men down there, they are dead."

The Abydan soldiers begin their own rain of death, hurling javelins and rocks. The stones clang into the Macedonian's helmets, staggering them. When the stunned peltasts drop their wicker shields, Abydan spears fly into their throats and torsos.

A huge Abydan stands at the top edge of the ruined wall, his black-bearded face contorted with rage. "I crush you all!" he bellows, laying down his war axe.

Groaning with effort, the giant levers a wall block up to his broad chest, his thick arms stitched with veins. With a mighty grunt, he straightens his bended knees and drops the stone upon the peltasts entering the breach. The boulder thuds into the back of three onrushing soldiers, crushing them into the jagged stones beneath him. Another block crashes down, and another. The invading peltasts pause outside the wall, staring anxiously at the Abydan above them.

"Zeus curse you, get him off of there!" shouts the infantry captain. A dozen Macedonians turn as one and hurl their javelins at the giant. Three spears strike home, piercing his chest.

The Abydan roars with pain. Bristling with spear shafts, he levers up another block and hurtles it onto the helmet of a Macedonian, caving in his head.

"Bring him down!" the peltast captain screams. He flings his spear at the Abydan. Dozens more follow.

A javelin crunches through the Abydan's eye socket, the spearhead bursting from the back of his head. Stone and man plummet down upon the enemy in a final act of defiance.

The peltast commander scrambles onto the top of the rubble. "That big bastard's dead! Now get up those steps!" He trots up the stone stairs to the right of the breach, with scores of his men following.

The Abydan militia rush to the head of the narrow passage. Standing shoulder to shoulder, the two militia in the front clash swords with the ascending Macedonians. The Abydans jab spears and swords over their compatriots' shoulders, eager to strike down their enemies. The peltasts fling spears into the men behind those dueling in the front, tumbling dozens from the walls.

The first Abydan militiaman falls from the front, pierced by a half-dozen spear thrusts. The other soon follows. The peltasts break onto the wall walkway and push the Abydans backwards. The Macedonians hurl the last of their spears into the walkway defenders, men packed so close together they cannot raise their shields. Dozens of Abydans hurtle down into the courtyard, thudding into the rubbled ground below them.

Vangelis stands behind his two front-line defenders, jabbing his javelin at the Macedonians. He studies the long line of enemy infantry waiting to ascend the walkway. *We're not going to fight our way through them. We've got to retreat to the inner wall.*

He leans into the man's ear in front of him, and squeezes his shoulder. "You men in the front have to hold them, Aco. Hold them for just a few minutes more."

The lean young officer looks over his shoulder. His teeth gleam in his blood-grimed face, belying the fear in his eyes. "We'll keep 'em here 'til they die from old age, Captain."

Aco's broad grin vanishes, replaced with a tight-lipped grin. "It was a good life while it lasted."

Tears well in Vangelis' eyes. "Go with the gods, warriors." He turns to the rest of his men. "Get to the inner wall!"

Vangelis barges through his men, shouting his command to retreat. He races toward the wall section that borders the Aegean Sea. *Gods help us, I hope Philip's men haven't found the walkway over here.*

He hears a scream behind him. Vangelis turns and sees Aco plummeting off the wall, a sword hilt protruding from his chest. His breath chokes in his throat. He pushes himself onward.

The Abydan captain rounds a curve in the wall. The sapphire sea looms below him, lapping at its jagged shore. Vangelis notices that Abydans are the only ones here, grouped about the rear steps to the inner wall.

"Down, down!" he shouts, gesturing with his spear. "Get inside the inner wall!" The men hustle down the steps and race to the right, seeking the side gates of the inside wall. The townspeople inside see them coming and fling open the foot-thick gates. Scores of soldiers rush inside, embracing their neighbors.

Vangelis stands atop the walkway, urging down the last of his militia. "This way!" Vangelis shouts. The last two men jostle past him and rush down the stone steps. Vangelis follows, hurling the last of his javelins into the shoulder of an oncoming peltast. The three Abydans dash frantically for the gates, the townspeople cheering them on from the top of the inner wall.

The Abydan commander hears the thunder of hooves behind him. Three spears whistle over his shoulder.

A spear lands between the lead man's shoulder blades. The soldier stumbles forward, dropping his shield and sword. Vangelis throws his shield over his back and shoves his arm around the warrior's shoulders, dragging him toward the gates.

Six older men hobble out from the inner city. Each lugs a dagger and a plate-sized shield, their bronze helmets enveloping their white-haired skulls. They march past Vangelis, their eyes fixed on the charging Macedonians.

"Get him inside, we'll take care of them," one elder says, his voice quavering with terror.

"No! You don't need to—" Vangelis says, but the old men are already past him.

The elders hurl egg-sized rocks into the oncoming Macedonians, their reedy voices shouting their defiance. The heavy infantry thunder towards them. With trembling hands, the elders raise their swords and shields.

The Macedonians trample into the old men. The six disappear under the stallions, their death cries quelled by the thundering hooves above them. Two lead horses stumble as they cave in the seniors' fragile frames, lurching sideways onto the ground. The other horses veer sideways to avoid the stallions, slowing the cavalry's assault.

A stout young woman rushes from the gates and grabs Vangelis' wounded soldier. "I have him, get inside!" She picks the wounded man up as if he were a child stumbling inside with him. Vangelis rushes in behind her, and the gates slam shut.

The Macedonians close in upon the gates. The townspeople fling tools, urns and rocks over the wall. Their children rush up the steps with tools and toys, grabbing anything they can carry. Beset with a storm of missiles, the riders veer about and gallop back toward the breached wall, seeking easier prey.

Vangelis smiles with pride, though his heart hammers with fear. *Look at them. They will die before they surrender.*

As dusk approaches, the Macedonians resume their assault upon Abydus' inner wall. Dozens of peltasts throw up ladders and scramble toward the top, only to be repulsed by the fanatic Abydans.

Philip and Philocles observe the attack from outside the breached wall. The king watches old men flinging themselves from the top of the wall onto the ladder men, crashing them all into the earth. His eyes widen as he watches women and boys hack at the Macedonians with hoes and rakes, heedless of the sword blades that cut them down.

The king purses his full lips as if he has tasted something sour. *Well kiss my ass! They're going to all kill themselves. Then there won't be anyone left to run the town. And they'll probably throw all their treasures into the sea!*

"Sound the recall," Philip tells Philocles.

The old warrior stares at him. "What? Why? We can have them all dead before nightfall."

"We have them cornered, and almost all of their soldiers are gone. We'll give them three days to decide their fate. Perhaps they'll surrender when they have a chance to think about it."[xv] He grins at Philocles. "But just in case they don't, get the slaves ready to dig another tunnel!"

At sunset, a lone Macedonian rider pauses before the inner gates of Abydus. Vangelis peers over the top of the wall.

"What do you want?" the Abydan demands.

"King Philip seeks to make terms with you. If you surrender he will spare all of you."

Gods be blessed, there is a chance for honorable surrender. "We are willing." He brandishes a small scroll. "We have prepared some modest terms," replies Vangelis. "We desire that the Rhodian ship in the harbor be given safe passage from here, and that our women and children—"

The messenger jerks up his hand. "Nonsense! You do not dictate terms to the future king of the world. King Philip demands your unconditional surrender."[xvi]

The young officer turns his horse about. "Three days to surrender. If not, we destroy you."

Vangelis watches him go, his shoulders slumped. *No terms. No honor. No other way.*

Philip has returned to his tent to find a red-haired young man standing inside, watched carefully by his captain of the guard. The young man is arrayed in full battle armor. His right arm cradles the red-plumed helmet of a Roman tribune. Philip's guard cradles the man's sheathed sword and dagger in his left arm. His right hand rests upon his sword hilt.

A Roman in my tent! Philip mutters to himself. *What a miserable day this has turned out to be!*

The Roman inclines his head. "Salve, King Philip. I am Marcus Aemilius, envoy from Rome.[xvii] I have come to notify you that Rome protests your advances into Greece. You should know that Athens, Delphi, and the rest of the Aetolian League have petitioned Rome to intervene on their behalf. They notified us of your attack on Attalus and the Rhodians, and your conquests of Maronea, Aemnum, and Serrheum, among other Greek possessions. We beg you to desist."

Philip slumps into his throne. He motions the young envoy to a stool.

"Bring wine," Philip says to his attendant. The slave fetches a tray from the map table. He hands Philip a golden goblet brimming with deep red Xinomavro wine. Philip glowers at the slave. He rushes back and fetches a bronze cup for the Roman.

The king takes a deep draft of the wine and smacks his lips. *Nothing like a good Macedonian red.* "Always nice to have a visit from the esteemed Romans, now that we have made peace with each other.[xviii] I do miss seeing my old friend Hannibal, though."

He smirks at the young man. "I thought the two of us would conquer the world."

"But you didn't," the tribune replies evenly. "Hannibal—and the men you lent him—they all fell at Zama."

The king shakes his head and takes another drink. "That was quite a feat, Scipio defeating him. Very ingenious how he did it."

Marcus nods. "He is as much a scholar as a warrior. I have never seen the like."

"I would enjoy meeting him," Philip says, his voice casual. "Is he planning to come over here on a diplomatic mission—or a campaign?"

The young man sips his wine. "I think not. Scipio has involved himself in civic activities." He smiles at Philip. "That is no secret."

Excellent! The king spreads his hands imploringly. "Your Senate thinks I am attacking Greece. I simply defended myself against an unprovoked attack by the Rhodians. Would they have me lie down and die?"

The young patrician smiles acidly. "I suppose these Abydans attacked you, too. Is that why you are preparing to murder them? Continue your invasion into Greece and you will provoke us, King Philip."

Philip glowers at the young man. "Your youth, your looks and, above all, the Roman name, make you too outspoken. As for me, my first preference would be that you Romans should remember our treaties, and keep peace with me. But if you attack me in war, you will realize that I also take pride in my kingdom and its fame; for Macedonia is not less renowned than Rome." [xix]

The young tribune blushes with anger. He pushes himself up from the stool, his face a stone.

"I must return to my troops. Rest assured, I shall relay your message, word for word, to the Senate." He smiles tightly. "You know, Scipio pleaded with them to give you a chance to desist, before they declared war on you. You have wasted an opportunity to keep your kingdom."

Philip looks at his guard. "Escort this bleating sheep to the foothills."

The tribune strides stiffly out the exit. Philip sips moodily from his wine cup, staring at the linen tent walls. *Romans! They are getting too cocky. They will need a lesson on who the real empire is. But first, I settle with Abydus.*

Three days later, the king leads his small army toward the gates of Abydus' inner garrison. While Philip watches from a safe distance, his messenger rides to the portal and booms his staff upon it.

"You in there, come forth!" The town is silent, save for the barking of several dogs. The messenger repeats his message. There is no answer.

Philip's face reddens. "Those shit-heeled farmers think they can ignore me?" He waves over Philocles. "We're going over the walls."

Twenty pairs of soldiers dash forward with ladders. Hundreds of

38

infantry follow them. The men pitch their ladders against the wall and scrabble to the top, swords clenched in their fists.

Philip watches the men leap onto the parapet. He sees them pause, staring down into the town. They abruptly lower their swords. Several walk across the parapet and disappear below.

A black cloud of crows suddenly rises up from the town, cawing their displeasure at being disturbed.

What? Don't tell me they—? Philip trots toward the gates, heedless of his guards' warnings. His officers and cavalry follow, their spears at the ready.

The gates creak open, pulled by two somber Macedonians. Philip rides into the entry. And stops.

The Abydus militia are strewn in front of him, their corpses filling the courtyard. The streets behind them are scattered with the bodies of the town's citizenry. Many are heaped into mounds, their chests blooming with the red flower of a single sword thrust.

Other bodies drape down from second-story windowsills and doorways, mute testament to the killing frenzy that overcame them.[xx] Dead women lie with their dead children cradled in their arms. Old men lie in peaceful repose, their hands crossed over their bloodied chests.

Captain Vangelis lies near the feet of Philip's horse, still clutching the sword that he pushed into his own heart. Philip nods to himself. *They killed the townspeople, then they took turns killing each other. He was the last.*

The king sighs. "Go house to house," he orders. "See if anyone remains."

Philocles rides to Philip's side. "The savages killed themselves, can you believe it? What now?"

"What now? Now we take over. This will be our new garrison for the upcoming campaign. We'll leave five hundred men here and return to

Macedonia. I have a meeting with Antiochus of Syria, to ensure he will not oppose my advances into Greece."

"We're going back? What about Athens?"

"Athens will be ours. But first we have to recruit more men. Many more men. And make sure Syria will not interfere."

Philocles sniffs disdainfully. "We don't need more men to beat Athens and rest the Aetolian League. They're nothing but a bunch of puny Greek cities."

Philip smiles to himself. "Most likely, we do not. But then, we're not worried about them any more, are we? Word of Abydus' destruction will travel like Mercury."

Philocles shrugs. "So?"

"Rome will know, my dear commander. Rome will know."

Antiochus III

II. EASTERN POWERS

TEMPLE OF CASTOR AND POLLUX, ROME. The supine ox bawls out the last of its life. Rome's foremost haruspex eases a silver bowl underneath the beast's pulsating throat and fills his sacrificial bowl with its lifeblood. The young man pokes his finger into the blood. He tastes it, then nods appreciatively.

Tiberius Sempronius Gracchus places the blood bowl on a white marble table, next to the ox's dripping liver. He grabs a sheaf of razor-sharp obsidian and deftly splits the saddle-shaped organ. Softly intoning a supplication to the gods, Gracchus pokes into the liver's right globe, studying it intently. He hears a man cough loudly—then another.

"Be patient, Senators," the priest says without looking up. "I must search for any sign that the gods do not favor your plan." The room is quiet.

Two senators in the back row are particularly attentive to the priest's ministrations. One is a sturdy little potato-nosed youth with flaming red hair. He fixes his gray eyes on his elder companion, a bony and angular man with a dark and pensive countenance, a man whose brown eyes are turned inward as if he were dreaming—or plotting.

"Why does he need to kill an ox?" Cato fumes. "Isn't a sheep enough? Curse these divinations! They are nothing but a waste of good livestock!"

"Shhh. This is important to our cause," Flaccus whispers. "The people don't want to fight a war with Macedonia. The haruspex needs to declare that the gods support it."

Cato eyes Flaccus. "You are sure he will come to that conclusion?"

Flaccus grimaces. "Who knows what he will say? The sanctimonious young fool wouldn't take a bribe!" He shakes his head. "Makes me wonder if he's working for the Hellenics."

"I am not a religious man, but I know a priest works for the gods and the good of the people," Cato replies testily. "I admire him, even if he is a friend of the Scipios."

"Scipio!" Flaccus hisses. "I wish that bastard was away at war. He has become too powerful. He's the one who formed that committee to give our local farmlands to war veterans.[xxi] Then he asked all the people to vote on the proposal, just so they'd know who did it!"

Flaccus glowers at Scipio, who sits on the temple's front bench. "The commoners think that Hellenic puff is a god!"

"Do not fret. I know he stole war plunder; he will get his due rewards," Cato says. "Look here, the priest is about to reveal his findings."

After exploring the left liver lobe, the haruspex grabs a snow-white towel and wipes his gory hands. He looks up at the expectant senators, who are sitting in semicircular rows about the marble altar.

"The signs are propitious," Tiberius Gracchus declares. "The liver has no signs of corruption. The ox's blood is pure and clean." He spreads his arms out and looks toward the ceiling. "The gods favor your decision to declare war."

There is an audible sigh of relief. "That will help," comments a senior senator, "but we still have to convince the people."

Scipio hears him. "I wouldn't blame them if they didn't, Senator," he says. There is no reply.

Flaccus rises and spreads his hands. "Too bad we can't perform an augury upon that Tribune of the Plebs who vetoed our war proposal!" A few senators chuckle nervously, but most are quiet. They know the two tribunes' power to control the people's mind.

The Senate Elder grabs his ivory cane and pushes himself from his seat. "Enough for now. We convene in an hour for the final vote."

The Senators exit the beautiful little temple, walking out between its twenty-foot stone columns and down its twelve marbled steps. Chatting and arguing, they head for the Senate chambers in the Curia Hostilia.

Cato and Flaccus stroll across the Forum square. They watch the pigeons surge across the gauzy winter sky, soaring over the towering statues that ring the plaza's temples and government buildings. Two members of the Latin Party join them.

"Scipio's over there," declares Fulvius, a portly senator from the Servilius family. "I wager he's gathering recruits for his political army!"

Scipio looks over his shoulder, noticing the patricians are watching him. He grins at them and turns back to his party members, jerking his thumb at the Latins while he talks. Scipio's colleagues laugh, several grinning over their shoulder at them.

"Look at him," snarls Flaccus. "I'd bet he's cozening votes against our war proposal."

Fulvius grimaces. "He thinks we can stop that snake Philip by negotiating with him." He spits on the ground. "You'd think Scipio had never fought in a war, much less been a general!"

"It is because he fought in two wars that he delays conflict," says Cato, disdainfully eyeing Fulvius. "Too bad you have not had that experience." Fulvius looks away, knowing better than to provoke the man called the Hound of Rome, for his relentless pursuit of truth.

"I have heard Scipio has a secret society of Rome's most powerful old families," whispers Junius, a diminutive junior senator. "Members of the Cornelii, Aemilii, and Curiatii have all joined him."

"He's probably trying to get money to build that cursed library he keeps quacking about," says Cato. "As if Romans need to waste their time with scrolls and statuary." He shakes his head. "If Scipio has his way, we'll all be speaking Greek."

"Only too true, Cato. Just when we rid ourselves of Carthage and prepare for Macedonia, we have to worry about a cultural invasion from Greece!" Fulvius replies. "We have to minimize his power before he wrecks our city."

Junius snorts. "If the Greeks would spend more time on military training and less on culture, they wouldn't come begging for help against Philip! That haughty Aetolian league wants us to help them fight Macedonia. Last year they declaimed our interference in Greece!"

"Ah, we talk overmuch," says Fulvius. "The war vote awaits." He waddles toward the Curia, Junius hurrying after him.

Cato watches them go, making sure they are out of earshot. "Is it true?" He asks Flaccus. "Scipio has organized some type of secret society?"

"Such a meeting has happened, that much I know. But he did not organize it. His bitch wife Amelia has picked up where his mother Pomponia left off; meddling in men's work!"

Cato shrugs. "Scipio's mother was a strong and noble woman, but I cannot say I mourned her death. I only hope his wife is less dedicated to raising taxes and lowering standards."

If she is, I'll kill her too. Flaccus thinks. He shrugs. "I would not worry about her if I were you." He stares up at the sky, watching the pigeons circle the Temple of Saturn.

"What do you mean?" Cato demands.

"I think she will soon be...inconsequential."

Cato's unflinching stare bores into Flaccus' eyes. "I have told you before, friend Flaccus. I will be not be party to any malfeasance. Ours is the party of virtus, of pure Roman values. You will not sully it with your vengeful intrigues."

45

Flaccus looks away, pursing his lips. *Hmmm. The boy is becoming overly full of himself. As old Fabius was. He might be next.*

"You are overly suspicious, Cato. I merely meant she doesn't have the determination to be a threat to us."

"I would rather be overly suspicious than overly incautious," Cato replies.

Flaccus slaps him on the back. "Come on, let's grab some flatbread and onions before the meeting starts. Luca's stall is over there on the corner. He has the best in the city!"

Within the hour, three hundred senators are gathered in the chambers, a rare full turnout. As First Senator of Rome, Scipio has the privilege of speaking first. He extolls the virtue of negotiating a peace with King Philip, to avoid the costs of war.

"You all know of my admiration of Greece, I would never let it fall under Philip's control," Scipio says. "But why waste our precious men and resources in an unnecessary conflict? We are yet recovering from Carthage!"

Cato rises from the back row. "You don't keep a mad dog around so it can bite you again," he replies. "We should destroy him now, before he gathers more power. That is what we would have done with Carthage, had you not made such a flimsy treaty. Carthage must be destroyed,[xxii] and Philip must be destroyed!"

Stubborn little shit, Scipio thinks. *He'd have us fighting everyone in the world.* He turns to the senators. "Do you remember Aesop's Fable about the Hart and the Hunter, that people despise what is useful because they do not grasp its true value?"[xxiii]

Scipio notices that scores of senators are nodding their agreement. *Good. They will not be horrified at what I will say.* "As repugnant as it may seem, Philip is very useful to us. Yes, he is ruthless, cunning, and unpredictable, but that is why he is so valuable!"

"Scipio is mad," Fulvius shouts, his jowls quivering with rage. "The censor should remove him from office!"

Scipio shakes his head. "Don't you see it? His ruthless hand keeps the east from falling into ruinous disorder. If Philip falls, Thrace, Egypt, Pergamum, Syria, and other nations would fight take his place. Chaos would reign for years. And the victors would battle to take Athens, Sparta, and the rest of Greece!"

He paces across the front row, becoming more animated with each step. "If we rid ourselves of Philip, others, many others, will rise to take his place. You call him a mad dog, Cato? That dog keeps the rats in place."

"He's not a dog, he's a demon!" blurts an elder Latin senator.

Scipio spreads his arms. "If so, he's but the demon we know. We have made peace with Macedonia after a bitter war with them. Let us not be so hasty to dissolve it."

Scipio's remarks set the senators to arguing among themselves. Listening to their discussions, Flaccus' eyes widen. *We are on the cusp of losing our majority!* He rises and shoves his right fist over his head.

"Enough of this gutless talk of diplomacy," he shouts to the Senate Elder. "We have been over this before. I call for a vote!"

The older man blinks in surprise. "Uh, very well, Senator Flaccus." He turns to Scipio. "Are you finished?" he asks.

"I am not finished until we abandon this addiction to war," Scipio replies. "But go ahead, call the vote."

"You know the procedure, senators." The Elder waves his arm toward the right side of the chambers. "All those who favor war with Macedonia, move to my right. Those opposed, move to my left."

The Senators leave their semicircular rows and step down to the main Senate floor. Cato, Flaccus, and their Latin colleagues move to the Senate Elder's right, along with a cadre of unaffiliated senators. Scipio and his Hellenic associates group to the left. The Latins are joined by a dozen more, most of them younger men.

Flaccus glances over at the Hellenics, comparing it to his own group. He grins triumphantly. *The youngsters made the difference. Those bribes were costly, but I'll recoup my losses on army grain sales when the war starts.*

"The motion carries," declares the Elder. "We propose that Rome declare war with Macedonia. On the new year next month, we will take the proposal to the People's Assembly for the final vote."

Scipio shakes his head. *Fools! They would have us at war forever!*

The senators begin to file out of the Curia, weary of the day's rituals and speeches. But Scipio does not go quietly.

"I tell you once again, you worry overmuch about Philip," Scipio shouts to the emptying room. "He is not our main threat."

Flaccus stalks past Scipio, giving him a sneering glance. "Who is?" He winks at his Latin colleagues. "Is it the 'mighty' Boii up north? You think they can sober up enough to conquer Rome?"

Amid the peals of laughter, Scipio shakes his head. "If only it were them! But it's not the Boii, or the fractious Iberians. I tell you now, a desert storm is coming, and it blows from the east. The Syrians are coming."

ANTIOCH,[xxiv] SELEUCID EMPIRE. 201 BCE. "Now who are *these* worthies, Zeuxis?" asks King Antiochus III.

The hawk-faced Syrian points at a column of slim Asian riders in loincloths and leather caps, each with a curved wooden bow on his back. As they ride past, the diminutive archers bow their heads toward Antiochus, lightly touching their foreheads.

The king's army commander squints out into the parade ground. "Those are Dahae horse archers. Their king sent you five hundred of them as a gesture of support. Supposedly, they can shoot the eye out of a bat at a hundred paces."

Antiochus runs his long lean fingers through his thick brown curls. "I swear to Zeus, I cannot keep up with all these different recruits. How many nations are in our army now?"

Zeuxis tugs at his wiry black goatee. "Hmm. If we count the Pamphylians and the Lydians, who are yet to arrive, we have nineteen nations and city-states."

"Nineteen? I have nineteen little armies joining me?" The king rubs his dark eyes. "What a headache this is going to be! Hannibal himself did not have to supervise so many peoples!"

Zeuxis looks puzzled. "You want me to send some of them back?"

"No, no, that would be undiplomatic," Antiochus says, stretching his sinewy arms. "Having them here binds their countries to our kingdom." He arches his eyebrows and grins mischievously. "The more allies I have, the fewer nations I have to conquer!"

And that many more I have to manage while we campaign, Zeuxis thinks. "You know, Hannibal was a genius at making his diverse army a single instrument of his will. Perhaps we should invite him over for a visit. He might welcome the chance to leave Carthage. I hear he has accrued some powerful political enemies."

"As all great men do," Antiochus replies. He rubs his chin. "Perhaps I will ask Hannibal. Or perhaps I'll just get me more Gauls and Thracians. Now those are men who can fight!"

"We could send the Pamphylians back," Zeuxis says hopefully. "They fight with each other more than our enemies."

"No, let's keep all the tribes. I know it's a pain to remember who's here and who does what, much less to find food for their different tastes. But our variety is our strength. Even Scipio himself would have a difficult time combating all their different fighting styles. And all their different weapons."

"Very well," Zeuxis says resignedly. His face brightens. "Look, here come your charioteers. Imagine them charging into the Romans!"

The two-horse chariots rumble into view. Hundreds of the bronze-sided war machines parade past in five-wide columns. The wheels' curved scythes whirl around the hubs, their razored blades glistening in the late morning sun. The Syrian charioteers extend their left fists in salute to Antiochus. Their spearmen raise their barbed spears over their bronze-domed heads.

Antiochus rises from his gold throne. His leopardskin robe pools at his silver-sandaled feet. He extends his right palm. *Where would I be without my chariots. They hacked the Egyptians to pieces. Wonder how they'll do against the Greek phalanxes? And Rome's legions?*

Antiochus lowers his palm and steps back toward his seat, smiling as he imagines his men wreaking havoc.

"Don't sit down, my King. The Galatians are coming. Their chieftains would take it as a slight."

Antiochus sighs. He straightens his long frame and raises his chin, trying to look as regal as possible.

The Galatians tromp into view, Gallic tribes who inhabit Thrace and the western edges of Antiochus' kingdom. The bare-chested giants wear their tribes' signature brown plaid pants. Their polished stone necklaces dangle beneath their long scraggly beards. Some carry head-splitting longswords on their broad shoulders; others heft hand axes next to their thighs.

Antiochus smiles at the grim-faced warriors. *They will make good shock troops. Now that they've arrived, I can attack Pergamum and take it back from the Egyptians. Those meddling Romans will be occupied with Philip's forces; they'll let me alone.*

"How many men do I have now, Zeuxis?"

"If we count the Cretan mercenaries, who will arrive at the next moon, we have well over a hundred thousand fighting men."

"Then I'll have the largest army in the world?"

Zeuxis shrugs. "I would imagine. Certainly, Philip does not have as many. Since we destroyed Ptolemy's southern army, the Egyptians are greatly reduced."

"That is good. We will need every man if Rome sends their legions at us."

"*When* Rome sends their legions, you mean," Zeuxis says. "We can lay ancestral claim to Pergamum, but they will not sit by if we attack the Achaen League of Greek cities. Or the Aetolian League. Scipio has made them friends of Rome."

"*When* we attack them," Antiochus rejoins. "I will restore our kingdom to the glory it had before it fell apart under my dear father." *I will show everyone that he was a fool to insist my brother be king instead of me.* He smiles. *Of course, the assassin dealt with Dear Brother, so we'll never really know how well he'd have done.*[xxv]

"Philip is ready to invade Greece, my King. He has taken Abydus. Our scouts say he will cross the Hellespont and march on Athens." He cocks an eye at Antiochus. "That will be close to our western borders."

"Philip?" Antiochus laughs. "I am not worried about Philip! He has the Romans to contend with. That will keep them both occupied."

He watches the last of the Galatians march away. "We can move on Pergamum and take Thrace. Then on to Greece. Rome will have exhausted its resources fighting Philip. After Greece, we cross the Adriatic land unopposed in Italia."

"Perhaps Philip will defeat Rome," Zeuxis observes. "Then he'd be a real threat."

Antiochus laughs. "That would make it all the easier for us—we'd only have to conquer Macedonia! Philip's army would be depleted after fighting Rome's legions. Either way we win."

The king rises from his seat. "Look, here come the cataphractii! I'd like to see the Romans try to deal with them!"

Eastern Powers

Three thousand Syrian riders prance into view, a forest of twelve-foot spears looming over their egg-shaped iron helmets. The torsos of horse and rider are covered in polished bronze scale armor, shining a blinding white in the noonday sun.

Zeuxis shades his eyes with his palm. "Whoo, they are like suns on earth! I think they win half their fights by scaring their enemies to death!"

Antiochus smiles. "Wait until the Romans see my cataphractii bearing down on them. The sight will strike them blind!"

As the last of the gleaming cataphractii rides past the king, a booming din of drums rises. A square of five thousand Parthian archers[xxvi] trots in, their multicolored feathers waving from the nipples of their bronze domes. Wearing only tunics and pants, the unarmored youths pound their cup-shaped war drums in unison, their curved horn bows slung across their backs. *Aiyee-ah-oh*, they chant, *Aiyee-ah-oh-ah-oh*!

"I bet Hannibal could have used some of them against Scipio's Numidians," Antiochus observes. "They'd shoot those slippery bastards right off their horses!"

"Better still, he could have used a thousand of your king's Friends.[xxvii] They are the best riders in the world."

"Here they come," Antiochus says, rising to his feet. He waves his hand like an eager boy, belying his forty years.

The Friends arrive in triangular formation, their movements so synchronized that the triangle seems to float across the parade grounds. Antiochus' prized cavalry ride the black stallions that have been specially bred for them, rangy and swift beasts that are strong enough to carry their heavily armored riders.

Antiochus' cavalry carry their thirteen foot lances straight in front of them, forming a giant arrowhead for their king. The spears bear pennants with the springing lion insignia of the house of Antiochus. Each bronze cuirass has a lion's head painted upon it, signifying their lifetime allegiance to the king.

"We can send some of these troops to the Colophon garrison," Antiochus says, "But I'm taking the Friends with me."

The parade of riders concludes with Antiochus' two thousand Arab archers, dark-robed men riding atop their wicker-covered dromedaries. The swarthy men stare straight ahead. Fiercely independent, they ignore the foreign king who temporarily presides over them.

They act like I have enslaved them, fumes Antiochus. *Very well, they can lead the initial charge instead of the Galatians. Let the enemy tire themselves out with killing them.*

The parade concludes with the Syrian king's prized beasts: sixteen gargantuan Indian elephants. An oak plank tower sways atop each of the strolling monsters, with a Syrian archer and lancer peering out from them.

"The Romans defeated Hannibal's little elephants at Zama," Antiochus tells Zeuxis. "But wait until they face my beasts! Mine won't run from a few horn blasts or spear pricks. They're trained better."

A bugle sounds, and the elephants halt. Slowly, ponderously, the elephants bend to one knee, paying obeisance to their king.

We will conquer the world! Antiochus muses, his heart pounding with excitement. *I'll show Father, I'll rebuild his kingdom and stretch it to the ends of the earth!*

As the elephants rumble out of sight, Antiochus and Zeuxis step down from the dais and mount their horses. With his royal guard around them, the two leaders trot out to a dozen mansion-sized tents outside the city walls, following the thousands of soldiers who are marching to the sprawling ceremonial feast that is already in process.

The army's tribes and nations scatter across acres of the dusty plains, each to its own section. The Gauls and Thracians sprawl next to each other, eyeing each other suspiciously.

Though every group keeps to itself for the feasting, the soldiers gather afterwards on the sloping hillside outside of camp, facing the large field beneath them. They murmur and shout excitedly: it is time for Antiochus' games.

The nations' contestants vie with each other in foot races, wrestling, javelin throwing, archery, boxing, horsemanship and boulder lifting, as thousands cheer and jeer. Antiochus places a golden wreath on each victor's head, reveling in the deafening cheers that cascade about him. *I have united them. They are ready to go to battle. Now for the climax!*

The Syrian trumpets sound three long, plaintive notes. A man strides into the empty ring, tying the straps of his conical helmet underneath the chin of his silver face mask. The crowd mutters excitedly—they know the reputation of the man who stands before them.

No one knows his real name, and he would never tell it. He is known only as Nicator, the Victor, because he has never lost—nor have any of his opponents ever lived.

The crowd sees a man of average height, with a lean, loosely-muscled build. He walks about the ring with the loose grace of a leopard, his sandaled steps both fluid and sudden, as if he were a dancer instead of the captain of Antiochus' royal guard. Thousands on the hillside watch him, rapt with anticipation for the coming duel.

The tan-skinned man pauses in the center of the ring, his limbs slack. The crowd hushes with anticipation, so quiet they can hear Nicator clacking his short, double-edged sword blade against his silver greaves. He waits silently. His plate-sized wrist shield hangs limply next to his thigh.

There is a clanking and shuffling from the side of the field. Three chained men emerge from a group of Antiochus' guards, dragging themselves into side of the ring. They are sturdily built men, their copper-colored bodies striped with the thread scars of countless nicks and slashes. They are obviously veterans of many battles.

A guard unlocks the men's wrist and ankle chains. The three warriors rub their arms and legs. They calmly look about them. Having seen death a hundred times, in all its guises, they are ready for whatever fate brings them.

The Syrian guard motions with his spear for them to approach the center. The three step onto the freshly-trampled earth, watching the staid silver warrior who stands before them.

A young slave scurries out toward the threesome, his arms cradling weapons. He gives each an iron sword shaped like a question mark and a tombstone-shaped wooden shield, the timeless armament of Egyptian soldiers. The men slide their arms into the shield grips. They heft the familiar swords, testing their balance. The youngest man ducks low and swoops his sword about him, practicing his moves.

Antiochus walks to the edge of his viewing platform. "Attend to me!" he shouts to the three, though the hillside is quiet as a tomb. As one, they turn and face the king.

"You kill him, you go free," he says in flawless Egyptian. The warriors nod, and turn back toward Nicator.

The silver-faced warrior says nothing. Nicator taps the tip of his blade against the brim of his domed helmet, as if saluting them. He spreads his legs and arms. Shifting his balance to the balls of his feet, Nicator stands immobile as a statue.

The seconds drag into a minute, then another. No one moves. "Go!" shouts an Arab, breaking the unbearable silence. "Fight, fight!" bellows a Gaul.

"Don't make me come down there," warbles an elder Syrian, prompting laughter.

The three Egyptians look at one another. The one in the middle nods to the other two. He slaps his sword against his shield.

The three dash forward. "For Monte!" they scream, invoking their god of war as they spring into action.

The Syrian does not move. The three close on him, raising their sickle-swords high. When the trio is within two steps of Nicator, he leaps into the space between the man in the center and the one to his right, angling his body sideways. Nicator shoves up his left arm. His small shield rams against the center man's downward cut, diverting the blade. His sword clangs against the Egyptian's thrust on the right.

As Nicator slides between them, he catches his foot around the right man's ankle and jerks it off the ground. The Egyptian tumbles sideways. Quicker than a striking serpent, Nicator's sword flashes. The point of his blade jams into the back of the man's neck, cleaving his spine. The warrior crumples to the ground, convulsing helplessly.

The other Egyptians spin about with swords raised, ready to slash into him. They find Nicator has already resumed his battle stance, arms and legs spread wide. The two step warily toward him, blades bobbing nervously at their sides, staring into his silver mask as if it would somehow show some expression.

"Fight him!" yells Antiochus. "Fight or I'll come down there and kill you myself!" The crowd roars its approval of his words.

"Together, battle formation," mutters the older Egyptian to his fellow. The two stand next to each other, their joined shields forming a wall in front of them. The lead Egyptian crouches low.

"At him!" he bellows.

The two march forward, shields locked in front of them. They raise their blades, ready to strike him simultaneously from different sides, knowing his small shield cannot divert both blows. They cock their arms for the strike.

Nicator does not move.

"Now!" shouts the elder soldier. The Egyptians swing their scythed swords toward the Syrian's bare neck.

Nicator springs to life. He turns sideways and jumps toward the younger soldier's sword arm, just as the elder's blade whistles past his back. The Syrian arcs his tiny shield into the Egyptian's fist, blocking his blow in mid stroke.

Nicator's razored blade slashes upward. The Egyptian's forearm falls to the ground, still clutching his sword. The man wails with pain, gripping his gouting arm stub. Nicator springs towards the wounded man, slashing his liver as he passes in front of him. The young warrior crumples, covered in blood. Nicator resumes his stance.

The senior Egyptian whirls to face Nicator. He stares into the eye holes of the silver mask, but sees only darkness.

Nicator beckons him with his blade. With a resigned shrug, the Egyptian marches in.

When he is within a few feet of the Syrian, the elder warrior flings his shield into Nicator's face and dives into his legs, yanking at his silver-sandaled feet. The Syrian stumbles sideways. His sword stabs past the Egyptian's back and crunches into the sandy earth.

With desperate strength, the Egyptian yanks Nicator's feet out from under him. The two tumble to the ground. Nicator's wrist shield falls off. The two roll about, grappling with each other's sword hands.

The hillside onlookers are delirious with excitement. Hundreds scream for the Egyptian to kill Nicator, while hundreds more scream for the Syrian to finish it. Fights break out among the cheering factions, and the onlookers begin to cheer the combatants.

The Syrian rises to one knee, grabbing his larger opponent's sword arm at the wrist. As he shoves the Egyptian's arm upward, his foot slips on the forearm of his last opponent, the stub slick with blood.

Nicator tumbles forward and lands on his face. He quickly rolls over, but the Egyptian is already upon him. His left hand grabs the chin of Nicator's face mask and yanks it off, ready to shove his poised blade into the Syrian's face.

The Egyptian freezes with horror.

Angry red eyes glare out from the wells of lumpy white scar tissue that surround them. Snaggled yellow teeth snarl from a lipless mouth ringed with pustulent red sores. The Egyptian gapes at the nightmare visage.

The moment's pause is all the Syrian needs. He twists his shoulder from under the Egyptian's relaxed grasp and buries his short sword into the side of the man's stomach. The Egyptian rears back his head and wails with pain. His sword drops to the ground.

Nicator saws a jagged rent across the Egyptian's convulsing stomach. The Egyptian's bowels spill out onto Nicator's chest. The Syrian shoves his groaning opponent backwards.

The Egyptian falls onto his back. He rolls onto his side, cradling his intestines in his hands, crying with agony and despair.

Nicator lunges for his mask, his head bowed into his chest. He slaps it onto his face and swiftly knots the rawhide strings onto the back of his head. Then, only then, does he raise his head and arms triumphantly. The hillside onlookers scream with delight and disappointment.

Antiochus walks down from his dais and enters the ring. He grabs the Syrian's bloody arm and holds it high, prompting more roars from the crowd. *Now to make them mine.*

The king steps back and draws his sapphire-hilted sword. Warriors of nineteen nations watch in amazement as the King of Syria faces off against his mightiest warrior.

The middle-aged king shrugs off his robe, letting it crumple to the blood-spattered dust. Antiochus stands in loincloth and sandals, his ropy muscled body glistening with olive oil. He bends over and lays his jeweled crown on top of his robe. His eyes flick sideways to the hillside, measuring his audience. *Now they will see that their commander is no soft-assed drunk, like my father.*

Antiochus whirls upon Nicator, his scythed blade flashing toward his neck. The Syrian captain rings his sword against his king's weapon. He jabs his sword at Antiochus, who sidesteps it while chopping at Nicator's thighs. The silver-masked warrior raises his leg just in time to take the blow upon his silver greaves. The crowd cheers each cut and block, now aware that they are watching a practiced demonstration.

Nicator and Antiochus continue their dance of thrust, parry, and block, moving to the music of steel edges ringing on bronze and iron. The two men pivot and spin. Their blades whirl toward a mortal blow to neck or chest, only to be blocked at the last moment. The crowd roars with each sequence. Many make note of a move they plan to use in their own fights.

Nicator slows his cuts the barest fraction of a second, giving his king more time to defend them. His own thrusts curve off from Antiochus' body before they can strike home, for all their apparent deadliness. Syria's greatest warrior knows that if he draws blood he will likely end up being roasted alive, however superficial the cut.

After several minutes of furious action, a sweat-soaked Antiochus steps back and raises his blade to his chest, saluting his opponent. Nicator lowers his blade and bows. The crowd roars its approval.

The half-naked king struts back up the dais steps and eases into his chair, still clutching his sword. Zeuxis sits alongside him, scowling his disapproval.

"You just had to do that, didn't you?"

"They need to respect me, as Hannibal's men respected him," Antiochus replies. "I wanted to show them that I am a warrior."

"You could have been killed."

"Yes, if Nicator wanted me dead," Antiochus replies with a smile. "And if he wanted his family and relatives burned alive, because he knows that would happen if I were."

He takes a deep breath and exhales. "Gods above, it felt good to fight again! I hate having to be such a cursed politician all the time."

"Don't worry, my King. If we take Greece, you will have plenty of opportunities for fighting. Especially if the Romans come to their aid."

"We are ready to defeat both," Antiochus replies calmly, fingering the serrated edge of his sword. "I will have a hundred thousand men ready for them, with legions of chariots and elephants. They will have never seen the like."

"They may call upon Scipio again," Zeuxis notes. "He is undeterred by being outnumbered. Look what he did to the Iberians. And the Carthaginians."

"All the more reason for the Macedonians to dilute their numbers! I go to Eretria to meet Philip," Antiochus says. "I will make him an ally. Then he can devote his energies to fighting Rome."

"Be careful. Philip is notoriously capricious and untrustworthy. He is a worthy general, even if he is no Scipio. I hope we don't have *him* leading an army against us."

Antiochus is silent for several moments, lost in thought. He raises his chin, his eyes gleaming. "Well, then. If they should send Rome's greatest general at us, we shall counter with his greatest opponent. Send an emissary to Carthage."

The king grins. "Tell Hannibal we would like him to pay us a visit."

TEMPLE OF BELLONA, OUTSKIRTS OF ROME, 201 BCE. "Ah, Cornelia, I can't wait to feel your buttocks pushing against me," young Cassius whispers.

The boy grabs Cornelia's tapered fingers. He pulls the auburn-haired girl toward the sacred grove adjoining the ancient temple.

"I want to see you naked in the moonlight! We'll lay together under the sacred fig trees, and consecrate our love."

Cornelia peers into the dark foliage about her. "Shhh. There may be someone about here." Her eyes widen in mock fear. "We'd cause a scandal if we were discovered!"

"Scandal? Because we love each other? I don't care if you are married. Just write him a letter telling him you want to be free, and then you'll be divorced![xxviii] We'll run away to Capua and buy a villa, surrounded by olive groves. We'll make love all day, and dance into the night!"

"Oh, I do want that," replies Cornelia, squeezing his hand.

He puts his arm around her hip. "And I want to be inside you, feeling you push against me." He reaches inside the armhole of Cornelia's ankle-length tunic and cups her breast, feeling her nipple swell against his forefinger. "So firm! I'd love to—"

"What are two you doing here?" a gruff voice growls from the trees. Cassius jerks his hand away, his heart hammering. Cornelia clutches his arm, angry and embarrassed.

"We—we were visiting the temple," Cassius stammers. "We like to make our devotions at night."

"You mean you like to make each other at night," the voice replies. "Why don't you go over to the Temple of Apollo? The meadow has tall grasses around it. You'll have more privacy for your 'devotions.'"

Cassius summons himself. "See here, why should we take orders from—" his bluster is interrupted by the steely scratch of a sword eased from its scabbard.

"There is an affair going on here, and it's not yours. Go now, young lovers, before I forget what it was like to be your age."

The two youths scurry off to the nearby temple of Apollo. "Don't come back, or I may take part. And I won't be going after *her*, boy!" the voice shouts.

Chuckling to himself, Laelius turns back toward the small temple, pushing his way through the seven sacred fig trees in front of it. He walks onto a tiled floor that leads up to the temple's torchlight stairs. Thirteen men sit upon the temple's wide marble steps. They wear only plain dark blue tunics, but their bearing indicates they are people of station and influence.[xxix] Scipio stands in front of them, looking over his shoulder at Laelius.

"All is well?" Scipio asks.

"Just a boy and a girl," Laelius replies. "I didn't have to kill anyone, in case you were wondering. They are gone."

Scipio turns back to the men. "I welcome you to our meeting. I will forego introductions—you all know each other. Every one of you is from one of Rome's most powerful clans. The Julii, Fabii, Cornelii, Scipiones, and more. We are all people of power. We shall need that in the months to come."

Scipio walks to the lowest step and sits down, folding his hands over his knee. He looks up at his peers, his face grave. "As you know, Philip rejected our emissary's overtures for peace. And we, the Senate, have foolishly voted for war against him."

"All true. Only too true," declares one of the elder Julii.

"Our respite from war has been all too brief," Scipio says. It has been less than a year since we made peace with Carthage. And now, if the People's Assembly approves our motion, we will find ourselves fighting in another foreign land. And while we're contending with Philip, Syria musters its forces to march on Greece. War with Macedonia would be a dangerous distraction from our real threat—the Syrians."

Cassius Servilius rises from his seat. One of Rome's wealthiest slave traders, he has never feared to speak his mind. "I don't understand the purpose of your words, General. Why cry about the inevitable? If we are going to fight Philip, let us do it with all our heart. To Hades with Syria." His words bring scattered shouts of assent.

"I am not here to whine about the inevitable. If we fight, we fight to win. But I am here to be clear about what we should be fighting for. If we must war with Macedonia, it's to make peace with them."

"Now *I* don't understand," remarks Laelius.

Scipio's face flushes. "My point is a simple one. If war is approved, we defeat Macedonia so that it ceases its advances. But we do not have the time or men to rule it. If we defeat Macedonia, we make it one of our *amici*, a friendly nation. Not a chattel of Rome. Just like the Aetolian league has united Athens and Sparta. And the Achean League has joined Corinth and Thebes."

"You forget, Imperator. Philip has broken peace treaties before," growls an elder senator.

"Philip is conniving and ambitious, but he is practical. If he thinks he will lose his kingdom, he will keep the peace."

"The Latins speak of empire," the older man says "They will insist on ruling Macedonia. And maybe Greece!"

"You are right, Sextus," says Scipio. "And that's why I asked us to meet here. It is to declare war."

"Against Philip?" Sextus says, confused. "Antiochus?"

"Neither," Scipio replies.

Scipio picks up the javelin he brought. Bracing his legs wide like a javelin thrower, he hurls the spear toward Rome. The spear whooshes through the torchlight and disappears into the darkness. The senators gape at each other, confused.

"Following the traditions of our temple, I hurled the spear to declare war.[xxx] War against the Latin party, and all those who place conquest over growth and security. Let us band together as a secret society, devoted to promoting Rome's welfare. We will promote our own candidates for political office, that they may seek to build overseas alliances, not possessions."

"I am with you," says Laelius, rising from his seat. "Who is with me?" Slowly, by fits and starts, the rest of the members stand up.

"Excellent," Scipio says. "We start with the upcoming election for consul. Who among us should run for consul?"

"You!" shouts an older patrician, prompting some nervous laughter.

63

"You are the most popular man in Rome!"

Scipio grins. "You know I cannot. Ten years have not expired since last I ruled. I will not break Roman law." He rubs his neck. "Besides, I am mainly popular with the commoners. Half the Senate still thinks I was too lenient with Carthage in my peace terms."[xxxi]

"Then who?" asks Quintus. "Who would you support, First Man of Rome?"

"It is for us to decide, not me," Scipio replies. "I will only say this: we need consuls who are diplomats as well as warriors, men who will build bridges to friendship even as they knock down enemy walls. Who would that be?"

After several hours of discussion, the nobiles decide upon Publius Sulpicious Galba and Aulus Atilius as their candidates. The middle-aged Galba is a veteran officer of the Carthaginian and Gallic wars, a lean and stern man known for his successes on the field of battle.

Atilius is a longstanding civil servant to Rome. Though his military record is unremarkable, he is a member of one of Rome's oldest and richest families. And a devout admirer of Scipio.

"Now, one last item. We have to ensure our candidates' popularity with the people," Scipio says. "The Senate has granted me leave to form a ten-man commission to allocate more Italia farmland to our veterans. We can give them retirement lands they so richly deserve. Giving land to our veterans will be welcomed by the citizenry."

"And its members will be welcome as well, eh?" asks Horatius, a elderly scion of the ancient Geganius family. He smiles. "You are clever—for a Scipione."

Amid the laughter, Scipio points to an austere young man. "Galba, you will be on that committee. And you, too, Atilius. Young Flamininus there, he will join it.[xxxii] He is a promising candidate for a future election. Will you three men serve?"

"If they don't, I will have words with them," growls Horatius, prompting further laughter. All three men readily agree.

Their business completed, the sleepy senators wander over to their horses and carriages. They are thankful to arrive home before the dawn citizenry finds them riding about on the streets of Rome, arousing suspicion about their activities.

Scipio and Laelius stretch out upon the steps. They watch the eastern horizon lighten from black to gray, listening to the birds rejoicing in the birthing day.

"I'm going to become a consul," Laelius declares, breaking the silence. "I'm better than either of those two mushrooms you've nominated."

Scipio's eyes widen. "You want to be the lead magistrate of Rome? You haven't even been a praetor yet."

Laelius wrinkles his nose at him. "I didn't mean *this* year, pumpkin head. I'm going to start the cursus honorum, and pursue the pathway of offices to consul."

Scipio bites his lip. "You are the finest man I've ever known, but you're an orphan from the docks. The patricians would never stand for it. Or stand for you."

Laelius studies the cottony dawn skies, tapping his sandal against the steps. "Then I will be the people's candidate." He throws his head back and grins. "I am a war hero, after all. The immortal Scipio made me a temporary admiral and cavalry commander! The citizens will love me!"

Scipio toys with the sleeve of his toga, avoiding Laelius' eyes. "You know that Rome prefers its consuls to be, uh, family men? With a wife and children."

Laelius bugs his eyes at Scipio. "Oh ho! So you think my taste for men means I can't beget children? I can be quite, eh, ambidextrous when the situation calls for it! I just need to marry a woman—I don't have to love her. It's nothing new. All the consuls have married for wealth or power—except you."

Scipio reaches into his belt pouch and retrieves the worn Nike figurine that Amelia gave him long ago. He lightly rubs his thumb over it.

"Amelia captured my heart early, when the three of us were childhood friends. We went from friendship to lust to love. But you have never burned for a woman."

"So what? I am willing to make the supreme sacrifice!' He laughs. "That is, as long as she is beautiful, modest, intelligent, open-minded, wealthy, and—"

"And enough!" interjects Scipio, grinning. "If your mind is set to it, I know I will not change its course." He grasps his friend's shoulder. "I will help you any way I can."

"Of course you will," Laelius says brightly.

Scipio smiles mischievously. "You know, Amelia has a cousin Lucretia. She is quite brash, but very kind-hearted—and attractive!"

"She sounds appealing." Laelius says, springing up from the steps. "But enough of marriage and politics! It's a brilliant morning, and I am in the mood for a wrestle and a bath." He crouches into a wrestler's pose, spreading out his smoothly muscled arms. "All this talk of romance makes we want to go grab a man!"

"A wrestle and a bath? In that order, I would assume. You go on, I have work to do."

"Work? Are you going to take the speaker's platform in the Forum, and extoll old Galba's virtues?" Laelius says, chuckling. "That will be a short speech indeed!"

"You are overly critical. Galba will prove to be a capable leader. No, I do not have to do that. Amelia will handle the propaganda for his election, and her artists will decorate the city with slogans and banners. I have some military training to direct." His eyes twinkle. "And I'm going to take a little trip down south. To Liternum."

Laelius cocks an eye at him. "Oh? Going to visit someone you know?" He grins slyly. "Someone Amelia shouldn't know about?"

"Your mind is still in the gutters from whence you came," Scipio retorts. "The new year is coming. This trip is to begin my plan."

"Your plan for what?"

"To begin my end, of course," he replies laughing. "Retirement. And I am looking forward to it!"

Hannibal Barca

III. Four Days from Rome

ROME, 200 BCE. Six-foot pennants dangle from the upstairs windows of Rome's gritty apartment district. The vermilion banners flap energetically in the drizzly winter wind, rippling against the drab gray walls of the three story buildings.

Some of the pennants declare *Galba for consul. Hero of the First Macedonian War!* in white painted letters. Others testify that *Aulus Atilius is a man of the people*. Dozens more are lettered in black, reminding people that *Gaius Aurelius Cotta is a tax dodger*, an obvious slander to the Latin Party candidate.

Amelia stands under the arch of a small temple dedicated to Minerva, surveying her work. "You have done a remarkable job," she says over her shoulder. She reaches into her shoulder satchel and extracts six mouse skin bags, each bulging with jingling coins. She hands the purses to the young artists behind her.

"I know you would rather be painting frescoes, but today you have supported a worthy cause," she says. "Galba and Atilius favor a grain tax for the arts, so that we may build public buildings and populate them with your works." She laughs merrily. "Think of your efforts as a means to gain future employment, along with our poets and actors."

"Thanks the gods I'm not rich. I'd have to take down all those banners!" quips a ragged young Umbrian. Amelia glares him to silence.

"Go home now," Amelia says. "There will be more work coming. We have candidates for several magistracies."

The Roman citizens shuffle through the narrow streets with their wool cloaks pulled over their heads, hurrying their convocation in the Forum square. They pay little notice to the familiar banners, having more immediate issues on their mind. Today, at the end of the year, the People's Assembly will vote on the Senate's proposal to declare war on Macedonia.

"Can you believe it," growls a dark-skinned man to a hunched passer-by, "they want to start another fuckin' war!"

"Aye, and put us in the front ranks," the other replies. "I almost got crushed by an elephant at Zama, and now they want to send me against some more of them! Let those sag-butt patricians stand there while one of those monsters roars down on them. Then we'll see how quick they vote for a war!"

The dark man glances at the banners waving on the walls in front of him. "We're supposed to vote next week on the consuls. Which one's against the war?"

"You jest, surely," replies the other. "Those senators, they're all looking for glory and money at our expense. Another war could take years, take all our food and money. But they'd get rich, you can be sure!"

"I suppose so," answers the dark man. He pulls his damp cloak down his forehead. "Maybe we shouldn't give them the chance..."

"I'm with you," the man replies. "I heard Scipio argued against it, and that's good enough for me."

ROME. 200 BCE. The two newly elected consuls stand in the center of the Senate chambers, wearing their purple togas of office. The Senate members chat and laugh, expecting that today will be a day of celebration, devoid of any serious dispute.

"I call this session to order!"

A leathery older man steps to the oak plank rostra facing the Senate. The Senate chamber quiets. "I, Publius Sulpicius Galba, hereby accept the consulship. Long live Rome!" Amid the cheers, the veteran commander spreads his arms and lifts his head high, as if making an invocation. "As my first act, I propose that I sail to Greece and confront Philip of Macedonia, before he moves any farther into Greece."

Amid the roars of approval, a young man steps next to him. "I agree with my fellow consul," says Gaius Aurelius Cotta. "*One of us* should sail for Macedonia as soon as possible. The other will march north to halt the Boii's advance."

A voice rings out from the rear of the chambers. "Maybe the one of you that goes to Macedonia should be the one that's actually been in a few battles!"

Cotta's downy face reddens. He glances sideways at his co-consul. "I think we should let the Senate decide who should go where, as Roman law dictates."

The wizened Senate Elder steps in front of the rostra. He bangs his staff of office upon the stone tiles. "Hear, hear!" he rasps. "Enough of this fighting Macedonia nonsense."

He glares at Galba and Cotta. "The Senate appreciates your initiative, but you both know that the People's Assembly has rejected our motion for war with Macedonia."[xxxiii]

He grins widely, exposing the dentures he made from the teeth of corpses.[xxxiv] "So you might both end up fighting the Gauls."

A young senator stands up in the back row, nervously clenching his hands. "Perhaps we can get the plebians to, uh, reconsider."

"How can we get them to reconsider when we don't even know why they voted against it!" snaps Horatius Julii, provoking a chorus of agreement.

"The Tribune of the Plebs is here to explain the people's puzzling decision," replies the Elder. The old man's face creases into a disapproving frown. "And to explain why he spoke against the war at the Assembly."[xxxv]

A lean, sinewy man lurches sideways into the room, dressed in battered armor. "Here comes the Broken Man," a senator whispers to his colleague.

"He may be crippled, but he won't take any shit from us. Just you watch," his colleague replies.

A decorated centurion from Scipio's Iberian army, Quintus Baebius' torso is skewed sideways, a testament to the back injury he suffered at the Battle of Ilipa, when the weight of the Celtiberian dead on top of him injured his spine. As one of the two Tribunes of the Plebs, he is the leader of the citizens' major ruling body, the People's Assembly.

Baebius makes his way to the speaking platform and leans into it for balance. His emerald green eyes fix the senators with an unblinking gaze.

"I see several of my former officers and commanders in this room. They will testify that I am not a man to run from a fight. I followed the immortal Scipio into Iberia, and thence on to Africa. My body was broken in defense of Rome, but I was glad to make that sacrifice, as any true Roman would."

"Then help us fight Macedonia, you woman!" yells Horatius.

"Silence!" barks Scipio, shaking his fist at the senator. "The man is more warrior than ever you will be!"

"But this war you propose," Baebius continues, "it follows the Carthaginian war without a break, and that is too much.[xxxvi] Too many Romans have died. Too many widows and children beg in the street."

He pauses, fixing his eyes on Flaccus. "Too many patricians have seized our humble farms for back taxes while we are out defending Rome. We are tired of our Gallic enemies burning our fields and destroying our towns while we fight abroad. Italia needs time to heal, Rome needs time to heal, and we will not bring any more havoc to either of them! I have said my piece."

Head held high, the old soldier hobbles from the chambers, ignoring the catcalls behind him. The Senate Elder pounds his staff. "There will be order here! You have heard Baebius. What do you propose?"

Scipio rises from his seat in the front. "You know I favor negotiation over war. Baebius has vetoed the Senate's war proposal. So, if we will not have war, we must try diplomacy. Let me go to Philip and convince him to withdraw from Greece."

He walks to the front row and stands over the senior senators sitting there, with Flaccus directly beneath him. "We are Rome, the mightiest of nations. The very threat of war may be enough to give him pause."

Flaccus hears the mutters of agreement. *Shit! We're going to lose our chance to take Macedonia.* He jumps from his seat and faces the senators, his back to Scipio. "Before we assume that war is impossible, let one of our new consuls speak to the People's Assembly. I don't think the people have really heard our side of the story."

Scipio starts to reply, but the Senate Elder hurries to the rostra, "Show of hands," the Elder orders. "A show of hands for Flaccus' motion." The senators raise their hands. "Flaccus' motion carries," the Elder says. "Now who will address the plebs, Galba or Cotta? That is our next item of business."

While the senators debate the merits of the two consuls, Horatius shuffles in behind Flaccus and pats him on the back. "A wise suggestion. I don't think the people understood the implications of their decision."

Flaccus nods solemnly, barely repressing a grin. *Now I have some time to persuade this prick Baebius to change his mind.*

The next afternoon finds Baebius in his apartment in the gritty Aventine Hill section of Rome, reading a scroll on farm property taxes. There is a heavy pounding on his door. Baebius opens it and finds two burly slaves facing him.

"You are Quintus Baebius?" asks the lead slave, a six-and-a-half-foot Gaul.

"Who are you to question a free man?" Baebius retorts. "Get out of here before I take a sword to you!

"It's him," the Gaul says to his Celtiberian companion. "Take him."

The slaves grab Baebius and drag him into the center of the Aventine street, next to a four-wheeled carriage covered by a gilt wood roof. As the Hill's denizens look on, Rome's two censors emerge from their carriage, men who are the chief morality officers for the city. Men who are accountable to no one but themselves.

The censors carefully shed their snow white togas and hand them to their accompanying guards. Wearing only simple gray tunics, the middle—aged patricians walk toward the kneeling Baebius, holding rawhide whips in their hands.

The censors flank the Broken Man. "Strip him," one says to the Gaul. The huge slave tears off Baebius' thick tunic as if it were gauze, leaving him with only his subligaculum.

"Why are you doing this?" Baebius demands. "I've done nothing wrong!" His eyes dawn with recognition. "Who sent you?"

"This man is guilty of betraying the public interest by speaking against the war," a censor shouts to the crowd. "He has betrayed Rome's best interests for his own self-aggrandizement. As such he is a public officer who has acted immorally. Punishment will follow."

"You know all about betraying Rome's interests for personal gain, don't you?" snaps Baebius.

The Gaul grabs Baebius' twisted shoulder and shakes him. "Be silent!" he bellows. Baebius spits on the back of his hand.

The slaves pull Baebius upright and pin his arms in front of him. The censors snap their whips into Baebius' back. Baebius contorts with pain, but he does not cry out. The whips lash again. And again.

"Leave him alone, you soft-assed bastards!" shouts a squat young plowman. He marches toward the censors. The Celtiberian takes a hand off Baebius' arm and pulls out his falcata. "Come on, pig." he growls in pidgin Latin. The plowman retreats, his eyes teary with humiliation.

Angered by the crowd, the censors rain their whips upon Baebius.[xxxvii] Summoning himself, he raises his head and pushes himself upright, his mouth clenched tight.

The Broken Man stands like a misshapen statue, his arms pulling against the slaves' confining grips. His bent body twitches with each lash. Blood streams from the ribbons cut into his back and chest but still he stands, staring silently straight ahead.

Long minutes later, the censors' arms tire; their lashes become slaps.

"Enough," says one. "It's time for dinner." He walks back to the carriage.

The other leans into Baebius' ear. "We know you have a family, traitor. Act accordingly at the Assembly." He strides back toward the chariot, only to be struck to his knees by a rock from the booing crowd. Baebius manages a blood-streaked grin.

A day later, the People's Assembly gathers at the Campus Martius on the outskirts of Rome. At the Senate's request, the people meet to conduct another vote about declaring war on Macedonia.

Consul Galba addresses the Assembly. The attendees stand in large familial groups, with one vote given for each group of a hundred. Galba is respectful but direct: he tells the Romans that their vote is not so much whether to war with Philip, because he will bring war to Rome regardless,[xxxviii] but whether they will bring it to him before he brings it here.

"Does anyone else want to speak?" asks the assembly leader. All eyes turn toward Baebius, who sits on the edge of the assembly platform, his tattered body cloaked in a lengthy gray robe. Baebius stares into space, saying nothing. The plebians stare at him, then at one another.

"Baebius!" cries one.

"Speak, Tribune!" implores another. Baebius quivers with repressed rage and shame, but he does not rise.

"Well, then, it is time to vote—again!" declares the assembly leader.

The centuries sprawl out onto the lawn and discuss the measure. An hour later, the assembly leader calls for a vote. Each century's designate walks to the platform and drops a waxed tablet into a five-foot urn. The tablets are shaken out and counted.

"The people vote to approve war with Macedonia," says the assembly leader. "Consul Galba, it is the Senate's mission to decide where and how the war will commence."

"We will meet tomorrow to determine that," Galba responds. "And we will not leave the chamber until it is done."

The Senate convenes early the next morning. Scipio steps to the rostra, his face grim. Consuls Galba and Cotta step back to allow Rome's First Senator to speak.

"As you know, I favored diplomacy over war. And I have not changed my mind. Not one bit." Scipio pauses, letting his words sink in. "But if we must war against King Philip, then he must be engaged before he gathers strength. Much as I hate to say it, we have to march on Philip immediately."

Senator Glabro rises from his seat in the front. "Is it really that simple? With more time we can recruit and train more legions. If we wait until he lands here—*if* he lands here—we can meet him with ten trained legions. Hannibal himself would tremble at such a force!"

Scipio shakes his head. "It is too dangerous. Carthage was four months travel to Rome," Scipio says. "Macedonia is four days from Rome.[xxxix] Four days. If Philip takes Greece and then he occupies Italia, Philip will not be stranded here as Hannibal was, without homeland resources to call upon. He could quickly access more troops, money, and food from his vast empire."

Glabro shakes his head. "If we had a few months, we could garrison the port cities. Our men would not have to fight in a foreign land."

"Suppose Philip does not land where we anticipate him?" Scipio retorts. "Do you want to wake up with fifty thousand Macedonians at our gates? Do you want to take that chance?"

"I am of Scipio's mind," Consul Galba interjects. "I have fought Macedonia before, so I am the best consul to fight him now. Give me my two consular legions and two more of allies, and I will have my army there by the beginning of the new year, ready for the spring campaign."

Scipio realizes that many of the senators look indecisive. *They need someone to tell them which consul goes where.* He sees Flaccus preparing to rise. *Seize the day before he takes it from you!*

"All in favor of Galba going to Macedonia, raise your hand," shouts Scipio. The Senate Elder flushes with anger at Scipio's intrusion. He totters toward Scipio, his staff raised as if to strike him.

"Give me this, honored Pontius," Scipio hisses. "Let me do this and you will not regret it, I promise."

The Elder steps back. He watches the senators raise their hands, his face impassive. In twos, threes, and then fours, three hundred senators vote for Galba."

"The vote favors Galba," the Elder declares.

"It's settled then," Scipio says. "Consul Cotta will have the north Italia territory. Galba, you have my leave to recruit the veterans from my army,"[xl] But I ask you, do not force them into service, take only volunteers. Many are still haunted by the thousands we burned alive when we raided Syphax's camp in Africa.[xli] Of the massacre we perpetrated at Zama." Scipio smiles sadly. "I know how they feel. I still have nightmares myself."

Galba bows his head. "As you say, First Senator. I will talk to your men immediately. As soon as possible, my army will be at Philip's tent!" He glowers at the Latin Party members. "But first I will negotiate with Philip. And if I fight, I fight to win a peace, not his kingdom."

Galba raises his hand, quelling the outbursts from the Latin senators. "I am consul, and that is my prerogative. I think Scipio has the right of it about making allies, not conquests."

Flaccus seethes when he hears Galba's words. *That bitch wife of his got Galba in, after all the money I spent. And look what he does! She cannot be allowed to work on next year's elections.* He glances over at Cato, who stands in the back row with the rest of the junior senators. *Cato won't be any help. He'd probably report me to the censors. I'd have to bribe them all over again.*

Flaccus rests his chin in his hands. He chuckles. *Well, then. This will be between you and me, Amelia. Just you and me.*

Consul Cotta steps to the rostra. "I bid you well, Galba," the young consul says glumly. "As for me, I fully embrace my assignment to North Italia."

Cotta shrugs, managing a slight smile. "Things have been quiet up there. Those tribes spend more time fighting each other than us!" The senators laugh.

Scipio does not smile. *The boy does not know how fearsome they can be. Thanks the gods they don't have a Hannibal to unite them.*

PO RIVER VALLEY, NORTHERN ITALY, 200 BCE. "They thought they'd seen the last of Carthage, didn't they, Luli?" gloats Hamilcar Gisgon.

His aged army commander nods vigorously. "Verily. The Romans thought Scipio's victory at Zama was the end of us, but we'll show them different. Our war with Rome's not over yet."

"The fools didn't bother purging the hundreds of us who were left up here in Genova," Hamilcar says. "It has taken me two years to recruit enough Gauls, but now the Placentia garrison is ours for the taking!"

"That town has strong, high, walls, Commander," Luli cautions.

"That's what stopped Hasdrubal Barca from taking it." He sees Hamilcar scowling at him. "It had to be mentioned, General."

"I know that, you dungheap. I was with him!"[xlii] But that will make our victory all the sweeter! I'll show Carthage that a Gisgon is as good as any Barca, including that overrated Hannibal!"

"Carthage will not like the idea of you breaking the peace with Rome," Luli says. "Perhaps it is best that they didn't know it was you. Let that Boii chief Lugos lead the attack, then they'll blame it on the Gauls."

Hamilcar grimaces. "And let the Gauls have the honor? Absolutely not. And Carthage, they can float to Hades for all I care," Hamilcar snaps. "I asked them for reinforcements, and they tell me to come home. They've lost their will to fight."

He taps his muscled chest. "They call me an exile, a renegade. When I take Placentia, they'll come to my side."

"But how are we going to take the walls?" Luli asks. "The Gauls are not patient enough for a siege. They are best when they are in full assault, wreaking havoc."

"Then they can charge the walls and wreak havoc! I have thirty-five thousand Cenomani, Insubres, and Boii; three tribes all lusting to revenge themselves upon the Romans. They'll tear the walls down stone by stone if they have to."

"Many would die," adds Luli.

"That's just it," Hamilcar says, his voice excited. "Hasdrubal was afraid to launch a full-scale attack on Placentia—he thought he'd lose too many men." He throws up his hands and grins. "But I'm not planning to march on Rome with *these* men, so I don't care! There are always more where they came from. Too many to feed now, anyway."

Luli looks away from his commander, hiding his expression. "Very well. I will talk to the chieftains, tell them to get their men ready for the assault."

Three days later, Hamilcar's army approaches Placentia, marching down the wide dirt road between the frost-limned stubble of Placentia's harvested fields.

Hamilcar rides in the lead position, surrounded by the two hundred Carthaginian soldiers who had remained with him at Genova. Tens of thousands of Gauls follow in loose columns, each tribe towing along wagons of weapons, belongings, and family. Hamilcar has brought only two day's food stores with his army. As Luli told the three tribes' chieftains: they will take Placentia quickly, or they will starve.

The Gallic army halts a quarter mile from the town. With Hamilcar directing them, the massive army slowly surrounds the twenty-foot walls of Placentia. By late afternoon, a sea of tents has sprouted around the garrison. Hundreds of legionnaires watch anxiously from walls.

Provincial Governor Quintus Anicius stands above Placentia's front gates, waiting for an envoy from Hamilcar's camp. *He'll want us to surrender*, he muses, *but he can go crawl in a hole. We have food stores for a year, we'll wait him out.*

By nightfall, no messenger has approached Quintus, though he can see Hamilcar and his chieftains standing in front of the Carthaginian's command tent, looking out toward him. The Roman commander comes to a realization that turns his stomach: Hamilcar is not here to negotiate a surrender, he is here to destroy the garrison. He turns to his lead tribune.

"Get all the catapults up here. Give every man and woman a sword, a spear, some kind of weapon. Tell them they are going to fight for their lives."

The next day dawns upon a Gallic camp that is furious with activity. The Gauls wheel in dozens of catapults while their warriors pile up the melon-sized river stones they trundled in from the Po River. The catapults encircle the town, facing the Roman machines that loom above the parapets.

Hundreds of Gauls ride into the forest and harvest limbs and branches for ladders. They ferry them back to camp, where their women and children tie them into ladders. When a ladder is finished, two young Gauls carry it the circumference of the mile-wide battle circle. By the end of the day, a thick ring of them encircles Placentia.

Night falls and scores of bonfires appear, accompanied by much shouting and singing. Quintus watches from the parapet over the gates. He studies the distant silhouettes of the large, thick, men dancing about the towering flames, swilling wine and waving swords.

The young governor sighs. *They'll be at us tomorrow morning, as sure as Jupiter dwells in the sky.* Quintus clambers down the parapet's wooden steps. He strides across the open courtyard and enters his stone block command house. Pulling up a stool at his command desk, he picks up his quill pen, dips it into a clay pot of octopus ink, and writes on his best papyrus.

Dearest Horatia:

I trust this letter finds you well, riding about the golden fields of our new farm, rejoicing in a bountiful fall harvest.

I thank the gods we decided to that you and Claudia would stay near Rome. I dream of you plucking fat purple grapes from our vines and popping them into Claudia's pudgy little mouth. I think of your happiness, and I am comforted.

Events here may mean I do not see you for quite a while, though my thoughts are ever with you. While I am gone, I only ask one thing: when you are about our villa, or playing with Claudia, or shopping at the merchants' stalls—stop for a moment and take me into your heart, with a memory of how we were.

I love you forever.

Quintus

The governor rolls up the papyrus and seals it with his wolf's head stamp. He stoops over, his shoulders quivering. A sob escapes his throat.

Quintus slaps his face. *Enough!*

"Coaxtus, come here!" A one-armed legionnaire appears in the doorway. "Bring me our three best riders, ready to fly."

The gray-haired soldier nods. "I know just the ones, Commander. He grins. "Not as good as I was in my prime, but you know how this new generation of soldier is!"

Quintus forces a laugh. "Bring them anyway, or I'll make you get on a horse yourself!" While he waits, Quintus pens out a note to the Senate, writing with quick, bold strokes. He quickly makes two copies of each message.

Three young equites step through the doorway, wearing their riding armor. "I need each of you to take two messages to Rome," he tells them. "I want three of you to go, that one may survive the trip. Take off that armor—it will only slow you down. I want you in dark tunics and leather caps. Gods be merciful, you will all soon be dining in Rome."

"Wh-when do you want us to go?" stammers a thin young patrician, his eyes anxious. "The Gauls are getting thicker out there."

"Now!" Quintus barks. "Now, while those drunken clods are wandering around in a stupor. Go!"

The three horsemen hurriedly jostle out the door. Quintus stares into the blackened doorway. *Fortuna bless them with safe passage. I cannot bear Horatia would never read my message.*

"Coaxtus!" he shouts. The old soldier appears. "Yes, Commander?"

"Bring me the Falernian," Quintus says. "The one with the golden faun painted on the jar."

"The Falernian?" Coaxtus' eyes widen. "As you say."

The assistant quickly returns with a sealed urn. He scrapes the thick sealing wax off the wood stopper and pulls it out. Quintus nods. "No water—just fill it up." He holds out his bronze goblet. Coaxtus carefully fills it with the fragrant, heady, white wine.

"You, too," Quintus says, pointing at another goblet.

"I get some Falernian?" Coaxtus says. "Now I'm truly ready to die!"

When both vessels are filled, the praetor pours a dollop onto the ground. "To the gods," he says. The two drink deeply, smacking their lips. "A drink fit for the gods," Coaxtus affirms.

Quintus raises his goblet. "To Rome, may she rule forever." The two drain their cups. Quintus toys with the rim of his goblet, tapping it against his left fist. "Such a life it has been, Coaxtus: a farm, a wife, a child, and service to Rome."

Coaxtus laughs and raises his cup. "Such a life it has been! Lots of wine to drink, women to fuck, and fights to win." he laughs. "I can say that my life cup was filled before it was drained!"

Quintus nods. "As it was for me. Now excuse me, friend. I must rest."

Coaxtus' eyes grow wistful. "Aye, it will be a big day tomorrow."

With Coaxtus gone, Quintus lays back on his sleeping pallet and stares at the wood-beamed ceiling. He thinks of how he will place his men on the walls, and how he will bolster the main gates. He recalls his years in the Sabina Hills near Rome—growing up, enlisting, fighting, marrying, and fathering.

After hours of tossing and turning, Somnus blesses him with relief.

The sun breaks the horizon, its sharp light crawling up the back wall of Placentia. Quintus stands on the walkway above the gates, his freshly polished breastplate gleaming in the bright morning sun. He pulls off his helmet and leans his elbows on the wall, watching the dawn illuminate the Gallic camp. He sees that there are thousands of barbarians still sprawled out in sleep, their weapons scattered about them.

They're all half drunk. If I had two legions of veterans, I could march out there and wipe them from the face of the earth. If, if—fucking if!

An hour drags by. The Gauls rouse themselves, grappling for their shields and long swords. They chew on dried meat scraps from their packs, washing them down with drafts from their wineskins. Many wander over to the latrine ditches on the fringe of their camp, shouting crude jests at each other as they relieve themselves. The barbarians wander back to their clan's places along the front lines, ready to attack.

Quintus spies an eagle soaring high in the sky, approaching the front of the town. *Come this way, spirit bird,* he prays. *Give us a sign that Fortuna is with us.*

The eagle wheels away from Placentia. It swoops low over the Gallic camp, drifting above the thousands of Boii who are massing opposite Placentia's main gates. Quintus' shoulders slump.

A horn blares out from the Gallic camp. Scores of others echo around the encirclement. Quartets of Gauls march out to man the catapults that encircle the garrison. They push them through the thick ring of waiting warriors, out into clear space in front. The barbarians crank back the catapults' ropes and load the baskets with head-sized river stones, readying them for attack.

Hamilcar Gisgon rides out from his men and pauses opposite the Placentia gates. He turns his horse about and faces his soldiers. The Carthaginian pulls out his curved sword and holds it high in front of him. The Gauls are hushed, expectant. Hamilcar swipes down his sword. The horns blare again.

From all directions, pairs of Gauls burst out from the ring and race toward the walls, each duo lugging a rude tree-branch ladder, the leaves and branches still dangling from its sides.

The Gallic army trots in behind the hundreds of ladder men, ready to follow them up the walls.

Watching his army advance, Hamilcar's eyes shine with murderous lust. *We'll see how tough you are now,* he gloats.

84

"Prepare a covering fire!" he yells to Luli. Moments later, the air fills with the groans of thick ropes being pulled to their breaking point. Hamilcar stares into the sky over Placentia, ready to enjoy the destruction he will unleash. "Loose!" he screams.

Dozens of snapping sounds erupt. The catapults jolt forward. Their lethal boulders fly at Placentia from all directions.

The large stones arc over the walls. They crash into Placentia's roofs and courtyards, bashing down its citizens and soldiers. Screams erupt throughout the town.

"Give the men on a walls a taste of it," Hamilcar commands. A second volley crashes into the parapets, knocking out gaping holes.

Unperturbed, Quintus shouts over to his men manning his catapults. "Back at them! Load and fire as fast as you can."

The groaning crack of catapults rattles across Placentia's parapets. A cloud of river boulders whooshes down upon the attacking Gauls. Dozens fall face first to the earth, their helmets bashed into their skulls. Scores writhe on the ground, hugging their broken shoulders and arms.

The Boii, Ligurians, and Cenomani continue their charge, leaving a trail of fallen kinsmen behind them. The Roman catapults release again, angled for shorter range. The rocks crunch into the front lines approaching the walls, knocking the huge Gauls down as if they are children.

Heedless of the carnage about them, the tribesmen continue their rush to the base of the walls, holding their oblong shields high above their heads. The ladder men fling their ladders onto the wall and scramble up, eager to receive Hamilcar's purse of silver as the first to land on the walkway. The warriors follow them up, their axes and swords at the ready.

The Roman defenders leap onto the first barbarians who appear above the wall, attacking them in groups of two and three. They chop at the Gauls with their double-edged gladii, ramming them off the ladder with their shields. Scores of warriors hurtle onto their men below.

85

More ladders clack against the top of the wall, too many for the Romans to cover. The barbarians flow onto the walkway, and a free form fight erupts around the perimeter.

The Romans' short swords serve them well in the close-in fighting. They step inside the Gauls' long swords and stab into their enemies' chests and thighs, felling scores of the them. But the fierce Gauls do not relent, so focused are they on killing their hated enemies. Mad with battle lust, many simply grab the legionnaire facing them and fling him off the wall, ignoring the thrusts into their chests and stomachs. More barbarians pour over the wall, hacking swathes through the Roman defenders.

A quartet of Boii plunge their swords into the two legionnaires guarding the steps above the gates. They fling the men aside and scramble down into the courtyard.

"The gates!" yells their Boii leader, a fleshy older man with a jawless skull dangling from his neck. "Open the fucking gates!" The four run toward the square timber barring the passage. Two rush to the short stairway at each end of the gate and grasp the waist-thick bar.

"Now! Lift together," the older man shouts, "get it off the—Aggh!"

A javelin crunches into the man's lower back, arcing him backward. The leader reaches behind with his left hand and yanks it out, bellowing with pain. He stumbles back to the gate timber and grabs it. Another spear clunks into the palisades above his head.

"Now, boys, before they finish killing me," he shouts, gasping for breath.

Groaning with effort, the brawny warriors lift the timber over its braces and watch it thunder to the ground. Another javelin spears the older man in the neck. He falls face first on top of the gate timber, where he lies still.

More spears rain in on the remaining defenders. The three tumble from the steps, spears jutting from their backs.

86

Four Days from Rome

"Get that gate closed!" Quintus yells. He rushes for the portal, leading a cohort of 480 legionnaires, the city's main force. While his men brace themselves against the gates, Quintus throws down his shield and grabs the center of the timber.

"Come on! Help me get this monster back up there!"

He hears the gates groan. A narrow opening appears. A dozen Gallic sword blades jut through the opening, stabbing at the air. "Hurry, hurry!" Quintus screams. He and his men waddle the timber toward the gate braces, ready to drop it in place.

The gates fly open, knocking the Romans backward. Lugos stands in the center of the opening, his brown hair flowing from his horned skullcap. The bearlike Boii chieftain swoops his tree-root war club over his head.

"Into them!" Lugos shouts to his men. "Kill them all!"

Hundreds of Boii stream through the front gates, led by their screaming chieftain. Quintus pushes himself to his feet and grabs his shield. *Mars, give me strength to kill him—then I am yours.*

Quintus strides toward the onrushing horde. His eyes are glassy with fear, but his step never falters.

"Here now, Governor. Don't be going anywhere without your best man." He looks over his shoulder and sees a grinning Coaxtus' limping toward him, his shield tied onto his arm stub. "I was good at getting rid of rats on the farm," he says. "Now it looks like I'm back to work at it way over here!"

Quintus manages a small smile. "Come on, old friend. Let's drive them out!"

Lugos spies Quintus' purple-plumed helmet. "He is mine!" the barbarian chieftain shouts to his men. He rushes toward Quintus, his war club raised for a killing blow.

Quintus raises his left arm and takes the chieftain's blow upon the boss of his shield. Even so, the force of the heavy club knocks him to one knee. He stabs futilely at the empty space between him and the Boii, as the chieftain again raises his club.

Coaxtus suddenly appears between the two combatants. The older man rams his shield into the chieftain's barrel chest, knocking him back. He stabs his blade into the Gaul's club arm, slicing it across his forearm.

"Stupid old bastard," Lugos growls. With a deft sweep of his foot, the Boii yanks Coaxtus' foot sideways. As Coaxtus falls, the Boii sweeps down his weighty club. It bashes into the side of Coaxtus' head.

The old Roman's eyes bulge. Blood spurts from his gaping mouth. He crashes to the ground, his lips spasming wordlessly as he chokes on his blood.

"Coaxtus!" Quintus screams, rising to his feet. Mad with rage, the governor sprints forward and crashes into the surprised chieftain's chest. The Boii's lethal club sweeps harmlessly over Quintus' back.

Quintus stabs into the Boii's ribs and breast. Bellowing in agony, the wounded chieftain drops his shield and shoves Quintus onto the ground. He leaps upon him and swings down his club.

The cudgel bashes into the top of Quintus' helmet, denting it into his skull. Blood spurts from Quintus' nose and mouth. His eyes glaze over. He crumples to the earth, twitching, and lies still. Lugos raises his bloodied club to the sky, screaming his triumph to the gods.

The nearby legionnaires see Quintus fall. Enraged, they leave their individual battles and swarm to protect his body, stabbing at any Gaul that nears it. The Gauls press into the defenders, hammering at them with their axes and swords. Mounds of dead combatants heap over Quintus and Coaxtus' bodies, but the Romans refuse to give ground.

Slowly, inevitably, hundreds of Boii surround the legionnaires. The victorious Cenomani and Ligurians descend from the walls and join the Boii. The Romans fight on top of an island of bodies, their numbers dwindling as their enemies tighten their circle.

A chorus of screams erupts from the streets behind the Gauls. Hundreds of townspeople run toward them, their faces contorted with fury. Men, women, and boys attack them, brandishing swords, spears, hoes, and mattocks—anything that can cut through flesh and bone.

The outer circle of Gauls faces the attacking citizenry. Some laugh, some chuckle. For others, a wolfish gleam comes to their eyes.

"At them!" shouts Lugos, flinging a Roman head at the townspeople. The other chieftains echo his call.

Hundreds of Gauls run forward. They scream out their renewed bloodlust, their axes and swords ready for the kill. The barbarians stampede through the citizenry, swinging their weapons to the right and left, heedless of who they strike.

Without shields or armor, the townspeople are easy prey. Many a Gaul extends his fight with a boy or woman, toying with them as a cat with a mouse, taunting them until he becomes bored and strikes a final blow.

Hamilcar rides through the gates, accompanied by Luli and his Carthaginian guards. He calmly watches the slaughter in the streets.

"Those people are spirited, I will give them that," he says to Luli.

"Do those savages really have to chop the heads off the women?" Luli says, tightening a linen arm bandage with his teeth. "They'd fetch a lot of silver in the slave market."

"You're right, we're losing money. Where's Lugos?" Hamilcar waves over the Boii chieftains. "Stop the massacre, we need slaves for the market!"

"They try kill us, we kill them," Lugos barks angrily.

Hamilcar shakes his head. "You're killing your money! Your plunder! Go on, now. Keep the women and children alive. The young women, at least. You'll make much money!"

The chiefs stalk back to the massacre. After a few shouted orders, the Gauls turn from slaughter to capture, roping their captives together about the ankles. The forlorn survivors are dragged into the stone meeting hall fronting the courtyard.

Now that's better! Hamilcar wheels his horse toward the Romans defending the gates, surrounded by a deep circle of Gauls. The soldiers stand exhausted and bloodied but unbowed, their feet planted atop a hillock of their fellows' corpses.

"Halt the attack!" Hamilcar shouts. He pushes his horse through the ring of barbarians and faces the legionnaires.

"Death or slavery, slavery or death," he chants rhythmically, "throw down your weapons, or breathe your last breath."

A lone centurion stands in the center of the defenders. He surveys the hundreds of Gauls around him. He throws down his sword, and the two dozen survivors follow suit.

"Put them with the rest," Hamilcar orders. His grin splits his face. *What a victory! Hannibal himself couldn't have done better. Wait until word gets out about my conquest, I'll have twenty thousand Carthaginians up here!*

Hours later, Hamilcar's captain comes into his tent and gives him the news. The Gauls have leveled the city and captured two thousand survivors.[xliii] Ten thousand townspeople and legionnaires sprawl dead beneath the hazy winter sun.

The Carthaginian commander pours himself a goblet of deep red Iberian wine. He sips it thoughtfully, reclining on his sheepskins. *No sense stopping now. The Gauls have the bloodlust upon them. Let's see if the Cremona garrison will capitulate.*

After two days of feasting and revelry, Hamilcar moves his army east toward Cremona, his back to the smoldering ruin of once-proud Placentia.

PLACENTIA RUINS. The Roman scouts dismount in front of the

shattered Placentia gates. Throwing a rope about their horses' necks, they lead them carefully through the wreckage, weaving between the fallen blocks and bodies. The four men pause before the mound of Roman corpses at the gates.

"This is where they made their last stand," says the red-haired young equite, his voice hushed with reverence.

"Look at this, Rufus," says a legionnaire. "The Gauls took away all their bodies, but they didn't have the decency to burn ours." He peers at the corpses. "But they had time to steal our men's' rings and bracelets. Even pried the gold out of their teeth."

He gingerly pulls up a dismembered hand resting on top of the bodies. "Looks like they cut the finger off this one here so they—what's that?" The equite strides over to a high mound of bodies. The other scouts rush over.

A hand sticks out from underneath the dead legionnaires. Its fingers twitch spasmodically.

Rufus stares at it, open-mouthed. "Fortuna be praised, one of them's still alive!" Two scouts grab the top bodies and roll them off.

"I can see his other hand," a scout yells.

"Grab them both and pull!" Rufus orders. "We've got to get him out before he dies..."

Quintus awakes in a darkness of stinking, rotting flesh, his mind clouded with pain. He feels rough hands grasping his wrists, his body being pulled forward. His face slides across cold bronze armor, then across colder flesh.

Sunlight explodes into his face. He blinks and grimaces, coughing violently. "Water," he rasps. "Water!"

A waterskin is pressed to his mouth. He gulps greedily. "Wh-where am I?"

"You are still at Placentia, sir," a young voice tells him. "You are the only survivor we have found." The voice softens. "Forgive me, but we must depart soon, before the Gauls find us here."

The legionnaires gently lift Quintus up. They wipe the clotted blood from his face and head, wrapping a bandage around his scabby chin. Two scouts ease him onto the back of Rufus' horse. They rope Quintus and the scout together about their middles.

A scout yanks Quintus' purple-plumed helmet from the corpse mound. *The praetor might want to keep this.* The young equite notices the deep dent in it and his eyes grow wide. *This man must be favored by the gods!* He straps the helmet onto the back of his horse and springs upon it.

"Back to the garrison," Rufus commands. "We've got to prepare for an attack. We might be next."

"Where are we going?" a bleary Quintus asks.

"To Cremona, Governor," Rufus replies. "Let's see those Gallic bastards try to come over our thirty-foot walls!"

CURIA HOSTILIA, ROME. The Senate chambers are hushed while the Senate Elder reads out the Placentia losses, his voice trembling with rage.

"This is the work of the Gauls, but they were led by a Carthaginian," replies the Elder. "This Hamilcar Gisgon thinks the war against Carthage is not over. He went on to attack Cremona, but the garrison was prepared and they have repelled his assaults—so far. Now Hamilcar is laying siege to them."

He turns to his fellows, his arms wide in entreaty. "What do you propose we do, Senators?"

Senator Sextus Fabius rises from his front-row seat. "Hamilcar is one of Carthage's own. We should send envoys to Carthage and tell them to recall him."

Four Days from Rome

Flaccus rises quickly from his seat. "Excellent idea! I nominate young Cato here. He is a man of impeccable character, as all of you know." Carthage-hating Cato starts with surprise, looking at Flaccus as if he were mad.

"Absolutely not," Scipio replies. "Cato has an unrelenting hatred for Carthage." He shakes his head. "Why, we can't have a Senate meeting without him saying 'Carthage must be destroyed,' as if it were some ritual prayer!" The chamber erupts in laughs.

Smirking bastard! Flaccus thinks. "I nominate Marcus Porcius Cato to be lead envoy," he repeats stubbornly.

Flaccus stands with his hands at his side, waiting for support. Several awkward minutes pass. The Senate Elder eventually steps in front of him. "We apparently have a vote of silence here," he says. "We will consider another candidate, Senator."

Flaccus sits down, his face flaming. He glowers at Scipio. *You are the Senate favorite now, but your time is coming. And I will bring it to you.*

A tall white-haired man rises from his seat, his back ramrod straight despite his girth and years. "You know have I no part in this Latin-Hellenic nonsense," bellows Publius Glabro, his deep bass voice reverberating through the chambers. "My death is too near for me to play favorites. I tell you now, there is only one man the Africans respect. You know who it is or you are a fool."

The Senate erupts with shouts of "Aye!" and "Scipio Africanus!" Without another word, Glabro resumes his seat. He glares at Flaccus, who averts his eyes.

A slight smile creeps onto the Senate Elder's seamed face. His ancient blue eyes twinkle with mirth at the mention of Scipio, his favorite. "Well then! Your suggestion has merit with the Senate, General Glabro." He raises his staff of office. "I call a vote. All in favor of sending Scipio Africanus as our lead envoy, stand up."

Hundreds begin to rise, and the Elder impatiently waves them down. "Enough, enough, I can see the vote is decided. Publius Cornelius

93

Scipio, will you accept the mission?"

Shit! I have so many things to do here! Our council was going to propose a new salt tax. He thinks of Hannibal, and Masinissa. *But I have unfinished business there.*

Scipio rises from his seat. "I will lead our envoys to Carthage on one condition: that we use the mission to gain material support for our wars with Gaul and Macedonia."

He eyes Cato. "Carthage's support will strengthen the bonds between our two great nations." Cato grimaces at him.

"I see no reason why we should not," says the Elder. Does anyone else?"

Cato rises from his seat. "We should owe nothing to those treacherous dogs. They will only use their support against us!" The chambers are silent. Cato glances over at Flaccus. *Sit down,* he signals. Cato resumes his seat, his eyes blazing defiance.

The die is cast, boy—why bother? Flaccus thinks. He smiles to himself. *Besides, if Scipio is gone, that gives me more latitude for my own plan.*

"Now back to the matter of north Italia." The Elder's mouth tightens. "Consul Cotta, that area is your responsibility. What do you propose?"

The consul steps to the speaker's rostra, his eyes downcast.

"Praetor Lucius Furius has five thousand Latin allies up there," Cotta says. "Their numbers are no match for Hamilcar's army." He looks anxiously at the Senate. "I, I imagine I should march up there and help him." His eyes beg the senators to agree.

Scipio gapes at the rotund little patrician. *My gods, this man has the heart of a lamb! He'll get them all killed!* Scipio rises from his seat. "I know Lucius Furius Purpo well, Consul Cotta. He is a fine officer, a veteran of many campaigns. You are right to have your consular army go to his aid." He looks at the Senate members, catching their eyes before his next words. "But perhaps you would be of greater service if you stayed here. After all, Consul Galba will be leaving for Macedonia, and we would lose another experienced magistrate if you are gone too."

Cotta sees that scores of senators are silently nodding their assent, their faces grim. He gulps, understanding Scipio's thinly-veiled command. "With the Senate's approval, I will send the praetor my two consular legions and two legions of allies."

"A fine idea," the Elder mutters. Cotta shuffles back to his seat and sits bent over, staring at his feet.

"Now, as to Macedonia. What news to report, Consul Galba?"

"My two legions are being assembled and trained. Many of Scipio's veterans have volunteered to join me."

He grins at Scipio. "They were quite amenable, once they heard their old commander would be helping me out! I have mixed the veterans with our raw recruits. Scipio's men will aid their training, which we are currently completing. When the fall harvest ends, I will sail to Greece and establish winter quarters at Appollonia. That will put us between Macedonia and Athens."

"Does anyone have any questions about that?" says the Elder. Hearing none, he pounds his staff on the floor. "We are concluded!"

The senators file out into the afternoon sun, wandering through the spacious Forum square. Scipio and Galba turn into a side street, looking over their shoulder to make sure they aren't followed.

"It's over here, on the left. " Scipio says, pointing to an inconspicuous wine bar at the intersection of the side street and the Avenue of Merchants. "It's my favorite popina."

Galba eyes the patio's crumbling wood overhang. "It looks like a stable."

"I know it's a bit rugged," Scipio replies, "But that keeps out the patricians! We can talk in private here."

Galba and Scipio pull up stools at a round stone table inside the rear of the bar. The new consul notices several workingmen glancing at them. "This is a rough-looking place," he mutters.

"Don't worry about the locals," Scipio says. "I came here often before I went to Africa. They just have to get used to seeing me here again."

The men share a bowl of the savory pheasant stew and a platter of flatbread covered with olive oil and mushrooms. A wizened little man in a grease-spattered tunic stumps over to their table, lugging a jug of water and a bronze pitcher of dark red wine.

"This is a fine Rioja, Senators. A gift in honor of General Scipio's conquest of Iberia." He bows and walks away.

"That's the owner. His son was a centurion in my first legion. He somehow credits me for his boy coming back from Africa."

Galba nods. "I can see why. Your victory at Zama saved a lot of lives. I would be grateful for your guidance on my upcoming campaign."

Scipio sips his wine, thinking. "I only have one bit of advice right now: add a new element to your army. One that has been very successful for our enemies."

"New swords? Assault tactics?" asks Galba.

Scipio shakes his head. "Nothing like that. It's a lesson I learned from two great generals: Hannibal and Pyrrhus." His eyes twinkle over the top of his cup. "Elephants."

Galba stares at Scipio. "Elephants? They've killed thousands of Romans. Our horses bolt at the sight of them, and so do the men!"

"I taught them both to behave otherwise," Scipio says, trickling some water into his wine. "Hannibal and the Greek general Pyrrhus used them to deadly effect against us. It's time we learned from our enemies. You should get your own elephant squadron."

Galba rolls his eyes. "And where am I supposed to get elephants?"

Scipio looks up at the smoke-blackened roof timbers. He smiles. "Oh, I just happen to have a few around," He grins at Galba's amazed look. "I brought four back for my triumph. I used them in Africa to accustom my soldiers and horses to them."

"Four is not twenty. They wouldn't be enough to lead a charge."

"Of course not. I'll bring you some more when I return from Carthage." His grin widens. "I'll get them from my old friend Hannibal!"

"Our mortal enemy?" Galba blurts.

"Hannibal is a man of honor. He fought us because that was his duty. And to fulfill a promise to his father." Scipio's eyes grow distant. "I know what that's like."

"You think they'll just give you the beasts? We have severely restricted their military force."

"Carthage is anxious to maintain the peace with us, they will be glad to give us a few of them." His eyes twinkle. "But that won't be the only thing. I give you something else to consider."

"More gifts from Carthage?" Galba asks suspiciously.

Scipio sips his wine. "Oh no. One is from Iberia!" He grins. "The other from Numidia..."

AVENTINE HILL DISTRICT, ROME. The city's torch lighters tread uneasily in this darkened section of town, often looking over their shoulders. They touch their brands to the eight torch sticks fastened to the posts around the Aventine's stable fences, as the horses eye them curiously. Their task completed, the lighters trot out of the narrow alleyway, anxious to return to the Capitoline neighborhood before one of the roaming Aventine gangs finds them.

The torch lighters do not notice the hooded figure that withdraws into the doorway of the stable master's hut, lurking in the shadows until they pass. They do not see the four burly slaves crouched among the horses, their hands at their sword belts, searching for any who might assault their master.

A squat, hairless, man enters the alleyway, waddling toward the stables. The Toad does not fear the gangs or the darkness; in the Aventine, he is the master of both. His three Gallic henchmen lumber along behind him, their wary eyes searching every darkened doorway in the rickety apartments that line these cobbled streets.

With the flood of immigrants that continuously flow into the Aventine's huts and insulae, there are always those who have not heard of the Toad, and might essay an attempt at robbery. Those who do are most often found at the Toad's patio in front of his Aventine manse, their fly-covered heads a testament to their folly.

The Toad pushes open the stable gate and tramps toward the hut. The cloaked figure moves out into the torchlight, briefly, and waves him inside.

"I have a new assignment for you." The hooded figure whispers.

A grin splits Toad's wattled face. "Got another senator for us to beat down? Give him some fist bumps on his face?"

"It is a she. And it must be done after her husband leaves."

"Ah, she wouldn't give you any, eh?" Toad chortles. "I know how that is. A view whacks with the club and they come around. She'll be on her back for you in no time!"

"This one is not to remain alive," the figure says. He extends a bony hand and drops two bulging purses into Toad's warty palms. "Scipio's wife. After he leaves for Africa."

Toad is silent. "Well, Senator, that is a very risky case. His veterans would flay me alive if they found out. Yes, very risky!"

"Two more purses when the job is done," the figure replies testily. "But get the right man. I need someone who can kill like a striking snake. This woman is skilled with blades, and she does not balk at killing."

"I know just the one," Toad says. "Six kills last month, all neat and clean."

"Good. But he had better not miss."

"He?" Toad replies, chuckling. "Who said anything about a 'he'?"

CARTHAGE, 200 BCE. "Look at it, isn't it amazing?" Scipio says, staring out from his ship's prow at the gigantic port of Carthage.

The trireme sails through the walled channel that leads into the center of Carthage's town-sized circular harbor. It eases into one of the hundred covered docks that line the inside perimeter, gliding past the marble statues that flank each side of the dock.

"It's like landing inside a temple," his captain says, his mouth agape. Scipio can only nod, staring at its wonderment. *I wonder if Rome could build something like this at Ostia? No, the Latins would think it a frivolous waste of money. They'd have us all dock at fishing piers.*

A statuesque gray-haired man stands at dockside, a leopard skin patch covering one eye. He wears a toga of pure Carthaginian purple, a sign that he is one of Carthage's leading magistrates. The man is surrounded by a score of Carthage's elite Sacred Band warriors, their glued linen cuirasses shining like polished eggs.

The trireme's gangplank thuds onto the spotless dock planks. A toga-clad Scipio walks down the dock, followed by three elder senators who are Rome's other envoys. As he approaches the Carthaginian, the man fixes Scipio with a single penetrating green eye, as if staring into his soul. He smiles.

"General Scipio," says Hannibal. "It is a pleasure to see you, now that we are not fighting each other!"

Scipio grasps Hannibal's rock-hard forearm. "I had the same thought, Commander. I am delighted to see you, and to return to your fair city. This time we do not have to wrangle out a peace treaty with your

Council of Elders, thank the gods!"

Hannibal chuckles. "You will find them as contumacious as ever, more so because you have befriended me! But first, we'll take a scenic tour through the main street."

He grins impishly. "You'll see what Rome could become some day, if you are very fortunate!"

The four envoys clamber onto padded benches inside a fragrant cedar wagon, its waxed sides roofed with gold-embroidered linen. Hannibal's guards mount their white stallions and lead the wagon down the avenue, rolling past hordes of brown-skinned onlookers.

The group moves through the wide main street of Carthage, a venue lined with statues to Carthage's gods and generals. Scipio peers into the side streets. *Let's see what the poor people live like.* He sees nothing but tree-lined streets that boast immaculate stone apartments.

This is better than Athens. The gods themselves could dwell here. And Cato wants to burn it to the ground! I can't let the Latins destroy it.

The envoys disembark in front of the Senate. They ascend the chamber's fifty steps and pass through the white marble columns that flank the Senate entrance, walking through twin columns of grim Carthaginian guards. They enter open bronze doors and walk into Carthage's inner chambers.

The Council of Elders are waiting there, seated along the circular rows that surround their Senate floor. Carthage's two ruling sufetes stand in the center, bald-headed elders in purple-bordered indigo robes.

"Ah, General Scipio, you have arrived earlier than we expected today," says one of the sufetes. "I am Hiro, the Senior Sufete." Hiro is a heavyset man, built like an aging wrestler.

"We are all anxious to know, why has Rome decided to grace us with your presence?" he asks sarcastically.

"I suspect you know why," Scipio says. "On behalf of Rome, I request that you recall Hamilcar Gisgon from North Italia. He is leading a Gallic insurrection that has cost us lives and money."

Scipio hears a number of the seated Elders chuckling. The lead sufete shakes his bald head. "We have tried to recall him, Senator Scipio, but he refuses to come back."

Hiro eyes the Romans. "Now, if you would let us mount an army and let Hannibal take them over to Italia, we could do something about him!"

Amid scattered laughter, Scipio's neck flushes. *Diplomacy can go to Hades—I will not tolerate this insolent shit!*

He steps toward Hiro and stares into his onyx eyes. "Have a care, lest I come back here with my veterans." He turns and eyes the others. "You know what happened the last time I did, don't you?"

Hiro looks past him, toward the Elders. "I am only saying we cannot do anything about it," he replies loudly. "We have confiscated Hamilcar's property and threatened him with exile,[xliv] but all to no avail. Isn't that right?"

Scipio hears the murmurs of assent. "So you propose to make *your* problem Rome's problem, eh? Well, that bird will not fly. You had best offer me a solution, immediately."

Hannibal steps to Scipio's side. "What about food? Our wheat crop was good this year. We can send wheat to Rome. Say, two hundred measures?"

"Two hundred measures, to Rome," Scipio replies. He sees the Elders start to smile. *No you don't.* "And another two hundred measures to Galba's army, which is currently at Epirus."[xlv]

"I am not sure we have that much to—" Hiro begins. Hannibal steps in front of Scipio. He fixes Hiro with a warning look. "It is done! I will personally oversee its transport!"

Scipio nods. "Good. That is all I want from Carthage—for now." He marches out the entryway, still seething, followed by the other three envoys. A tall, gaunt man appears outside the doorway, his hands tucked into his floor length white robe.

"That was an unsavory little event, was it not?" the man says.

Scipio eyes him. "I remember you. You are Durro, chief emissary of Carthage's council of judges, the all-powerful Council of 104."

"They *were* all powerful," comes a voice behind Durro.

Hannibal steps into the doorway. "They were too powerful. I roused the people against them. Instead of lifetime appointments, they have a one-year appointment and a two-year term limit.[xlvi] Now we can get rid of them if they misbehave." He laughs. "The citizens love it. And me."

"Many of the Elders would cheerfully gut you with a dull knife," Durro replies dryly.

"Psh! They hate me no more than before," Hannibal says. "The Gisgons and Magonids, they've always resented the Barcas' success. I've just given them a few new friends to join them!"

"I think it is more than a few, General," Durro says. "I would watch out for treachery, especially from those who claim to be on your side."

"Let them watch out for me!" Hannibal retorts. "I will follow my father's dream. We will make Carthage a true democracy. I have the people on my side."

That's often not enough, my friend, Scipio thinks.

"I think I have the people of Rome's hearts," Scipio says. "But the Latins fight me every step of the way." He grins tiredly. "It looks like we are still at war, General. Just not with each other!"

Hannibal nods. "We've only shifted the theatres. Now we're at war within our own cities." He laughs heartily. "Ah, Fate! What will you bring us next!"

"Fate may have more surprises awaiting me in the next few days,"

Scipio replies. "I must ride to Numidia and visit King Masinissa. We did not part on the best of terms." He shrugs. "I may get a crown on my head or my head on a spike."

Hannibal winks at Durro. "Well, then, Commander Scipio. If your head ends up on a spike, I may have to come out of retirement!"

Scipio laughs. "Just do me a favor, and get those twenty elephants you promised me. I have to take them to our new consul, Galba." Scipio bows his head slightly. "I'll also give him a few tactical tricks, some of which I learned from you!"

"I am honored. You'll get your wheat and elephants, and the ships to take them wherever you are going." He shakes his head. "New tricks, eh? Gods help the Macedonians if you are scheming against them!"

AVENTINE HILL, ROME. *Thank Hera I finally get to kill someone again*, Spider thinks, smiling to herself. *I was going to have to kill myself just to keep in practice!*

The elfin young woman skips through the dark streets of Rome's toughest neighborhood, eyes alight with anticipation. *This contract will bring me a fat purse full of denarii. I don't know who is paying for this, but he surely pays well! He should marry me. I'd kill for free, and he'd save himself a lot of money!*

Dozens of Aventine toughs pass the raven-haired girl, but they give her a wide berth. Spider's skill with sword and dagger is well known among the Aventine mobs from whence she sprang. After killing several of the Hill's most prominent thugs, the sicaria has earned peace from the rest of them.

She glowers at several who walk past her, just to see them avert their eyes. *You're fucking right to stay away. I'm not a child any more. I'll kill any of you pukes who try to rape me now.*

Spider turns into a dark alley and arrives at the front of a rundown stable. She sees one of the stable's eight torches is not burning. She walks over and stands under it, waiting.

"I am here," comes a muffled voice in the shadows, behind a swaybacked horse standing next to its fence.

"Scipio has landed in Carthage," Spider declares. "I came to you as soon as I found out, as ordered."

A well-manicured hand extends a bulging goatskin purse. She takes the purse and stares into the shadows, a question in her eyes.

"In the purse," the voice says. "It's in the purse."

Spider pulls open the purse and extracts a slip of papyrus. She walks over to a stable torch and holds it up to the light. She glances back into the shadows and nods. "I know who she is," Spider says. She grins. "She's made life miserable for the Latins, eh? Is that why it's her?"

"You won't know why. Just make her die."

Spider holds the scrap up to the torch until it catches fire, then drops it at her feet and watches it turn to ashes.

"When?" she asks.

"Soon, before Scipio Africanus returns from Africa," replies the voice.

"Don't worry, it will be done within days," she says. She extends the purse toward the shadows and jingles it. "As you know, I will not spend a coin of this until the task is done. And I am eager to buy some wine and men."

"There will be another purse if you make it extremely painful," the voice says. "Now go."

Spider stalks down one of the narrow, crooked side streets, weaving her way between the tatty mud brick apartment houses. *A lot of money to kill a woman*, she thinks. *Maybe we are coming up in the world!*

EASTERN NUMIDIA. "Come on, get out of here! Masinissa's men are coming!"

Vermina races through the burning Massylii village, slowing only to shove his lance through the back an escaping villager. As the man falls, the Masaesyli king shouts out his orders again. A hundred Masaesyli riders quickly gather around him.

"Out onto the plain," he shouts. "Back north toward the mountains!"

The west Numidia warriors gallop away on their swift little ponies, heading for the sheltering heights of the coastal Atlas Mountains. They race from the screams and wails of the smoldering village, their grisly task completed. The riders enter the wide, windswept plains in front of the mountains, riding through a scrubland of scattered shrubs and grasses.

Minutes later, the Masaesyli close in upon the mountains' pine-forested foothills. *We'll go to the caves for a couple of days*, Vermina decides. *Then we will hit another of Masinissa's villages. If their people don't come over to me, they get the same.*

The deposed king pulls back the leopard's head cap that covers his domed helmet, and unbuckles the side strap. He cradles his helmet in his sword arm, letting the breeze dry the sweat from his tightly curled black hair. *I hate hiding like a rat in a manger. But that will change soon. I'll get my father's kingdom back. I'll put Masinissa on a cross in front of my palace. Watch him rot until he is nothing but stinking bones.*

Vermina's reverie is interrupted by a scream from the rear of his horsemen. "They're coming!" one of his riders yells. Vermina looks to his right. A large dust cloud billows toward him from the foothills, with hundreds of galloping riders shadowed within it.

He knew we'd head back here. He's going to cut us off! The rebel king turns to a dusky-skinned rooster of a man riding next to him, his tan wool tunic spattered with the villagers' blood.

"Eshmun, I need to get into those trees or I am dead. My father Syphax's kingdom will be gone forever. The Massylii will rule us."

Eshmun bows, resigned to his fate. "I'll take half the men, my King.

We will detain them."

"May Ammon bless you," Vermina says, raising his hand over Eshmun's head. "I'll see you back at the caves."

Eshmun laughs bitterly. "Of course you will." The wiry little commander barks several orders to his nearby riders. The rear half of Vermina's force veers off to the right, heading for the men closing in upon them.

Vermina sees that a tall, rangy warrior leads the Massylii cavalry, a lion's head topping his helmet. *Masinissa! Probably came to kill me himself.* Vermina kicks his heels into his mount. It surges toward the hills. Vermina peers over his shoulder as he rides.

Eshmun's fifty riders gallop into Masinissa's cavalry. Horses thump into each other, whinnying in terror and pain. Riders of both tribes tumble from their steeds, to be speared by a passing enemy before they can rise.

Eshmun spies Masinissa in the center of the whirling horse duels, his back to him. Eshmun's heart quickens. *Kill him and they'll retreat. We'll live to fight another day.* He races at the Numidian king, his six foot spear aimed at Masinissa's spine.

"King! Your back!" shouts a Massylii rider. Masinissa whirls to face Eshmun, and kicks his horse into a gallop.

The two Numidians ride straight at each other, spears leveled. Eshmun crouches alongside his horse's neck, knowing his diminutive size makes him a difficult target. Masinissa rides bolt upright, his lance cradled under his elbow. He watches Eshmun's eyes. *He's looking at my chest.*

The Masaesyli captain shoves his spear forward, aiming it at Masinissa's bare breast. In a flash, Masinissa drops to the side of his galloping stallion, his left hand gripping his horses' mane. Eshmun's spear passes through the space he had been sat in, gashing a cut in the stallion's haunch.

106

Slippery bastard, Eshmun thinks. He whirls his horse about for another charge, but he is already too late. Masinissa's flying lance skewers him from breast to back. Yelling in pain, Eshmun arcs his head back. His neck becomes an easy target for the king's flashing blade.

Seconds later, Eshmun's head rolls to the ground. It is quickly squashed to a pulp by the hooves of the stampeding riders.

The outnumbered Masaesyli are slowly encircled. Two dozen survivors stand in the center of a wide ring of Massylii cavalry, a hundred spears pointed at them.

"Halt!" Masinissa bellows. He trots through the circle and faces his enemies. "Swear loyalty to me and I will let you live," he states.

The Masaesyli glower at him, knowing they will live as slaves. They shake their heads, readying themselves for a final charge.

*It's not worth losing more of my me*n, Masinissa decides. "I promise you will live as free men," Masinissa adds. "But you must swear never to draw sword against me."

The warriors look at one another. An older rider throws his javelin into the dirt, then his sword and shield. The others follow.

Masinissa looks back toward the snow-capped Atlas Mountains. He sees a dust cloud settling at the base of the foothills, marking the place where Vermina's men passed. *They are into the trees—we won't find them now.*

The victorious Massylii trot back toward Cirta. Three hours later, Masinissa passes through the iron-studded gates of his fortress city. He finds a handful of town dignitaries waiting for him in the city square, their faces anxious.

"The Romans are here!" blurts one of them. "They are some kind of politicians!" declares another, as if he were describing fearful animals.

"All will be well," Masinissa replies. "We are amici, legal friends of Rome. Remember, they helped to restore our kingdom." He turns to the lead elder. "Tell them to come to my throne room in half an hour."

The king gallops up to his palace and quickly trots up the steps, his heart hammering. *He cannot have come all the way over here*, he thinks. *Ammon, please, do not let it be him. I don't know what I'll do.*

Masinissa hurries into his upper bedroom. He stands in the middle of his spacious chambers, arms and legs spread wide. "Bathe me," he says to his Masaesyli slaves. "And be quick about it."

The attendants strip off Masinissa's dusty loincloth and sandals. They lave his lean body with eucalyptus-scented water, drying him with a thick, soft, camelskin robe. Masinissa stretches his nude body onto a padded platform. The slaves rub grapeseed oil into his limbs, lightly pounding his muscles before they towel him off with squares of fine linen. His toilet complete, the king drapes himself in a lush lionskin robe and strides from his chambers.

Masinissa marches down a statue-lined corridor to his throne room. He takes his seat on his high-backed throne. It adjoins the one he keeps empty for Sophonisba, his dead queen—the one in which her poisoned corpse once sat, grinning at the legionnaires who came to drag her to Scipio.

Masinissa reaches into his robe's sleeve. His sinewy fingers caress the wavy-bladed dagger he hides there, its razored edges carefully wrapped. He strokes the blade and thinks of Scipio, imagining him gushing blood from the second mouth that gapes in his throat.

The king stares at Sophonisba's empty throne. He studies the spots of blood that bear testament to her final minutes of anguish. *Remember what she told you after she passed,* he reflects, her smiling face in his head. *She said your destiny is to unite Numidia. To fulfill your father's dream. You cannot accomplish that from a Roman cross.*

The lead courtier opens the throne room doors. The heavily muscled giant stamps his bronze staff upon the floor. "A delegation from Rome," he announces in his deep bass voice.

"Send them in," Masinissa orders. He feels his pulse throb in his neck.

Four Days from Rome

Control yourself. He is only a man.

Outside the chamber, Scipio and another envoy recline on a settee that faces the other two dignitaries, the four of them clad in purple-bordered white tunics. Scipio feels his right hand twitch nervously; he presses it against his side. *Wonder what he'll say when he sees me? Is he still angry about Sophonisba? It wasn't my fault—our laws demanded I bring her back to Rome!*

His eyes roam across the twenty-foot high chamber, at the mounted elephant heads and the tall marble statues of war gods. His eyes fix on a carved triptych of three Numidian infants riding horses bareback, their fathers holding them upright. *No wonder they are the finest horsemen in the world—they ride before they can walk! We need his men in our army. Our cavalry will never learn to ride like them.*

The courtier enters the chamber waiting room. He points his staff at the seated Romans. "You are summoned," he intones, and walks back through the chamber doors. The four envoys walk into the house-sized throne room. They march quickly toward Masinissa. Six armored guards appear in front of them, bared swords at the ready. The delegates halt.

Masinissa sees Scipio standing in front of him. *Gods, he's here!* He rises from his throne and walks down from the dais to meet them.

He's still muscled like a leopard, Scipio thinks. *But he has the early gray hair of a ruler.* He laughs to himself. *As do we all.*

"Masinissa, my heart sings to see you," Scipio says, walking forward with his right arm extended.

The Numidian's face is a mask. He briefly shakes Scipio's forearm. "Welcome to Numidia, Imperator," he says tonelessly.

Masinissa returns to his throne. He rests his chin on his hand and studies the envoys. "How may I be of service to Rome?"

Scipio's stomach wrenches. *He still hates me.* He forces a smile. "It is good to hear you that you are still a friend to Rome, because we have need of your assistance. King Philip is on the move again, and Antiochus gathers his men to oppose us. Can you provide some men and food for our armies?"

Masinissa glances at the other three envoys. They nod mutely. "Rome helped me regain my throne," he says to them, looking past Scipio. "I have not forgotten it."

His looks back at Scipio. His eyes bore into him. "I am still a friend—to Rome."

"And we to you, my King," Scipio replies stiffly. "I do remember how valuable your riders were to me at Zama." He manages a tight smile. "Back when you and I fought together."

"Those days were long ago. I try not to dwell on them," Masinissa replies. "Times of love and friendship, now lost forever."

Scipio feels a great sadness descend upon him. "Ah, well. The poets say that what is lost can oft be regained, in time." Scipio hears no response. *I am dead to him.* "How much can you give us," he says curtly.

"I can give you two thousand of my best cavalry," Masinissa states. He looks away, his eyes distant. "In honor of what we once were."

"A thousand will suffice,"[xlvii] Scipio replies. "That will provide us with three turma of riders for Macedonia. He laughs softly. "Besides, one of your riders is worth ten of someone else's."

"As you wish, Imperator," Masinissa replies. "I will send you enough grain to provide for them."

"Carthage is sending two hundred measures of wheat," an envoy says.

Masinissa sniffs disdainfully. "Carthage! Since their defeat, they have become a nation of small-minded businessmen. How can you expect honor from such as these? I will send you 200,000 measures of wheat, and as many of barley."[xlviii]

The envoys gasp. "You are most generous, my King," a young senator replies.

"I merely repay the debt I owe," says Masinissa. He stares over their heads, as if they were no longer there. "And I now consider that debt repaid."

"May we speak alone for a minute?" Scipio asks.

Masinissa shrugs. "A minute, yes. I have my own war to wage."

The three envoys return to the antechamber. The doors boom shut behind them. Masinissa stares at the door.

Scipio shifts about, summoning his courage. He takes a deep breath. "Masinissa—my friend—you must understand. What I did, I had to do, according to our laws. To them, Sophonisba was Syphax's wife—the wife of our mortal enemy. They would have come after her if I didn't, and taken her as part of the spoils of war."

The Numidian king's eyes blaze. "'Spoils of war?' As if she were some golden trinket, or a prize mare? Do you have any inkling what she was to me?"

He vaults up from his throne, his hands gripping its arms. "I have never married. It takes all my will just to lie with another woman, that I may reproduce heirs. Heirs who are all bastards. Sophonisba was more than 'spoils' to me!"

"I have more than an 'inkling' of what you feel, my King," Scipio replies levelly. "I fear losing my Amelia more than I fear losing my own life. I intended no harm to Sophonisba. I would have sent her back after she was paraded through Rome during my triumph. But I had to take her. Gods be my witness, I have paid for that act with a hundred sleepless nights."

"My debt to you is repaid," Masinissa says, his eyes stones. "Your debt to me—that can never be paid. May you live forever, General."

Masinissa sits down. He stares into the space above Scipio's head.

Scipio looks at the king's hands. He notices them clenching the throne handles, his knuckles bulging. *Such pain I have caused him—am causing him. He does not deserve any more. But he has to understand what happened.*

Scipio takes a step toward Masinissa, reaching out with his right hand.

"Go now," Masinissa says, his voice quivering. "Lest Rome destroy my kingdom for the murder I commit."

"As you wish," Scipio says bitterly. "You talk about my debt to you? Just remember, were it not for me you'd still be hunched over a campfire in the mountains, hiding from Syphax's men." Scipio Africanus stalks from the room, tears filling his eyes.

Masinissa watches Scipio yank open the doors and disappear. The king slumps down in this chair, his body quaking with released tension. He recalls the times when he, Laelius, and Scipio would celebrate their victories over Syphax, Gisgo, and Hannibal: three brothers in arms with common purpose. His eyes moisten. He grabs a pomegranate and flings it at the closed doors, spraying its blood red seeds across the tiles.

You rule-brained clod! We could have ruled the world together!

Two days later, Scipio is standing at the African transport ships next to the Cirta docks. He watches the Numidian cavalry lead their horses into the dockside troop transports, each rangy young rider dressed in leather loincloths and caps. Scipio peers out onto the emerald green bay. He observes a score of broad-beamed transports floating low in the water, their holds weighted with Masinissa's grain.

Scipio feels his neck tingle. He looks over his shoulder. Masinissa is still on the hill behind him, watching the last of his men being loaded. Scipio stares hopefully at him, but the king does not meet his eyes.

One of the Roman envoys appears next to Scipio. "Is it time to go back to Rome?" he asks. "Our trireme is sailing over from Carthage. It should be here by nightfall."

"Scipio slaps the senator on the back. "Yes, Egnatius. It is time for us to leave." He flicks his eyes back toward Masinissa. "There is nothing more we can do here."

"Then we'll leave tomorrow morning?" says Egnatius.

"You will, but I'm not going with you," Scipio says. "I have to ride back to Carthage. Hannibal has some gifts for me. Large gifts. I have to take them to Galba's camp in Appollonia, after a stop at Sicily."

He points toward the Numidian-laden transports. "The Africans are going with me to Appollonia. They'll wait for me in Sicily so we all leave together."

Egnatius crooks his head. "Sicily? What's in Sicily? More wine?"

Scipio smiles. "Oh, I have a cache of weapons there, including some specially made swords. I think Galba could use them in Greece. You go on. Send my love to Amelia, please."

When the gangplank is pulled up on the last transport, Masinissa turns his horse away from the scene, pacing down from his overlook. He races across the plain toward Cirta.

A half hour later the Numidian king pulls to a stop in front of a large pyramid-shaped stone tomb, its center block inscribed with a dancing elephant. He dismounts and walks slowly to the base of the tomb. He kneels.

"I am here, Beloved. See what I brought you?"

Reaching into his saddle bag, he carefully extracts a large bouquet of dark purple passion flowers. He lays them gently in front of a marble urn bearing withered flowers.

"Here. A bouquet of your favorites." He extracts the urn's dried hibiscus and replaces them with the spiky-leaved bouquet. *I've got to bring you fresh ones more often. They dry up so quickly out here.* He empties his waterskin into the urn.

"My Queen, I have fulfilled my promise to you. Numidia is a united country. Now I can join you." Masinissa stands, waiting, his hand on his sword pommel. "It won't take but a moment. One thrust, and we're together!"

A breeze caresses Masinissa's face. It whispers through the feathery leaves of the tall cedars above him. "You think I still have purpose here? Yes, I *know* Vermina is still out there, but someone else can finish him. Numidia is mine; the large work is done."

The breeze wafts by his face again. He stares at the dancing elephant and laughs sadly, shaking his head. "I know, I know. 'Dance when the task is finished, or the music rings sour in the ears.'"

His voice chokes in his throat. "You are still my wisest counselor. You are still—" He raises his head to the heavens and sobs. "Ah, aah! Oh what a queen you would have made!"

The king of Numidia prostrates himself, burying his face into the sand, futilely pounding it.

A hawk screeches from a nearby tree. Masinissa raises himself, brushing the damp sand from his face, and remounts his horse. "Very well," he says to the elephant carving. "I will finish it. But then we dance together—for eternity."

He slaps the side of his horse's neck. The stallion races off for the mountain road to Cirta, heading home. As Masinissa rides up the rocky switchback trail, he looks north toward the Mediterranean, hoping to glimpse his donated fleet.

A thousand of my best men out to Macedonia, while Vermina still lurks about! Ah, it's all for the best. This Philip seems to have larger designs than Greece. He might be on my shores next. Let the Romans handle him.

The king crouches next to his horse's neck and gallops away, riding as fast as he can.

Roman Women at the Baths

IV. Assassin

ERETRIA, MACEDONIA,[xlix] 200 BCE King Philip and King Antiochus recline on thickly padded couches inside Philip's palace. Both men wear the ankle-length purple tunics that Philip provides his guests of honor. The remains of a feast are sprawled about the table between them, scattered bowls, pitchers, and platters of finest silver.

"I hope you enjoyed the food," Philip says, picking his teeth with a bone shard. "I gave you only the finest, in recompense for you making the trip to my capitol."

"It was a glorious meal," Antiochus replies. He reaches into a bowl filled with fruit slices, his emerald rings sparkling. "I particularly like these Egyptian melons. They are food for the gods!"

"You may have the chance to get all you want. I heard that Ptolemy is dead.[l] If that's true, Egypt is ripe for our conquest. We could divide it up, if we can figure out how to split it."

"That would be a happy problem," Antiochus says. "It's like deciding how to carve one of these delicious melons. Should we cut it north to south, or east to west?"

Philip spreads his hands. "I am open to your suggestions. Myself, I am more interested in the two of us clarifying our intentions for Greece and Asia."

"As I am," Antiochus says. He pops another melon slice into his mouth. "Hmm. Perhaps the Nile could be the dividing line. Then we would both have access to fresh water. The west side would have much more land, but the east side would have the sea."

Assassin

"I wish I would have thought of that; it's a splendid idea!" exclaims Philip, expecting just that response. "I can see why you are called Antiochus the Great." *Although you gave yourself that title.*

"I am glad we agreed to meet and work out a treaty,"[li] Antiochus says, sipping from his goblet. "The world's big enough for both of us to share." *For now.*

Philip bobs his head, his filigreed crown falling over his brow. "Oh, most certainly. I plan to regain the Greek territories that were once part of the Macedonian Empire, when Alexander was king. That is all I want." *For now.*

"I understand regaining lost possessions," Antiochus says. "Under Seleucid, Syria ruled Thrace and Pergamum. I intend to take them back."[lii]

"Understood," Philip says. "I see no problem in that." *If he invades Thrace, I can get them to fight against him."*

Smiling, Philip reaches for the bronze wine pitcher. "Then it's agreed. We have a nonaggression pact between our kingdoms. As allies, we will move on Egypt after I take Greece." *And Italia.*

He drinks deeply, and grins at Antiochus. "Come on, old fellow, let's get drunk. Our ministers can work out the details for us." *I'll take it all anyway, after I'm done with the Romans.*

"I'm not ready to move on Egypt, anyway," Antiochus says. "I need to take Teos and Banias, the two citadels in Pergamum. They are too near my borders. I can't leave them at my back when I advance into Thrace."

"I understand," Philip says. "Beating the crazy Thracians is tough enough, without Roman-loving Attalus attacking you from behind."

Philip's eyes narrow. "Besides, I have a score to settle with Athens. They refused to acknowledge me as their king, like the rest of those fools in the Achean League." He snorts. "Old Philip II would have burned them alive by now!"

117

Antiochus waves his silver goblet in the air. A slave boy rushes in and refills it with ruby red wine. The king drains half of his goblet and swirls the rest about, watching it lap against the glistening silver.

"We are victims of our ancestors," Antiochus says, still watching his wine. "Reputations to live up to and territories to reclaim. Kings can never be their own man."

He's getting maudlin. "Be of good cheer, Antiochus. Now is the time to act. The Romans have diverted forces to north Italia. With a little luck, the Gauls up there will keep them occupied while we pursue our own interests."

"True enough," Antiochus says, brightening. "They've been fighting the Boii and Ligurians forever. With a little luck, they'll be tied up in a campaign there for several years, wasting their men and money."

"Well, *I'm* not going to wait" Philip says. "Half their men are out fighting Gauls, and Scipio's far away in Carthage. I'm going to take Athens while the Romans are distracted."

Antiochus pounds his chest; he burps loudly. "Sounds like those Achean Greeks will regret they ever rejected your offer to join you."

Philip grins. "Oh, they will regret it. How they will regret it!"

PORT OF APPOLLONIA, ILLYRIA.[liii] The mighty elephants step lightly down the foot-thick gangplank that extends from the transport to the dock, docilely following their mahouts. Scipio and Galba stand at the dock entryway, watching the Carthaginians unload the beasts.

"I hope they don't fall through the dock timbers," Galba says, staring in wonder at the enormous pachyderms.

"It's built for heavy loads, Consul," says Scipio. "We just have to take them down it one at a time,"

"I still don't know what I'm going to do with them," Galba says.

"I do. And I'll show you."

The mahouts lead the twenty elephants past the walls of wheat sacks that were previously unloaded, parading them past the wide-eyed townspeople. The elephants are soon foraging in the fields around the ancient port, using their trunks to pull the tall grasses into their mouths.

The empty transports sail from the sheltering bay, anchoring in the open water.

"Where are those ships going now?" asks Galba.

"Back to Carthage, where I just came from. They were on loan to us. They'll leave when that last ship unloads."

Galba stares at the remaining ship. "What's in that last transport? It floats low in the water."

"Swords from Sicily," Scipio says. "Thousands and thousands of swords."

Galba looks quizzically at him. "Swords? I have plenty of swords."

"Not like these. Ah, here they come!"

The dockside transport unloads large straw-filled sacks into the wagons waiting next to them. "Come on, take a look," Scipio says. He and Galba walk out to the nearest wagon. Scipio grabs his belt dagger and slashes open a sack's rawhide strings. He gropes through the straw for a moment, then pulls out a gleaming, wasp-waisted sword, its twin edges glistening from a recent sharpening.

Grasping its hilt, Scipio cradles the blade in the palm of his other hand, staring lovingly at it. "This is the *gladius hispaniensis*, the sword I used in Iberia and Africa.[liv] I modeled it after the Iberians' falcata, a deadly blade that I have long admired."

"My men are used to the standard army sword, General," Galba replies stiffly.

"Not the thousands of my veterans who are with you," counters Scipio. "They conquered Iberia and Africa with this sword! It will do everything our old swords would do, and more. It can slash and chop, as well as stab!"

A long silence falls between the two commanders. Scipio puts his hand on Galba's shoulder. "I backed you to be consul because I know you are willing to embrace progress. Do not make me regret my choice."

Galba blows out his cheeks. "Well, if your men want to use it, I do not see the harm of it." He grins awkwardly at Scipio. "You did win two wars with it, it can't be all bad!"

"Oh, it's bad," Scipio says. "But it's bad in a good way. You will see."

Galba purses his lips. "As you say, we shall see. Now what am I supposed to do with these elephants? Am I supposed to train them to fight? We are marching on Philip, I don't have much time."

"Come with me," Scipio says. The two march to the field where the elephants are grazing, their mahouts following behind them.

Scipio takes a sarissa from one of the mahouts, and walks to the front of his beast. He raises the twelve-foot spear up to the elephant's forehead and taps it twice. The ten-ton beast lowers its head and kneels. Scipio pets its table-sized forehead. "Now, for attack mode," he says.

Scipio taps the beast's head again and it rises. Its intelligent eyes look expectantly at Scipio. Scipio steps to elephant's right rear leg and whacks it on the haunch. The elephant rumbles forward, with Scipio trotting alongside, goading the twelve-foot beast onward.

Slapping the spear against the elephant's right shoulder, Scipio turns the beast about and herds it back toward Galba. As the beast closes on him, Galba dashes sideways, gaping over his shoulder as he runs. The mahout yells an order in Carthaginian. The beast rumbles to a halt, trumpeting its excitement.

Scipio trots over to Galba, smiling mischievously. "Nothing to fear, General. I was in total command of the beast." He looks back at the elephants and shrugs. "Then again, I sometimes forget the correct command. Perhaps it's best you ran!"

Galba exhales loudly. "You have made your point, the elephants are already trained." He glances over at the harvested grain fields that encircle the port. The Numidians gallop wildly across the terrain, exercising their horses. "Are those wild men used to elephants?"

"Since childhood," Scipio replies. "You do not have to worry about the Numidians, but you do have to train your own army. Train your horses and men to get used to them. My veterans can help you. And train the elephants to get used to your bugles. That will profit you greatly when you fight Philip."

"Elephants and Numidians and Iberian swords," Galba says shaking his head. "I respect your genius, and appreciate you helping get me elected consul. But you are asking me to employ aspects of the very people you defeated."

"Learn from your enemies or fall prey to them," Scipio says. "I triumphed over the Carthaginians, Numidians, and Iberians, but only because I took the best of what they did and used it against them."

Galba is silent for a moment. "I will write to you. We can talk further about this, if you will."

Scipio bows his head slightly. "It would be an honor. For now, I must return to Rome. The Gauls are gathering strength under that Carthaginian renegade Hamilcar. If we don't stop him now, he may soon be at Rome's doorstep!"

Galba watches Scipio march away, lost in thought. *Elephants and Africans? What kind of Roman army is this? What good can come of them against Philip? What good can they be at all?*

CREMONA, NORTH ITALIA, 200 BCE. *Aryeenk, aryeenk, aryeeeenk!* The mighty elk raises its bearded head to the dawning sky. It bugles out its mating call, echoing his need across the miles of spelt wheat fields that carpet the pastoral Po Valley. The elk's herd grazes along the lush riverbanks of the Po, savoring the knee-high grasses that line its crystal waters.

The lead bull abruptly spins his head to the south. His ears flare out to the side of his head. He cranes his neck skyward, lifting a crown of antlers as tall as boy. He trumpets a warning. The elks raise their heads, ears pricked, listening. The bull repeats his order and trots toward the sheltering foothills. Within minutes, the stately beasts have melted into the forest.

Soon, the quiet valley fills with the machined tramping of hobnailed sandals. A ten-wide column of Roman infantry appears from the south, marching along the twenty-foot roadway that bisects the grainfields.

Governor Lucius Furius Purpurio rides in the vanguard, a man as wide as he is tall. Nicknamed "Crispus" by his admiring soldiers, the bull-bodied magistrate is anything but curly-haired—his head and face are as hairless as an egg. Furius Purpurio ignores the jibe; he knows he has the men's respect.

Furius leads his army toward the plumes of black smoke rising miles to the northeast, where the Cremona garrison is located. His army marches with a pace which mirrors their leader's conduct in battle: steady and unrelenting, always forward. There is little talk among the Romans: they have marched all night to get here and they are far too weary for conversation. They dream of a hot porridge breakfast, with a drink of wine to wash it down. And sleep, blessed sleep. In the meantime, they nourish themselves with dried cheese and fruit, knowing they may be fighting at any minute.

The governor eyes the faint plumes of smoke. "Those are too small to be a burning city, Quintus."

Quintus rides next to the governor. His head wrapped in bandages beneath his new helmet, protecting the wound he received at Placentia. "Those fires are too big to be cooking fires, though," he says.

"Perhaps they are the smoldering remains of another Gallic celebration," Furius remarks. "The brutes celebrate all the time. I only hope it is not a victory celebration."

Assassin

The lead scouts race in from the direction of Cremona. They rein in their lathered mounts in front of Furius and Quintus, their eyes alight with excitement.

"Good news! The town is still intact!" a scout says.

"The Gauls are strewn all over the fields there, they are busy gathering food," the other adds. He cocks an eye at Furius. "Their camp is almost empty."

"They could be very vulnerable to a surprise attack," Quintus says. We could catch them in the fields."

Purpurio shakes his head. "There's still forty thousand of them, from what I hear. That's a lot to fight without preparation. And my men are exhausted. I will wait until we make camp."[lv]

He eyes Quintus. "You are exhausted, too. When I met you returning to Rome, I should never have agreed to let you come along. It would be better if you stayed out of this."

"They killed my men. They killed my friends. Was I supposed to sit idle without any chance for revenge?" Quintus growls. He looks away from Purpurio. *I am sorry I didn't come home, Horatia. I could not live with myself if I didn't do this.*

"As you wish, Quintus. Just remember, you promised to stay out of the fight."

Quintus eyes the smoke plumes, his mouth tightens into a line. "I will do my best."

Miles to the north, two scouts race in to the Gallic camp, seeking their commander. "General Hamilcar! The Romans are coming! They are only a few hours away!"

Hamilcar nods to Luli. "Now it starts—the battle for north Italia. Sound the recall."

Riders gallop out into the field, blaring the call to prepare for battle.

Thousands of bare-chested Gauls raise their heads from the fields they are harvesting with their swords, listening to the summons. They drop their loads of forage and trot toward camp, blade in hand.

They come upon Hamilcar circling his stallion at the front gates, waving the warriors into the pentagon-shaped camp. "Inside, quickly. Get to your weapons!"

The men line up outside the crosshatched logs that serve as the camp palisade, ready for a Roman assault. More of Hamilcar's scouts return. They report that the Romans are occupied building camp, and pose no immediate danger. Hamilcar laughs with relief.

"Fools! They should have got at us while we were dispersed," he tells Luli. "That will be their fatal mistake." He jumps from his horse and paces about, excited. "Go get the chieftains. We have to prepare for a full assault tomorrow. We'll hit them quickly, before they have time to organize. What a victory it will be!"

The three tribes' chieftains are in Hamilcar's tent within the hour. "We have more than twice their numbers," says Hamilcar. "If you rotate your front lines, we can hold them in place and eventually outflank them."

He glares at the three Gallic officers. "That means your men must be ready to fight all day. No drinking tonight! When the sun rises, everyone must be ready and sober. Do that, and north Italia will soon be yours!"

The chieftains nod solemnly, and rush out to prepare their armies. Hamilcar turns to Luli. "You know, I have changed my mind—we can take Rome. After we destroy this army, no one blocks our path south to it. We could do what Hannibal never did: throw down its walls!"

"We shall see," Luli says. "The Gauls can be temperamental. If they thinks their lands are secure from Roman incursions, they may just want to go home."

"Pah! When we tell them about all the plunder, all the soft patrician women, all the slaves that are there for their taking, they will run to

Rome!" He rubs his hands together. "I'd love to see the faces of that Carthage's Council of Elders when they have to negotiate with *me* instead of Scipio and his ilk! Ignore me, will they?"

The next day's dawn finds the Gallic camp swarming with activity. Thousands of Gauls strap on their helmets and weapons, cursing about rising so early in the day—and about their dearth of wine the night before.

Forty thousand infantry pour into the field and group themselves by their nations: the Boii are in the center, Ligurians on the right, and Insubres on the left, each tribe grouped about their clan's standard bearer. The field is filled with tall poles holding the heads of bears, wolves, elk and other beasts, with multicolored squares of fabric flapping beneath them.

Hamilcar rides out to the center of his army, his black stallion caparisoned with blood-red ring mail. He holds a silver sarissa over his head, the twelve-foot spear glinting in the sharp morning sun.

The rams' horns sound behind him. Hamilcar slowly trots to the head of his men, his silvered armor gleaming. The Gauls march forward, following Hamilcar's shining spear.

As his army closes upon the Roman camp, Hamilcar speeds up his trot. The Gallic horde follows at a rapid march, flowing toward the somnolent castra.

Lucius Furius Purpurio's attendant shakes him from bed. "The Gauls are coming! They'll be here within the hour!"

"Sound the call to arms," orders a bleary-eyed Furius. "Get my lead tribunes in here immediately. And bring the allied commanders." The praetor's officers soon gather about him, strapping on their bronze cuirasses and greaves.

"Listen carefully, we don't have much time. Claudus, your allies will form the front line, and Marcus' cohorts will back them up.[lvi] Julius, you will lead the allied cavalry on the right, and Lucius will command our equites on the left."

125

"The allies will be in the front instead of us?" says Marcus, irritated. "You are using our two legions as backups?"

"They are from north Italia." Furius replies coldly. "They fight to preserve their homeland. They will not break."

"What's the strategy, then?" asks Quintus.

Furius rubs his forehead. "We can't set a strategy, we don't know what they're doing yet. We'll have to formulate one as we go." He smirks. "Our plan is, don't have a plan! Be ready to adjust! Now go!"

The officers race to position their troops. Furius turns to Quintus. "Stay with me, Quintus. We'll be at the back of the front line, to see how the allies fare. If they can hold the Gauls, our legionnaires might hit their wings and get behind them."

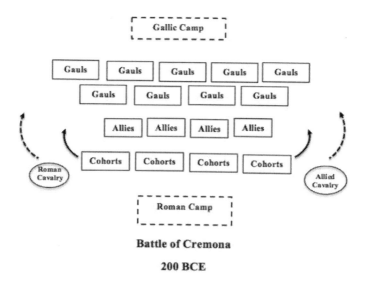

Battle of Cremona

200 BCE

"I'll stay near you," Quintus says. He notices Furius looking expectantly at him. "And I'll stay out of the fighting," he adds morosely.

The two trot in behind the two front lines of allies. They join Furius' two lead tribunes there, Gaius Laetorius and Publius Titinius.

"All right, let's get out there and get into formation," Furius orders.

The Romans form ranks with expediency and efficiency. Furius' army is soon arrayed in battle formation a quarter mile from camp. They watch a mile-wide line of Gauls approach them, with Hamilcar riding front and center.

The Gauls draw within a spear's cast of the Romans. With a wave of his hand, Hamilcar halts the advance. He surveys the Roman lines, trying to peer behind the Roman allies who face him. *Why are the Romans in the rear? Their ranks are deep, but not wide. If we hold them in place we can surround them.* He turns his horse toward his men and points his silver spear at the Romans.

"Victory!" He shouts, kicking his horse forward. The Gauls dash out, toward the Roman lines, screaming as they run.

The Umbrians and Etruscans stare wide-eyed at the wave of giants hurtling toward them. "Hold up your shields," the allied centurions command. "Dig your feet into the ground."

The soldiers extend their right legs behind them and dig their sandals into the soft earth. They raise their shields to their noses, nervously peering over the edges. Men void themselves in terror, gaping at the Boii, Ligurians, and Insubres who thunder down upon them. The odor of urine and feces wafts through the air.

With a chorus of delirious screams, the barbarians crash into the allied lines. They batter their swords and axes against the allied shield wall, shoving out their own shields to knock the soldiers backward. The disciplined socii counter with javelin stabs, pricking the Gauls' legs and arms. The allied centurions roam behind the front line, shoving men into gaps. The Gauls cut down scores of their opponents, only to find each opening quickly filled by a fresh fighter.

Assassin

Allied commander Claudus rides his horse across the two-hundred foot gap between his men and Roman cohorts. "Stand your ground," the rangy old warrior yells. "They will tire out soon if you just stand your ground." After an hour of furious fighting, the barbarians have pushed the Roman allies back a dozen feet, but have not broken their lines.

Hamilcar rides behind the Boii occupying the center. He can see the Roman cohorts readying themselves to replace them. *We can't break their center; we'll have to outflank them with our numbers.*[lvii] He waves over Luli.

"Get the chieftains to send their back lines to the side. When the horns sound, I want them to run out past the wings of the Romans and circle back inside. We'll catch them on three sides." Lucius starts to ride off, but Hamilcar grabs the shoulder of his tunic. "Get Lugos over here immediately."

The massive Boii chieftain marches in from the front line, where he is leading the attack on the allied center. "I need your men to hold the center for an hour, Lugos. You don't need to beat them back, just hold them off until we can circle around to the Romans."

Lugos nods. He grins through his gore-spattered beard. "They no get by us. Anyone run from fight, I bash their head in."

Minutes later, Hamilcar's trumpeter blows three long blasts. The Gauls in the rear trot to the right and left, spurred on by their tribe's chieftains.

Furius hears the battle horns sound. *They're up to something.* He pushes his horse closer to the front, peering through the dust. He spies movement within the whirling dust clouds, shadows of men flowing to his flanks. *They're going to outflank us! If they get behind us we're dead.*

Furius can see the center line Boii are now only two deep, though they continue to furiously attack the allies. He waves over Quintus. "They're going around our wings. We don't have enough men to stretch past

128

them, our lines would be too thin."

"But their lines are thin, too," Quintus replies. "We can cut through the middle. Their front has got to be tiring, and they don't have many reserves."

Furius looks across at the moving Gallic lines, and back at his own men. He looks back and forth again. His eyes glaze with confusion. *He doesn't know what to do*, Quintus decides.

"Believe me, Governor, their center is vulnerable. You have two fresh legions, let's go after them!" He leans closer to Furius' ear. "You have to call the attack, Sir. And you have to do it now!"

The stout old warrior shakes himself, as if waking from a dream. His eyes relight with determination. He whirls upon his attendants, his face flush with excitement. "Get Lucius, Julius, and Claudus over here!" He bellows. The three commanders arrive within minutes, irritated at being called from the fight.

"They're going to circle around our wings," Furius explains. We have to stop them or we're dead. Lucius, send your equites at any who cross outside our infantry flanks. Julius, do the same with your allied cavalry."

"There'll be thousands of them coming at us," Julius says. "We only have about twelve hundred each."

"Listen to me—this is important," Furius says. "You don't have to drive them back, you just have to keep them from going forward. You hear that? Just hold them! Claudus and I, we will drive them back in the center."

"And if you don't?" asks Lucius.

Furius smiles one of his rare smiles. "Then you should be glad you've got horses, because you'll be the only ones to get away. Go!"

The two cavalry commanders disappear. Furius faces Claudus. "This is it. We are marching straight through that center. Your legions had better be as good as you say they are."

Claudus puts his hand on his heart. "If my men cannot break that line, I will fall on my sword."

Furius smiles again. "Don't worry. If they can't break that line, some Gaul will do the job for you. Get the men ready."

The Roman cornu sound a long, plaintive blast. The Roman legions move forward. The young hastati march in the front, backed by the veteran principes, followed by the senior triarii. The legionnaires step sideways through the three-foot gaps separating the allied soldiers, slithering toward the battling Boii.

The Boii have begun to tire in the warm sun, their energies drained by their extended fighting. They hear an unfamiliar clattering, which grows ever louder. Then they see the Romans pushing their way to the allied front lines, endless columns of fresh soldiers stepping to the front.

Before the Boii can draw back and regroup, the Romans are upon them. The Romans push past the exhausted allies and march straight into the waiting Gauls. They ram their bossed shields into the Boii's bodies and stab out their pila from between their shield wall, gouging their enemies' limbs and torsos. The tiring Boii gamely bash back at the attacking Romans, but the legionnaires' punctures and cuts take their toll. The Gauls' shield and sword movements slow. Hundreds fall to the relentless Roman.

"Halt," the Roman centurions shout. The legionnaires stop their advance. The Gauls step back from them, grateful for the respite. Many reach for their wineskins, eager for a deep drink.

"Loose!" the centurions shout. The Romans hurl their javelins into the back line of the Gauls. Scores of unwary enemies fall, groveling and moaning. "Forward!" the centurions shout, blowing their attack whistles. The Romans draw their swords and march forward, tramping toward the regrouping giants.

Lugos shoulders his way to front of the Boii. He plants his feet in the short clearing between the lines and waves his enormous cudgel at his men.

"Romans come to take our lands!" He screams. "We kill them now!" He rushes toward the Romans, a human juggernaut hurtling toward the arrow-straight lines of the advancing hastati.

A red-haired Gaul steps out behind Lugos, totally naked, to show his disdain for his opponents. "Come on, you women!" he shouts, and runs in after his leader. The weary Boii charge out again, screaming their defiance. The Ligurians and Insubres follow them from the sides.

Lugos rushes up to a young hastati and batters him backward, driving him into the man behind him. Kicking them on top of one another, he bashes the skull of the man on top. Another swing and he crushes the shoulder of the man beneath the dying legionnaire. The young soldier rolls on the ground, moaning piteously.

A gladius blade slashes across Lugos' melon-sized shoulder. He roars angrily and swipes his club sideways, knocking the legionnaire away. Grinning with battle lust, he reaches under his loincloth and shakes his penis at the legionnaires. "Come fight me, little cowards! I put this in your ass!"

The Boii swarm in about Lugos, battering at the Romans. The Roman line becomes jagged. Sections give way to the rejuvenated Gauls.

Furius rides back and forth in the clearing between the lines of hastati and principes. He sees dozens of his young soldiers fall, and his men ease backwards. *They're tiring after that long march, and losing their will.*

The praetor catches the attention of his lead tribune, and gestures with his thumb toward the principes waiting behind him. The tribune nods his understanding. He shouts an order to his nearby centurions. The battle whistles blow again.

Javelins swoop over the heads of the embattled hastati. The principes march in to the front, edging their way between the retreating hastati. The veteran fighters agilely deflect the Gauls' blows with their shields, patiently waiting for an opening in which to thrust their swords. Hundreds fall to the principes' practiced blades, and the Gallic advance halts.

Furius and Quintus follow in behind the principes. The two gallop from one cohort to another, shouting encouragement. As he returns to the center of the battle line, Quintus notes the dwindling number of Boii. *Their center is thinned—we can break through them.* He grabs Furius' cape and tugs on it, leaning in so he can be heard over the din of the fray.

"Furius, we can break through if we charge," he says. Furius nods. "I'll get my guards. We'll form a wedge." He looks about him. "We have to tell Claudus. Where is he?"

Quintus scans the front lines. He points to the right. "Over there. The fool's going after that big naked bastard with the blue tattoos."

Claudus steps out in front of his principes and rams his shield against the red-haired warrior, knocking him back from the legionnaire he was battling. The Boii jumps forward and swings his long sword at Claudus' knees, aiming to cut his legs off.

The veteran fighter crouches with his shield held low, taking the brunt of the blow on its iron edge. Even so, the force knocks him sideways. Claudius lands on one knee, his shield falling from his numbed arm. The Gaul raises his sword back for a decapitating blow to Claudus' neck.

Claudus plants his numbed left hand in the dirt and lunges forward on his knees. He jabs his gladius into the Gaul's foot, splitting open the top of his arch. The red giant screams and totters sideways, hopping on one foot. Claudus scrabbles to his knees and plunges his sword into the Boii's bowels, yanking it sideways.

Bellowing in agony, the relentless Gaul swipes his sword sideways at Claudus' neck. His weakened blow clangs off the boss of Claudus' shield. The tribune swings his sword with all his might. There is a crunch, and a scream. The Gaul's arm falls off at the elbow, geysering

132

blood. He falls screaming onto the earth, grasping his bleeding stump.

Claudus drops his blade to his side, gasping to catch his breath. The principes cheer. With renewed heart, they charge into their opponents.

He hears footsteps coming toward him. He turns just in time to see a wide-eyed Lugos running at him, his club clutched in both hands.

"Yeaaaagghh!" the Boii warrior screams, his eyes glazed with murderous lust. He swoops down his tree-root cudgel. A fist-sized tree knot bashes into the side of Claudus' forehead. Claudus' eye pops from its crushed socket, dangling on his cheek. Blood gushes from his gaping mouth. His sword falls from his hand as he topples forward, dead before he hits the ground.

Lugos screams out his triumph. The Boii echo his victory and storm back into the Romans.

Furius and Quintus watch Claudus' triumph and fall. Quintus leans over the side of his horse, retching. "We have to break through now!" Furius blurts. "They are rallying."

He studies Quintus, concern on his face. "We'll have to lead them."

"Don't worry about me—I am fine," Quintus shouts. "Just get your guards up here and let's go!"

Furius waves over the two dozen elite veterans that serve as his mounted guard. "We're going right through the middle," he shouts to them. "You three get behind me. The rest form a wedge behind them. There is no turning back—we make it to the open or die in the trying!"

Quintus grabs Furius' forearm. "I'm ready. See you on the other side!"

Furius spurs his horse forward. "Make way, make way!" he shouts. The riders crash into the front line of Boii. They slash furiously at the enemy warriors who surround them, edging their horses ever forward.

Lugos spies Furius' black-plumed helmet. He instantly grasps the

Romans' plan. The Boii chieftain stalks over to the battling cavalry, gripping his bloodied club. *I kill him, they all quit* he thinks, his black eyes fixed on Furius.

Lugos ducks under an attacking equite's spear thrust. He swipes his club sideways and bashes in the Roman's kneecap. The guard careens away. Lugos stalks on, fixed on Furius' red-caped back in front of him. He sees the unprotected gap between the governor's cuirass and sword belt. He can see the bumps of his naked spine. *One stroke there.* The chieftain scurries forward, grasping his club with both hands.

A spearhead bites into the back of Lugos' neck, at the join of head and spine. Even as he jerks his hand back to pull it out, the javelin plunges into his back again, and again.

Lugos' club drops from his numbed hand. He crooks his head over his shoulder. Quintus stands behind him on his horse, his dripping lance clutched in his hand.

"You're not killing any more men, you piece of shit," Quintus spits, his face flaming with anger. With a lightning jab, he crunches the spearhead deep into Lugos' ear hole, letting the pila dangle from the Boii's head.

Lugos scrabbles aimlessly at his face, his mouth working like a beached fish. He staggers through the battling equites and Boii, his arms twitching limply at his side. Finally, the dread barbarian falls onto his face. With a final kick, he lies still.

His warriors pause in their assault, horrified at the death of the man they thought invincible.

"Lugos is dead," shouts a Boii. Other Boii take up the cry.

Quintus hears it. "Lugos is dead!" he shouts in Gallic. "Lugos is dead!" The news echoes across the lines. The Boii mill about, confused and dismayed.

"Now!" Furius shouts to his men, "Full speed." He digs his heels into his horse and barges through the quiescent Boii. Quintus and his guards follow, their wedge formation widening the gap in the front-line Boii.

Sensing victory, the principes barge into the gap, beating the Gauls aside. After stabbing down the second line Boii, the Romans break into open space.

"Into their backs!" a centurion shouts.

The principes turn about and attack the Boii from the rear. Now the barbarians are caught between Roman assaults from the front and the back. The Boii panic, colliding with their own men in their haste to escape. The Romans cut through them relentlessly, destroying the center of Hamilcar's army.

On the Roman left flank, the Ligurians march rapidly around the Roman wing, hastening to outflank the allies and attack the Roman cohorts behind them.

Lucius' cavalry stampede out from behind the allied line, aiming straight for the surprised Ligurians. Twelve hundred riders rampage through them, following Lucius' directive to concentrate their attack there. The equites fling their spears into the lead infantry. They draw their swords and plunge through the disorganized barbarians, hacking at them from all directions.

The Ligurians' rear lines jam into their disorganized front-liners, limiting the Gauls' use of their long swords and axes. Cutting into the edges of the Ligurian mob, the equites hew them down from every side. Hundreds of Ligurians fall.

The Ligurians' erstwhile flank attack turns into a chaotic, desperate rout. The Roman cavalry stampede the Ligurians back toward the Roman infantry that penetrated the Boii center.[lviii] The remnants of the Gauls' rear lines break and run toward camp, flinging off arms and armor.

On the Roman right flank, the Insubres fare even worse. Marcus has led his twelve hundred allied riders into the side of the oncoming Insubres. Most of his men are north Italians, people who have long been victims to the Gauls' predations. The Italians cut into the barbarian infantry with a vengeance, striking down hundreds before the Insubres retreat.

Directing the battle from the rear, Hamilcar watches his flank attacks break apart before his eyes. He notices that Furius and his men are destroying the Boii's rear line, and he realizes the day is lost. *I'll have to rebuild my army. Another two years lost. Shit!*

"This day is theirs, Luli," he says to his commander. "We've got to get to camp and get all our money. Then we get out of here!" The two wheel their horses about and gallop away.

The Ligurians see the flash of Hamilcar's silver armor behind them. "Hamilcar has deserted us!" shouts one.

"That fucking Carthaginian has run away!" screams another.

As the message circulates, the fierce Gallic army loses their last taste for fighting. They run toward camp, joining the thousands of Boii already fleeing toward its fragile safety.

Furius watches Hamilcar's army dissolve. He sees the Roman and allied cavalry roaming across the plains, stabbing down their unarmed enemies. He feels a jolt of pity for the victims, but he quickly quells it. *Now to finish it. Give the tribes something to remember.*

"Looks like you have beaten, them, Furius" says an elated Quintus. "They're running like dogs."

"Not yet," replies Furius, his eyes fixed on the retreating hordes. "Hamilcar is still on the loose." He turns to the two tribunes standing to his left. "Call the men to order. We are marching on their camp."

"When?" asks one of them.

"Now! I don't want anyone getting away," Furius barks. The chastened officers gallop off to seek the other tribunes. A half hour later, the exhausted allies and Romans pause to reorganize their ranks. The soldiers refresh themselves with water and food, sprawling out a stone's throw from the field of the dead. The battle horns sound again.

Assassin

The troops march toward the Gallic camp, spread out in a miles-wide line across the plain. The soldiers methodically stab into any enemy felled by their cavalry, be they moving or still, ignoring any pleas for mercy. Furius and Quintus follow along in the center, directing the slaughter.

Rufus rides in and salutes Furius. "There's something you'll want to see, Commander," the scout says, nodding his head toward the enemy camp.

Quintus and Rufus follow Rufus out to the right, galloping ahead of the advancing Roman army. The scout pulls up to a dead stallion, its body covered in blood red mail. A man in silver armor lies spread-eagled next to it, an Umbrian spear jutting from his spine. Another in Carthaginian armor lies next to him, staring at the sky. His motionless chest is dotted with six spear punctures.

Furius dismounts and walks over to the corpses. He grab the shoulder of the one in silver armor and rolls it over. He stares into the face, then rolls the body back over.

"It's him all right." He smirks. "The Gauls didn't even stop to plunder his body. They must have been really scared." He points to Luli's body. "That little bastard must be his second in command. We got them both."

"What do we do with Hamilcar's?" asks Rufus.

Furius bites his lower lip. He looks back toward the Roman camp, at the scattered mounds of Roman and allied dead. His eyes grow cold.

"Cut his head off and stick it on one of the Gauls' standards," he growls. "Maybe it'll make them think twice before they try this again." He looks at Luli's corpse. "Put this one up, too. And that big bastard with the tree club. Maybe it'll help prevent any more rebellions."

"Speaking of preventing rebellions, if I would you I would send Hamilcar's head to Carthage!" says Quintus, smiling. He looks toward the Gallic camp and his smile vanishes. "Come on, Governor, the camp's just ahead of us. We have one more battle this day."

The two join the Roman and allied cavalry, heading for Hamilcar's camp. With the hour, Furius' cavalry have completely encircled the enemy camp. The equites sit on their horses, a fresh set of javelins in their hands.

Lucius rides out and meets Furius. "There's thousands of them holed up in there, Commander."

Furius nods. He eyes the rude pile of timbers and branches. "I daresay they don't have much water stored in there, because the river is so close. We'll use the ring of fire."

Lucius raises his eyebrows. "Ring of fire? No attack?"

"No. I'm sick of my men dying and their men living. You know the rules: capture any without a weapon, kill any who carry one. The infantry will back you up."

Lucius sticks up his right arm, palm down. "I hear and obey."

A half hour later, dozens of cavalry gallop around the camp perimeter, hurling burning torches into the palisade. The logs' branches crackle with flame, slowly igniting their parent trunks. The thick logs turn into walls of flames, flames that leap into the tightly bunched huts and tents inside. Screams and shouts erupt within. Anger and despair echo from every corner.

The Roman army stands quietly, every man facing the camp. The commotion inside grows. Minutes later, the gates fly open. Hundreds of Gauls race out from the burning camp, scattering in all directions.

The Roman and allied cavalry spring to life. The rush into the herd of fleeing Ligurians, Boii, and Insubres. Those who brandish a sword or spear are swarmed over and killed. Those without weapons are ordered to kneel and wait. Several chieftains refuse, standing unarmed but proud. They are lanced down.

After scores of Gauls are killed, the rest drop their weapons and kneel. The hundreds more flee from their burning camp. They see their compatriots being led away and drop their weapons. A few storm out,

138

roaring their defiance. They rush at the nearest enemy they can find, seeking a warrior's death over a slave's life.

By dusk, the camp is in ashes. Hamilcar's army is only a tale to be told. Thirty five thousand Gauls lie dead.[lix]

Two thousand Roman and allied bodies burn on the plains outside the Roman camp. Furius' army solemnly watches the gigantic pyre. Many clutch a clay statuette of a dead comrade's wife or child.

Furius, Lucius, Marcus, and Quintus stand in front of their men, watching the charnel flames soar into the night sky. The officers wear sandals and simple gray tunics. Tonight, everyone is just a soldier, saluting their deceased brothers in arms.

"We've got to get back to Arminium tomorrow," Furius says, "and begin setting up winter quarters for the army." His lips wrinkle with disdain. "Now that the Boii are vanquished, perhaps Consul Cotta will deign to pay his men a visit, if his 'pressing affairs' in Rome are resolved."

"I'll go back and give them the news," Quintus replies. "It will be a pleasure to tell the Senate. I can finally see my wife Horatia." His eyes start in panic. "My gods! I have to send her a message that I am alive!"

He rubs his wounded jaw, chuckling. "I am alive, after all this madness!"

"You are Fortuna's child, there is no denying it," says Marcus. "What will you do in Rome, Favored One? You should go to the Capitoline Baths and put some money on their dice games!"

Quintus laughs. "Well, one thing for sure, I will venture to the baths as soon as possible. I'd give a year of my life to be soaking in a big hot tub, far from these stinking Gauls!"

ROME. Amelia rubs the back of her neck and looks at her fingers. *Ugh! I'm oily as an Etruscan pig!*

"Lucretia!" she shouts, "let's go take a bath!"

Assassin

The curly haired young woman appears in the atrium doorway. "Why tell me? Do I look like your servant? I'll tell your slaves to fill the wash basins."

"No, no," says Amelia, waving her hands. "I want a proper cleaning. I'm going to the public baths. I'm spending too much time with the new baby. I want to be with people—grown up people! Let's take a soak in the big pools at the Capitoline Baths."

"It's a farther trip than Minerva's Baths behind us," Lucretia says.

Amelia winks at Lucretia and smiles. "The Capitoline will suit you. cousin. The main pool is for both sexes. There are sure to be some handsome bachelors there!"

The dark-haired young woman laughs. "You say you are doing that for me, eh? Your husband had better return soon, cousin, lest he find you've ridden off with some young tribune!"

Amelia rolls her eyes. "You will make a wanton woman out of me yet!" She grins. "Now you have to come with me. You have to keep an eye on me, lest I become the wanton woman you wish you could be! Tell Caldus and Nascus to meet us by the door."

A half hour later, Amelia and Lucretia are strolling down the narrow sidewalk that abuts the main street of Rome, accompanied by Amelia's two house guards. The group passes through the Forum and enters the bustling marketplace that surrounds the front of the Capitoline, heading for an enormous rectangular building bordered with tall granite columns.

"Magnificent!" exclaims Lucretia. "It's beautiful enough to be a temple."

"Look, there's a bunch of soldiers on top of the Tarpeian Rock," says Amelia, pointing to the precipice behind the bathhouse.

"I heard they're preparing for another execution," Lucretia says. "They're going to fling a Macedonian spy off the cliff."

Assassin

"Another spy?" Amelia says. "They're getting to be as bad as the Carthaginians."

The two women walk up the limestone steps that lead to the entryway statues of King Neptune and Queen Salacia, Rome's favorite sea gods. Caldus and Nascus stroll four paces behind them, looking about for anyone who seems suspicious. Neither guard notices the petite woman that walks to the right of them. She skips lightly up the steps, her long olive tunic flapping against her slim tanned legs.

Caldus and Nascus pause at the entryway, facing the ox-sized Thracian that guards its wide bronze doors. "No sense paying for you two," Amelia says. "We'll meet you out here in a couple hours," She turns to Lucretia and holds her palm out. "Give me two denarii. I'll pay you back when we get to the house."

"Hmph! I have heard that before." Lucretia drops two newly minted bronze coins into her palm. Amelia looks at them and grins. Scipio's profile is stamped on one of them, the back side depicting him on a rearing stallion. She grins. *The Latins must hate this. They'll have to stare at his face every time they give out one of their bribes!*

Amelia gives the coins to the burly Thracian. He pulls open the thick iron doors. The women pass through the vestibule and enter the women's dressing room, its walls built of pink marble slabs. They slide out of their robes and loincloths and hang them on a peg.

Amelia considers Lucretia's slim, firm body. *I'll have to get her married soon, while her breasts are still high. She'd be the perfect match for Laelius, if he wasn't so...disinterested.* She chuckles. *Lucretia's so hot-blooded, she'd probably cheat on him a month after they were married! At least Laelius would have children then—that would help his run for consul.*

She looks down at her full breasts, and squeezes her bicep and shoulder. She runs her hands down her slightly curved stomach—down to her nether regions. *Look what children have done to me. I'm bigger and looser—everywhere! I've got to start lifting the heavy ball again, do some gymnastics.*

Two male slaves appear to pick up their clothing. A nude Amelia grabs back her robe and shakes it under one slave's nose. "You put that in a safe place!" she barks, knowing the capsarii are notoriously light-fingered. "If anything's missing, I'll cut your dicks off!"

She reaches into a hidden pocket inside the robe's midriff, feeling the hilts of the two throwing knives she's cached there. *Wish I could keep my knives. But I'd look pretty silly wandering around naked with a knife in my hand. The balneator would probably throw me out.*

The two women pad through the dressing room exit and step into the frigidarium, whooping like children when they enter its cool waters. "I wish I had a man could make my nipples this hard," Lucretia declares. "My luck, I'll marry some old senator who only wants boys!"

"This is bracing, but I've had enough of being cold," says Amelia, rubbing her arms. "Let's go warm up."

They rise from the chill pool and pad into the tepidarium, plopping onto two of its padded stone benches. The women stretch out languorously on the leather pads, savoring the warm air that radiates from the heated floor.

"Oooh, I could stay here all day," Lucretia says, stretching out her arms.

"So could I," replies Amelia, "but I have to get my staff busy on some propaganda for the property tax increase."[lx] She sighs with pleasure, her hand resting lightly on her lower stomach. "I want to get the notices done before Scipio comes home. So we'll have some time together."

"You should get yourself a well-endowed slave to keep you serviced, like I do," Lucretia says. "Or hire one of those lean young gladiators." She rubs her lower stomach and smiles. "Mmm. I wonder if they're as good with their tongues as they are with their hands."

Amelia laughs merrily. "Gods, you are as horny as a Sicilian! Come on, let's get in the caladarium, before you get me aroused!"

They stroll through a side door and enter the center of the baths,

142

dominated by a field-sized hot pool bordered with marble statues of gods and warriors. The women step down the immersed stairs and stand waist-deep in the pool's hot waters, splashing each other like children. They stare across the water-level wall that separates the men's and women's section, watching the men lave themselves with sponges.

"Gods above, it's all I can do to keep my hands off myself," exclaims Lucretia. "Look at that stallion with the bandage on top of his head. I'd love to take *him* for a ride."

"That's Quintus, you goose! He's recently returned from Cremona, where he killed some famous Boii chieftain. His wife Horatia would probably kill you!"

"I don't care what he did to some Boii. I only care what he could do to me," Lucretia purrs. She dips her hand underwater. "Mmmm, I'll have wet dreams of him!"

Minutes later, Amelia and Lucretia stagger into a large marble room adjoining the caladarium, woozy with warmth. The two stretch out on two marble benches that lie on opposite sides of the room, ready for an olive oil massage and scraping.

"Where's the attendant?" Lucretia says, looking about the empty chamber.

"I'm coming," comes a voice from a curtained alcove in the rear. "Just disposing of something." The gauze curtains part and a petite young woman walks into the room, carrying wool towels and a bronze pitcher. She wears a drab gray tunic and a wide oxhide belt that holds two scraping horns.

"Where's the woman who was here last week?" Amelia asks. "She said she was just hired."

"Oh, she was called away," the attendant replies, "and I have rushed in to take her place." The attendant places her towels and pitcher upon the rectangular stone pedestal that separates the two benches. She smoothes back her close-cropped black hair and smiles impishly. "Don't worry. I'm very practiced at what I do."

"I'm sure you are," replies Lucretia. She rolls over onto her stomach and wiggles her buttocks. "Here, do me first!"

"That's fine by me," Amelia replies. "I need to cool down anyway."

The attendant grabs the pitcher and fills her cupped hand with olive oil. She slides the oil over Lucretia's back, buttocks, and legs, then rubs it vigorously into her back muscles.

"My, you're a strong little thing," Lucretia says, "but I like it!" She smiles coyly. "I can't wait until you do my front!"

"By the gods, Lucretia!" Amelia blurts. As she stares at the floor's tiled images of ships and sea monsters, she feels her eyelids droop. "Somnus is calling me. I'm going to drift off. Wake me when it's my time."

"I'll let you know," the attendant replies.

Amelia closes her eyes. Images flit across her mind as she lies half awake. She snores softly.

A slight gurgling noise stirs her attention. *Juno's cunt, what's Lucretia doing now!* Amelia turns her head toward Lucretia. She vaults up in horror.

Lucretia lies on her back, spasming on the marble bench. Her eyes and mouth gape, fish-like, as blood spurts from the new mouth that blooms in her throat. The attendant strides toward Amelia, a blood-stained dagger in her fist.

Spider's dark eyes lock onto Amelia's. She smiles. "All right, it's your turn!"

Assassin! Amelia rolls off her bench and crouches behind it. Her arms splay across its top as she crouches down, preparing to dodge to either side.

Spider springs to the top of the bench. She flashes her knife down toward Amelia's head. Amelia pushes away from the bench, flinging

144

herself to the floor. Spider stabs at her as she falls, gouging her blade across Amelia's back. Amelia cries out, but the sound is quelled by the noises from the bath rooms.

Amelia scrabbles on hands and knees to the other side of the bench. The assassin springs to the floor and scurries after her, her arm cocked for a fatal stab. Amelia springs into a crouching run. Spider runs after her, staying between Amelia and the exit.

I need a weapon! Amelia thinks, her mind racing. *Anything!*

"Come here, patrician bitch, before I decide to make this really painful."

Amelia grabs the towels and flings them into Spider's face. Momentarily blinded, the killer steps sideways. Her right foot steps into the pool of Lucretia's blood. She slips sideways, landing on a knee, but instantly springs back up.

The instant's respite is all Amelia needs. She grabs the bronze pitcher and swings it into Spider's chest, knocking her onto her backside. Amelia dashes for the exit. The assassin jumps up and runs after her.

"I'll carve your guts out for that!"

Amelia sprints out the arched exit and barges into the male side of the pool. "Assassin," she yells, "Sicarius!" Naked and streaming blood, she dives into the pool, splashing down among a group of disconcerted men. Spider bursts from the entryway. She glances at Amelia in the middle of the pool.

"Fuck!" Spider snarls. She dashes back into the massage room.

Hours later, Amelia is back in her home. She sits in the atrium, quaking with fear, a robe thrown over her head and shoulders. A contingent of sword-wielding servants encircles her.

Laelius runs into the atrium, stumbling upon the hem of his snow-white toga. He rushes to her couch and kneels before her, clutching her knees. "Gods above, Love, are you injured?"

Amelia shakes her head. "It's just a cut and some stitches. I'll live." She frowns with disgust. "I didn't have my knives. The assassin knew I carry them—that's why she waited until I was naked in the bath."

"Who was it?" Laelius says, his face clouded with anger. "I'll break her neck myself."

"I don't know," Amelia replies, her voice quaking. "The assassin slipped away. They found the real attendant stuffed into an empty amphora, her throat sliced from ear to ear. And Lucretia—my gods, Lucretia...!"

Amelia lowers her head and cries. Laelius grasps her shoulder. Tears well in his eyes. "You lost your cousin! Oh, my poor dear heart."

Amelia's head rises up. Her face is contorted with anger. "I should have beaten that bitch to death with that pitcher! Curse it, that's the last time I go anywhere without a weapon on me. Anywhere!"

"I do not doubt you are capable of killing someone," Laelius says softly. "I know you have killed men before. But next time, there may be several of them. Maybe you should stay at home more, with your people around you."

"I'm not hiding from whoever tried to do this!" Amelia spits. "And I'm not abandoning my work!" She laughs bitterly. "What good would hiding in the house do? One of them tried to kill Pomponia at my wedding. At my wedding, in this house!"

Laelius nods. "Nor would I hide, either, if I were you. Still, you need someone to stay with you, someone who can go with you, wherever you go."

"Huh! Lucretia was with me. What good did that do?"

"Oh, someone more, uh, skilled than dear Lucretia." Laelius stares out toward the exit of the house. "I still have friends from the docks, from all parts of the country." He winks. "With all sorts of backgrounds."

Amelia's eyes grow cold. "I want someone who is not afraid to kill.

Or torture someone, if needs be."

Laelius nods. "I understand. Let me talk to Scipio about it. I'm due to meet him when he docks in Ostia next week."

He shakes his head. "Gods, I hate to think what he'll do when I tell him what happened."

OSTIA DOCKS, ROME. "*What! When did this happen? Who did this?"*

Laelius spreads out his hands. "Easy, brother. She is fine. There is a deep gash on her back, but the medicus says it will heal. She was attacked last week, at the city baths."

"Let's get out of here," Scipio snarls, his face florid with anger. He trots down the gangplank of his trireme, past the marines roping it to Ostia's dock pilings.

I was a fool to leave her alone. I've got to get home. The ship's captain appears at the side railing. "Where are you going, Imperator?" he says.

"I have to get to Rome," Scipio says. "Get the grain sacks into port as soon as possible, and take them to the city granary. I want to see them there by tomorrow."

Scipio springs onto the mare Laelius has brought him. The two friends gallop down the cobblestoned road that leads to Rome, following the Tiber River pathway. Twenty miles later, the two race through the Porta Collina, the gate guards scrambling to get out of their way. Scipio pulls up in front of the Scipio manse and rushes inside.

"Amelia, Amelia!" he shouts. "Gods take me, where are you?"

Amelia pads out from the inside garden, tucking her trowel into a belt on her green wool tunic. She smiles into Scipio's anxious face. "Do not shout so, Husband. You'll wake the children, and I'll make you walk them to sleep!"

Assassin

Scipio rushes to her and enfolds her in his arms. "Carissima, are you all right? I heard a woman tried to kill you, and Lucretia died, and..."

Amelia presses a finger to his lips. "I am fine. That bitch was lucky I didn't kill *her*." She grins impishly. "I swear to Juno, that's the last time I get naked without a knife, even with you!"

"What about the children?" Scipio blurts. "Are they safe? Is Publius well?"

"They are fine; Publius is fine. I'm the one they wanted, but it won't stop me from working. We have already started to campaign for Laelius to become aedile."

She studies his face. "He didn't tell you that, did he? Typical of him." She shakes her head. "Lucretia would have made a good match. So full of life, just like him."

Scipio shakes his head. "Poor Lucretia. And you were almost killed!"

"But I wasn't. And I won't be. Next time I'll bring my guards inside, even if they have to take a bath with me!" She pulls his hand. Come now, it has been months since we have seen each other. Let me show you my new scar..."

Hours later, Scipio joins Laelius at the baths. The two walk through the women's chambers, ignoring the nude women who stare curiously at the famous personages.

They stop at the massage room. Scipio notes the faint pink stains that encircle one of the tables. *That must be where Lucretia bled out her life.*

He looks at the other table. *Then the assassin came after Amelia. Probably thought she'd be terrified. Thank Mars she didn't know her!*

"I have asked around. I think I know who did this," Laelius says. "They call her Spider, because she has a venomous bite." He looks at Scipio. "But she only kills for hire. I don't know who ordered her to do it."

"Amelia has her enemies, as do I. But only the Latins bear us enough enmity to hire someone to kill her," says Scipio.

"Cato?" asks Laelius.

Scipio shakes his head. "He is an honorable man, however outdated his values. He would be too ashamed of himself to try such a thing."

"Flaccus, then," Laelius says. "Honor would not be an issue with him."

Scipio nods. "He would be the type. And the type to try it again. I still think he had something to do with my mother's death. Would that I knew, I would strangle him myself."

"You know, Amelia thinks she can handle anyone who comes after her," Laelius says. "But I am not so sure. The next time it may be two or three men—or women!" He sighs. "I wish were still here; no one would come within a block of her!"

"Marcus is gone," Scipio says. "But I have someone else in mind."

He grabs Laelius by the shoulder. "Say, can you take a trip with me to Capua?"

"Down south? Whatever for?"

"Why, for the Capuan Games, of course. They have someone there I'd like you to meet.

Philip V, King of Macedonia

V. The Wrath of Philip

ATHENS, GREECE, 200 BCE. General Sulpicius Galba slows his horse to a walk, so he can better take in the carnage about him. The consul shakes his head forlornly. "What kind of man destroys the beautiful and sacred, Lucius? Why would he wreck all this art, and desecrate the dead?"

"Philip hates Athens," his lead officer replies. "He couldn't get inside the city, so he destroyed all that was outside it."

"I can see him taking slaves and plunder—that is part of the fortunes of war." Galba says. He stares at the white-specked mounds of the children's cemetery. "But this, this is...unholy."

Lucius and Galba trot through a furrowed field of dismembered skeletons and corpses, plowed from their resting places by Philip's raiders. All about the two men are detached heads, limbs, and torsos, garbed in their rotting burial raiment. Other bodies lie at the mouth of their tomb entrances, dragged into the light of day before their crypts were destroyed—further evidence of Philip's determination to desecrate the Athenian dead.

Gigantic stone heads sprawl among a ghastly expanse of bodies, parts of the gods' statues that were strewn there when the Macedonians leveled the temples and shrines.[lxi] The Temple of Hercules smolders in the distance, its graceful marble columns lying in broken chains about the rubble of its once-proud carvings and walls.

Galba turns his horse back towards the Roman camp. "I cannot bear to see any more of this," the veteran commander declares. "It's as if he declared war on the dead, and then the gods themselves. What madman would risk invoking their revenge?"

"You just said it," Lucius replies. "A madman. With a vision of conquering the world." He looks below him, where the marble face of Minerva stares up at him, noseless. "He will do the same to us, if given the chance."

"We can't allow this atrocity to go unchallenged," Galba splutters. "We march on him tomorrow."

Lucius stares quizzically at Galba. "Do you know something I don't? Because I don't know where he is."

"I don't either, but we will find him. His path of destruction indicates he is heading back to Macedonia, taking the road toward Lyncus. That's all we need to know."

Two days later, the Romans pack up their camp and head north. They march into the saw-toothed mountains, stumbling and climbing through its rocky passages. The path is steep, but the legions maintain pace, moving quickly toward Macedonia.

Three days later, Galba's army descends upon Philip's garrison at Lyncus. They find a fort populated only by a handful of militia and thousands of terrified townspeople.

Galba pauses before Lyncus' open gates. He flings a rock into its timbered walls, watching it bounce off. *The snake has slithered away.* He calls on his cavalry leader Sergius to join him in his tent for a breakfast meeting.

"Sergius, I think we are closing in on Philip, but I cannot be sure of his whereabouts. Send out three hundred of our best men to find his camp. We'll camp here until we find out."

He bites into the top of a roast canary, then points the headless bird at Sergius. "They are not to return until they find him. He's out there somewhere, hiding in these cursed mountains."

Forty miles away, Philip sits on his throne inside his tent, camped in the sprawling Lyncus Mountains. He is drops a handful of bronze obols into a bulging mouse skin purse, and pulls its drawstring tight.

"There, that is more than enough for you," he declares. Philip holds the purse out toward the stoop-shouldered Athenian shepherd standing before him. The man reaches for the purse, but Philip snatches it back.

"You know, if this information is false, your wife will be placing these obols upon your eyes, that Charon may guide your journey to the underworld."

The dark little man swallows. "I swear, they were but three or four days' march down the road when I left them." He points. "Back south, toward Lyncus, by the Bevus River, far north of Athens."

"Ah, Athens. I will have to get back there soon. I have unfinished business with them." He turns to Athenagoras, his second in command. "There are enough trees near Athens for ten thousand crosses, wouldn't you say?"

The officer grins. "Aye, and enough firewood to burn the rest of them alive. Haughty little bastards, we'll see what good their Aristotle does them when we set their feet afire!"

Philip waves his hand, his jeweled rings flashing. "Send out four hundred of our best riders. Tell them to comb the area until they find the Romans."

The king pulls out his dagger and idly cleans his fingernails. "Oh, yes. They are to kill any Romans they find. But bring a few back for torture—we need information."

"I'll take them out myself," Athenagoras says. "I'm bored with sitting in camp."

Athenagoras hurries out. When he is gone, Philip walks over to face his informant. He wipes the dagger on his thick fur robe and holds its gleaming edge under the Athenian's nose.

"You will be my, ah, guest until we find out if your information is true," Philip says. He grins wolfishly. "You can keep your coins, farmer. I can always get them back if I need them, now, can't I?" The wide-eyed man can only nod.

Athenagoras' men race out toward Lyncus, galloping down the roadway between the valley's fertile grainfields. The Macedonian cavalry soon enter the Bevus hill country outside their camp. The cavalry rides single-file along the threadlike upper trails, looking below for signs of Roman incursion. After an hour of fruitless searching, Athenagoras leads his men onto the river plain that connects with Lyncus.

Sergius' cavalry contingent is riding down the same roadway. His advance scout race up to him. "Sir, the Macedonians are coming down from the hills. There must be hundreds of them. They are only a few miles away, and coming fast."

The veteran warrior only nods. "Macedonian cavalry, eh? Let's give them a Roman welcome! Tell the men to prepare for an assault." Sergius listens to his order being passed along to his riders. He unties his helmet's chin strings and knots them more tightly, shoving his black plumed dome more tightly upon his head. *There, now I'm ready!*

Sergius pulls out the wasp-waisted gladius hispaniensis he so recently acquired from Scipio. He cups the double-edged steel blade and feels its razor sharp edges. *Let's see if you are all that Scipio claims you are.*

"Sound the charge," he orders his trumpeter. The man pulls his cornu to his lips and blows two long blasts, the sound echoing into the distance. As one, the Romans charge across the plain in a sweeping arc of three hundred riders, stampeding toward the Macedonians.

Having descended to the base of the hills, Athenagoras has halted his cavalry, reorganizing his men along the wide road to Lyncus. "We'll take the road to their camp," Athenagoras tells his captain. "Send out some men to see what's ahead."

The words no sooner leave Athenagoras' mouth than he hears the rumble of hooves coming from the road in front of them. He sees a wide dust cloud growing in size, billowing around the road.[lxii]

"Romans!" he shouts back to his men. "Get ready for them!" He pulls out his ivory-handled sword and points it forward. "No quarter, no mercy!" Four hundred riders thunder across the plain, their spears lowered at the Romans.

Sergius watches the silhouette of a broad line of cavalry heading toward him. *They're going to try to encircle us.* "Spread out!" he shouts. "Don't let them get around our flanks!"

The cavalries close upon one another. Without breaking stride, the squadrons fling their spears, bringing dozens on both sides crashing to the earth.

"Into them!" Sergius screams. "Trample them into the earth!" The two forces crash into each other, knocking horse and man onto the earth. With the lines too mixed to hurl spears, the conflict becomes a freewheeling swordfight between skilled warriors who jab and dodge at one another.

Sergius' horse takes a spear into the neck. Whinnying with pain, the beast crumples to its knees. Sergius slides off the side of his mount and lands agilely on his feet, his sword at the ready. A Macedonian rider hurtles toward him, leaning to the side of his charging mount, ready to spear Sergius' chest.

Sergius twists sideways and shoves his parma out in front of him. The spear grates across the front of the small round shield, turning it away. As the rider passes, Sergius swings his gladius into the rider's bronze chest protector, hoping to knock him off balance. The Iberian steel hews through the bronze and into the man's ribs. The Macedonian drops his spear, bellowing with pain. He gallops away, his hand futilely covering his spurting wound.

Sergius watches the rider fall sideways off his horse. He stares at his bloodied blade. *Gods above, this thing is like a butcher's cleaver. It cuts through anything.* A decurion trots up to Sergius, towing a horse. Sergius vaults into the saddle and grabs his young cavalry officer by thc shoulder. "Tell the men to use their swords like axes! Tell them to chop, not thrust! The damned thing will cut right through their armor."

An hour later, both sides' men and horses stagger about, weary with battle.[lxiii] Sergius realizes that his men are beginning to hold their swords and shields low. *They outnumber us, and they can catch us if we flee. I have to do something.*

He spies Athenagoras riding about in his rearmost line, directing men to attack points. *His guards are a spear's throw from him. There is a chance.*

Sergius waves over the young decurion. "Spartus, if I do not return, I want you to lead a retreat back to camp. Full speed—let the gods take any that fall."

Sergius snaps the reins and plunges toward Athenagoras. A Macedonian rider angles in from his right, aiming his spear at Sergius' exposed throat. At the last instant, Sergius ducks his head next to his horse's neck. The spear passes by him. Sergius swipes his sword at the Macedonian as he rides by, and hears the satisfying crunch of blade chopping into bone. The Macedonian screams, clutching his shattered kneecap. Sergius races toward the Macedonian commander.

Athenagoras notices Sergius weaving his way toward him. *Ah, he wants to kill the commander. We'll see about that.* The Macedonian cradles his long spear in his arm and gallops straight at the oncoming equite.

Sergius turns his horse sideways, forcing the Macedonian to break his charge. As Athenagoras wheels his mount around, Sergius plunges in and swipes his deadly blade at the Macedonian's unprotected head. Athenagoras parries the cut with his spear. There is a loud *crack*. The front half of Athenagoras' spear cartwheels to the ground. He stares dumbly at the stub in his hand.

"What a piece of shit!" he swears. He hurls the stub at Sergius' face.

With a swipe of his shield, Sergius deflects the cartwheeling spear shard. He urges his horse forward, his gladius raised high. He swipes it down at the Macedonian's shining helmet. Athenagoras raises his thick round shield.

Sergius' blade hews through it to the boss in the middle. He yanks his sword out and aims another blow at Athenagoras' shield. The gladius chops a wedge out of the Macedonian's shield.

Athenagoras gapes at the hole in his shield. *To Hades with this! We know where the Romans are.* He wheels his horse about and races away. "Guards, guards! Come to me!" he shouts, galloping toward the Macedonian camp. The riders trot in behind Athenagoras.

Sergius watches the Macedonians close about their leader. *I've got to get out of here before they spear me to death.* As he turns to ride away, he hears Athenagoras shout an order to his men. The horns sound. The Macedonian cavalry retreat from the fray, flooding out into the descending dusk.

"Should we go after them?" asks Spartus.

Sergius glances into the night sky. *We don't know the terrain like they do.* "Night is coming. Let them go for now."

Hours later, a bedraggled Athenagoras stands before Philip, reporting the day's events.

"You left the bodies on the battlefield?" Philip asks. "Why didn't you bring them back?"

"We were outnumbered," Athenagoras lies. "We could have been overcome."

Philip shrugs. "No matter. We'll bring them back tonight. We'll show the men what the Romans have done to their fellows."

The next day, Philip's army gathers around the border of a natural amphitheater outside of camp, looking down at a large, shrouded mound in the center of the bowl. When all have gathered, Philip struts in, wearing his ceremonial armor. His purple-crested plume nods high above his head.

"I know you all to be men of grace and morals, men who seek to bring the Macedonian way of life to others. But the Romans, they are nothing but barbarians, beneath your contempt. See what they have done to our colleagues!" Philip nods at two attendants. They grab the corners of the shroud and whisk it back.

The soldiers gasp. The warriors are used to seeing their dead with the puncture marks and stab wounds of traditional spears and swords. The bodies before them are a grisly jumble of decapitated corpses, torsos missing entire legs and arms—stomachs with their internal organs exposed.[lxiv] These Macedonians have never before seen the deadly effects of Scipio's Iberian sword.[lxv]

"You see what they are," Philip shouts. "You see what those savages did? They cut our men to pieces, like they were hogs for the slaughter."

The warriors stare at the horrific tangle of heads, bodies, limbs, and organs. One vomits, then another.

"Gods above," mutters one, "I didn't sign up to have my guts cut out!"

"Look at that, that poor devil had his entire arm cut off at the shoulder!" exclaims another. "What kinds of demon weapons are they using?"

Philip notices the look of horror spreading across his men. *This was a mistake. Now they're scared of the Romans! I'll get us more men. If we outnumber them, that will bolster their spine.*

"Summon my officers," he says to his attendant, and strides back to his command tent. His infantry and cavalry commanders soon gather about him: Macedonians, Cretans, and Thracians.

"Hmm. Perhaps I have underestimated the Romans," Philip says, rubbing his chin. "Our phalanxes should make us their superiors in battle, but it is best we do not tempt fate. I am going to bring back my son Perseus and his army, and retrieve the men we stationed at Pelagonia."[lxvi]

The Wrath of Philip

"And then what?" asks a Thracian captain.

"Then we march on this upstart Galba, and wipe him out," says Philip. "We won't kill them all, though. We will take lots of prisoners." He bares his teeth in the rictus of a smile. "Our men will give the Romans what they gave our men, with their own swords. We'll see who the butchers are, then."

ROME. "You failed, woman. Give me my money back."

Spider peers into the darkened stable entry, trying to make out her shadowy client's face. "I failed *that* time. But I have not given up. Give me another chance."

"It is too late. The bitch's machinations have gotten the salt tax approved. Now I'll pay a fortune in higher taxes!"

"So what? You said she was a constant thorn in your side. I'll kill her so she won't be working against you in the future."

There is no response from the man. Spider purses her lips. *I can't give him his money back; it'll ruin my reputation.* She peers into the darkness. *He sounds old. Just jump in and kill him.* Her legs tense, preparing to spring.

"Do not plan any mischief," the voice rasps. "People know I am here."

Spider pauses. *Don't be stupid. Word gets out you killed a client, you'll never get another job.* She sighs. "I tell you what. I will do another assignment for you, at no charge. You will have two for the price of one!"

"Two?" replies the voice. "No further charge?"

Cheap bastard. "That is the sum of it. Just tell me who."

"Scipio Africanus," the voice replies immediately.

Spider hoots with laughter. "The Savior of Rome? Even assassins have a code of honor. Pick another."

Moments drag by. "Manius Aemilius. He is a Senator—a Hellenic party organizer."

"And that is reason enough to kill him?" Spider asks.

"My reasons are my own," the voice replies. "You must take care of this before the next Senate session—that is all you need to know."

Spider shrugs. "Well and done. It will be soon."

"When?"

She smiles. "Sooner than you expect, my bloodthirsty friend. Sooner than you expect..."

* * * * * * *

Saturn Day dawns clear and sunny. The dawn light streams inside the slot window that opens into Manius Aemilius' bedroom, waking him from his fitful dreams. The tall, angular man rises and stretches. He flaps his arms about his white-haired chest and bends to touch his toes, working to loosen his aching joints.

Manius rubs his eyes. *Ah, I stayed up way too late last night, fussing over that slave tax proposal. Why do I bother? The Latins will savage it, regardless. Probably insist on lowering the tax rate to one percent. I think I have the votes to counter it. I'll twist Publius and Cassius' arms. They owe me a favor after I kept the censor from dismissing them.*

"Toga!" he says to his empty bedroom. A house boy materializes in the entryway, cradling the purple-bordered garment in his spindly black arms. Manius spreads his arms. The slave carefully wraps the snow-white toga about him, throwing the last wool flap over Manius' bony shoulder.

"Mulsum!" Manius says, straightening the folds about him. A kitchen boy hurries in with a small bronze cup. Manius downs the spiced honeyed wine in one gulp. He shoves his shoulders back and straightens up. *There now, ready for business!*

The Wrath of Philip

Manius strolls into his atrium, bowing toward the Aemilii death masks that line the wall above his family altar. *Good morning, ancestors. Bring me good fortune today.*

"Marcus!" he shouts. "Get yourself ready, boy. I've got to go to the Forum Boarium!"

A short young man strides in, cinching a wide leather belt across his unadorned gray tunic. Manius smiles at him. "Ready as always, weren't you?"

Marcus shrugs. "This is your favored day for shopping, Father. I expected as much."

"Purchasing, boy. I am doing purchasing. The women shop."

Marcus' mouth twitches with the hint of a smile. "Of course. Purchasing."

Manius smiles at his son. *Always so taciturn. I thought he would be more voluble, like me.* He glances at his flaccid arms. *I am built like a gangly old heron, but he is a block of stone.* He smiles. *People must think my Proserpina was cheating on me! If they only knew!*

"Come on, then," Manius replies. "We need some cattle for the farm. And there's a new play at the Avenue of Poets."

Marcus' eyes wander to the ceiling. "Oh, joy. Another new play. I can hardly wait."

The two men step out from the Aemilius manse and enter Rome's busy Via Sacra. They stroll down the wide, cobblestoned street, with Manius' two Gallic guards following behind them. An inveterate shopper, Manius pauses frequently to purchase minor items that strike his eye: a bag of fresh figs for tonight's dinner, an ivory carving of Venus as a gift to his wife, a small bag of turmeric from far-off India.

He hands each purchase to two hulking Gallic attendants. They somberly place the new items in one of the large wicker baskets they lug along in front of them, occluding the short swords hanging from their belts.

Manius stops again, closely examining a cage with two Ethiopian monkeys. Marcus pulls him away. "Mother would boil you in oil if you brought them home," he says.

With a final wistful glance, Manius turns from the chattering little beasts. "Very well. I suppose we should get to the Boarium."

Marcus and Manius walk to the edge of town and enter the fenced portal to the cattle market. After several hours of intense bargaining, Manius arranges for several calves to be carted to the family villa near the Sabina Hills.

"That's it for the day, Son," says Manius. "Let's go see the latest performance."

"Can't we go watch the gladiators practicing?" Marcus retorts, pointing toward the Campus Martius. "I might learn something new to show my legion."

Manius tugs his son away. "You have had the greatest teacher in Rome. I doubt those pot-bellied louts know something he didn't." He grins. "Besides, you are going to be a senator some day. You have to attend public cultural events. You have to be seen among the people!"

"I'd rather be seen among my men," Marcus growls. "Preferably when we are kicking Philip's ass back to Macedonia! "

"You won't be a tribune for the rest of your life. You are coming with me to the play. Plautus has a new comedy,[lxvii] and I have to see it!"

The two men wander through side streets lined with vegetable vendors and food stalls. Manius stops to buy a sausage on a stick, much to Marcus's disgust. "You eat too much meat," he says to his father. "We don't eat any when we're on the march, and we do fine."

The two Amelii pause at the entryway to the Avenue of Poets. A crude wooden stage dominates the entrance. Two frenetic young actors cavort on it, wearing only helmets and loincloths. One sports a purple

Roman helmet and the other a battered Carthaginian dome; clearly they are meant to be Scipio and Hannibal. The Scipio character has an enormous leather penis tied about his waist. He uses it to slap the buttocks of the Hannibal character, who dashes about to escape him. The crowd roars with laughter. Vendors ply the crowd, selling chickpea cakes and pork sausages from wicker baskets that dangle from their necks.

Manius stands with his guards at the edge of the crowd, raptly watching the comedy unfold. Marcus prowls about the edges of the burgeoning crowd, watching the people that surround his father and his guards.

From the corner of his eye, Marcus sees a dirty young man reach inside his belt purse as he pushes through the crowd toward Manius. In a flash, the young tribune is standing beside the man, his hand on his dagger.

The man yanks out a crust of spelt bread and bites into it, spitting crumbs as he guffaws at the onstage spectacle. Marcus' shoulders relax. He steps back toward the edge of the crowd, continuing his watch.

"Man down!" someone screams from the crowd. Marcus whirls about and sees his father lying on his back, a red spot blooming from the snow-white cotton of his toga. Manius' guards lurch about with swords drawn, searching for the perpetrator.

Marcus barges through the crowd, flinging men aside as if they were children. "Father, Father!"

He drops to one knee in front of his father, grasping his blood-streaked hand. Manius' mouth gapes like a fish's. "I tried to be as good as your father," he stammers.

He grips Marcus' trembling hand. "You will always be my son." His hand falls from Marcus wrist.

Marcus leaps up, staring through the press of humanity. He watches a tiny figure slide away from them, a mere flash of dark green weaving between the forest of onlookers.

The Wrath of Philip

Marcus plunges after the escaping figure.

Twenty paces ahead of Marcus, Spider hurries toward the edge of the crowd, her bloody dagger tucked inside her olive colored cloak. She hears several protesting yells behind her and turns to see the thick crowd parting like a wave. She sees a blocky young man shoving them aside, his baleful eyes fixed on her.

Spider fingers the hilt of her dagger. *That one won't kill easy*, she decides. *He could delay me*. Pitching away her cloak, she dashes up the steps of a nearby temple. Arriving at the temple landing, she wedges herself through a narrow space between the ten-foot statues of Castor and Pollux, disappearing into a dark space behind them.

Marcus dashes up the steps. He jams himself into the narrow space, but he cannot squeeze his thickly muscled body through the opening. "Gods curse it!"

Digging his sandaled feet into the limestone steps, Marcus shoves his upper arms into the legs of the two statues and pushes outward. His face darkens with effort, his arm veins swelling to the top of his iron biceps. The statues begin to lean sideways. They sway.

"Madman! Blasphemy!" shouts a temple priest. He jumps onto Marcus' back. "He sullies the gods!"

In an instant, a bevy of temple priests swarm over the young man, yanking at his arms and legs. Marcus tumbles to the floor.

"Get off me, fools!" he bellows, flinging priests off him. He springs up and sprints along the marble-tiled corridor that runs the length of the building. His yellow-green eyes search every space and nook, but he sees no one.

He has to be here, somewhere. He dashes past the columns that line the perimeter. He cannot find anyone there, just a slim young girl begging for alms.

Get back to Father's body. There is no revenge today. You will find the assassin. And the one who hired him.

Marcus walks back to the statues. Pushing aside two glowering priests, he picks up the olive cloak and returns to his father's corpse.

As he walks, he rubs the cloak between his fingers. *Smooth. A finely knit wool.* He brings the cloak to his nose and sniffs it. *Roses. Am I dealing with a woman?* His eyes widen with realization. He sprints back down the corridor, seeking the beggar girl. There is only an empty cup where she sat.

Marcus slaps the side of his head. *Fool, fool, fool!* He forlornly returns to the murder site.

Swords drawn, the two guards have cleared a space around Manius' body. Marcus bends down and kisses the old man upon his cheek. He reaches out and gently pulls his eyelids down. "I will find whoever is responsible for this," Marcus says. "The gods will weep for the woe I bring to whoever that did this."

The guards pick up Manius' body and carry it on their shoulders, returning to the Aemilius manse via the Forum. Marcus follows behind, lost in thought.

As they walk through the Forum, they pass the announcements platform, where Rome's public speaker announces the news of the day.

"Mischief is abroad," the barrel-bodied praeco announces. "Philip of Macedonia has ravaged Athen's sacred places. The estimable consul Galba pursues him. Retribution is certain to follow. The savage Celtiberians have taken the Poulo garrison and burned it to the ground. Antiochus of Syria has invaded Pergamum, leaving destruction in his wake. He marches on the seaport of Teos."

Marcus raises his head at the news. *Antiochus? He's heading toward Greece? Gods above, how many tyrants will we have to fight?*

TEOS, KINGDOM OF PERGAMUM. "It doesn't seem fair, Zeuxis," Antiochus says, "but I do love watching it."

The Seleucid king stands atop a small hill outside Teos, watching his Syrian charioteers cut through the last of the city's defenders.

The Wrath of Philip

The chariots wheel through the disorganized infantry as though playing a game of catch-and-tag. The chariot's spearmen shove out their eight-foot spears to lance into the Greeks' bodies. The cruel scythed wheels hack into the unfortunate's legs. Scores of disabled Greeks crawl upon the ground, begging for death.

The Galatians march in behind the chariots, chopping down any who have escaped the chariots' charge. The huge Gauls pull off the wounded soldiers' helmets. Using a practiced tribal gesture, they grab their victim by the hair and pull his head back. With one slash of their heavy long swords, they strike the man's head from his body, waving it aloft while their tribesmen cheer.

An hour later, the frenzied battlesite has become a somnolent cemetery field, covered with a thousand men and boys. The chariots rumble slowly through the corpses, bumping over the bodies that lie in their way. The Syrian spearmen eagerly search for any signs of life, their spears held ready. Occasionally a chariot halts, as the driver or spearman spots a corpse yet unplundered by the Galatians.

Hundreds of disconsolate captives squat among the weeds at the edge of the carnage, roped together like cattle. They stare hopefully at Teos, hoping someone will come to rescue them. No one does.

Antiochus rides his white stallion to the edge of the killing fields, with Zeuxis at his right hand. The king summons one of his Syrian infantry officers to his side. "Bring up the four catapults. It's time to convince them to surrender."

Zeuxis rides over to the Galatian chieftain, who is busy prying some gold teeth from a defender's mouth. "We need the heads. Bring them to the front, by the catapults."

While the Teos townspeople look on, the Syrians hurl one head after another over the city's twenty-foot walls, bashing them against buildings, animals—and townspeople. The townspeople wail in sorrow when a familiar face thuds to the ground near them, their voices supplicating the gods. Tears streaking their face, they scrabble about the city, cloaking the heads for burial.

166

The Wrath of Philip

The town's twelve elders step up to the parapets, watching the Syrian's grisly onslaught. They see Antiochus riding out near the front of the city gates, just out of spear range. He waits there, facing the elders, an unspoken question on his face.

Antiochus raises his right arm and waggles his fingers. A white-cloaked messenger rides past his king and pauses under the city's front watch towers, looking up at the rulers. "Surrender now, and all will be spared," he barks. "Resist, and we burn you to the ground."

The town rulers quickly confer. Most of them shake their heads. They resume their post and watch the Syrians.

Antiochus grimaces. *We must do this the hard way.* He rides back to the catapults. The elders see him gesturing angrily at his men. Soon, the Syrians march the captives out in front of the catapults, their hands bound behind their backs.

The Syrian king rides back to his place in front of the gates. While the city elders look on, four Galatians stride out from behind the catapults. They each grab a captive and push him to his knees, ignoring his pitiful cries for mercy.

One by one, the Gauls chop the heads off of their prisoners and shove the bodies to the earth. Carrying each head by its hair, they hand them to the catapult operators. The operators drop them into their catapult buckets, already swarming with flies from the previous missiles.

A Syrian officer barks an order. The catapults release their ropes and shoot their load toward the elders. Four heads arc into the city. Four more soon follow by four more. And four more. The elders watch in horror as the dripping skulls arc over their heads.

"That's enough for now," Antiochus says. "Have the men take food. We will wait."

An hour later, the twin gates creak open, then widen. The Teos survivors file out, their heads bowed.

"Bring them in, Zeuxis," Antiochus says. Minutes later, the deadly chariots roll into the city, followed by the Galatians and the Syrian infantry. Soon, the town reverberates with crashes and shouts, as Antiochus' men gleefully plunder it.

At sunset, Antiochus is sitting comfortably in Teos' main hall, clad in his favorite lionskin robe. He chews on a roast boar snout while he watches his men roll in wheelbarrows of coins and jewelry.

"Sort out the types of coins, you fools," Antiochus says. "We have to use them for bribes to different peoples."

The twelve elders stand against the far wall, surrounded by guards. They watch glumly as their townspeople's treasures pile up before them.

Picking his teeth with a porcupine quill, Antiochus turns his attention to the elders. "I gave you a chance to surrender immediately, and you refused it. And look what you made me do! I had to kill a dozen fine warriors just to convince you. You took their lives. That cannot go unpunished under Syrian law."

He watches the fear wash across their faces. He smiles. "Oh, I won't kill you old cows." He taps his grease-spattered chest. "I promised I would spare your lives if you surrendered, and I am a man of my word!"

He sits quietly for a moment, watching them. When he sees the relieved look on their faces, he continues. "Then again, I did not say everyone would go *unharmed*, did I?"

He turns to the captain of the guard. "Take them out to the courtyard. I want you to cut the right hand off every one of them, except that fat one on the end. I saw him using his left." He smirks at them. "Now you'll have to learn a new way to wipe your ass!" The guards drag the pleading old men from the room.

"Old pisspots," Antiochus says, "they made my day harder than it needed to be." He bites into a thick slice of plundered bread.

"I am glad we didn't have to knock down their walls," says Zeuxis, sipping from his wine goblet. "If we cross the Aegean and attack the Aetolian league, this place would make a good base of operations."

Antiochus burps loudly. "Zeus' balls, what do they put in their bread here? I'll be having spirits in me for days." He waves his hand airily at Zeuxis. "Oh, we're not going to Greece for a while. We still have to take over all the towns around here. Build a firm base in the south."

"King Attalus will not take lightly your conquest of part of his kingdom," Zeuxis says. "We should send out some scouts to track his movements. Those Pergamum cavalry can move fast."

"Attalus? That old goat-fart? He's busy fighting the Galatians up north. He cannot bother us as long as we stay down here. From here we will gather strength."

Zeuxis shakes his head. "Why wait? We have the largest army in the world now. Let's take it all the way to Italia!"

Antiochus flings his bread slice at a passing slave boy. "We do not yet have the best trained army in the world. Hannibal will see to that, when I lure him here. Besides, the time is not propitious. We'll wait until Rome and Macedonia have depleted their forces from fighting each other. Then we strike."

"What about our pact with Philip? He will lay claim to Pergamum, because his ancestor Alexander conquered it. Maybe we should fight him first."

Antiochus vigorously shakes his head. "No, we will honor our pact with him, Zeuxis. We aren't ready to war against both of them—yet. Let's see how Philip fares against the Romans. That will tell us much about our next direction."

He bites into the boar snout, chewing slowly. "I'm not worried about Macedonia. I think Philip is going to be very busy with the Romans for a while."

EORDIA REGION, NORTHERN MACEDONIA, 199 BCE. "This is the place. We can keep an eye on them from up here."

The Wrath of Philip

King Philip trots along a plateau two miles east of the Roman camp. He pauses on the lip of the flat hill, looking down at the bustling Roman encampment. He can see the camp is divided into perfect rectangular sections by its arrow straight streets, the tents uniformly spaced apart. *I don't believe it, who would have thought those farmers could make such an orderly camp?*[lxviii] *They're not as crude as I expected.*

"Philocles!" Philip shouts, summoning his stocky infantry commander. "We'll build camp here. I want a sturdy palisade surrounded by a deep ditch. Get it done by dusk. I don't want those shit-heeled Romans sneaking up on us."

Twenty thousand infantry and two thousand cavalry flow up the winding pathway toward the top of the plateau. Scores of disfavored Macedonian soldiers start on the onerous task of ditch digging. Hundreds more march into the surrounding forest. They hack down hundreds of young trees and hurry them back to the camp site, knowing Philip's penchant for punishing laggards.

Two days later, the Macedonians finish a sturdy camp parked in the center of the plateau. The army carpenters raise the log gates into place, while the sentries watch from the guard towers above them.

Philip sits on the edge of the plateau, watching the Romans' muster their forces below. *They are going to come out and confront me*, he decides. *Fine. Now I can show them why Macedonia once ruled the world.* He mounts his horse and trots back to his command tent in the center of camp. Philocles is waiting for him there, poring over a map of the region.

"The Romans will be coming out tomorrow," Philip says. "Likely for an opening skirmish. We should give them a taste of our best fighters, to dampen their morale. I want the Companions to go after them, after the skirmishers open the combat."

"The Companions will send them running," Philocles says. "They are the best cavalry in the world!"[lxix]

170

"I would think so. I don't just want a victory, I want a humiliation. Get the allied commanders in here," Philip orders. "We have an attack to plan."

As Philip meets with his officers, Consul Galba holds a war meeting in his own tent. The veteran commander paces about in front of his tribunes, uncharacteristically nervous.

"This is our first time against the Macedonians, but Philip knows our strategies. He is a friend of Hannibal's, is he not?" He clenches his hands behind his back. "His army outnumbers ours, and he has the high ground. We'll have to do something he doesn't expect."

Octavius Septimus steps out from the officers. The slim older man is bent over, favoring the abdomen wound he suffered at Zama. "We have the elements of a real surprise for him, Consul. Those Numidians that general Scipio sent here? They whirl about like Zephyrus' wind! I daresay Philip has never seen their like. And the elephants—he doesn't know we have elephants to fight him, does he?"

"No, but that is what worries me," replies Galba. "They could trample our own men. Our horses are still shy of them."

"We who fought with Scipio are used to them," Septimus says. "Put us on the front lines."

A gray-haired tribune steps next to Septimus. "He speaks the truth. Scipio had us march with the elephants when we trained in Africa. And the Numidians—they have been raised with them!"

"And we fought Philip's phalanxes at Zama," Septimus adds. "We know how to fight his spearmen. And his elephants, if he has any."

Septimus notices that Galba is still wavering. *Don't make this about Scipio!* Septimus chides himself. He slightly bows his head. "Please, it would be our privilege to fight them for you, General. And for Rome."

Galba purses his lips, he glances sideways at his waiting officers. *Scipio said his men are the best in Rome.* "Very well. Septimus, your cohorts will take the front lines. The Numidians will back your skirmishers. But no elephants! That's too many new things going on at once."

Do not push it, Septimus tells himself. He sticks out his right arm. "I hear and obey, General. We will be ready for tomorrow."

The next morning, a Macedonian sentry shakes Philip from his wine-induced sleep. "The Romans are mustering for battle! They will soon be out in the field!"

Philip rubs the sleep from his eyes. He grins. "Well and good. Let's show them how real warriors fight." He rises and stretches, massaging his neck. Bending over, he yanks the fur cover off his sleeping pallet. A naked girl stares up at him, her eyes wide with apprehension.

"Your sexual naiveté no longer amuses me." Philip points a finger at his chief attendant. "Give her a purse and send her back to her parents. I'll be out at the front of the camp."

Philip is soon at the edge of the camp plateau, watching the Romans mass their forces a half-mile away. Athenagoras stands at his side, already clad in full battle armor.

"Being Romans, they'll open with their skirmishers, " Athenagoras says.

"More than likely. Romans are quite predictable." Philip rubs his chin. "Mmm. Just to be safe, let's make this a skirmish, not a full-scale engagement. We'll see how Galba's men fight before we risk a battle."

"As you say," Athenagoras says. "But the Gauls will be disappointed. They are itching for another fight."

"They can go to Hades! They kept me up last night with all their carousing! We'll use the Illyrians to skirmish with their skirmishers. They're swift and elusive—the Romans won't be able to touch them. Then we'll have the Cretan archers go right behind them. They can rain arrows upon the Romans before the Illyrians hit them."

"We should have our cavalry follow up after them," Athenagoras says. "They can cut the infantry apart. And we'll destroy their plodding cavalry, if they send them out."

Philip nods. "We'll use my King's Companions, just like we talked about. Big Borko can take them out." He smiles. "Their army can watch us defeat their cavalry and light infantry. That will weaken their will before we give them a full scale assault."

As morning eases into afternoon, the Macedonian gates creak open. Four hundred Illyrian skirmishers trot out, sinewy young men with six foot spears and circular shields, wearing only knee-length tan tunics. Three hundred Cretan archers follow them, easily keeping pace with the swift-footed Illyrians. The leather-clad soldiers carry their U-shaped horn bows and a quiver full of barbed arrows, with a neck-length helmet as their only armor.

The Illyrians line up at the base of the plateau, preparing to charge. The Cretans stand a spear's throw behind them, looping on their sinew bowstrings.

Seven hundred King's Companions[lxx] stand in rows behind the Cretans, riders who are the heart of the Macedonian cavalry. The proud young men carry their eleven-foot spears on the shoulders of their bronze cuirasses, their black capes flowing behind them. Each of their wide-brimmed helmets carries a series of black X's upon it, each mark a tally of a slain enemy.

Athenagoras and Borko stand in front of the Companions. Borko is a wide-bodied, loose-limbed giant. His thick forearms are tattooed with the faces of Acteon and Artemis, the god and goddess of the hunt. Borko's silvered helmet is webbed with black kill marks.

Mounted in front of his infantry, Galba watches Philip's forces massing for an attack. *He is holding back his full army. He wants to test us. Very well, he shall have it.* He looks to his left. "Septimus, prepare your forces. Let's see what Scipio taught you."

Septimus can barely repress a smile. "Yes, let's see. I promise we will do honor to you, General. By your leave, I will join my men."

Galba stares at him. "You want to fight with the velites? On foot?"

He taught me to fight with my men, not behind them," Septimus replies testily."

Galba raises his eyes heavenward. "Be your own man, then. I will have my cohorts at the ready, should you need them."

"I won't," Septimus replies. "Our cavalry will see to that." He dismounts and walks to the front of the heavy infantry, facing the Macedonians.

The Illyrians march thirty yards out from the Cretans. They turn sideways and crouch forward, ready to sprint. The Cretans nock an arrow into their bows and look out toward the Roman lines, picking their targets. They chatter about the force and direction of the breeze, formulating the best angle for their shots.

Waiting with the Companions in the rear, Athenagoras sees the Roman light infantry sliding up between the three-foot gaps that separate the infantrymen. The velites are unarmored men with spears, shields, and domed helmets, blooded veterans of the Iberian and African campaigns. Scores of them have wolf's heads covering their helmets, honorifics that Scipio awarded to them for bravery in battle.

Athenagoras watches Septimus step out in front of the velites, conferring with a group of centurions as he looks over his shoulder at the Macedonians. He sees the tribune wave his arm to the right and left, sending his centurions to man each flank. *They're getting ready to charge us,* Athenagoras decides. *We should seize the initiative.*

"Ready, Borko?" Athenagoras asks. "Let the Illyrians wear them down, then our Companions will cut into them before the Roman cavalry can reach us. The equites are slow riders."

"We'll spear down whoever is still standing," the huge cavalry captain replies. He laughs. "Those Romans ride around like turtles, all covered in a shell of armor. If they come out to get us, we will kill all of them."

Athenagoras chops down his right arm. A ram's horn blasts three times. The Illyrians dash out, running pell-mell at the waiting velites.

Septimus' heart thuds in his chest. *Here they come! Remember what General Scipio said: you fight pandemonium with organization.* "All together now, and hold your lines!" he shouts.

Septimus' skirmishers trot out from the front and arrange themselves in a two rows. The centurions step out in front of them and beckon their men forward, with Septimus leading in the middle. The velites march forward as one man. The gap between the two enemies begins to close.

The Cretans trot in behind the Illyrians. On command, they halt and nock their arrows into their bows.

"Fire!" their commander shouts. Their bows thrum like a hive of bees. A torrent of arrows swarms in upon the oncoming velites. Dozens of the light infantry stumble and fall, arrows buried in their faces and necks. Their compatriots gaze at them, tight-lipped, vowing vengeance.

Holding his shield over his head, Septimus feels an arrow thunk into its center. "Testudo!" he shouts to his officers. The centurions direct the light infantry into turtle shell squares, with shields held over their heads and in front of their bodies. The Romans march forward, their shields bristling with arrows.

Screaming and shouting, the Illyrians close in upon the Romans. "Formation! Get into formation!" shouts Septimus. The velites break out from their testudos and reform as a two-deep line of seven hundred men.

"Loose two!" shouts the lead tribune. The Romans fling two rounds of javelins into the onrushing Illyrians, bringing scores of them rolling to the earth. But still they come on.

"Wait for the signal," Septimus orders. The veterans hold on to their last javelins, arms cocked and ready. The onrushing Illyrians draw within a hundred feet of the Roman line, then fifty.

"Loose!" Septimus shouts, drawing his sword. The Romans fling their last round into the faces of their onrushing assailants. Dozens of

Illyrians crumple to the earth, javelins jutting from their faces and chests. But still they advance.

The centurions blow the defensive formation signal on their neck whistles. The velites draw their swords and pull their shields next to their bodies, bracing for the Illyrian charge.

With a resounding crash, the Illyrians collide shields with the Romans—and bounce off their shield wall. Septimus steps out from his men and cleaves his gladius into the collarbone of an Illyrian stumbling backward. The man falls onto his back, writhing in pain. Septimus stabs his blade into the man's unprotected chest.

"Come on, women!" he shouts. His men move out and surround him. "Attack!" he screams, beckoning them with his bloodied sword.

The Romans slash out with their Iberian swords. The steel blades split the Illyrians' small round shields, leaving the warriors vulnerable to the Romans' biting thrusts into their bodies. Within minutes, dozens of Illyrians lie upon the ground. The Romans march forward to engage more of the disorganized enemy, stabbing down the wounded as they tramp past them.

"Forward!" shouts Septimus, as he gouges his sword through an Illyrian's sword arm. The Romans cut through the second line of Illyrians and head toward the archers.

The desperate Cretans shoot arrows straight at the faces of the Romans, but their velites' shields protect them well. Within minutes, the legionnaires cut into the front row of the Cretans. Armed with only a sword and helmet, the Cretans are chopped to pieces by the double-edged Iberian swords.

"Retreat!" screams the Cretan captain. The archers run for the camp, joining the Illyrians in flight.

Athenagoras watches in stunned disbelief. *They're running like sheep! It hasn't been an hour!*

"Send the Companions!" he orders.

Borko charges out ahead of his men. He grasps his heavy lance with both hands, leveling its barbed spearhead at the foot soldiers in front of him. The hetairoi thunder in behind them, spears lowered, a wave of lances bearing down toward the Roman light infantry.

"Shield wall!" Septimus barks. The Romans genuflect and dig their shield and right foot into the earth, ready for the onslaught.

Borko's heavy mount crashes into the shield wall, knocking two velites onto their backs. Grinning with triumph, Borko pushes his long lance through the chest of one fallen youth, pinning him to the earth.

"See? They're all weak!" he bellows at his men. "Follow me!" Borko plows his horse into the second line.

The Companions batter into the resolute Romans. Dozens break through the shield wall, pushing their lances into the soldiers' sides and backs. The velites strike back, but their sword blows glance off the heavily armored riders. The Roman lines start to break apart, as men turn from the front turn to defend themselves from a rear attack.

Septimus ducks under a charging Companion, slashing at the horse's haunch as it runs by him. He sees the velites turning in all directions to defend themselves, charging at the rampaging riders. *They can't hold their ground forever. Best to hit them now, while they are engaged with the foot soldiers.*

"Sound the cavalry attack!" Septimus shouts to his trumpeter. The cornu sounds the call.

Hundreds of Numidians burst out from the main army's flanks and storm across the plain, galloping madly toward the Macedonians. With only a spear and shield, the tunic-clad Africans cross the gap in minutes. The Africans whirl into the flanks of the slow-moving Companions.

The hetairoi are brave and skilled riders, but they have never faced an opponent like the acrobatic Africans and their nimble Numidian ponies. Guiding their horses with their knees, the African riders duck under the Macedonians' heavy two-handed spears. They jab their cone-headed

177

javelins into their shieldless opponents' legs and feet as they hurtle past, drawing first blood. Before the Macedonians can spin about to face them, the Numidians charge back to inflict more wounds.

The Numidians attack the Companions from every side, their spears flying into them from all angles. The Macedonian cavalry reel about, bleeding from front and back wounds, not knowing which way to turn.

Borko rages on in the middle of the velites, ignoring the Numidians' flank attacks. "Break their center," he screams to his men. "Follow me into them!"

Borko rams his spear into the helmet of a centurion. The officer topples to the earth, feebly trying to raise himself. Borko lowers his lance and aims it at the centurion's face.

A rock clangs off the side of Borko's helmet, bringing stars to his eyes. Borko looks over his shoulder and sees Septimus striding toward him.

"Coward!" Septimus shouts at him, flinging another rock. "Sheep-fucker!"

"You die today, old man," Borko snarls. "I feed your head to the pigs!" He spins about and charges toward the tribune, his spear leveled at Septimus' breast. Too late, Borko notices Septimus is looking past him.

Borko feels a sharp, blinding pain in his lower back. A spearpoint emerges from his stomach then quickly disappears. A rangy Numidian bolts past him, whooping with triumph as he races after new prey.

Septimus closes on Borko. "We'll see who feeds the pigs," he says, drawing his sword. With one strike, his gladius cleaves Borko's thick lance in half, leaving him with a stub.

"Roman pig!" Borko bellows, ignoring his bloodied stomach. "Now you see your gods!"

The Macedonian flips the stub away and reaches for his curved sword.

His bloodied hand slips on the hilt. He pauses to wipes his hand before he grabs it. It is a fatal mistake.

Septimus hurries to the side of Borko's horse and plunges his blade into Borko's thigh, severing his artery. Bright red blood gushes from the Macedonian's leg. Borko reels his horse about and swipes at Septimus' head, but the veteran combatant blocks it with the edge of his shield. The wounded Macedonian strikes at him again; his blow is feebler and Septimus easily deflects it.

"You are dead," the Roman commander says to Borko. He trots away.

"Coward! Come back and fight!" Borko puts heels to his horse and gallops toward Septimus. Tottering in his saddle, Borko raises his arm for another sword blow. Septimus hears Borko's hoofbeats. He looks over his shoulder and turns back, ignoring Borko's charge.

Borko topples backward, rolling off the rear of his horse. He crashes onto the ground.

Septimus halts his horse, watching Borko twitch out his last seconds. *Pig meat, eh?* He rides back to the front line of his men.

General Athenagoras fights in the center of the maelstrom, using his sword to strike at infantry and cavalry alike. A Numidian darts in behind him. The African shoves his dripping spear deep into the shoulder of Athenagoras' horse. The animal rears up on its hind legs, pitching Athenagoras to the ground. The Macedonian captain sits up and rubs his forehead, trying to clear his head. Four of his Companions dismount and encircle him, bared swords at the ready.

A Companion stuffs his horse's flowing mane into Athenagoras' hands. "Here, my King. I will double with another." Athenagoras woozily clambers onto the mount.

"This way, Commander. We must get you back to safety!" The captain is meekly led from the battle, surrounded by a contingent of his riders.

Seeing their leader depart, the dispirited hetairoi soon follow. The

Macedonian riders leave a hundred of their dead upon the plain, joining hundreds of brutalized Illyrians and Cretans. The Numidians chase the Companions across the plain, flinging their spears into their slow-moving opponents.

Best we get our men back, before Philip's entire army comes at them. "Sound the recall," Septimus barks. The recall sounds, and the Numidians and Romans head back to the waiting cohorts. The cohorts erupt with a mighty shout, knowing their men have won the day.

Galba rides out and joins Septimus on the front line. "You acquitted yourself well today."

"Gratitude, Consul," says Septimus. "General Scipio taught us that surprise can be your greatest ally. They thought our velites would fight and run away, like most skirmishers. But these men have learned to fight like hastati." He grins. "They fight quicker than the regulars, without all that armor."

Galba nods, his face pinched. "And the Numidians?" he asks sarcastically, "I suppose Scipio taught them to fight?"

Septimus chuckles. "Gods above, he had no hand in that. They are like a force of nature. They blow in and surround you like a desert wind. He only taught us how to defend against them."

"I see," Galba replies. "Tomorrow, we will try out those elephants you wanted. Maybe that will be another surprise for these Macedonians."

The next day, Septimus marches his entire army up to Philip's camp, with the elephants leading the way. [lxxi] The army arrays itself in front of the Macedonian ramparts. And they wait. An hour later, Galba himself rides out toward the Macedonian gates, determined to challenge them to battle.[lxxii]

"Philip! King Philip! Come out and fight! Why do you hide behind your ramparts like a rat in a wall? Alexander the Great would be ashamed of you!"

Philip watches Galba and his army from one of the gate's

watchtowers, dismayed at what he sees. *They're using elephants! They've never had elephants! What's going on here?* He notices the dusky-skinned Numidians are whirling about outside the flanks of the Roman lines, chasing each other as if they were children playing a game of tag. *And he's got all those Africans with him! I need more time to figure this out.*

Philip's sticks his head out of the tower's window. "Go back to camp, peasant. I will be the one to pick the time and date of our next encounter, and you shall not be so lucky then. Go back and celebrate your little victory, while you still can."

Galba removes his helmet, glaring at Philip. He spits on the ground and trots back to camp, riding over to the waiting Septimus. "He's not going to fight."

"He will, eventually. Philip cannot let our win go unchallenged; he will lose command of his men. He will have to do something soon. And it will likely be a sneak attack. We must be very careful."

"I hear what you say, but we need food. We have to gather what's left of this spring wheat while we can," Galba says. "We will have to go outside of camp, no matter what he plans."

"He may ambush our foragers." Septimus says. "Just as his friend Hannibal did. Let's not make it easy for him to do it."

Galba rubs his forehead. "Hmm. Let's pack up and move north. Our scouts say there is much grain to be had near some place called Ottolobum. We'll quickly fill our stores and return."

"What about Philip?"

"Our scouts will keep an eye on him. When he moves, we will move after him. And end this thing."

Two days later, the Romans decamp and move eight miles north of Philip's fort, lugging the palisades from their old camp. They settle into the fertile wheat fields of Ottolobum province, where they rebuild their camp next to a river in its valley.

The Macedonian scouts follow the Romans to their new site. When they see Galba's men digging the wall trenches, they hasten back to inform Philip. The king receives the news with great equanimity.

"Good, they are near enough for an attack, but far enough to give them a false sense of security. They probably intend to ransack the area, and don't want us bothering them."

"And will we bother them?" asks Athenagoras.

"Oh, most certainly," Philip replies. "Most certainly, indeed. They like to give me surprises. Well, I have one for them."

ROME. "Here now, Publius, that's not for you!"

Scipio gently pulls his swordbelt from his young son's grasp, laying it atop his goatskin traveling satchel. "You'll be wearing one of those belts soon enough," he tells the chubby boy. "Gods willing, it will be during peaceful times."

Bobbing his son on his hip, Scipio stuffs more clothing into his bag. With one arm around Publius, he continually drops and retrieves his items. *This is next to impossible to do with one hand. How does Amelia get anything done with him and Cornelia about? Thanks the gods I can escape to the Senate!*

"Here, lay down and stay out of trouble!" Scipio plops Publius onto a sleeping pallet. He hands him a soldier doll of tied rags. "Amuse yourself until Uncle Laelius comes."

"What, you want me to tell jokes to a baby?" comes a voice from the doorway.

Scipio grins. He turns, spreading his hands in mock exasperation. "Your humor is usually at Publius' level, Laelius. Why not?"

"Careful, old man. I have no reason to go to Capua other than to keep you company. I'd sooner be wrestling in the gymnasium than plunking along on some leaky old trireme!"

"I do need your company," Scipio says. "Little Surus there is not much of a conversationalist." He glances at the family molossus. The enormous puppy is dozing in a corner. He raises his seamed, jowly face at the sound of his name.

"He *is* a bit easier on the eyes than you, though," Scipio says.

An elderly red-headed slave hobbles into the room, leaning on his carved ivory cane. "Apologies, Master. There is someone asking for you."

Scipio folds a green tunic into his satchel. "Who is it, Rufus? Not another one of those artists? I told them I don't want any statues made of me!"[lxxiii]

"It is a woman of noble birth, I would say," the elder slave replies.

"Jupiter's balls, it's impossible to get anything done around here!" Scipio eases his shaving blade into his satchel's side pouch and ties the valises' top strings together. "There. That's ready!"

"Hurry it up. We have to get to the docks soon." Laelius says.

"Yes, yes, we'll get there," Scipio snipes. "let me tend to this woman." He stalks from the room, muttering to himself.

His frenetic pace eases when he sees who is waiting for him. She is a tall and thin woman, her blonde hair elegantly coiffed above her head. Wearing a long burgundy gown, the woman has the aura of a queen, beautiful despite her advanced years.

Scipio walks up to her and takes her hands in his. He kisses her lightly upon both cheeks. "Proserpina! This is an unexpected honor." His eyes moisten. "I am so sorry to hear about Manius. He was a true man of the people. I admired him deeply."

"Gratitude, Imperator. Manius always spoke well of you." She stares into Scipio's eyes. "He said I could come to you if I ever needed help."

"Of course. Anything that is within my power."

183

Proserpina squeezes Scipio's hands. "I want you to send my son Marcus away. I fear he will kill himself in his quest to find Manius' assassin."

Scipio blinks with surprise. "Uh, yes, of course. Manius mentioned Marcus. He was very proud of him. I am sorry I have not met him."

"How could you? Marcus was fighting in Gaul when you were in Iberia and Africa." She smiles. "Marcus is a tribune in the Sixth Legion now. He is a fearsome fighter, but he roams the Aventine at night, looking for my husband's assassin." She grasps Scipio's forearm. "Who knows what could happen to him in that den of thugs?"

Scipio nods. "I appreciate his determination, but I have seen good men come to grief in their quest for revenge. Yes, I will get him reassigned. Perhaps to Greece. I hope to go there, and I can keep an eye on him. Is he in the city?"

"He is outside," Proserpina says. "I wanted you to meet him."

"I would be delighted."

Proserpina's face grows anxious. "There is something you should know about him, something important." She glances at a sitting couch. "May we sit?"

A puzzled Scipio leads Proserpina to the couch. She leans close to Scipio, her eyes searching his face as she talks.

"Manius and I had a wonderful marriage; I loved him with all my heart. But we never produced a child, though he so wanted an heir to follow him. After years of trying we decided to take, how shall I say, another course of action." She looks away from him. "To let someone else be the genitor of his child."

Scipio is silent for several moments. "It is understandable. And you are not the first to do that. Many older men have taken that path, and raised the children as their own."

"Manius wanted the father to be someone strong, and moral. A man of strength and honor. Someone he truly respected. And he found him. After much cajoling, the man agreed, for the good of Rome."

"And you?" Scipio says.

Proserpina looks at her feet. "I knew the child would become a scion of the powerful Amelii family. That he would carry on our name." She raises her chin. "I did my duty, and I am proud of it. Marcus has turned out to be a wonderful child, and a better man."

Proserpina places her hand on Scipio's shoulder. "Now I ask you, for Manius and myself—take our son under your guard, that he may live to pursue an honorable course in life as a soldier."

She rolls her eyes. "He wants to fight King Philip, and says he is the real threat to Rome." She throws up her hands. "Macedonia is so far away! At least it would get him away from the Aventine!"

Scipio grins. "Young men want adventure. Where is he?"

"Wait here." Proserpina walks out the arched doorway. She soon returns with a solidly built, auburn-haired youth. The young man's eyes roam across the room, taking in every detail as if he were scouting it for threats. He fixes his yellow-green eyes on Scipio.

"General Scipio," says Proserpina, "I would like you to meet my son, Marcus Aemilius."

Scipio is struck dumb. He stares into the face of a young Marcus Silenus, a boy with the unflinching demeanor of Scipio's beloved commander. *My gods, he has come back to us!*

Still gaping at the young man, Scipio extends his forearm. "Salus, Marcus," he says, the words catching in his throat. He feels his forearm crushed in an iron grip.

"Salve, Imperator," Marcus replies. "I am deeply honored. My physical father spoke often of you. And well."

Scipio stares at Proserpina, a question in his eyes. "Oh yes, he knows who his *body father* was. Whenever Marcus was in Rome he would spend all his time with our son, training him in the ways of the warrior."

"He had the finest teacher in the world, then," replies Scipio. He scratches his head, bewildered. "I just can't believe it. Marcus never told me about you," Scipio stammers. "I, I just never knew."

"Of course not," Proserpina replies stiffly. "He swore not to tell. And he was Marcus Silenus—what could ever make him break his word?"

She's angry I even hinted he might break his promise, Scipio thinks. *She must have cared deeply for him.* "Of course," Scipio replies.

"Gods curse you, Scippy." Laelius strides into the room, frowning with mock anger. "We have to be in Ostia by the next watch and you're out here chatting with—" Laelius pauses when he sees Marcus. He stares at Scipio.

"Laelius, I would like you to meet Tribune Marcus Aemilius of the Sixth Legion, son of Manius and Proserpina Aemilius. We will be talking to Marcus about his future when we return from Capua."

Laelius gapes at Marcus. "Jupiter's beard, he looks like..." Scipio nods at him. "Yes, he is Marcus' body son."

Tears in his eyes, Laelius grabs the young man's forearm with both hands. "Oh, I am so happy to see you, Tribune! I hope we will see much of you when we return."

"It would be an honor," Marcus replies, discomfited by Laelius' outburst. "Especially if we are working to defeat the Macedonians."

"You will certainly have your chance to do that," Scipio replies, "unless we can make peace with Philip."

Marcus grimaces. "Apologies. From what I have heard, he is an oily character. Always sneaking about. Best we stomp on the snake, before he can bite." He taps his chest. "I am looking forward to fighting him. Philip must be destroyed!"

The Wrath of Philip

"Sounds like 'Carthage must be destroyed'," Laelius says, chuckling. "You're sure he's not Cato's son?" Proserpina glares at him.

"He will learn diplomacy in time," Scipio replies. "For now, it is enough that he knows how to fight. We need officers who will fight Philip before he gets any closer to Italia."

Marcus fidgets, his hands balled into fists at his side. He looks at his mother, then back at the two famous commanders. "You must excuse me. I have to go to the Campus Martius; it's time for me to lift some boulders. Father Marcus taught me the importance of daily conditioning." The young tribune marches out without a backward glance.

He is Marcus' son, all right. Scipio stares into the empty archway. He turns to Proserpina. "You know, I have a gift for him, something that will carry him through the hard times he will undoubtedly face. Something he will treasure."

Laelius looks at Scipio, puzzled. His eyes light with recognition. "You're going to give him that?" he says.

Scipio grins. "Of course. I had my Nike figurine to inspire me, and he will have the most inspirational gift any soldier can have!"

As dusk creeps in from the east, Marcus limps back to the Aemilius manse, his body aching from hours of lifting and swordplay. *I have become a better man today, but I'm ready for a dinner, a bath and a bed!* He enters his bedroom and finds a scarlet cloaked hump resting in the middle of his sleeping pallet.

Marcus fingers the rose-red covering. *This is a sagum, an officer's cape,* he thinks, puzzled. Marcus whisks the cape away.

A battered tribune's helmet lies on the bed, an immaculate red horsehair crest towering above its battered surface. A folded square of papyrus rests next to it. Marcus opens the message.

This is the war helmet of Marcus Silenus, Rome's greatest warrior. Every scratch, every dent is a record of the many encounters in which he triumphed.

The helmet does not evidence the times he risked his own life to save a fellow, or the times he aided the poor and vulnerable in Rome's humblest neighborhoods. He was a man of unwavering honesty, courage, and loyalty; the greatest man I ever knew.

Publius Cornelius Scipio.

Marcus unlatches a large wicker basket in the corner of his room. He raises the lid and extracts his unscathed helmet from the bed of armor and weapons it rests upon. He gingerly lays the battered helmet inside the basket, running his fingers over its worn cheekpieces.

Marcus slowly closes the lid, shoving the wood latch through the loop. The young legionnaire rubs a forefinger into one eye, then the other. He takes a deep breath and strides out from the house, heading back to the Campus Martius. *I'm not that tired; I can get in one more lifting session.*

OTTOLOBUM, 199 BCE. "Look, Athenagoras. They've reaped all the spelt wheat that's along the road. They're moving inside to the farther fields."

"Farther from their camp, too," notes Athenagoras.

King Philip grins. "Good. Now we can exact our revenge."

Philip turns his horse about and trots down a steep hill overlooking the Ottolobum valley. Athenagoras and his guards follow along the twisting passage, their eyes wary for Roman scouts.

When he comes to the plain, Philip forces his stallion into a gallop, anxious to return to camp. Athenagoras pulls up alongside him. "Why are you hurrying?" he shouts. "There aren't any Romans around."

"That's just it!" Philip replies. "They aren't watching us any more. For days I've waited for them to let down their guard. We can strike while they're busy harvesting!"

The Wrath of Philip

Athenagoras breaks into a toothy grin. "I'll get our raiders ready. We'll make them regret they ever left Italia."

At dawn a dozen scouts ride out from the Macedonian camp, stationing themselves at overlooks above the river valley's hillsides. They watch thousands of Romans march out along the roads, carrying the baskets and sacks they will use to gather grain. Scores of trundling wagons follow them, ready to take the winnowed grain back to camp.

The Romans tramp through the flattened fields of last week's work, which ends in a straight line of tall wheat. The soldiers line up opposite the tall plants, in formation as if preparing for a battle. The centurions blow their whistles, and the legionnaires march into the fields.

Using their Iberian swords as scythes, the Romans whisk down the neat rows of grain. Working industriously, the men lose themselves in their task, moving ever farther from camp. Hundreds of disconsolate soldiers stand around with threshing baskets, waiting to do the slave's task of winnowing the harvested wheat from the chaff.

Philip and Athenagoras stand alongside their horses among a copse of hillside trees, three miles from the Roman camp. A scout joins them, his face excited. "The road is totally free of enemy, my King. The Romans are at least a half-mile from it in either direction."

"Excellent!" replies Philip. "Time for revenge!"

Two thousand Macedonian cavalry follow Philip onto the main road. Five hundred Cretan archers trot out behind them, led by Athenagoras.

Following Philip's orders, the Cretans are now armored with breastplate, shield, and sword, prepared for hand-to-hand combat. They march slowly, conserving their energy for the murderous task ahead of them.

The small army moves unnoticed down the wide main road to Ottolobum, as scouts return with news of the Roman's current position in the fields. An hour later, when the Macedonians are within a mile of the Roman camp, Philip summons Athenagoras.

The Wrath of Philip

"You know what to do," Philip tells him.

Athenagoras nods. "I'll take the northern fields, and my captain Nikolas will take the south."

"I'll have the main road," Philip replies. "Remember the plan. No mercy. Take them like sheep to the slaughter." The king trots back to the front of his men.

Five hundred cavalry depart with Athenagoras, and another five hundred with Nikolas. Philip leads the archers and remaining thousand cavalry down the road. They halt a half-mile from the Roman camp.

Philip calls over his two infantry captains. "Spread out a spear's throw to the right and left. I want a long wall across the sides of the road—no escape possible!"

The cavalry position themselves across the road, with the Cretans standing behind them. And they wait.

Athenagoras' and Nikolas' cavalry fan out across the edges of the north and south fields, lurking among the hillside trees that border the busy Romans. The two commanders ride back and wait near the roadway, waiting for their signal.

A scout rides up and bobs his fist twice. The leaders nod and repeat the signal to the officers nearest to them. The officers gallop back to the waiting cavalry.

Minutes later, a wave of battle cries erupt from the Macedonians. The armored riders fan out and race across the barren fields, heading toward the distant shapes of the harvesting Romans. They pull out their curved swords and lean next to their horse's necks, ready for slaughter.

The legionnaires hear the distant rumble of hooves. They raise their heads and gape at the hordes of enemy cavalry descending upon them.

"Attack, attack!" a centurion screams. Hundreds of harvesters run for the roadway, clutching their swords. Others form maniples of shieldless, unarmored defenders, grimly facing the waves of impending attackers.

Whooping and shouting, the Macedonians stampede through the fleeing Romans. They lean sideways and slash into the soldiers' heads and bodies, hewing them down in their own grim harvest. Scores of battle-tested veterans fall into the alien soil, bleeding out their lives in a farmer's field.

Many legionnaires see the futility of escape and turn to face their pursuers, their gladii at the ready. They are quickly trampled down by the unrelenting Macedonians. Their bones and bodies broken, they worm through the emerald green stalks, mewling for help.

Hundreds of Romans reach the roadway and run toward their fort. They round a bend in the road and see Philip and his men straddling the road, lances at the ready. They next thing they see is a cloud of Cretan arrows rocketing into them.

"Don't let them get away!" Philip screams. The king charges forward and his Companions follow, lowering their long spears toward the backs of the fleeing legionnaires. The Macedonians rampage down the roadway and its stubbled fields, spearing every Roman in their path, paving the way with the dead and dying.

Seeing Philip's horde approaching, two young legionnaires run sideways from the road and dive into the tall green stalks. Caesar and Lucretius crawl toward camp, slithering past the roadway's waiting soldiers, flattening themselves each time they feel the rising thunder of hooves underneath their trembling hands. Soon the two Romans are past the Macedonians and their deadly harvest. They rise into a crouch.

"Lucretius, we've got to get to camp," says Caesar, so nicknamed for his hairy torso. "Our men depend on us."

Lucretius throws down his sword. "This will only slow us down. And it won't do us much good if they catch us."

"No weapon?" Caesar says, gripping his hilt. "It's sure death."

"Every minute we tarry, someone dies. It's camp or death!" Lucretius unbuckles his sandals. He rises up and dashes out onto the roadway, loping toward camp.

"Wait! I don't want to die alone!" With a wistful glance at his gladius, Caesar throws down his sword and runs after Lucretius.

The goddess Fortuna smiles upon the brave young warriors. They soon stumble into the gate portal. "They're killing our men!" Lucretius screams, falling exhausted into the ground.

"Macedonians! They're everywhere!" Caesar gasps out. He bends over and vomits, his chest heaving.

The Roman horns sound the call to muster. Within minutes, two thousand heavy cavalry rumble out the gates and down the roadway. Septimus gallops ahead of them, strapping on his bronze cuirass as he rides. General Galba soon follows, leading his entire infantry toward Philip's murderous raiders.[lxxiv]

Minutes later, Septimus hears the cries of the victimized harvesters. He waves over his squadron commanders. "You, and you. Take your men to the right. You two, go to the left. Kill every one of those Macedonian bastards, and don't come back here until you do!"

Twelve hundred riders scatter out into the fields, chasing the sounds of their men's distress. They veer off at random, rushing to succor anyone who cries out.[lxxv]

By now, the entire Macedonian attack party is milling about the fields, killing at will. The Cretan archers take particular delight in finding groups of Romans massed to defend themselves. The archers casually shoot down each one, making wagers on who can hit a chosen Roman. When all the men in the group have fallen, the Macedonian cavalry ride in, lancing each body before they dismount to rob it.

Back on the main road, Philip trots his lathered horse over to Athenagoras, who is directing his men toward two flocks of fleeing Romans. "How many are left to kill?" Philip asks, his eyes bright with delight.

"How in Hades would I know?" Athenagoras snaps. "These fields go on forever!"

"Just keep hunting, until no one's moving but us." Philip waves the tip of his bloody sword in Athenagoras' face. "Then take heads. I want some heads to put on our spears."

"Cavalry!" shouts a nearby rider. Athenagoras looks over Philip's shoulder. "Their cavalry are coming across the fields, my King. They're all over the place!"[lxxvi]

"Shit!" says Philip. "Just when we were almost done! Well, we'll stop them. I'm going back to my men on the road. Get the archers to join me."

A furious cavalry fight erupts in the wheat fields. Romans and Macedonians swarm across the landscape, dodging and pursuing each other. The remaining harvesters rush in to attack their tormentors, stabbing at the Companions' legs and backs. The tide of battle turns. The Romans begin to hunt the Macedonians.

Philip rejoins his roadway forces as the first of the Roman cavalry stampedes toward them. "Fire at them, curse you, fire!"

The Cretans unleash a barrage of arrows, followed in quick succession by three more flights. Dozens of Romans and horses sprawl onto the roadway.

"Riders, attack!" commands Philip. Heedless of the danger, the king spurs his horse toward the armored wave of Romans.

The Macedonian cavalry ride in to engage the outnumbered equites. The Companions drive back the Roman riders, charging into them with a wall of spears.

"Regroup, face front!" Septimus screams wheeling his mount through his milling riders. In spite of Septimus' commands, the Roman cavalry flee toward camp.

"After them," Philip cries, exulting in his triumph. He grabs a spear from a nearby Companion and flings it at the fleeing Romans. *I'll run them all back to Rome!*

Minutes later, the Roman equites ride into Galba and his oncoming legions. "Halt!" Galba commands. The equites barge into each other, milling about in front of the Roman infantry.

Galba glares at the arriving cavalrymen. "Reform ranks," he shouts at them. "Get back out there or I'll crucify the lot of you!" The fleeing riders halt. They stand silently, avoiding Galba's fierce stare.

Septimus rides up to Galba. His face flushes with embarrassment. "They were too scared to listen to me," he says. "It is my dishonor."

The consul points his forefinger down the roadway. "You will regain your honor now. Lead the charge back." Septimus nods. He rides to the front of his men.

Septimus trots over to a veteran cavalryman. He draws out his sword, and places the point of it against the man's throat, drawing a trickle of blood.

"I will personally kill the next coward who flees in battle." He raises his head high. "Decurions!" he shouts to his officers. "You are free to kill any man that turns his horse to retreat. And that includes me!"

Septimus shoves his sword into its scabbard and puts heels to his horse. He gallops down the road.

"Come on, women!" shouts a decurion, racing after his commander. The cavalrymen plunge forward, shouting and screaming.

Septimus' cavalry storm back down the roadway and thresh into the oncoming Macedonians. The chastised equites fight furiously, their swords mowing down scores of the tiring Macedonians.

Though mounds of his Companions lie in the dust about him, Philip rides around the front like a madman, goading his men to beat back the equites.

Nikolas draws near Philip, his limp sword arm bleeding from a slashed triceps. "I can see a field of Roman standards coming down the road towards us, my King. Their entire army's here! Thousands of them!"

Philip grimaces. *Ah Gods, why do you hate me? I almost had them!* "Back to camp!" he orders. "Get all the men back to camp!" The cavalry race down the roadway. The Cretans trot behind them, pausing to loose volleys of arrows.

After a half-dozen of his riders fall to the hails of arrows, Septimus halts his pursuit. "Wait until Galba gets here," he tells his officers. "There may be an ambush ahead."

Galba and his men soon join the waiting cavalry. "I am ready to take our men and assault the camp," Septimus blurts. "And this time we won't turn back, though we all die."

The consul shakes his head. "For that we need to get the elephants and the siege machines." He looks at the scores of dead Romans lying about the roadway. "Tomorrow, we're going over the walls and burning his camp to the ground."

That night, as Galba shares a pitcher of watered wine with Septimus, a Macedonian messenger arrives. "King Philip desires to have a conference with you," the messenger announces, handing Galba a sealed lambskin scroll. "He wishes to discuss peace terms."

Galba blinks in surprise. "He wants to make peace?"

The messenger's face is blank. "I only know my king wants a conference with you. He requests that both sides cease hostilities until then."

He looks doubtfully at Septimus. "Should we do it?"

Septimus shrugs. "If it's a chance for peace, why not? Just double the scouts and guards, in case of treachery."

Galba peers at the wine dregs in his goblet, as if reading them. "Tell him to come to my camp tomorrow morning. We will meet then."

"Forgive me, Consul," the messenger answers, nervously twisting his robe. "My king requests he have tomorrow to gather his fallen soldiers—to give them a proper burial."

Galba stares at the tent ceiling. "Jupiter's cock, he's already making demands!" He dismissively flings up his hand. "The morning after this one, then. But no longer!"

"Gratitude, General," replies the messenger. He walks backwards out of the tent, bowing as he leaves.

Two days later, Galba sits in his tent with his officers, clad in his purple-bordered toga of office. His tribunes are with him, as well as Septimus. The morning turns into the early afternoon, and still they wait.

"What would be keeping him?" Galba says, playing with the ink pot on the table next to him. "Is this some new treachery?"

"Fuck him," growls a grizzled veteran of Scipio's army. "Let's march over there and tear them to pieces. That's what we'd do in Africa."

Scipio, Scipio. Will I ever step out from your shadow? Galba turns to his attendant. "Get the cornicen to stand outside the tent. I want to be ready to make a call to battle, just in case."

"I think we are being duped," Septimus says. "Scipio told me about a trick Hannibal once played on Fabius. He left the camp fires burning while his army packed up and left during the night." He stares at Galba. "Philip is a friend of Hannibal's. He could be playing the same trick."

Galba's face flushes. "Get a messenger over there immediately," he orders. "Tell Philip I demand we meet, or something like that. Just get someone over there and find out what's happening!"

An hour later, Galba's messenger enters the command tent. Only Galba and Septimus remain. Suspecting what the messenger will tell him, Galba has sent his officers away.

196

"I rode up to the front gates. No one answered my request to parley. No one appeared in the guard towers, even though I slandered the Macedonians' manhood and courage."

Septimus grimaces. "I bet that snake has slithered away!"

"Send the laddermen over there," the consul orders. "I want those gates open within the hour." He pushes himself up. "Come on, Septimus. Let's get our horses."

Galba is riding towards Philip's camp when one of his scouts rides in to meet him. "They are gone, General. The king only left some men to tend to the campfires. When we captured them; they told us he had sneaked out in the night."[lxxvii]

Septimus shakes his head, laughing to himself. "Hannibal's old trick! I should have seen it coming."

"That liar!" Galba splutters. "Where did they say he went?"

"They said they don't know."

"Let's put their feet to the fire," Galba fumes. "We'll see what they know then!"

"Their story makes sense, Galba," Septimus says. "Philip is smart enough not to tell anyone."

Galba grabs his scout by the forearm. "Send out all our scouting parties. I want to know which way they went. Don't come back until you find his army!"

After days of fruitlessly searching the plains and valleys, two scouts return with news: Philip has led his army up a ridge trail and into the mountains, heading back toward his central garrison in Macedonia.

Galba receives the news with curious equanimity. That night, he calls in his officers. "The Macedonians have retreated toward their stronghold. We will pursue them, but our primary objective will be to reclaim all the towns and cities enroute, to restore them to Grecian rule."

"What about King Philip?" asks a tribune.

Galba frowns. "He will retreat every time we approach him. I fear he will prove too elusive to catch in my time remaining as consul."

He looks at his men and smiles bitterly. "I envy Philip being king, he can make war plans for the long run. He does not have to resign his post after a year."

The meeting ends with plans to march toward Bruanium, Philip's apparent destination.[lxxviii] The officers slowly file out.

"Septimus. A moment, please," says Galba, bringing him back from the tent's exit flap.

Galba snaps his fingers. A Carthaginian slave brings brimming cups of watered wine to the men. Galba raises his goblet to Septimus. "You were right. He played an old trick upon us. I should have seen it coming."

"As you say, Consul." Septimus replies. He stares into his half-empty cup. "Apologies for my cowardice back there," he mutters.

Galba raises his cup toward Septimus, toasting him. "You overcame your fear, though." He smiles. "What is it the playwright Plautus tells us? 'If you have overcome your inclination and not been overcome by it, you have reason to rejoice.'"[lxxix]

Septimus' eyes glaze with tears. "Gratitude, General."

The consul drains his cup and motions for a refill. "Well, I have learned much about Philip these past weeks. He is brave, but treacherous. Impetuous, but surreptitious. Proud, but dishonest." He chuckles. "He is a broth of many spices."

"A clever man, not easily fooled," Septimus replies. "I knew some of what he was doing, but I had the benefit of Scipio's advice to help me know his mind."

"Well, Scipio is not here now. I am," Galba huffs. "And I will try to break King Philip before I go." Septimus says nothing.

Galba senses the tribune's reserve. "This Scipio's becoming more of a politician than a soldier, if you ask me. He's probably cozying up to some Hellenic Party senators even as we speak."

Septimus feels a tug of irritation. He shrugs noncommittally. "If he is, it's because he has Rome's safety in mind. One thing I know, he is the best at finding people to defend it."

Female Gladiators in Combat

VI. GLADIATRIX

CAPUA, ITALIA, 199 BCE. "He's had it!" the arena crowd chants.

Bleeding from a dozen cuts, the brawny gladiator props himself on an elbow. He raises his right index finger to the crowd, imploring them for mercy. The hoplomachus' sword and shield lie alongside him in the red-dappled sand, mute testament to his forced capitulation.

"I surrender," the gladiator tells his victor. "In the name of Clementia, goddess of mercy, I beg you spare me! The goddess will bless you for it!"

A lean, bronze-bodied warrior stands above the fallen combatant, holding a Roman shield and sword at the ready. The murmillo's face is concealed by a mesh silver mask under the gladiator's visored helmet, but the fighter's stance conveys readiness to kill the hoplomachus, should he reach for his sword or spear.

The murmillo looks up at the crowd and sees that most of them are pushing their thumbs downward, seeking the fighter's death.

The chief magistrate of Capua leans down from his gilded throne. His rheumy eyes size up the crowd's mood, estimating which decision will most favor him. He extends his bony arm straight out, his fleshless fist closed. He holds his hand there, letting drama build.

The magistrate jerks his thumb downward. The crowd erupts with anticipation. The fallen warrior wails with despair.

"Compose yourself," the murmillo growls, "you are a gladiator."

The young man swallows. His eyes shining with tears, he lifts his head back, exposing his pulsating neck.

"Kill him!" the crowd screams.

The murmillo's blade flashes down. It plunges into the stinking sands, digging in next to the warrior's ear. The hoplomachus gapes in amazement. He embraces the gladiator's lean, muscular calves. "Gratitude, oh, gratitude," he tearfully babbles.

The murmillo throws off the visored helmet, then the faceplate. The gladiator's long auburn hair cascades down, framing her defiant blue eyes.

"Fuck you!" she shouts, glaring up at the audience. "He fought a good fight. I'm not killing him." The gladiatrix casts away her shield. She spits disdainfully into the earth and marches toward the arena exit, ignoring the food scraps that fly past her.

"Prima, come back here," quails the praetor. "I command it!"

"Go suck a slave," she yells, not deigning to turn around.

Walking with the fluid grace of a trained athlete, the young woman strides into the arched portal that leads to the gladiators' quarters, shouldering her way through the column of fighters waiting their turn at victory or death.

"You let Niklas live?" a nervous young gladiator asks, his gladius quaking in his uncalloused hands.

Prima sniffs disdainfully. "He is unskilled but he kept coming at me, even when he did not have the strength to lift his blade. What is the honor in killing such as he?" She laughs. "No matter. He may die of his wounds before the night is over."

"The crowd wanted you to kill him," says another fighter.

"Those idiots want everyone to die! No matter how good the match, they want the fallen one killed. Would any of them give a single sestertius to the victim's owner, who trained and fed him all this time?

202

Gladiatrix

The crowd can stick a temple up their ass! Same for that that milk-spined magistrate!"

A Thracian retiarius chortles, grinning at his fellow fighters. "Leave it to a women to go soft at the crucial moment!" The hefty gladiator stabs his trident into the ground, swooping his net over it. "Me, I would have wrapped him up and stuck him like a frog!"

Prima spins about and stares up into the Thracian's face. "I have twelve kills, Leo. Would you like to be my thirteenth? We could go out there right now."

Leo looks away. "I already have a match." He murmurs. He bares his snaggled yellow teeth. "Another time, when I can take my time killing you."

Prima grins. "Mm. Yes, it will always be 'another time,' won't it?"

The gladiatrix turns a corner and enters one of the spacious underground cells reserved for the elite fighters. A boy waits for her there, holding a goblet of deep red wine. Prima cradles it with her long-fingered hands. "Good you had it waiting for me, Cassius. I have to wash the taste of that crowd out of my mouth."

While the young woman drinks, her slave bends over and unties her knee-high silver greaves. "Go get my weapons from the arena," she tells him. "Pollux would have gathered them up before the next fight." She gives him a coin. "Here, give this to him so the fat old bastard doesn't give you any trouble."

The boy dashes off. Prima refills her wine cup and places it on a stone shelf. She reaches behind her and tugs loose the leather strings of her breast band.

The felt band falls from her small, firm breasts. She takes a deep breath and lets it out, massaging herself. *Hades take me, I hate being squeezed in like that. I'm going to fight bare-chested next time, like the Amazons do.* She grins. *Maybe my opponent will stare at my tits—that would give me a tactical advantage!*

Gladiatrix

Prima stoops over and begins to unwind her linen subligaculum, letting the loincloth's linen strands snake down her long, tanned legs.

"Prima?" says a voice from the dimly lit entryway. "You are Prima Julia? Of the Julia family?"

"What of it?" she asks. Prima pulls away the final linen strand and drops it to the floor. She steps over to the shelf holding her wine and dips her hand into a bowl of light green olive oil. She rubs it vigorously onto her nude body, oblivious to the two shadowed men standing outside her cell, their armor glinting in the candlelight.

"I would have words with you," the voice says. "I would like your services."

Another rutting beast! "Why don't you and that other slug crawl over to the Avenue of Maidens. You can get a wallow there for a few denarii." She smoothes the oil down her thighs. "Now get out before I cut it off."

She bends over to rub oil into her shins. The man gazes from the shadows, watching the flex of her rounded, muscular buttocks, their cleft outlined with the faintest wisp of hair. He feels himself swell.

"You would cut the throat of the man who saved Italia?" says the other voice, tinged with sarcastic humor. "If so, don't do it for free. There's lots who will pay you to do it!"

"I am not looking for sex, gladiatrix," says the first voice. "But I do have need of your help."

The two men step inside the cell. Prima stares into the first man's face and gasps. She grabs a plush emerald robe off its hook and holds it in front of her, her face flaming.

"You are Scipio Africanus!" she blurts. She dips down and slides the silk robe over her head, smoothing it over her body. "I was there at your triumph. Gods forgive me, Commander, I did not know it was you!"

"I would like to think not," quips Laelius. "I know the Julii have a reputation for being snooty, but that would be a bit much!"

She studies Laelius. "Huh! You must be Laelius. Your reputation precedes you."

"But it does not exceed me!" Laelius replies, grinning. He bows deeply. "I am at your service. Although I don't mean 'service' in the way you seem to take it." He snorts. "Avenue of Maidens, indeed!"

Prima chuckles. "It's just that men come in here all the time, and they want..."

Scipio raises his hand. "I fully understand. You are a strikingly beautiful woman—a beautiful, deadly, woman. And that's why I am here." He glances around him. "Is there somewhere we can talk?"

"My house is not far from here, if you would be good enough to join me," Prima responds. "Go on out. I will follow in a minute."

Laelius wrinkles his nose. "With pleasure; it smells like a butcher's waste wagon in here. To think, I considered fighting as a free gladiator. Now I know, I couldn't take the stink!"

Laelius and Scipio stride down the dank arena tunnel and emerge into dazzling sunlight. Their guards stand in front of them, holding Scipio and Laelius' horses. Surus, Scipio's molossus puppy, is held on a rope by a guard—his doleful expression evidences his distaste for his assignment.

The two friends mount their horses and face the tunnel entrance. "Do you think she'll be long?" Laelius asks anxiously.

"She is a woman," Scipio replies, "but she is a warrior, trained to be quick. So who knows?'

Prima soon emerges from the tunnel entrance, wearing a dark blue robe. Prima walks to a small carriage and springs effortlessly inside it, her robe billowing about her slim ankles.

The driver snaps the two horses' reins and the carriage rumbles down the cobbled road towards Capua's main entry portal. The Roman retinue follows the carriage, Surus happily loping alongside his master. The train moves past dozens of immaculate three-story mansions, each with one of Capua's famous bronze statues interspersed among the palm trees and rose bushes. The carriage trundles past a twelve-foot stone watch tower. The tower guards wave heartily at Prima's carriage.

"Salve, gladiatrix, may Victoria smile upon you!" bellows a one-eyed veteran, his smile contorting the face scars that seam his face."

"She must be very popular," Laelius observes.

"Fighters always are," says Scipio. "At least the ones who live."

The carriage enters Capua's bustling forum and turns off into an avenue, passing through another avenue lined with trees and statues. It halts before the House of Julii, an mansion fronted with a collonaded portico the size of a small temple.

Laelius and Scipio pull up behind the carriage. Prima jumps from her seat and strides toward the door. "Come on," she says, "I'm always hungry after a fight."

She barks a few words to the twin Nubians guarding the Senate-sized double doors. The Nubians sheathe their curved swords and pull open the doors.

Scipio and Laelius stroll through the house-sized atrium and follow Prima down a spacious corridor, savoring the elegant frescoes that line the walls.

"This place is twice as big as yours, Scippy," whispers Laelius.

"The size of a house is not the measure of a man," snaps Scipio. "How large a place do you need to take a sleep and a shit?"

Laelius rolls his eyes. "That sounds like something Marcus would say. He must have rubbed off on you."

The pair enter the Julii atrium. Prima eases onto a gold-edged couch, reclining next to a gushing fountain in the midst of a pink marble fish pool. "Come on, recline yourselves." She claps her hands. "Food will be here in a minute."

"Where is your father?" Scipio asks.

She looks about, as if he might be hiding. "Oh, I don't know! He must be out on business. Father has taken his exile hard. He works all the time, trying to make us the richest people in Capua." She grimaces. "I think he's trying to make us the richest people in Italia, as if that could be balm for his wounds."

The two stretch out on couches on each side of Prima. She holds up a strand of lush purple grapes and bites one off, then proffers it to Scipio. "Try these. They are from Neapolis. The grapes make good wine, too."

Scipio bites two off and gives the strand to Laelius. He picks one and chews it slowly. "Food for the gods," he proclaims.

The three are soon dining on roast goose, shrimp, and emmer bread, washed down with watered white wine. Laelius' eyes rove over the paintings and statues that line the walls. "I swear, Prima, I cannot fathom why you seek the stinking pits of the arena, when you have all this luxury around you."

Prima's green eyes flare. "And what would you have me do? I am not of a mind to devote my life to several squalling brats. I cannot join the army or hold office—apparently, having breasts disqualifies me from both! As a gladiator, I have fame and achievement—and the chance to fight."

"I can promise you a chance to fight—in defense of my wife," Scipio says. He twists his hands together. "She was attacked by an assassin."

Prima eyes Scipio speculatively. "And you want *me* to hunt down this assassin for you?"

"Not 'hunt down;' protect. I need someone to accompany Amelia wherever she goes, to protect her in a way that no man could."

Prima shakes her head. "Sorry. I would need more of a life than that, to give up what I have here."

"I doubt your life will be smooth here, after you insulted Praetor Camillus," Scipio says.

Prima sniffs. "That old gasbag? He can kiss my ass."

"A delightful prospect, were my tastes so inclined," says Laelius, digging his spoon into a pomegranate. "But still, that 'gasbag' can make life difficult for you. And Rome awaits you, with all its splendor."

The gladiatrix turns toward Scipio. She bows. "Apologies, General. I just can't walk around like someone's slave all day."

She raises her chin and stares into Laelius' eyes. "I am well aware of Rome's 'splendors.' I am a Julii, one of Rome's oldest families. Were my father not sent here for his financial peccadillos, we would still be one of its ruling clans."

"Then come back with us," Scipio replies. He summons himself for what he says next. "I promise your father will gain a seat in the Senate. And become a praetor within two years."

She laughs, and looks sideways at Scipio. "How can you promise such things?"

"Did you not already answer that question?" Scipio replies. "I am Scipio Africanus, the most famous man in Rome." He chuckles. "I have not yet spent all my political capital, though it dwindles by the year."

"And if *he* doesn't do it, I will!" adds Laelius. "Because I am going to become a consul!"

She looks at Laelius, then back to Scipio. "Is he serious? This moon-head?"

"Please, at least talk about it with your father?" Scipio asks, staring into her eyes.

Prima looks at her feet, shuffling her big toe across the marble tiles. She abruptly raises her head, eyes alight with fervor. "No, no, I do not need to talk with him—I accept. If you give him all that you promised, I will go there." Her eyes flash. "And if you don't..."

"If I don't," Scipio interjects, "You can go join Flaccus, Cato and the Latin Party. They will be delighted to help you get your revenge upon me!"

Laelius chuckles. "They certainly will!"

Prima claps her calloused hands. "Oh, Father will be delighted, and so will Mother! She misses Rome so much. We will be there as soon as we can, I promise you."

"Then it is done," Scipio says. He rises to leave.

Prima raises a forefinger. "Not yet. There is one condition."

"And what would that be, Domina?"

"I get to fight in Rome's next gladiatorial games, at the Circus Maximus."

Scipio's mouth tightens. *She could be killed as soon as she gets back.*

He notices the determined set of Prima's chin. *She is a Julii. She is not yours to command.*

Scipio glances at Laelius, who gives the barest of nods. "Very well. If you can get permission to fight at the games, have at it. But I will not use my influence for you!" He waggles his finger. "And no fights to the death!"

Prima's smile splits her face. "Wonderful! You needn't worry about losing me in some contest. The man hasn't been born who can kill me in a fair fight!"

Scipio starts to open his mouth, but Laelius tugs on his tunic. "Leave it!"

Scipio sighs. "It's done, then. Come to our house as soon as you arrive. Amelia has heard all about you, and she is anxious to meet." He turns toward the door. "Now, if you will excuse me, I have to visit another town south of here."

"You seek another gladiatrix?" Prima says. "I am the only one in the region." She grins impishly. "At least the only one that's any good."

He shakes his head, smiling. "This concerns plans for my retirement. And my family's safety."

"I hope you find your dream." says Prima, bowing her head.

The two men stride toward the door. Two Iberian house slaves pull open the twin doors, averting their eyes as a show of respect. As Scipio walks out, Laelius turns around and paces back to Prima.

"I'm heading back to Rome now. Scipio's on his own down south. When you get to Rome, I would love to show you about."

Prima blinks in surprise. She sniffs haughtily, repressing a smile. "I know my way about Rome, Admiral Laelius. I have been there many times."

"You haven't been to the places I've been," Laelius says. "Ostia has some of the best illicit boxing and wrestling matches in Italia. There's broken bones every night!" He taps his chest. "I used to fight there!"

"I will give you this, you are a man after my own tastes," Prima says. "You are not one of those womanish men."

"And you do suit me," Laelius says with a grin. "Because you are such a mannish woman! Come on, let's do it! Who knows what will happen?"

LITERNUM, SOUTHWEST ITALIA, 199 BCE. "Come on, Surus. Quit sniffing everyone's butts!"

The molossus puppy reluctantly turns away from the mangy road mongrel. He hurries over and trots next to Scipio's horse, his wide tongue lolling from his pot-sized head. Scipio grins at the huge brown dog.

"Your sire Boltar, he would have loved these forests," Scipio says to Surus. "He so loved to roam the wild places. I only wish I was at home more, then, so I could have taken him on some boar hunts."

He raises his right arm. "Things will be different with you, dog. I am home now." He looks east toward the walls of the small town facing him. "At least, I am at our second home."

Scipio has ridden the twenty miles from Capua in two days. He has taken time to survey the hilly countryside about this seaport town, talking to dozens of the local shepherds and farmers. Now he rides through the arched stone portal of Liternum, passing into the tree-circled town square.

He finds a large group of middle-aged men waiting for him in the middle of the square, their grins splitting their faces. Hundreds of men and women line the narrow streets behind them. Dozens fling flowers at him, and many others wave frantically.

Two boys dash out to pet Surus. He rolls on his back, ecstatic with their attentions.

A rangy older man steps out from the group, cradling a bouquet of roses in his hinged wooden arm. He hands the flowers to Scipio.

"Welcome, noble General. I am Tiberius Longius, former centurion of the tenth legion. I am also the magistrate of our fair town."

"Gratitude, Magistrate." Scipio slides off his horse. He gives the flowers to one of his guards. "Then you were with me in Africa, Tiberius?"

"For certain. We showed old Syphax and Hannibal what Roman swords can do, didn't we?

"We certainly did. I am here to see how our veterans are faring at the farms we have allotted them."

"You mean the farms you demanded for us," Tiberius replies, his eyes twinkling. "Oh, we know. The Senate voted the land to us, but only because you demanded it."

"I but knew the will of the citizens, and acted upon it," Scipio replies. "Our men certainly earned their farms, especially since so many of theirs were seized for back taxes while they were away at war. I hope they find their new homes satisfactory."

"Satisfactory? Look at all of us who showed up to greet you! We love working the land down here! No wars, no enemies—and very few criminals, we have all seen to that! It is peaceful and lovely, General."

Tiberius' face clouds. "Some of us still have nightmares, and some sleep with swords under their pallets. But we are content. Losing the fear of death will do that to you."

"I sympathize," Scipio replies. "I still have nightmares myself, legionnaire."

"Do you still have your visions?" Tiberius asks. He waves his hands at Scipio. "Oh, we knew. We all talked about how you communicated with the gods. We knew Somnus had blessed you with their counsel. That's why we would have followed you to the underworld, had you wished it!"

"I have not had those dreams lately, I am happy to say," Scipio replies. "My last was the night before we fought Hannibal."

The old centurion favors him with a wooden-toothed grin. "I bet they'll come again, just when you need them. The gods are on your side." Tiberius looks at his feet, suddenly embarrassed. "General, would you like to see my farm? It's not very big, but it produces well. You should see my hogs. And my olives!"

Scipio hesitates. *This is all the man has to be proud of*, he reminds himself. "I would be honored, Magistrate."

Within the hour, Scipio is riding up a gentle incline that divides two wheat-laden hills. The topaz-blue Mediterranean glimmers off to his left. Tiberius rides next to him, gaily chatting about the warm weather and clean air of the Campania region, bragging about the veterans' excellent harvests of olives and figs. Surus lopes alongside when he is not bounding into the roadside wheatfields, chasing every rabbit he sees.

Scipio observes the white-sailed fishing boats bobbing along the coastal waters. He smiles at the sight of children running along the beach, kicking balls and rolling hoops. *This is everything I heard it would be. This is the place.*

He halts his horse. "Tiberius, are there any lands available near town? I would like a home here. A place to rest from the travails of Rome and war."

The centurion's jaw drops. His brown eyes light up. "Oh, most assuredly, my commander, most assuredly! I know a lovely stretch near the city, with excellent soil and water. It can be yours for nothing!" He flaps his arms excitedly. "We can go there now!"

"Not yet. Let's see your farm first." Scipio replies. "Time enough for my dreams later."

Two hours later, Scipio is standing in a field tall grasses outside the Liternum walls, walking through the gangly pine trees scattered across the rolling landscape. *There. That could be the main house. Over there, by the stream, that could be where we put the cooks' and slaves' quarters. Maybe a wine press and storage bins over there. And that shallow depression, I could put benches there for my students!*

"You say these acres are available?" Scipio asks, not believing his luck.

Tiberius grins. "If they weren't, I'd kill whoever owns them, just so you'd take it!" His smile vanishes. "In truth, the owner was from one of the older Liternum families—they all died from the plague. No relatives have come forward to claim the land—and none will now, I assure you!" He sweeps his hand across it. "Take it, Imperator. It's yours!"

"Well and good. But to avoid any improprieties, I will pay for the land. Perhaps you can put the monies into the town coffers." He grins. "Or distribute it to our veterans, as a final bonus for their services."

Tiberius closes his eyes, overcome by the gesture. A moment later he looks directly into Scipios eyes and grins. "I expected you would say something like that. It will be done."

"Let us return to town and finish the details. Just give me a minute alone." Scipio walks over to the site he has picked for the house. He pauses beneath an enormous stone pine tree, its broad, flat canopy stretching out high above him. Surus ambles over, pawing at the loamy soil.

Scipio draws out his dagger. He bends to one knee and digs in the dirt beneath the roots, hollowing out a foot-deep depression.

Scipio fumbles inside his belt purse and closes his hand upon two objects. Stretching his fist over the hole, he drops two figurines into it: a clay likeness of his father and a worn stone miniature of Nike, goddess of victory. Scipio kneels above the hole. He gently scoops dirt back into it.

Rising, he bows his head and clenches his hands together. *You have been with me through my journeys into Iberia and Africa, at my side in all my battles and wars. Father, you reminded me of my promise to become a general and defend Rome. Goddess, you reminded me that victory is always possible to the bold and inventive. Your duty is done. Now you can rest here, in our new home. Amelia and I will join you soon.*

Scipio strides back to Tiberius and his guards, Surus galloping along next to him. Scipio climbs onto the back of his horse. "Let's go!" he says. A coughing spams seizes him, forcing him to cover his mouth with his fist.

"General! Are you well?"

"It comes and it goes," Scipio replies, waving his hand dismissively. "On to town, now. I need to start building a life." *Before I lose it.*

Tiberius peers into Scipio's face. "You will be long and far away from Rome's doctors if you should move here," he says.

Scipio stares out into the Mediterranean, his eyes fixed on nothing. "No matter. I have done others' bidding far too long. Too long, my promises have delayed my dreams."

He looks back at the home site he has picked. "Here, it will be otherwise. Here, I will study and teach. Here, I will flourish."

War Chariot

VII. SHIFTING ALLIANCES

TEMPLE OF BELLONA, OUTSKIRTS OF ROME. 199 BCE. Scipio spreads his arms toward the senators lolling about on the temple steps. "It's the end of the year, my comrades. The consular elections are coming. My wife will aid in publicizing our candidates, but we have to give her two worthy candidates. Whom will we select?"

"Aulius!" shouts one senator. "Valerius!" echoes another.

"You pick them, Scipio," adds a third.

Scipio watches the men argue with each other. He says nothing, nodding each time a candidate is voiced. *Let them decide, or they will resent you. If they pick a fool, push them away from him.*

"Who do you want, Scipio?" asks an elder Hellenic.

"I am a senator like yourselves, not a king," Scipio replies. "I would not deign to give you candidates. But I will say this: We need men who will favor diplomacy over conquest. Who are more interested in developing alliances than commanding countries."

"You have someone in mind, Senator?" the elder persists. "Go ahead, tell me. I promise not to be unduly impressed by the fact you have nominated him!"

Amidst the laughter, Scipio points to a slender, dark-haired young man in the back row. "Titus Quinctius Flamininus has served on the veteran's committee. He is a veteran of the Boii wars and has three admirable children. I think he is a natural leader."

The Hellenic Society senators break into small groups, muttering and

Shifting Alliances

arguing amongst each other. Scipio watches from his place on the side of the temple steps, sitting next to his brother Lucius.

"You watch," he says to Lucius. "They will call me over to talk to them. Then I can work on them about nominating Flamininus."

Lucius stares out into the trees, his face flat. "Why didn't you nominate me? I fought in the wars. I'm a family man, too—I finally have a child on the way!"

Oh gods, here we go again! "You are not ready yet, little brother. You need to become a praetor, or at least a quaestor." *Jupiter help us all if you are managing Rome's money!*

Lucius' face flushes. "You have been consul twice already, and here I sit. Fortuna did not give me the opportunities she blessed you with."

You are lucky to be a senator. Scipio thinks. Then: *You promised Mother you would take care of him.* "I promise I will help you become consul. But now is not the time."

A group of elder senators beckons Scipio over. He stifles a sigh of relief. "We can talk more of this later."

After two hours of speeches and debates, the Hellenic society nominates Flamininus and Sextus Aelius Paetus, an unremarkable man who happens to be one of the richest people in Rome.

Scipio rubs his weary eyes. *Curse it! Aelius couldn't lead a one-horse chariot. Philip or Antiochus would eat him alive. At least he stands a good chance on getting elected: he's rich enough to bribe his way to the consulship.*

His eyes blink with realization. *That little bastard probably bribed his way to the nomination.* Scipio smiles wryly. *He'll at least know how to win over Flaccus and the rest of the Latins. Bribe vs. bribe! But I've got to keep him from destroying our men in a war.*

Scipio faces the group, smiling stiffly. "We have our men! I rejoice that we have two fine Hellenics for candidates. I can see Sextus leading

218

our troops up north, and young Flamininus going to Greece."

Senator Galba, recently returned from Macedonia, rises from his seat. "That is a bit premature, noble Scipio. The Senate will decide who receives the assignment to go to Greece and fight Philip. Regardless, we must work to ensure that whoever goes there can stay there until Philip is defeated, not for just a year."

He shakes his head. "I had to return after one year there, when my consulship expired. I was one battle away from ending Philip's threat, yet I had to come back."

"Galba has the right of it," Scipio says. "The Senate will decide who goes to Greece." *But I will make sure they pick Flamininus. I still have that much Iberian silver to spend.*

Their business concluded, the Senators take their horses and carriages back to Rome. Scipio rides to the Aemilius town house. The house slaves lead him into the atrium. Scipio sits on a silk-covered couch, watching two peacocks strut about the garden, Proserpina enters, and warmly embraces Scipio.

"This is an unexpected pleasure! Will you have some wine? A little cup before bed is good for the spirit."

Scipio waves away the offer. "Apologies for arriving unannounced, Domina. But tonight I have been thinking about my obligations, and I remembered mine to you. Is Marcus here?"

"He will be here shortly," Proserpina replies. "He's with an African doctore, learning new knife fighting techniques." She smiles and shakes her head. "Always studying the art of war. Of certitude, he is Marcus Silenus' son!"

"You wanted him out of Rome. I think I can get him to Greece, where he would be needed. Are you still agreeable to that?"

"More than ever," Proserpina says. "Last week he beat up two Aventine thugs, trying to find out if they knew who killed Manius." She hugs herself and shudders. "The Aventine gangs will mark him for death, Scipio. I am sure of it."

Scipio stretches out on the couch, leaning on one elbow. "In that case, I will wait and talk to him. And yes, I will have some wine..."

A half hour later, Marcus steps into the atrium, his gray tunic bathed with sweat. "Apologies, Mother. I stopped for some wrestling at the gymnasium." He grins proudly. "I pitched Great Praxus onto his big ass! You should have seen the look on his face!"

Marcus nods solemnly at Scipio. "It is an honor to see you." *He looks a bit sickly,* Marcus thinks, studying Scipio's lined face. *He has an ill spirit inside him.*

Scipio eases up from the couch. He walks over and clasps arms with Marcus.

"Marcus, there is a strong likelihood that Quinctius Flamininus will be elected consul and be sent to fight Philip. He will need all the veteran help he can get. I could get you attached to Flamininus' army as tribune. Are you willing to do that?"

"If he is fighting the Macedonians, I will join him," Marcus says. "Consider it done."

"I will," says Scipio with a grin. *He is as taciturn as his father. Can he fight like him?*

"My gratitude for your hospitality," Scipio says to Proserpina. "Now I must get back home. Amelia will be wondering where I am." After a final embrace, Scipio strides purposefully from the house. He takes his horse's rope from the house slave and springs onto the nondescript gray mare.

Scipio rides to the edge of the block. He suddenly veers right, trotting in the opposite direction of his house. He pulls his cloak's hood over his head and hunches forward.

Soon, Scipio is easing his horse through the dark narrow streets that separate the rickety Aventine insulae. He dismounts in front of a tall mud brick apartment building and knocks upon a dark green door that fronts the street. The thick door creaks open. Two enormous Gauls fill the doorway, their hands upon the hilts of their daggers.

"I seek audience with Celsus," Scipio says.

"Give him entrance," rasps a voice behind the guards.

Scipio walks into a lavishly furnished interior, filled with armor and statuary from a dozen nations. Bags of foreign currency sprawl on a thick camel's hair rug, resting next to pyramids of silver bars.

A tall, lean Sicilian reclines on a gigantic stuffed bag, his frame draped in a brown robe of thick Egyptian cotton. He draws upon his long-stemmed clay pipe and blows out a cloud of wispy smoke. A skunky-sweet odor permeates the room. The man smiles dreamily at Scipio, waving his pipe at him.

"Good evening, General," Celsus says, his words fumbling from his mouth. "Would you like to try some of this kannabis?[lxxx] It's a filthy habit I picked up from the Scythians, but it does make me feel quite...relaxed."

Coughing violently, Scipio waves away the proffered pipe. "No, my health is bad enough as it is. We have business to discuss. An exchange of treasure for Roman coin."

Celsus gleefully claps his hands. "Oh yes, of course. I'm always delighted to make an exchange. I always give you the most denarii for your treasures. I hope you know that!"

Scipio bores into the man's watery onyx eyes. "I know that you had better. If I find you defraud me, those two over there won't save you. I am a censor. I can have you scourged and exiled."

Celsus flutters his hands in front of his face. "Of course, of course, I know who I am dealing with." He smiles craftily. "Then again, I *don't* know who I'm dealing with, isn't that right?"

"It had better be," Scipio replies. "Meet me behind the Campus

221

Martius entryway at the end of the third watch tomorrow. Bring coins. Many bags of coins." Scipio spins on his heel and walks out the door, shouldering his way through the towering Gauls. He gallops away, heading towards the low stone buildings that line the commercial section by the Porta Collina.

Scipio trots his horse through a narrow passageway between two buildings, constantly looking over his shoulder. He dismounts in front of a stone block granary with a narrow oak door.

He reaches into this belt, pulls out an iron key, and unlocks the weather-beaten wood door, leaving him to face an iron door inside it. Scipio checks the lock for scratches. Seeing none, he unlocks the heavy door and steps into a cool, dark, room. Striking iron to flint, he kindles a torch inside the doorway and holds it in front of him. The torch illuminates a fantastic trove of treasure.

There are sacks of Carthaginian coins, surrounding finely wrought Numidian statues and sculptures. Iberian silver bars are stacked neatly against the wall, fronted by a tower of painted wood panels from Libya. A small hill of Gallic coins and gold neck torques are mounded next to mounds of gold-plated armor.

At the back wall of the room lie Scipio's most valuable treasures; a small pile of diamonds, sapphires, spinels, rubies and fire opals, most embedded in gold necklaces and rings. Two stoppered amphora rest next to the pile, sealed in wax. The jugs' lettering indicates one contains cinnamon and the other is filled with saffron, spices more valuable than gold.

Scipio smirks. *I am fortunate King Syphax brought so many of his possessions with him to his camp.*[lxxxi] *It made it easy to plunder them.* He waves his torch across the pile and watches the light dance across the shining surfaces. *That battle with him on the Great Plains proved most profitable to Rome—and to me.*

He turns to his right and holds his torch high. The light glints off a stack of a dozen trapezoidal gold bars, each the size of a large brick. *There they are, the last of my plunder from Carthago Nova.*

He looks back over the half-empty room. *Most of our wealth is gone now, Mother, but it helped us elect the right people. And pass the right proposals. Our people benefitted more than if we had given it to the thieving Senate.* His mouth tightens. *I hope the gods do not judge me too harshly. I saw no other way.*

Scipio sticks the torch into a pewter wall bracket. He picks up two gold bars and a large sack of Iberian coins. Waddling toward the door, he knees the doors open and dumps his trove into the saddle bags that straddle his mare's back. With a final glance about him, Scipio locks the granary doors and trots his old horse down the dark cobbled streets, heading finally for home.

That night, as he tosses fitfully, Febris comes to Scipio. The fever goddess brings him chills, night sweats, and—finally—fever dreams. Scipio tosses in his sleep, clutching at the linen sheet that covers him.

Amelia rises from their bed and pads softly to the atrium couch, listening to the patter of rain falling into the fish pond. She knows he is in the grip of the gods, and that a vision will come to him if he is not disturbed.

Scipio dreams he is in standing in chains in the center of the Forum, the site of Rome's public trials.[lxxxii] Two Tribunes of the Plebs stand in front of him, reading a list of accusations to the purple-togaed consul who presides as judge.

"He stands accused of diverting money and treasure from the public coffers," intones one tribune.

"And using it for his own personal gain," adds the other.

Grim-faced Cato stands behind them, his arms crossed over his grimy tunic. Flaccus is beside him. He grins with delight, a bloody dagger in his hand.

"These are serious accusations," the judge intones. "How do you plead, Publius Cornelius Scipio?"

"I did what I did for Rome," Scipio says pleadingly. "To make us a

great nation, like Greece and Carthage. I took not a penny for myself! It was all for you, my people."

The citizens jeer and laugh at him. Turnips fly at his head. One strikes him on the cheek. The senators and citizens laugh uproariously, as Cato grins at him.

"Guilty as charged," says the smirking judge. "Take him from my sight!"

Scipio is led in chains to the other end of the Forum, marching through a gauntlet of booing citizens. He dragged down the street to the squat and blocky Mammertine Prison.[lxxxiii] The guards stand him next to the lip of the empty cistern in the center of it.

Scipio is released from his chains. The guards tie a rope about his middle and lower him to the bottom. Scipio squats in the empty center, ringed by mossy stone blocks.

Cato's face peers over the edge, smiling fatuously. "Die in darkness, swine."

Scipio hears a loud scraping sound. The guards lever up a thick wood lid and edge it across the top of the cistern.

"Stop, stop!" Scipio cries, watching the lid slice away his circle of light. There is a heavy clunk, followed by absolute darkness.

Scipio's eyes flash open. He stares dazedly at the wall frescoes in his candlelit bedroom, gasping for breath. Amelia pads back into the room. She places her arm across her husband's sweat-soaked back, hugging him close.

"I am here. You are safe. You are fine," she murmurs. "Did the gods send you a vision?"

Scipio rubs his eyes. He feels his right hand twitch with anxiety. *The elections are coming. I'll have to pay more visits to the granary.*

"More like a warning than a vision," Scipio says. "A warning that I must ignore."

SABINA HILLS, ROME. "Ah, what a nice day to be in the garden!" Flaccus stretches his legs out and leans back on one of his villa's marble benches. He bobs his cup at a house slave.

"Here now, fill this up with wine, turnip. I have to toast Rome's newest magistrate!"

The girl holds a small bronze pitcher with dancing centaurs painted upon it. She pulls a horn knife from her belt and carves the wax off the pitcher's conical stopper. Holding the pitcher with both hands, she carefully fills Flaccus' silver chalice with amber-colored wine.

When his cup is full, Flaccus nods his head at the stern man sitting opposite him, a knot-muscled redhead wearing a sweat-stained work tunic. The man dangles an empty silver chalice in his lap, clearly uncomfortable with holding the expensive cup.

"Give some wine to Cato there. He is the guest of honor," Flaccus declares.

The slave begins to fill Cato's cup. When it is half full, Cato pulls it away. "Put lots of water in there, girl. I've got field work to do this afternoon."

Flaccus eyes him. "This is a twenty-year old Alban, the best wine in Rome."

Cato shrugs. "I am quite versed in wines, but the wine my field workers drink is good enough for me. We are all men of the plow."

Gods, he is such a self-righteous little shit. Flaccus stands and raises his gleaming chalice. Cato rises slowly, reluctantly, and does likewise.

"Congratulations, Cato. You are now an aedile. The honor was richly deserved." The patrician Senator hugs his ward, who stiffly receives the embrace.

"I am pleased to get it," Cato replies. "Now I can eliminate Rome's wasteful spending on festivals and celebrations. As if the gods cared about drunken revelries and public fornications!"

"Have a care, my friend," Flaccus replies, taking a sip of his drink. "The gods may not care for such celebrations, but the people certainly do—they love their bread and circuses. We don't want another work stoppage on our hands; the last one shut down the city for a week." *And I make a fortune on selling wine for the festivities.*

"Mmph," Cato grunts. "They can learn to do without."

"Just don't change too much too soon," Flaccus adds. *I spent a lot of money getting you elected, boy. You had best not betray my interests.*

Cato makes a sour face. "Our people spend too much time idling about the city. They belong in the fields, indulging in good, hard work. Not sitting on their ass watching horse races and wrestling matches. A few less revelries will do them good."

He looks at the girl, who averts her eyes. "There are too many slaves doing freemen's work."

"Perhaps so, but do not do anything that will jeopardize our party's popularity. It's bad enough the new consuls are both Hellenics! And the People's Assembly elected that cursed Scipio to be a censor—he's the shitpot that got them elected consul!"

Flaccus shakes his head. "Can you imagine, that thief Scipio with the most dignified office in the state, with the power to regulate public morality." His eyes widen. "Now he can evict Senators from office!"

"Well, at least the slave tax was not approved," Cato replies. "When old Manius was killed, the Hellenics lost their champion." Cato stares into his cup. "A good man. His death was unfortunate, but propitious."

Yes, very propitious. "I was lucky," Flaccus says. "With all my slaves, I'd be paying a fortune in new taxes. I'd have been better off killing them and hiring freemen!"

"That would not be such an evil thing, Flaccus. Too many of our citizens lie idle because imported slaves have taken their jobs."

There he goes again! "You win a war, you get slaves! Cheap work! I must say, though, my Carthaginians are not half as good at farming as my Iberians. I might sell a few of the young ones to Pontius' brothel."

"We have more pressing concerns than the size of your purse," growls Cato. "I have heard that Titus Flamininus and Sextus Paetus will run for consul next year. They're both Hellenics. With two consecutive years of Hellenics, our taxes will be raised to Olympus! They'll probably put a Greek temple in the Forum!"

"Two more young progressives!" Flaccus sighs. "I daresay both were hand-selected by Scipio."

"They will be a serious threat to our own candidates, Flaccus," says Cato. "Senator Quintus Metellus does not have the military record of either of them. And old Castor, he is a good policy maker, but he does not have their speaking prowess or presence."

"Even worse, Scipio's wife will be using her propaganda to get them elected," Flaccus says. "She is a constant danger to our cause."

"Hmph! A Thracian or Sicilian husband would not allow his woman to perpetrate such nonsense," Cato says. "Men rule their wives, yet we, who rule all men, are controlled by our wives."[lxxxiv]

"Too true. By letting her run loose, Scipio is a danger to our traditions," Flaccus says.

Cato throws up his hands. "The fool does not see it. He argues to protect Greece from Macedonia's depredations, because Greece is such an *educated and cultured* country. But the reason they are weak is because they became *so* educated and cultured. They have fallen far from the earth that sprung them—we cannot allow Rome to follow their path! Our strength is our agricultural heritage, the roots that gave us Dentatus, Cincinnatus, and Horatius. Yet he would take that from us, and leave us as weak as once-mighty Sparta!"

"Calm yourself, Cato, all is not lost. I have already started a rumor campaign about the candidates' misappropriation of Senate funds," Flaccus replies, ignoring Cato's disapproving look. *Amelia will not be a problem. Spider will have her.*

"You should start a campaign about *Scipio's* misappropriation of war plunder," Cato says. "At least that would not be a lie. I saw it with my own eyes when I was his quaestor, him shipping treasure off on some midnight ship."

Cato pours out the rest of his wine, watching it splatter on Flaccus' marble tiles, oblivious to his host gaping at the expensive puddle at his feet. "I am going back to the plow, Patron. But I promise you, when I become censor, I will prosecute him—you wait and see."

He would throw Scipio in prison? Perhaps Cato is worth keeping around, after all. "A wonderful idea! But hold it for now. Scipio is a war hero—he is too popular right now, and people will not tolerate any accusations about him."

"Truth remains, through time and flames," Cato says. "When these wars are over, I will turn my attention to him."

Flaccus' eyes shine. "When his sun dims, his time will come, Cato. Him and his brother Lucius."

"I am off to work my fields," Cato says. "But bear this mind. Scipio may be a soft-handed Hellenic, but he knows how to defeat an enemy." Cato stalks from Flaccus' manse, his shoulders tense with purpose.

That night, a small cloaked figure rides near Cato's sturdy little farm house. He ties his horse to a shadowed olive tree and pads softly to the arched entryway. The man sidles along the side of the house, staying in the shadows. He comes upon Cato, sitting on his tiny patio while he writes by candlelight.

The man eyes Cato's broad back. He reaches into his satchel and softly steps into the light.

An aged house slave appears. "Master, there is someone to see you." A stern young man walks onto the patio, wearing his purple-bordered tunic of office.

"Senator Ennius!" Cato declares. "Why come you unannounced, at this late hour?"

Ennius frowns, his fists knotted at his side. "I have to talk to you about this Scipio, and his Hellenic Party. I just heard they are proposing to add two more holidays to our calendar. Two more days when my men lie idle, and the state pays for games to entertain them!"[lxxxv]

"The idle rich are disgusting enough," Cato replies, "but the idle poor are intolerable!" He gestures toward a split log bench. "Seat yourself. Let us figure out how we can defeat this silliness."

Inside the shadows, the cloaked figure's head slumps with frustration. He slides backward, easing himself off the patio, and pads back toward his waiting horse.

OUTSKIRTS OF ROME. "This place smells like a toilet sponge," Prima declares. "These fights had better be worth it."

"Oh they will," Laelius says, squeezing her green-robed shoulder. "You will be quite surprised, I promise you!"

Laelius and Prima sit on a worn splintered bench deep inside the bowels of an abandoned warehouse, surrounded by hundreds of working men—and a handful of patricians. As the only woman in the place, the beautiful Prima fetches many an admiring—and inviting— glance. She meets each set of male eyes with a disdainful gaze, until the men look away.

Laelius shifts about uneasily, pulling on his tan tunic. *Come on, boy. Make conversation.* "So, how do you like being Amelia's guard?"

Prima shrugs. She repositions the tortoiseshell comb in her elegantly piled hair. "Oh, it is more like being out with a friend," she confesses. "We go to the marketplace and the baths, and then I return to my manse when she is home for the night."

She smirks. "She is not comfortable with having a guard, I tell you

that. I think she wants a chance at the woman who tried to kill her."
Prima stares into the distance and smiles. "Maybe I can teach her a few
things about how to do that."

"Mars' balls, don't let her try!" Laelius says. "I couldn't stand to lose
her. I've loved her since childhood. Besides, she has to direct my
campaign when I run for consul!"

"You for consul?" Prima asks, feigning incredulity. "You are barely a
senator, with little political experience." Her mouth tightens. "And you
are not from one of the ruling families. Now, if you were a Julii, or a
Fabii..."

Laelius taps his chest. "*I* am a war hero! The plebians love me; I am
one of their own. Just you wait, I'll soon be—never mind, we are
starting!"

Two men walk into the circular dirt ring. One is a large, loose-limbed
Carthaginian, as smoothly muscled as a seal. He tattoos the air with
punches, ducking and weaving as if he is fighting some invisible
opponent.

The other combatant is a square-bodied Iberian, every muscle and
vein visible upon his chiseled body. The Iberian bends down and grasps
his ankles, stretching. His long black topknot falls over his head. He
rises and massages his iron-thewed thighs, smiling faintly to himself.

"This will be a good match," Laelius says. "Both have won bouts
here. They fight for money to buy their freedom." He points at the
squat Iberian. "That's Lagunas. I like him, he is most eager to fight."

Prima nods. "I have fought many a man like that. They are oft too
eager. I always felt sorry when I did them in. I tried not to kill them
whenever possible."

Laelius blinks. "Uh, that was very considerate of you."

Standing on opposite sides of the ring, two men hold out their bare
fists. A stern-faced older man inspects each of their hands.

"What's he doing?" Prima says. "Where are their fist wrappings?"

Laelius grins. "Oh, did I neglect to tell you? We are not watching a boxing match; the gloves are off in this one. This is pankration. It's become very popular in Rome, though it's still quite illegal."

"Pankration?" Prima says.

"Yes, 'all forces.' Boxing, wrestling, kicking—you can do almost anything to win! It's just become part of the Greek Olympics. They think it's the ultimate test of a warrior."[lxxxvi] He grins and pokes her shoulder. "See what you missed living out in the hinterlands?'

Prima digs her elbow into Laelius' ribs, making him gasp. "Capua is hardly a pig's sty, Pretty Boy. We shall see what I missed."

The older man calls the two men into the center of the ring. "You know the rules: no gouging, no biting—he glares at the Carthaginian—and no grabbing someone's balls, Matho!"

The Carthaginian grins maliciously. "Sometimes they just find their way into my hand!"

Lagunas and Matho separate and crouch down, legs akimbo. They spread out their arms, looking as if they are ready to grab their opponent and throw him to the ground. The crowd tenses with anticipation. Dock workers exchange bets with noblemen, throwing their money into the bet-takers' pottery bowls.

The referee claps his hands. The two men rumble toward one another, still crouched low.

Matho grapples for the Iberian's left wrist, aiming to twist it behind his back. Lagunas snaps a quick punch to the side of the African's jaw, jerking his head sideways. Roaring with anger, the Carthaginian leaps upon his smaller opponent. The two fall to the ground, wrestling and punching.

"It looks more like a street brawl than a sport," Prima sniffs.

"Yes, isn't it wonderful?" Laelius replies, his face rapt.

Lagunas shoves his opponent away and springs to his feet, his hands balled into fists. The Carthaginian approaches him warily, waving his open hands in front of the Iberian's face to distract him. His right fist flashes out, catching Lagunas on the jaw.

The Iberian flicks his head sideways, reducing the blow's force. Shaking his head, he grabs Matho's wrist and elbow and bends his arm inward. Twisting the Carthaginian's arm behind him, Lagunas leaps onto the African's back and kicks him in the back of his knee, plowing him face first into the crumbly dirt. Instantly, the Iberian wraps his left arm about Matho's throat and pulls his chin back, cutting off his wind.

The Carthaginian bucks and twists like a man gone mad, rolling about the earth as he gasps for air. He grapples for Lagunas' crotch, but the wily man draws up his knees to protect himself.

The Iberian grits his teeth. His arms tighten his hold. His shoulders and triceps bulge against his veined skin. He closes his eyes, lost in the focus of maintaining his grip.

Time and again the mighty Carthaginian tries to rise but the Iberian kicks his legs out from under him. His efforts weaken. Finally, his arms splay out to his side and his face darkens. The Iberian turns to the referee, a question on his face.

The referee nods. "Victory!" he declares, pointing to the Iberian. "Vanquished!" he adds, pointing at Matho.

Lagunas immediately releases his hold. Choking violently, the defeated Carthaginian rises. The Iberian raises his arms and flexes his biceps, grinning at the crowd. He walks to the open portal that serves as the ring's entry and exit.

An elegantly togaed man walks out from the stands and wraps his arm around Lagunas' shoulders, leading him out from the ring. "You did well," he says. "Tonight there will be wine and women for you."

"Well, it was certainly a spirited match," Prima says, her face flushed.

"I will have to learn how to fight like that, kicking them in the back of the legs." She lays her hand on top of Laelius' sinewy fingers. "You were right. That was a nice surprise."

Laelius feels himself stir. *Really?* he says to himself. *A woman? Why not? You've done it before, and she's more a man than half the ones you've been with.*

He manages an awkward grin. "Well, that wasn't the main surprise, it's still coming," he says. Prima arches her eyebrows, but she says nothing.

For the next hour Laelius and Prima watch a series of boxing and pankration matches. They cheer their favorites and hiss when their foes win.

Laelius stands up and stretches. "Wait here, I'll be right back," he says. He soon returns, handing Prima a honeyed blackbird on a stick. "Sorry, they didn't have any peacock," he says.

"This is just as good," she replies, crunching into the roasted bird.

"I like it. I only wish I had a cup of Thracian beer to go with it!"

Prima wrinkles her nose. "Beer? Gauls drink beer!" She shakes her head. "You are truly a street rat."

"And you are a prissbutt patrician, in spite of all your gladiatorial bravado," replies Laelius good-naturedly.

The events turn to wrestling. Two dwarves open the contests, followed by several wooden-sword bouts between boys training to be gladiators. Laelius glances over at a yawning Prima. "I could whip them all," she muses, "with or without weapons."

She's becoming bored. Well, it won't be long. "Here's someone you'd find challenging," he says. "The hordearii are going to fight."

Two ex-gladiators enter the ring, wide-bodied men known as the "barley-eaters" because their barley and bean diets gave them the fatty layers they use to advantage in the ring.[lxxxvii] The two men grapple upright for minutes, each striving to topple the other by shoving at them. The crowd jeers. Several throw scraps of turnip and pumpkin into the ring.

Finally, the older man crooks his leg behind the other's knee and drives his shoulder into the younger man's underarm, crashing him to the earth. The elder wrestler flops upon his prone opponent's back, driving the breath from him, and twists his arm behind him until he yowls his surrender.

The referee declares the younger man vanquished, amid the crowd's raucous cheers. The elephantine warriors stumble out from the ring, their arms draped across each other's shoulders.

"Formidable men," Prima says, suppressing a yawn. "A bit slow, but formidable."

Another enormous hordearii stalks into the ring, a dark, iron muscled behemoth covered with matted hair. "Where is the Roman who will fight me?" he roars. "Does any man here have the balls for a grapple?"

"This is one of the challenge matches," Laelius says. "They call that ox Nero, 'the strong one,' because he is as strong as two men. With that hair and attitude, he's obviously a Greek, eh?"

Laelius rises from his seat and steps down toward the ring.

"Where are you going?" Prima says.

"I've got a match to win!" Laelius declares gaily. *And it cost me a slave's fortune to arrange it.*

"Quit being silly," Prima says. "You can't beat that ox."

Laelius slides over the wood slat railing that encircles the ring. He pulls his tunic over his head and drops it inside the railing. He eases off his sandals and stalks to the center of the ring, wearing only the black leather subligaculum of a trained fighter.

"What are you doing?" Prima shouts, clasping her hands to her mouth. She grins with bewilderment and delight.

"I'm proving to you that a man can be silly and still be strong!" Laelius shouts back. He jerks his arms behind his back, loosening them up.

Prima chuckles. *What a fool!* She stares at Laelius' v-shaped back. *He is well constructed, though. Smooth muscled, like a swimmer. This is like a seal fighting a bear.*

"Ten denarii on the big one," she hears behind her. "I'll take that bet," comes another voice. "I've seen the pretty one fight before."

"I'll take the pretty one, too," Prima finds herself saying. "At a hundred denarii!"

Laelius stalks toward his large opponent. He spreads out his arms and grins at the glowering Greek. "Come on, ox-face. Let's see you give me a tumble."

Nero pivots his right leg forward and grabs for Laelius' shoulders. Laelius ducks under the Greek's grasp and grabs his heels. One quick jerk, and Nero crashes onto his back. Laelius scrambles on top of him and grabs his head in an arm lock, rolling his body to the side of Caesar's head. His biceps bulge as he constricts his grip.

Nero' face turns a dark red. His lips flap, spitting out silent imprecations. The giant plants his feet and elbows, raising his back and thighs from the ground. In one violent twist, he wrests his body sideways within Laelius' grasp.

He grabs Laelius about the midsection and raises him high off the ground. Laelius tightens his grip, his neck veins popping with the effort. Nero leaps forward, collapsing on top of Laelius.

Laelius' breath whooshes from him. He rolls weakly under Nero, struggling to push himself upright. The wrestler wraps both arms about Laelius' midsection and pulls him off the floor, raising him over his head. Laelius hangs limp in his arms. Nero braces his legs for a final throw, intending to land Laelius face first into the dirt.

That monster's going to break his neck, Prima thinks. Her eyes narrow. *If he does I'll kill him.*

Laelius springs to life. He rams his forearm under Nero's chin, shoving it backward. Laelius' other hand grasps his wrist for leverage. He pushes his forearm deeper into Nero's jawline.

Nero's head arches backward. The Greek tightens his grip about Laelius' back, his face a rictus of pain and effort. Laelius' eyes bore into Nero's. He pushes the giant's neck ever backward, grunting with effort.

With a gasping roar, Nero loosens his hold and grabs for Laelius' offending arms. Laelius drops to his knees and darts between Nero's tree-trunk legs, popping up behind him. He grabs Nero's right ankle and shoves his shoulder under his knee. With a yell so loud it silences the crowd, Laelius jerks Nero's leg up over his head, crashing the back of his head onto the ground.

In a flash, Laelius wraps his legs about Nero's throat and tightens them. The stunned wrestler grapples at Laelius' viselike grip, to no avail. Nero gurgles and rolls his eyes, slapping at the ground.

The referee steps forward. "Victor!" he says, grasping Laelius' arm. "Vanquished!" he says, pointing at Nero.

The crowd erupts in cheers and curses, with most of the noise coming from the bettors. Roses fly in from the audience, mute testament to the onlookers' approval of Laelius' prowess. Laelius reaches down and pulls the wrestler to his feet, patting him on the back. "You earned your money today, Hairy One," he whispers.

Bathed in sweat, Laelius staggers over to the railing and dons his tunic. He teeters up the steps and plops himself next to Prima, his eyes bright with excitement. She says nothing, her eyes fixed on the next two entering combatants.

"Well?" he says, frowning at her. "Do you still think I am a frivolous person?"

"You smell like a summer fish market," she snaps.

"That's all you have to say?" Laelius says, shaking his head in amusement.

Prima looks sideways at him. She smiles and squeezes his forearm. "Oh, all right. You were magnificent. But tell me the truth. You paid him to throw that match, didn't you?"

"Nothing of the sort!" Laelius retorts, wrinkling his nose at her. "When I was a dock orphan, I used to wrestle men like him for money." He taps his damp chest. "I could have made a living at it."

"At least until you got as fat as that one," Prima replies. She smiles coquettishly. "I am not unaccustomed to the sport myself. Perhaps I could give *you* a tumble."

His eyes wander over her body as if inspecting a horse. "Hm! You are overly confident of yourself, gladiatrix."

"You are certainly not the first man to tell me that—and be wrong. I have won much from your cocky breed—so to speak."

"Win what? What would we compete for?"

Prima stares at him, then smiles. "Why, truth and honor, of course. And maybe something else..." She puts her hands on her knees and pushes herself upright, rubbing the back of her neck. "Let's go. I'm getting bored watching these slum-dwellers roll in the dirt."

"As you say, Sweet."

The couple enter their waiting carriage and trundle down the cobblestoned road to central Rome, the moonlit Tiber glistening alongside them. A half hour later the carriage pulls in front of the Julia manse. They walk to the large green double doors.

Prima looks up at the starred sky. She inhales deeply. "Ah, it is so good to be back in the greatest city on earth. I am so grateful that

Scipio got us here." She stares into Laelius' eyes and touches his cheek. "And that I met you, my strong and silly fellow."

"Silly?" Laelius blurts. "You are just like the rest. You think anyone with the intelligence to have a sense of humor is weak or superficial! Well, I can whip any—" Prima leans forward and kisses him deeply upon the mouth, interrupting his tirade.

"I think nothing of the sort," she says. "If I did, you wouldn't be here. Have a pleasant evening." Prima bangs her fist on the door until a slave opens it. She glides inside and booms it shut.

Laelius turns to walk away. The door creaks open behind him. Prima's head pops out. "Do not think I've forgotten about our match," she chirps. "We'll see how you do against a real gladiator!" The door slams.

Laelius stares at the door, dumbfounded. He rubs his chin. *She does stir me—a woman, of all people!* He rubs his sore left shoulder and smiles. *A wrestling match could be fun.*

Laelius takes the carriage to the Scipio domus. He finds Amelia clipping off hyacinths and marigolds in the open-air garden in the back of the manse. Publius and Cornelia toddle behind her, lugging small wicker baskets of the harvested blooms.

"Ah, my favorite woman!" Laelius says, hugging her tightly.

"Where have you been?" she asks, gently disengaging from him. "Have you been rolling around in the stables?"

"Well, I was herding an ox for a bit." he says. "Where is old Scipio? Out slugging wine with the Hellenics?"

"He has his own livestock duties," Amelia returns, smiling tightly. "Our new censor is driving a hog from our garden."

ROME, 199 BCE. Scipio welcomes Flaccus with a warm smile, but his eyes are cold as ice. "Senator Flaccus, it is a pleasure to finally talk privately with you. Will you sit?"

Scipio sweeps his hand toward the steps of the Temple of Bellona. Eyeing Scipio suspiciously, Flaccus eases his bony frame onto the marble steps. Scipio gathers up the hem of his purple censor's toga and sits an arm's length away.

"I will be brief. At tomorrow's Senate meeting, Consul Lucius Lentulus will offer you a praetorship, with an assignment to Sicily. It is a prestigious position, with luxurious accommodations in a beautiful setting. I suggest you take it."

"I will do nothing of the sort!" Flaccus sputters. "All my work is here!"

"You mean all your mischief is here!" Scipio retorts. "I know what you have been about, Senator, and I suspect you of far worse. You can take the Sicily assignment or I will remove you from office."

"What? You can't do that. I am a senior senator, next in line to be Speaker!"

"As Rome's morality officer, I can and I will," Scipio folds his hands over his knee and looks calmly into Flaccus' eyes. "I will arrest you for bribery and theft. I have already removed Cyprian and Felix for their many offenses."

His eyes harden. "I suspect you have had a hand in several attempted assassinations, too. Were I sure of it, you would be on a cross right now."

"I won't go," Flaccus spits, raising himself from the steps. "Do your worst, Hellenic."

Scipio leaps up and grabs Flaccus' throat in his hand, shoving him backwards onto the steps. Flaccus grapples feebly at Scipio's cabled forearm.

Scipio stares into Flaccus' bulging eyes. "Oh, you do not want to see my worst, man. My worst will leave no skin on your roasted body."

He shakes Flaccus as a dog would shake a rat. "I will be at the Senate tomorrow. If I hear you refuse it, you will not live to see the morning sun, though you rouse a hundred minions to defend you."

Scipio pitches Flaccus sideways and stalks from the temple. Rubbing his bruised throat, Flaccus curses him under his breath.

The next afternoon finds Flaccus exiting the Curia Hostilia, surrounded by dozens of congratulatory Latins.

"Praetor to Sicily!" one says. "What a fine place to be governor!"

"You certainly deserved it," replies another.

Flaccus glares at the man. "What do you mean by that?"

The man blushes. "Nothing! I only meant..."

"Leave me, all of you!" Flaccus barks. "I have matters to attend to."

Flaccus quickly repairs to his city home. That evening, he eases out a side door and takes the back streets toward the Aventine Hill stables, his tattered gray cloak pulled about his head. He eases into a shadowed recess inside one of the stables. And he waits.

A half hour later, Spider walks into the stables, her eyes wary. "You had better have come alone," she growls.

"I come alone, as always. But I am not happy that your 'assignment' is still alive."

"Amelia has remained in her house," Spider says. "But now she has begun to venture out with her attendant. It will be soon."

"Make it sooner. Another purse if you do it before the new moon."

Spider smiles. "Your words are honey to my ears. It will be done this week."

Two days later, Amelia and Prima are wandering through the chain of stalls that lines each side of the main street into the Forum. Amelia's two house slaves follow behind them, each lugging a wood slat shopping basket.

The two women chat gaily, trying on various baubles and robes. Prima smiles, enjoying Amelia's company, but her eyes roam the stalls about her. She notices a petite young woman follows behind them, the same woman she saw when they entered the street. Prima watches the woman's eyes.

I have seen that look before, she thinks. *That one looks at nothing but sees everything.*

"Look, Amelia. There are some lovely dinner plates at that metalsmith's shop. I could use some for the next Saturnalia feast."

Prima and Amelia stop at the stall. Amelia fondles a long silver-beaded necklace. She drapes it around her neck and then about her waist. Prima picks up a polished silver plate and holds it up to the light, examining its surface.

"Those are purest silver," the young metalsmith says. "They shine like old Sol, the sun god himself."

"Yes, quite beautiful," Prima says distractedly. She holds the plate higher, admiring its shiny surface. The plate's blurry reflection shows the small woman easing toward them, her hand tucked inside her cloak.

"I'm going to get some thyme," Prima tells Amelia. She steps to an adjoining spice merchant's stall. She bends over and examines the open sacks of spices.

Spider eases toward Amelia, weaving through the scores of people who flow through the wide street. She reaches into a side pocket of her cloak and grabs the hilt of her dagger, being careful not to touch its poisoned tip.

The assassin approaches the side of Amelia and eases her blade from its hiding place, letting it dangle next to her thigh. She cocks back her arm.

Spider gasps, arching her back with the blinding pain she feels in her kidneys. An iron arm clamps across her throat and jerks her head back. She stabs furiously behind her, seeking to strike anything, but the iron arm jerks her off balance. Spider feels the serrated bronze blade saw into her neck, cutting deep into her jugular.

The next instant she is on her knees, gurgling out her life as screams erupt about her. A tall lean brunette stands in front of her, holding a dripping dagger.

"Asasino!" the woman declares. She points at Spider's fallen blade. "Sicarius!"

"That's her!" Livid with anger, Amelia stalks toward the fallen assassin, holding one of her throwing knives at the ready. She grabs Spider by the hair, ignoring the blood that spurts onto her robe.

"Who did this? Who sent you?" she screams, shaking the dying woman's head. Spider bares her blood stained teeth in a grisly smile. She spits several clots onto Amelia's jeweled hand, then collapses onto the street.

Amelia kicks the corpse, sobbing with fury. She turns to her two slaves. "Burn this body and dump the ashes in a public toilet," she orders.

Prima grasps Amelia by the shoulders. She leads her gently from the stunned crowd. "Let us go home now, Sister. She will threaten you no more."

An hour later, Scipio is stalking about the Scipio atrium, his fists balled into knots. Laelius sits on a couch with Amelia, his arms about her shoulders.

"Who did this?" Scipio demands.

"How would I know?" Amelia snaps. "I have many enemies—men who blame me for getting their opponents elected."

"If I had to bet on who it was, I'd bet Flaccus was somehow involved," Laelius replies. "Or Cato."

Scipio shakes his head. "Treachery is not Cato's way. Flaccus might do it. Maybe it was that snake Cyprian, or Felix. I ran them out of the Senate, and they have sworn revenge."

"I have friends in the Aventine gangs," Laelius declares. "I will make some inquiries. I'll find out who hired her, you have my word. And I'll start now."

Laelius stalks toward the door. He stops at the atrium and pulls on his dark green riding cloak. He feels a soft hand upon his shoulder. Turning, he sees Amelia standing behind him, with Prima at her side. Amelia gives him the tiniest of smiles, a pleading look on her tear-stained face.

"Laelius, you know my husband is not well. The night sweats come to him more frequently. And the dreams, those cursed dreams drain him." She squeezes his forearm. "By the love you bear me, I ask you not to tell him if you find out. He would kill whoever did this. That would kill his career. Rome would lose its greatest leader."

Laelius stares at her. "You ask me to betray him? It was always the three of us, united. I love him, too."

"If you love him, you will save him from this. Promise!"

Prima slides her hand over Laelius' forearm. "I see the wisdom in what she asks." She tightens her grip. "We can take care of it. Scipio can find out later."

"Later, you say," Laelius responds dully. "After I have hidden the truth he most desires from him."

"Rome needs his guidance. We can't lose him to a vengeance killing, when we war with Macedonia."

"Flamininus is an able general," Laelius mutters. "He can handle him."

"Then what of the Syrians?" Amelia replies. "That cur Antiochus is cutting his way through the Egyptians at Pergamum, preparing to sail on Greece. How long before he sets eyes on Rome? You must save my husband from himself, Laelius. He has a greater purpose ahead."

Laelius stares at the ceiling, his hands knotted into fists. He looks back at Prima and Amelia, who watch him expectantly. A hint of a smile crosses his face. "Well, I guess deception is good practice for my career in politics. Scipio will not know the killer until he is dead. He can devote his attention to Philip and Antiochus."

BANIAS, PERGAMUM,[lxxxviii] 199 BCE. "This isn't looking good, Zeuxis. Our infantry's stalled down there."

"We should have given those Galatians more training on attacking phalanxes," Zeuxis replies. "We're lucky those aren't Macedonians fighting them."

Antiochus sits atop his black stallion on a rise above the battlefield plain. The hawk-faced king is quite displeased.

General Scopas' Egyptian phalanxes are repelling his prized infantry. Bristling with eighteen-foot sarissas, the squares of 196 men tramp forward one step at a time, shoving out their spears to push the Galatians backwards. The Gallic warriors curse with frustration but still they retreat, edging into the mocking Syrian infantry behind them.

"Get at them, you women!" The Galatian chieftain screams, pounding his hand axe on his shield. Scores of Gauls rush at the forest of spears, seeking to break their ranks.

The front-line spearmen shove out their thick lances, knocking the Galatians' shields sideways. Their rear linemates jab their sarissas deep into the Galatians' exposed chests. Soon, the grassy plain is littered with dying Gauls. The implacable phalanxes march over the felled barbarians, every man fixed on maintaining the order of their impenetrable lines.

"If this keeps up, my men are going to break and run," says Zeuxis. "Should I bring up our Syrians? "They've got more experience in fighting phalanxes."

"No, we can't break them with a frontal assault," Antiochus replies. "We'll have to get into their sides, or the rear."

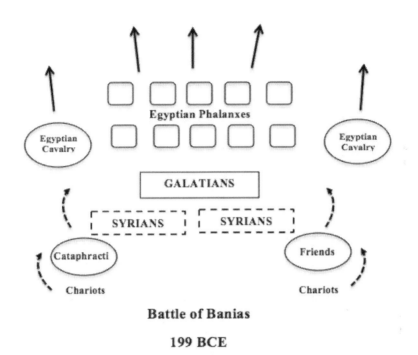

Battle of Banias

199 BCE

"Their flanks are protected by their cavalry, my King. There are thousands of them."

"Yes, but they are lightly armored cavalry," Antiochus says. He winks. "And we have just the men to break them. Get Antiochus the Younger over here."

A tall rider soon approaches the two commanders. His is body covered in bronze scale armor, as is his horse. He pulls off his domed helmet to reveal a sharp-featured youth with jet black hair and beard.

"What is it, Father? Can we attack now? The men are growing restless. They need heads and plunder."

"It is time. We have to break those phalanxes or we're lost. You will attack the left flank cavalry with your cataphractii, and penetrate their infantry. I'm bringing my King's Friends in to the right."

"I'll tell the Galatians to prepare for a counterattack," adds Zeuxis. His eyes gleam. "I'll let Nicator join them; he'll keep them fighting."

"By all means, turn him loose," the king says. He waves to his left. "Get your men ready, Son. But wait for the signal."

Antiochus the Younger salutes. "Their heads will be ours before nightfall." He trundles off, his armor jingling.

"Let's get my cavalry over to the right flank, Zeuxis. It's time to do some fighting!"

Minutes later, the Syrians' curved bronze horns sound across the ranks. Three thousand cataphractii thunder down the hillside, each horse and rider covered in heavy scale armor. They pound across the grassy plain, with Antiochus the Younger in the lead.

Thousands of Egyptian cavalry charge out to meet them, agile riders wearing a only helmet and cuirass of thick flax. The riders cradle their seven-foot spears in their right arms, a small round shield on the forearm of the hand that grips their horses' reins. They dart through the cumbersome cataphracti, striking at them from every angle.

On the right, Antiochus and Zeuxis boldly charge out ahead of their thousand elite cavalry. When they approach the Egyptians, the practiced riders move into wedge formation, with Antiochus at the head of them, eager to fight. They level their thirteen foot spears at the center of the cavalry riding column guarding the phalanxes' flank.

Antiochus barges between two riders and plunges toward the infantry, drawing in in his riders behind him. The Syrians cleave through the enemy cavalry, spearing dozens as they cut deeper into them. The Syrian wedge splits the cavalry apart, jamming them together.

King Antiochus plunges onward, crashing into the flanks of the Egyptian phalanxes. The infantrymen try to lever over their long sarissas to defend themselves but the Syrians are already stampeding through them, easily dodging the cumbersome poles. Wheeling about and stabbing at will, they cut deep into the ranks of the foot soldiers, slashing hundreds down.

Now the right side phalanxes have become a milling mob, jamming against each other in their madness to escape the killing riders that swarm all about them.

While Antiochus' riders penetrate the phalanxes, his son's cataphractii rampage through their lightly-armored opponents. Time and again, an Egyptian rider dodges an oncoming Syrian's lance, only to break his spear on his opponent's armor.

The Egyptians throw down their broken shafts and draw their sickle-shaped swords. Scores of Egyptians jump from their horses and leap upon the backs of passing Syrians, pulling them to the ground for a fatal sword blow.

"Run them down!" Antiochus the Younger bellows. The cataphracti charge into the Egyptians on the ground, their heavy beasts trampling their bodies.

After a brief fight, the Egyptian cavalry run from the field, knowing their heavily-armored opponents cannot catch them. The cataphractii give chase, eager to kill more of their vulnerable opponents.

Antiochus the Younger grabs his hornsman. "Sound the recall!" he bellows. "Get those fools back here!"

The horn bugles out its command. The lumbering cataphractii turn about and ride back to join the prince. When he sees his men returning, young Antiochus charges at the left flank of the phalanxes. His men thunder after him, lowering their spears as they close.

The Egyptians hear the thunder of approaching cavalry. They feel the rumble of thousands of heavy hooves striking the ground. Looking over, they see a wave of shining bronze descending upon them, lances bristling along its front.

The Egyptians on the flanks kneel down and turn their spears toward the onslaught of armored riders, leaving their front-line men to fend for themselves.

Hundreds of cataphractii crash through the scattered spears that face them, deflecting them with their shields and armor. They rear up their horses and bring them down upon the kneeling Egyptians, battering them to the earth. Hundreds more riders dash into the wide opening between the front and rear phalanxes.[lxxxix] They strike into the backs of the defending Egyptians, sowing further turmoil within their ranks.

The Galatians can see gaps appearing in their enemies' impenetrable front spear wall, with most of the backup spears pointed at the cavalry assaulting the flanks. The Galatians roar with triumph—and the lust for revenge.

The Gallic chief mimics a pumping motion. "Grab their spears and yank them away!" The brawny Galatians dash toward the phalanxes' disintegrating front line.

The Gauls slide in between the gaps in the front row spearheads and grab the middle of the spears. They shove the long poles aside and bash their thick shields into the Egyptians' bodies, knocking them off balance. The Galatians' long swords plunge into their foe's bodies. Screams erupt across the Egyptian lines.

In the midst of the melee weaves a lean and muscular warrior with silver plated armor—a man who is eager to kill. Nicator resents all men with unmaimed features, but he bears a particular resentment for the handsome, copper-skinned warriors of Egypt, men more beautiful than any of the women he has paid to tolerate his gruesome features.

Snaking his way through the spear front, the Syrian dashes to the left corner of the phalanx, knowing that is where the infantry captain would be stationed. Nicator soon spies the red plume of the captain's helmet. He hurries toward him, pausing only to slash the hamstring of a spearman who is engaged with a Gaul.

A mob of Galatians storm into the spearmen in front of Nicator, halting him in his tracks. Nicator hears sandaled feet behind him, crunching on the sandy soil. He spins to his right, raising his shield to his head.

The blade swooping toward his neck thuds into the edge of his shield. Nicator bends low and darts in his blade, slicing open the midsection of the attacking Egyptian. The infantryman falls to his knees, howling with pain, his bowels cradled in his shaking hands. A gap between the combatants opens in front of him. Nicator dashes through the opening, heading toward the bobbing red plume at the end of the line.

The Egyptian captain notices the silvered warrior weaving toward him, gracefully sliding between combatants. He instantly grasps his purpose. *That's the Syrian champion. One of us is going to die very soon.*

The officer's stomach churns, but his lips tighten with determination. He plants his feet. His sword beckons Nicator forward. "Why do you wear a mask? Are you too ugly to show your face?"

Behind the mask, Nicator's face flames with embarrassment—and fury. He ceases his rush and slowly steps forward, measuring the Egyptian. *He is well balanced, but his left leg is too far behind him. Let's see how he moves.*

Nicator stabs out with his short, double-edged sword. The captain's blade flashes, blocking the blow. Nicator hops backward, easily evading the Egyptian's sweeping counterthrust. He steps to the captain's left and rams his plate-sized buckler into the Egyptian's tombstone shield. The captain pivots to his left and slashes at Nicator. But he is not there. Nicator has rolled past the Egyptian's shield and now stands behind the captain.

Quick as a striking snake, Nicator darts out his foot. He scoops the Egyptian's left foot out from under him as he pushes into his shield. The captain topples to the ground. Nicator's blade delves through the underside of the Egyptian's wrist. Howling with pain, the captain reflexively grabs at his hand. His sword drops beside him.

Nicator stoops down and shoves his blade through the Egyptian's cheek. He whips the sword out and plunges it into the captain's eye and then his mouth, transfixing his head to the earth. The young officer's eyes bulge with agony, then fix into a glassy stare. The Syrian springs upright, his dripping sword hanging at his side.

"Who's the ugly one now, Captain?" he snarls.

Within the hour, the Gauls have destroyed the front row phalanxes. The Galatians' back lines dispose of the remnants as the lead Galatians crush into the next row of phalanxes. An hour later, the Egyptians drop their lengthy spears and dash across the open plains, seeking solace in the forested hillsides miles away.

On the right, King Antiochus and his Friends have threshed their way to the center of the Egyptian infantry, cutting them down to the right and left. He spies the rear phalanxes fleeing across the open plains. *Make sure there are none to regroup.*

"Bring down the chariots!" He yells at Zeuxis. His commander wheels about and gallops up the hillside. Minutes later, the Syrian horns sound a new attack call.

Hundreds of chariots trundle down the hillside, their deadly blades pinwheeling about their hubs. The charioteers ignore the dwindling infantry conflict in the center of the battlefield—their prey are the Egyptians fleeing across the plain.

The chariots catch up to the waves of escaping phalangites—and the slaughter begins. While the drivers steer their chariots toward knots of fleeing Egyptians, the archers nock arrows into their bows. They shoot into the back of the nearest enemy and quickly nock and loose another, frantic to kill as many as possible. Scores, then hundreds, then thousands litter the plains, breathing their last in the sweet spring grass.

The most bloodthirsty charioteers turn their chariots toward the men who fall, carefully aiming their wheel's serrated blades. The chariots draw next to the stricken warriors lying in front of them. There is a thump, followed by an agonizing scream, followed by fountains of gore. The chariots lurch sideways and rumble on, seeking their next victim.

Dusk mercifully descends. In the main battle site, the once-placid fields are clumped with thousands of dismembered bodies, as far as the eye can see. The Galatians and the Syrians step from body to body, swords at the ready, seeking more kills and plunder.

Antiochus, Zeuxis, and Antiochus the Younger are atop the hill, surveying their grisly victory. "How many got away?" the king says to Zeuxis, his tone expressionless.

"Maybe a couple thousand out of twenty," Zeuxis replies. "Not enough to mount any serious threat in the future."

"What of General Scopas?"

Zeuxis laughs heartily. "Him? Their brave Aetolian leader? He was one of the first to ride his horse out of here! I do not doubt that Egypt's King Ptolemy will give him his just reward for this defeat."

"It were best he receives it from us," says Antiochus. "Send out a dozen scouting parties. A purse to the man who brings me his head. Two purses if they bring him back alive."

"Father, that is the last of Ptolemy's armies in this region. We have regained all of our ancestral lands in Pergamum. Do we move on to Egypt?"

"We will, son, in time. Philip and I agreed to join forces and divide it. But let us see how Philip fares in his next encounter with the Romans. Egypt could be ours alone for the taking."

"Philip may fare better against this new consul," Zeuxis replies. "I hear this one is a young man, without Galba's experience. He could be another sop like that Villius was."

"Either way, we win," adds Antiochus the Younger. "If Philip wins, Rome will be weakened for us. If the Romans beat him, we can take all of Egypt."

He grins. "Or maybe they'll just destroy each other!"

BOUTHROTOS, EPIRUS, 198 BCE. Titus Quinctius Flamininus pulls his red cloak about his shoulders, trying to ward off the chill sea wind that blows across the bow of his quinquereme. The newly-minted consul paces the oak-timbered deck, trying to calm his nerves.

We're almost there. I'll be at the Roman camp by nightfall. When Villius leaves, I'll be in charge of the entire army. Then what do I do with Philip? Negotiate or fight?

General Flamininus had set sail for Macedonia as soon as he was elected, far earlier than the consuls before him.[xc] He heeded his mentor Scipio's advice: *do not delay your command. Galba had to relinquish command when he was on the cusp of victory. Then Villius came in and did nothing. Do not waste your opportunity.*

Flamininus is determined to give himself enough time to resolve this war before his year-long consulship expires. He has braved the Adriatic's treacherous winter winds to organize his army for an early spring campaign.

An hour after the ship docks, Flamininus is riding east with this guards, heading toward the Roman camp at the foot of the Pindus Mountains. As he races through the region's rugged terrain, the young consul's mind boils with indecision: should he try negotiating a peace with the notoriously devious Philip, losing months in the process? Or should he march into Macedonia and challenge him to battle?

Remember Scipio's dictum. Philip is the man who keeps our other foes in check. Stop him but don't lose him.

Hours later, Flamininus' party encounters a group of Roman sentries from Villius' camp, a dozen men scattered atop the limestone ridges that flank the narrow roadway. The guards see Flamininus' purple plumed helmet, and somberly extend their right hands in salute. He returns the respect, chuckling to himself. *I still can't believe it. I am a general!*

He looks at his shaking hand. *You'd better believe it, boy. You have twenty-five thousand men waiting for you.*

The consul's party rides through a narrow passage and emerges into a wide plain backdropped by the six-thousand-foot peaks of the Pindus Range. The Roman camp lies in the middle of the plain—an immaculate, timber-walled rectangle the size of a small town.

As Flamininus draws near, the watch tower horns sound his arrival. His party slows to a trot, then a walk. Young Flamininus knows he must enter the camp with the dignity expected of a general.

Consul Villius is waiting for him by the front of the open gates. Flamininus dismounts and embraces his short, stout predecessor.

"Salve, General Flamininus. I trust your trip went well?"

"Salus, Consul Villius. Getting here was like sailing over a boulder field, but we didn't have any Macedonian ships to harass us. How fare you?"

"I am ready to go home!" laughs the older man. "Gods above, I do miss Rome. Especially the baths and the brothels!"

Flamininus smiles awkwardly. *The man's done nothing this year, after Galba brought us so close to ending this. Why Scipio got him elected is beyond my ken.* "You have served long and honorably," Flamininus says, his eyes avoiding Villius. "Let me give you your well-deserved rest. I am ready to assume command."

Villus claps his hands together. "Wonderful! I will leave first thing in the morning. He notices Flamininus staring at him. "What? You think I am leaving too soon? Look, Titus, there's nothing to running this camp. I will brief you tonight on the main issues, during the big feast in your honor!"

"Uh, gratitude," Flamininus replies. "I will be sorry to see you go—so soon."

Villius rubs his hands together. "Come on, let me give you a quick tour of camp. Wait until you see the elephant pen...!"

Three days later, Flamininus sits at the head of a split log banquet table, surrounded by his army's tribunes. His eyes scan the seamed faces of the gravid older officers, and he feels his stomach roil. *Many of these men were with Scipio in Africa, when he conquered Hannibal. Will they fight for a treaty instead of a conquest?*

"I have talked to all of you, and listened to your opinions about what we should do next. I tell you now, whatever we do, we will do soon, within days. We can end this war this year."

Amid some scattered ayes of agreement, the officers nod silently. "And what do you propose we do?"

Here goes. "I propose to meet with Philip and discuss peace terms with him. His camp is in the mountains above us—it should not take him long to get down here."

"You want to *negotiate* with that murderer?" jeers one officer. "He killed hundreds of our men at Corinth. Let's go kill *him!*"

"You don't make your bed with a snake, General!" barks one.

A barrel-bodied man pushes himself up from his stool. He splays his hands on the table and leans toward Flamininus. "May I speak?"

"You are the First Tribune, Sextus," says Flamininus. "You have more than earned that right."

"For a year we have languished here, fighting skirmishes with the Macedonians and their Aetolian allies. And that's all! We are the finest fighting force in the world; thousands of us are veterans of Scipio's invincible army. But we are growing older, Consul, and we are weary of doing nothing here, far from home. Our army is losing its edge."

Amid a chorus of agreements Sextus raises his hands. "But I see your point. I fought with Scipio, the greatest man I have ever known. I was with him when he made his peace proposals to Carthage, though he could have destroyed them all. He was ever a man who worried about losing his men's lives in needless combat."

Sextus stares across the table at the other officers. "Scipio was always ready to extend the olive branch, but his other hand was always on his sword, should the branch be denied. When words failed, action quickly followed."

He's giving you a way to get them on your side. "My sentiments exactly" Flamininus declares hastily. "I will ask Philip to meet with me at a neutral site. I will propose he forfeit all control of Greece. In return he gets to keep his kingdom."

Flamininus notices that the tribunes looking at each other, trying to judge what their fellows think. "We have nothing to lose," he adds. "I will meet with him for one day, and give him a non-negotiable proposal. If he does not agree to it, we will attack him within the week. And we will not quit until Philip's minions are totally defeated."

"Good," Sextus growls. "Let's end this thing and go home!" None voice opposition.

Thank the gods! "It is decided. I will go to my tent and draw up the treaty. You men are to meet and plot an attack, that we may be fully prepared for combat."

A sturdy young tribune stands up from the table. "I served as a foot scout in the Alps, General. I volunteer to explore the mountains where the Macedonians are camped. A single man can go far unnoticed."

Flamininus gapes at him. "You want to venture out there alone?"

The tribune nods. "I only require a cloak and dagger. The locals do not flee from a simple peasant, all alone."

The consul studies the tribunes' faces. He nods. "That is a brave thing you would do, Marcus Aemilius. Are you sure you want to take the risk?"

Marcus' face twitches with the hint of a grin. "The only danger is to the Macedonian who encounters me."

KING PHILIP'S CAMP. "There is a messenger from that new consul?

Philip smirks. "That, what's his name, Titia Querulous?"

Philocles rolls his eyes. "Titus Quinctius Flamininus, my King. Yes, it's a messenger from him. He says it is urgent."

"Urgent, is it?" Philip grabs a handful of olives and bounces them, one by one, off his tent walls. "Well, let's show this new consul who's in control here. Tell him I have gone to Thessaly. Find out what he wanted to talk about, though. Tell him you will communicate his message to me."

The king stretches out on his tent's eight-foot couch, watching his attendants scoop up the olives. "Too bad Consul Villius has departed. I will miss his dithering inaction."

Philocles returns an hour later. The veteran commander has a surprised look on his face. "The messenger says that Flamininus wants to discuss peace terms with you."

"Peace, eh? Perhaps Rome has recognized the futility of disputing my ancestral rights to Greece. Or perhaps they are afraid of fighting a real army!"

"They did lose a lot of men fighting Carthage," Philocles says. "But the Romans, they are terribly persistent fighters."

"Persistent, but stupid. Even so, it cannot hurt to talk to this new man. Perhaps he is more reasonable than that iron-headed Galba."

"This new one may be a man of action," Philocles says. "He may attack immediately if these talks fall through. We should be prepared."

Philip's eyes light with a new plan. "I'll buy us some time. Tell them I won't return for a month, but that I seriously desire to talk peace with him then. While they wait, we will prepare."

"You are going to prepare to attack them?"

"Oh my no," Philip replies, rolling an olive in his fingers. "I'm going to prepare for them attacking us. That's what will lead to their defeat!"

CARTHAGE, 199 BCE. "I'm not sure how long I can protect you, Hannibal," says Kanmi Barca. "I have called in all the favors owed me, but the Council of Elders still demands that you stand trial for malfeasance."

Hannibal paces about his uncle's meeting room, hands clasped behind his back. "They are trumped-up lies! You know what this is about, don't you? When I was the lead magistrate, I convinced the people to demand that the Council members be elected by the people, rather than let them be appointed by the aristocracy. And we made their terms for a year instead of life. [xci] Now they want me dead."

"As do many Rome's senators," adds Kanmi. The gray-haired general stares pleadingly into Hannibal's angry eye. "If you stay here, I fear they will collude to bring you misfortune. It would break my heart to see you go, but it would be for the best."

"I should flee from a pack of lies?" Hannibal splutters. "Flee from a pack of jackals? I did what was right for our people! For years, the Elders have stolen from our treasury. They hid money to avoid their share of taxes, knowing their life terms protected them. I am proud of what I did. If I die, I die with a clear conscience!"

"And deprive us of our greatest general? We may need you. Rome may yet start another war with us. Just go away for a while, Commander. Antiochus wants you to visit him. He must be an admirer."

"He has sent me some laudatory letters," Hannibal says. "What of it?"

Kanmi lovingly fingers an ancient skinning knife on his wall. "Our Phoenician ancestors talked about bending with the wind so that you can spring back up. You could do much worse than to visit Antiochus for a while. His army is vast. He has the capability to defeat anyone, including the Romans."

"He is busy ravaging Egypt. Philip of Macedonia is the one warring with Rome."

Kanmi shakes his head. "Macedonia is a dying ember, but Syria will burst into flame. Our spies tell us Antiochus plans to eventually take over Greece and invade Italia—even if it means betraying his alliance with Philip."

"You speak of betrayal. If I were to visit him, I could betray *our* trust. We have a peace agreement with Rome."

Kanmi cocks an eyebrow at Hannibal. "Carthage has a treaty with Rome, not you. Carthage cannot be held responsible for the actions of one of its wayward citizens. Remember when the Roman delegates asked us to recall Hamilcar from north Italia? Once we told them he was beyond our control, their legions went after him and they let us alone." Kanmi frowns. "Unfortunately, they killed Hamilcar before he could get to Rome's walls."

"Hamilcar would not have defeated them, I know. His army was composed of the mercurial Gauls. What he needed was thousands of dependable Iberians or Libyans, men who never abandon the fight. Even I could not defeat Rome with that bunch."

"You must leave now," Kanmi says, his mouth set. "I worry about your welfare, nephew. And Carthage's safety from Rome. With your genius guiding him, Antiochus could conquer Italia and remove that threat. And you could revenge your defeat by Scipio!"

Hannibal shakes his head. "I bear no ill will toward Scipio. He was a soldier following orders." He smiles sadly. "We are kindred spirits. He had to fulfill a promise he made to his father, as I had to do."

Kanmi's eyes narrow. *The promise—that is my lever.* "You promised your father you would protect Carthage from Rome. That pig's ass Cato still calls for Carthage to be destroyed at every speech he gives.[xcii] He may become consul some day, then what will happen to us? He will burn Carthage to the ground! If you and Antiochus conquer Rome, you would truly fulfill your promise. Think of it, our ships and armies would be restored to us. We would again be an empire!"

Hannibal is silent. Finally, he raises his head. "I am weary of war, of plotting the destruction of humans. If I stay here, I can improve our people's lot in life."

"You do the people no good if you lie dead in your tomb, the victim of an assassin's hand." Kanmi snipes. "You are only forty-three; you have your mind and strength. Keep your promise. Save Carthage from Rome. Your father would want it that way."

Hannibal studies a purple flag of Carthage nailed to the opposite wall, surrounded by the Roman standards that Kanmi captured in Carthage's first war with Rome.

"You were ever true to Carthage's welfare, dear uncle—that much I know." He glances toward the chamber exit. "By the next new moon I will set sail for Syria. Gods help us all, I will war with Rome again."

AOUS RIVER, EPIRUS. Forty days after Flamininus' proposal for peace talks with Philip, the two commanders ride out to meet each other.[xciii] The men meet on the grassy banks of the wide Aous River, a place where the plain rises to meet the mountains.

Flamininus dismounts and stands near the front of a narrow old bridge that spans the crystal green waters. Philip dismounts and strides over to meet him, wearing a flowing black robe embroidered with gold.

He looks every inch a king, Flamininus thinks, noting the handsome man's upright bearing. *But he has that mocking smile on his face, as if he is being polite to the village idiot. It must disconcert those who meet him—is that what he planned for me?* He looks down at his belted wool tunic. *I should have dressed up. I look like Cato.*

"Greetings, King Philip. I am glad that we can *finally* meet to discuss a cessation of hostilities," Flamininus says.

"Hail, Consul Flamingius," Philip says, deliberately mispronouncing his name. "I am glad to have finally returned from my travels." He rubs his neck. "It is exhausting work, restoring Greece's towns and garrisons to rightful Macedonian rule."

Ignore that. Just get to the point. Flamininus points to a large sheepskin blanket sprawled out on the ground. Two bronze goblets and two stoppered pitchers rest on top of the blanket.

"Will you sit with me and take wine, my King? I find the elixir of the grape facilitates friendly communication." He grins. "At least during the first two cups!"

"I would welcome it," Philip replies, plunking himself onto the thick mat. *Hera above, a Roman with a sense of humor! Must have Greek blood in him.*

"Forgive me, but I find the matter quite simple. Rome will cease all hostilities against you, if you will remove your garrisons from the Greek cities you have taken, and recompense those which were plundered." Flamininus drinks deeply of his wine, hoping it will quell his hammering heart.

Philip barks out a laugh. "All the towns and cities? You jest! I have hereditary rights to those places. I will not give them up."

A peace without honor is no Roman peace, the consul reminds himself. "Then we cannot come to agreement," Flamininus replies evenly. "I have a legion of Scipio's veterans with me. They will help me settle the matter."

"Oh, you brought some old men to scare me," Philip replies. "They must all be old enough to be triarii!"

"They are old enough to have defeated three armies on three continents," Flamininus says. "Including the phalanxes you sent to Hannibal!"[xciv]

Hm. Scipio's legions were Rome's finest. "What about arbitration?" Philip says. "I would accept the decision of some arbitrators from neutral nations."[xcv]

"I see no need for arbitration. You were the aggressor in all these cases, taking towns and cities against their will."

"You say I have to give up *all* of them? Even those in Thessaly, which was part of our empire? You are being silly."

Flamininus' face flares. "The Thessalians were first on my list," he blurts, his face reddening. "They came to Rome and *begged* us to intervene."

"You would steal land that which is rightfully mine? We have owned Thessaly for a hundred and fifty years!"[xcvi] Philip flings his cup into the field.

The king rises, his hands clenched into fists. "Why, Titus Quinctius, you could impose no heavier demand on a *defeated* enemy!" [xcvii]

Philip stalks away. "Remember your words when you are hanging on my cross!" He strides over the bridge and takes his stallion's reins from a waiting guard. He springs onto his mount and gallops away, his guards following.

Flamininus sits on the blanket, toying with his cup. *I am sorry, Scipio. Perhaps you would have been more diplomatic about it, but I tried.* He flips his cup onto the sheepskin and pushes himself up. *Who knows? Maybe I just wanted to fight that mocking bastard. Get it over with before I have to leave.*

"Come on, men," he shouts, as he heads toward his tribunes. "It's time to plan our attack!"

ROME. "Are you sure you want to do this? I won't go easy on you."

Laelius lifts his embroidered black tunic over his head and slips off his sandals. He stands with legs spread, wearing only a tan leather subligaculum.

"It's not me you should be worrying about, gutter boy," Prima replies good-naturedly. She shrugs off her flowing green gown, leaving herself in a linen breast band and loin wrap. A girl attendant folds up Prima's gown and skitters from the ring, sitting on one of the padded benches that borders Julii House's gymnasium.

"Oil!" Prima commands. An aged crone limps over with a bowl of olive oil.

"Gratitude, Juna," Prima says, cupping her hand in the bowl. She slowly rubs the oil over her wiry torso and limbs, smiling impishly.

"What are you doing?" Laelius declares. "That isn't fair!"

"My house, my rules," Prima snaps. "Prepare yourself."

"Cheat! I should paddle your behind!"

She arcs her head back and laughs. "Oh really? Let's just see if you can do that!"

Prima spreads out her sinewy arms and legs. She stalks forward, her eyes fixed on Laelius' face, looking for signs of his next move. Laelius matches her stance. He edges sideways, circling around her.

Prima dives down and grabs Laelius' left ankle. She quickly jerks his foot up and pivots it sideways. Laelius hops about the dirt floor, trying to balance himself on one leg. "Let go, she-dog!" he howls, grabbing for her hands. Prima skips around in a circle, his foot raised to her chin, thoroughly enjoying herself.

Laelius drops to the ground. He snakes out his right foot and scoops Prima's legs out from under her. She thumps onto her ass. Laelius pivots forward and lands on top of her, reaching out to grab her wrists.

Prima dodges his grasping hands and plants her palms onto his chest. She pushes him backwards. Twisting sideways, she whips her right foot into his chest, kicking him to the floor.

Laelius raises himself, rubbing the small of his back. "You'll pay for that."

Prima springs up, grinning. "Well then, you'd better come and collect."

Laelius strides toward her. Prima jumps at him. She quickly wraps her left leg under his knee and shoves her forearm under his chin, bending his head back.

Laelius grabs her forearm and pushes her arm away as his other hand reaches underneath the back of her loin wrap. His hand splays across her muscular buttock, his fingers digging into her cleft.

"Mmm! Nice!" he whispers in her ear. Laelius heaves her sideways. Prima lands on her side and rolls over, springing lightly to her feet. She rubs her bottom, her eyes flaring.

"Now it's you who will pay," she says. The gladiatrix darts toward Laelius, her eyes fixed on his loins.

Oh no you don't, Laelius thinks, lowering his hands to cover his crotch. At the last second, Prima dives between his feet and grabs his ankles, yanking his feet from under him.

Laelius falls face first onto the gymnasium floor, the breath knocked out of him. He quickly props himself up on one elbow, but Prima is already upon him, grasping him about his middle and hoisting him up from the floor.

Strong little thing, he thinks, his feet barely touching the floor. Laelius grips Prima's wrists and pulls her arms from his midsection, tumbling him back to the floor. A grinning Prima leaps on top of him, ready to pinion his arms with her legs. But this time Laelius is ready.

Laelius spins around to grab Prima's back. He locks his hands across her stomach, raising her up off the ground. Prima kicks at his thighs but Laelius only raises her higher.

"Are you ready to raise your finger?" Laelius gasps, urging her to yield.

"You think you have me?" Prima says, laughing. She raises her arms over her head and twists her oily body sideways, wriggling through Laelius' grasp. As she squirms from his grip, the back of her breast band catches on his locked hands. Prima lands on her feet, her bare breasts heaving. She spreads her arms apart and waggles her fingers at him, beckoning him to attack.

Laelius crouches low, splaying out his arms and legs. He scuttles forward, crablike, his sinewy fingers ready to grab her. Prima steps forward and locks hands with him.

Laelius pulls her arms down. They close together, their breasts heaving against each other.

Laelius lowers his lips onto hers. Their mouths open. After a moment, Prima pulls her head back.

"That will be all for tonight," she says to her assistants, her eyes fixed on Laelius. "Close the door when you leave."

The gymnasium door closes. The combatants make one more move. Their loincloths whisper to the floor.

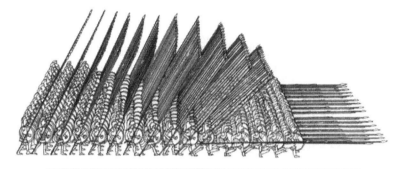

The Macedonian phalanx, here shown in its fighting formation of 256 men, the syntagma.

Macedonian Phalanx

VIII. Philip's Match

FLAMININUS' CAMP, 198 BCE. General Flamininus stands in the empty main street of Philip's camp, slapping his sword against his thigh. He glowers at the dozen Macedonians roped together in front of him.

"Where did Philip go? When did he leave?" Flamininus barks. "It means your life to answer me truthfully."

A terrified infantryman shoves his arm toward the rear gates. "My king left under cover of night two days ago. He is stationed in the Aous Gorge." He drops to his knees. "Spare us, Commander! We were left to walk the parapets and keep the fires going. We were only following orders."

He's holed up in that narrow canyon, the consul decides. *With cliffs protecting him on three sides. Shit!*

"Take them to the stockade," Flamininus says, waving his hand toward camp. "We may need more from them later."

"Now what do we do?" asks Vibius Tertius, one of his senior tribunes.

"Return to camp. We will have a war council at the third watch."

Flamininus stalks out the camp gates. *Where's that cursed horse of mine?* In the distance he sees his legions arrayed before him, perfectly aligned rows of men, their javelins upright at their sides. *My entire army waiting for battle. How embarrassing!*

"Send them back to camp," Flamininus says. "There will be no fighting today, Jupiter curse it."

That night, the lead tribunes gather around Flamininus at the map table. They stare at the map's serrated lines in front of the Roman camp outline, lines depicting the jagged terrain around them. Philip's camp is marked in a narrow open space between the serrations, with the thick blue line of a river drawn through it.

"That looks like flat land inside the cliffs, but it's actually broken ground," says Vibius, running his finger up toward the Macedonian camp marker. "The entrance goes uphill to his camp, with the river on the left, flanked by steep, rocky hills."

"The foxy bastard's blocked the pass to Macedonia," says Vibius. "We have to go through him."

"We can go north around him and take Macedonia while he holes up in his roost," replies an officer.

Flamininus shakes his head. "That cuts us off from our supply lines at the port, and there's no food to forage in that rocky land. Worse, it leaves Philip here to attack the port." He bites his lip. "If we don't get at him now, he could retreat into the wilderness, and hide for months." *And I'll go home without a victory.*

"Then I don't see how we can attack him," Vibius says. "He's in a perfectly defensible position."

"Not perfectly defensible, Commander," comes a voice from the rear. "There is a way."

Marcus Aemilius steps into the torchlight by the map table, his eyes alight with enthusiasm. "As my fellow officers know, I have roamed those mountains for days. I met a tribal leader up there, a man named Charopus. He introduced me to a shepherd that takes his sheep down to graze in that valley.[xcviii] The shepherd says he knows a way in."

"Then we could sneak in behind him," Vibius says.

"You can't take an entire army up those mountains. How would you get the packs and wagons up there?" says another tribune.

"We have to do it," Vibius growls. "What other choice is there?"

Flamininus' heart races with indecision. "Marcus, I want you to go back up there and get this shepherd. Ask this Charopus how much we can trust this man."

Marcus nods solemnly. "I will return at dawn." He salutes and strides out from the tent, his fists clenched at his sides.

"You heard him," Flamininus says. "We'll meet after breakfast tomorrow, to hear what this peasant says."

The officers file out, muttering and arguing among themselves. When they are gone, Flamininus leans over the map table, his face cradled in his hands. The young consul sighs deeply. *What can we do? I can't take an army up those steep hills. But it's suicide to attack him up the valley.*

Flamininus remembers Scipio's words when he handed Flamininus a wicker basket filled with scrolls. *These are my best military histories. Study them closely. They are your sage advisors.*

The young commander gently pulls out three of the yellowed papyrus scrolls that Scipio gave him. He fingers the thick parchment. *So thick and soft. Must be Egyptian papyrus. Scipio always paid for the best in books.*

Flamininus unrolls the first on the map table. He begins reading, running his forefinger down the fabric. An hour later, he puts the three scrolls away and extracts three more. Then three more.

As the dawn slices a bright blade through the tent flaps, Flamininus stabs his finger into the middle of a yellowed scroll, so old it crumbles under his finger.

"There it is!" he exclaims. "Thermopylae. The tale of the three hundred Spartans!" He kisses the scroll. *Gratitude, Scipio.*

Flamininus is chewing on a slice of honeyed bread when Marcus pushes his way through the tent flaps, pulling in a bedraggled rooster of a man. "Here he is," the beaming young tribune replies. He sniffs and glances down at his sandals. "Apologies, Consul. He was in among his sheep."

"You know a way into the ravine?" Flamininus says.

The shepherd looks at the ground, twisting his wool skullcap in his hands. "Several ways, my General. The mountains are full of animal trails. They go down to drink from the river." He grins shyly. "Animals always know the best way down!"

Flamininus heart leaps. "Any wide enough for, say, four men to go down together?"

"Oh yes," he replies. "There is a wide one that switches back and forth to the back of the canyon."

Flamininus keeps his face calm. "Marcus, what does your friend Charopus say about this man?"

"He says he can be trusted. He would wager his life on him," Marcus says.

"You there! How many days would it take to lead troops from here to the bottom of the canyon?" Flamininus asks.

"Two, maybe three days," quails the shepherd. Marcus nods. "It is a day and a half to the high terraces. We could descend from there."

Flamininus takes a deep breath. "Marcus, I will give you a legion and three hundred cavalry. Take this one with you, and do not let him out of your sight. March by night and rest by day. On the third day I will look for a smoke signal from you. When I see that, I will press our attack. Is that clear?"

Marcus bends to one knee and bows. "On my life, I will be ready by the third morning from this one."

"That is good news, indeed." Flamininus says. "Because we will be at the point of no return when you send it."

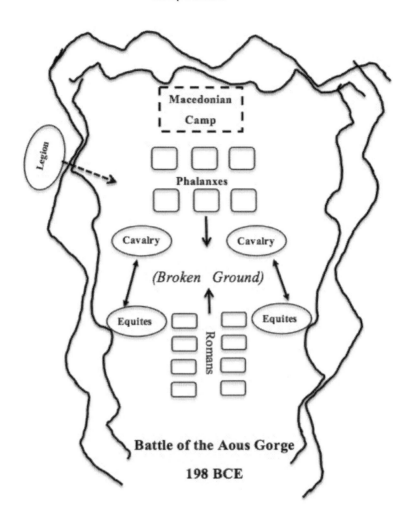

Battle of the Aous Gorge

198 BCE

For the next two days, Flamininus sends his infantry and cavalry into the mouth of the canyon, distracting the Macedonians with several extended skirmishes. On the third morning of Marcus' departure, Flamininus rides out from the camp gates, leading sixteen thousand soldiers behind him. His cavalry ride alongside the flanks of the columns, ready to engage any attacking riders.

Marching in two six-wide columns, the Romans quickly cover the five miles between their camp and the canyon entrance. Flamininus watches the sun rise higher, creeping over the gorge's forested cliffs. *Victoria, give us time for a victory before dusk settles.*

The army draws within eyesight of the cloud-clawing peaks. Flamininus jerks up his right hand. The Roman columns grind to a halt.

The young commander stares up into the mouth of the craggy ravine, its steep floor carpeted with rounded river stones and sharp-edged avalanche rocks. Philip's spear-studded phalanxes wait for him halfway up the canyon, ready to attack if he should venture inside it.

He sees hundreds of Macedonians strewn along the rocky terraces that loom high above the floor. Scores of men stand next to catapults and ballistae. Hundreds more hold spears and rocks. His heart quails.

What am I doing? Am I leading us to slaughter?

He looks back at the front columns of his army, stern-faced men who stand immobile, waiting for his commands.

What if I return to camp, with Philip free to attack Greece—and Italia? If I returned without fighting him, would I be another Man Who Sits in the Back, a senator whose words carry no regard?

Vibius appears at his side. He sees Flamininus' hands are trembling. *He's wavering,* Vibius thinks.

"You know, Marcus Aemilius is a man like no other I have seen," Vibius says. "Whatever he has said he will do, he has done. I trust that he will be ready to break into their rear."

"I, I don't know," Flamininus replies. "We're marching into hell."

"Act quickly, Consul. The Macedonians are on full alert. If they discover Marcus' legion up there, they will destroy them. All of them."

Flamininus straightens his back. He turns to an attending centurion. "Get a bugler back behind the columns," he orders. "He is to sound one long and two short when he sees the smoke signal." *If he sees it.* He looks at Vibius. "You're right. We have to protect our men up there. And I'm tired of standing on the fence. It's time to end it. Sound the call."

A smile cracks Vibius' weathered visage. "That I will gladly do, General." He motions to one of his centurions. "Sound the call to arms. Now!"

The cornu blare out the command. The front-line centurions shout for their men to advance. The columns tramp forward as the cavalry race past them, heading toward the Macedonian riders that are flowing down from the flanks of the phalanxes.

Thousands of riders clash inside the ravine's narrow mouth, javelins flying through the air. With little room to maneuver, the cavalry fight turns into hundreds of individual duels. The riders fight face to face, their horses pushing against each other, stabbing and hacking with their swords. Those who fall are indiscriminately trampled in the milling confusion, slain by friend and enemy alike.

The Roman infantry advances into the gorge, heading directly into cavalry milieu.

"Sound the retreat!" Flamininus commands. The cornu sound the withdrawal, and the Roman cavalry gallop to the flanks of their advancing columns, leaving the Macedonian riders to face the legionnaires.

"Pila!" Flamininus barks. The Romans hurl a cloud of spears at the Macedonian riders, bringing scores of them screaming to the earth. Another rain of spears follows. The Macedonians retaliate with the few javelins remaining to them.

The enemy riders scramble back up into the gorge. The Romans tramp past their victims' bodies, heading toward the implacable phalanxes.

Fifteen hundred feet above the valley floor, Marcus Aemilius and the shepherd are wending their way along a wide plateau stippled with thick stand of scrub oak. Four thousand men follow silently, the army edging their way to the precipice that overlooks the gorge.

Philip's Match

Marcus waves his hand at the men, signaling a halt. He pulls his forest green cloak about his armor and edges through the trees toward the point where the path switchbacks to the valley floor.

Two Macedonian guards stand with their backs to him, enraptured with the battle unfolding below them. Marcus retreats into the scrub and quietly removes his arms and armor, then his sandals. He grabs his dagger and slips through the trees next to the guards.

Marcus studies the two men's backs, looking for openings in their armor. He notices that one has a curved horn dangling from his belt. *The army might hear that horn above the din, but if those two scream, no one will hear them. I cannot let them fall down below.* Marcus crouches down, coiling himself for the spring.

One guard turns and looks back over his shoulder. He walks back from the precipice, heading toward Marcus. The young tribune freezes, daring not to breathe. The man steps to the side of the path and lifts up the hem of his tunic. He urinates on a nearby boulder, his back to his Marcus. Marcus slowly exhales. *Fortuna smiles upon me!*

Marcus tiptoes out from the trees' shadow. He darts across the space between himself and the guard who stands at the precipice.

The Macedonian hears footsteps. He whirls around. Marcus Aemilius rams into his cuirassed chest and knocks him flat. His dagger saws into the man's throat. Marcus rises and rolls the gurgling body away from the precipice.

"What? What's going on over there?" yells the second guard, fumbling himself back inside his tunic. He draws his sword but he acts too late—Marcus is upon him. The tribune grabs the Macedonian's sword arm and bends his arm backward. He rams his head into the Macedonian's jaw, knocking him dizzy. A split second later the guard is facing the ground, clasping his serrated jugular.

Wiping the blood from his blade, Marcus peers over the edge of the precipice. He watches the thick rectangles of the Macedonian phalanxes flow down toward the Roman columns. He sees the soldiers on the lower crags hurling missiles of every type at the legionnaires. His heart races with desperation. *We have to get down there. Our men's backs are completely exposed.*

He glances at the hills directly below him. *There are only two guards down there. They are all that separates us from the battlefield, unless someone's hiding in the trees.*

Marcus spies a figure in silver armor at the rear of the phalanxes. The tall man is seated upon a black stallion, a black robe flowing from his shoulders. His heart quickens. *King Philip! That one will be mine!*

The tribune dons his armor and races back to his legion. He drags the shepherd over to the precipice and points at the trail below. "Is that it?" he demands. "Is that the path down? You had best be truthful, because you are coming with us!"

The shepherd furiously bobs his head. "Yes, yes, the path widens as you go down!"

Marcus returns to his men. "Tiberius, send up the smoke!" The young legionnaire grabs his iron firestarter and runs over to a mound of branches topped with dried fungus. He strikes his iron tool against his flint stone and showers sparks onto the tinder. A fire springs to life. When the blaze is full, he heaps damp grass upon it, sending billows of smoke skyward.

"Glaxus!" Marcus shouts, waving over his First Centurion. "I want you to count to a hundred after I leave. Then bring the men down the trail. I'll be waiting for you near the bottom." The stocky young man pulls his forest cloak over his head and disappears into the trees.

After he finishes counting, Tiberius leads the army down the path, weaving through the dense pines and oaks. On the way he passes one dead sentry, then another, their bloodied throats yawning.

Tiberius emerges onto a wide rocky terrace just above the Macedonian rear. Marcus pops out from the trees next to the path and waves him over.

"Line the men up here as soon as they come down," Marcus hisses. "No talk until we are all together."

"We are going sneak up on their backs?"

"Gods, no!" Marcus says softly. "I want our men screaming like a bunch of drunken Gauls! We want to make the noise of a force ten times our size. They'll think Scipio himself has come to kill them!"

While Marcus' men filter into the trees, Flamininus' columns close upon the waiting phalanxes. Marching with his front-line hastati, young Flamininus studies the rocky ground beneath his feet. He notes they are negotiating a particularly uneven stretch of steep rocky ground, forcing his men to weave among its head-sized boulders. *This is the place.* He signals for Vibius to approach him.

"We are going to fight and retreat, Vibius." Flamininus tells him. "When the Macedonians are over this ground, we counterattack. Tell the officers." Vibius trots off.

Minutes later, the Romans close in on the bristling spears of the Macedonian front. Flamininus draws his sword and steps out in front of his men. "Into them, Romans! Today is victory or death!" He steps forward and rams his scutum against the thick spear wall.

The Romans rain javelins upon the bristling rectangles. There are scattered screams as the spears strike home, but the phalanxes hold. The Romans march steadfastly into the sarissas, shoving their scuta against them. A few brave hastati manage to slip between the spear thicket and cut into the vulnerable Macedonians holding them, but they are quickly punctured by the spearmen in the rear rows.

The Macedonian horns sounds. The phalanxes tread forward, one step at a time, pushing the battling Roman backwards. Dozens, then scores of legionnaires fall from every place in the columns. Many are casualties of the jutting spears, still more fall to the hail of rocks and spears thrown from above.

Flamininus nods toward Vibius. "Retreat in order!" Vibius yells to his nearby centurions. The Roman horns sound the signal. Slowly, grudgingly, the Roman columns back up, dragging their wounded comrades with them.

Watching from the rear, King Philip's vulpine face splits into a grin. *We'll push them out into the open plains. Then the cavalry can get into them. We'll wipe them out! I'll have a clear path across Greece.*

He trots his horse to the back line, where Philocles is slapping a wayward officer. "Leave off him. Get the rear phalanxes ready to replace our center when we enter the open plain. The cavalry will attack their flanks."

Philip's barrel-bodied old commander shoves away the officer. He raises his blood-smeared palm. "It will be done."

Satisfied, Philip trots back for his overlook. He notices a dark gray splotch in the sky. *What in Zeus' hell is that smoke up there? If those locals started another fire up there I'll have them roasted over it!*

"Perseus, see what's going on up there," he tells one of his senior guards.

On the plain of battle, the Romans have backed into the treacherous boulder field. Many stumble and fall as they walk backwards, trying to hold up their shields against the prodding Macedonian spears. Their comrades reach down and yank them upright, though many are wounded for exposing themselves. The columns edge backward like giant worms, twisting around the rocky wreckage.

The Macedonian phalanxes enter the rocks. The phalangites stumble over the uneven terrain and hundreds drop their ungainly twelve-foot spears, trying to keep themselves from falling onto the sharp rocks.

Flamininus peers intently into the wall of spears. He notices that many of the front spears are drooping low, and many of the rear ones are tilting to the side. *Their wall is breaking. Marcus, where in Hades are you?*

For the hundredth time, Flamininus glances up into the cliffs. This time he sees thread of smoke snaking skyward. His heart leaps into his throat. *He's coming in behind them!*

"Lines forward," Flamininus screams, his voice cracking with the effort. "Attack, attack, attack!"

The legionnaires halt. The veteran principes shoulder to the front, edging between the hastati. The principes are the battle-tested veterans of Scipio's army, victors over a dozen types of warriors and weapons. They are not dissuaded by spear walls.

A Roman horn sounds. The legionnaires fling their pila into the wearying and disorganized Macedonians. They immediately hurl out their other two javelins, the missiles coming so close together it seems as if a river of spears has washed upon the Macedonians. Hundreds fall, victims to the javelins that pierce their bodies while they are blocking the ones that preceded them.

The principes stride into the broken spear wall. Many ram their shields sideways to deflect the front spears, while others team with their fellows and yank the sarissas out of their way, enabling them to slide behind the Macedonians fronting them.

The phalangites drop their spears and grab their swords, widening the gaps in the spear wall. The Romans cut into them, wielding their gladii hispaniensis with deadly accuracy. They stab and slash their way into the second line of the Macedonians, leaving a trail of bodies behind them.

Perseus is just entering the hillside trees when he hears a horn sound above him. The Macedonian stops in his tracks, listening. Suddenly, the trees erupt with hordes of attacking Romans. The last thing Perseus sees is the flash of a spear hurtling at his face.

Marcus and his men flow down from the trees and onto the plain, dashing across the open space between them and the rear ranks of Philip's infantry. They fling their spears as they run, screaming for all they are worth.

The Macedonians turn and see wave after wave of Romans pouring out from the trees, flinging javelins. Screams erupt about them as the spears strike home.

"At them, at them!" Marcus screams, sprinting toward the phalangites with his sword in his hand. The Romans draw their blades and rampage into the confused Macedonians, screaming taunts and curses as they hammer at them.

"Romans in the rear lines!" the Macedonians cry. The alarm spreads like wildfire amongst the rear ranks. Hundreds of phalangites drop their arms and dash for the sheltering hillsides opposite the Roman attack, as much unnerved by the Romans' uncharacteristic wildness as by their numbers.

The front-line phalanxes hear roars and screams behind them. They look over their shoulders and see their army dissolving before their eyes, their compatriots running in every direction as the screaming Romans cut through them with their flashing Iberian gladii. The rear lines completely break; thousands run across the narrow plain to their left and scrabble up the boulder field into the succoring trees.

King Philip hears the yells of attackers behind him. He watches the Romans stream out from the nearby forest. Minutes later, he gapes in horror as his men flee the battlefield. *Ah, my gods, we are undone! I'm going to die in this stinking little gorge!* The king's mind fills with a single thought—*Escape!*

"Philocles, we have to get out of here!" he bellows. Philip puts heels to his horse and bolts for the mountain pass opposite the Romans, fleeing without a backward glance.[xcix]

Flaminius is directing the line changes in the space between the principes and hastati. He watches the vaunted Macedonian army disintegrate before his eyes, dropping spears, swords and shields as they disappear into the pines. His breath catches in his throat.

Steady. It's not over yet! "Maintain your ranks," he shouts to Vibius. "They may counterattack."

The consul sees scores of Macedonians dropping to their knees, begging for mercy. *Don't turn this victory into a slaughter. They could yet be our allies.* "Take them prisoner," he commands.

Flamininus runs his horse through the broken ground above him, seeking Marcus Aemilius. He finds him with his men, battling a knot of Macedonians who have refused to retreat, his green cloak still draped over his armor. Flamininus dismounts and strides toward the young tribune, who is deftly slicing the right hamstring of a rangy Macedonian who faces him.

"Marcus, over here!" he shouts. The sturdy little soldier tramps over, a smile beaming in this blood-grimed face. "We have them, General," he bellows over the clash of arms behind him.

"You have done well, Tribune, " Flamininus yells into his ear. "Now call your men back. We want the rest alive."

Marcus strides back toward the surrounded Macedonians. "Cease!" he orders. His men step back from the terrified infantrymen.

Marcus steps into the space between the phalangites and his waiting men. He drops his sword and shield. With arms spread wide and hands open, he walks within a sword thrust of the warriors.

"Drop your arms or you will die. If you do, I promise none will be killed." He stands there, hands spread, waiting. One, then another, then all drop their swords. The legionnaires rush to rope them together.

The cornu sounds the call to restore ranks. The Romans cease their murderous pursuit, leaving the field littered with two thousand Macedonian bodies.[c]

Flamininus looks up the steep rise at the back of the gorge. He notices that the Macedonian pennants are still waving above the timbered ramparts of Philip's camp. *They didn't even pause to take their flags. All their baggage and animals must be up there—and all their food!*

"Get our men into that camp," Flamininus orders. "Bring me every weapon, every foodstuff, anything we can barter with."

The long shadows of eventide flow down from the steep peaks about the gorge, signaling that the day's end approaches. The Romans march out from the Macedonian camp, exhausted but happy, leading a miles-long baggage train of Macedonian plunder. [ci]

Five miles from battle, Philip finally reins in his panting horse. *They can't follow me in this terrain*, he decides.[cii] Philocles draws his horse near to his king.

"Gods, what a mess!" Philocles blurts, rubbing his eyes. "Those cowards sneaked in behind us!"

A clever move, Philip thinks. "Send out all our messengers and scouts. They are to comb the woods and get the survivors back here. The Romans won't come after us—yet."

"Will we counterattack?" Philocles says.

Philip grimaces. He shakes his head. "I would love to go back and destroy them, but we have lost too many men and too much equipment. No, we will take the pass back to Macedonia and reorganize. We will burn every town and field on the way. That will slow their advance."

"Even our allied towns?" Philocles says.

"Anything or anyone that would give them strength will be removed," Philip says. "We take the town's men with us and burn the rest. The townspeople can keep what they can carry—we will take the rest." [ciii]

That night Flamininus takes pen to papyrus and writes a letter to his mentor Scipio.

General Scipio:

Gratitude for your advice about fighting phalanxes on broken ground, using the column formation. Both stratagems worked perfectly. I have won my first major victory, and I owe you much.

I will soon set out in pursuit of Philip. I will destroy his army, though I must follow him over every crag and mountain in his domain.

I know the march will be slow, but I will persist. I only hope to meet him again before my term expires and I am recalled to Rome. Please sacrifice a goat for me at the Temple of Mars, that Fortuna will favor my campaign.

Your grateful pupil,

Titus Quinctius Flamininus

A week later, as Flamininus leads his army through the mountains of Thessaly, a dust-covered messenger rides up and salutes him. He hands Flamininus a small scroll of finest goatskin, sealed with the wax impression of an owl. "I rode all night to get you this. It is from the Imperator himself."

The consul breaks the seal and carefully unrolls the scroll. He reads the brief message. Then he reads it again.

My Friend:

Congratulations on your defeat of Philip. I am grateful I was able to provide some assistance to you, however small the measure.

I understand your distress about your yearly term ending. I will not allow time to become your enemy; desperation has undone many a commander.

Take all the time you need to finalize your victory. I will ensure that you have enough of it.

Publius Cornelius Scipio

Princeps Senatus and Censor

"Is it good news?" says Vibius.

"Good news indeed, if it comes true," Flamininus replies. He shakes his head. "But I am at a loss to see how it will be accomplished."

ROME, 197 BCE. Scipio shakes the new consul's shoulder so hard his head rocks. "That won't work, fool! If I tell the Senate that Flamininus must stay in Macedonia, the Latins will strike it down as quickly as if I asked for a vote to make me king!"

"But they won't listen to me!" consul Gaius Cornelius wails. "Let Quintus Minucius do it."

Scipio shoves him. "Gourd-head! Quintus is a senior in the Latin Party. You have to do it. I helped you get elected. Now it's time to repay your debt."

Scipio releases his hand from the senator's shoulder and steps back, breathing heavily. He runs his hand through his thinning hair. "Apologies. I am overwrought. It's just that it's so important for Flamininus to stay there and finish the war. The Senate extended my command and look what happened—we won the Carthaginian War!"

"I know that," Gaius petulantly replies. "But Flamininus is a known consort of yours. The Latin Party doesn't want him to defeat Philip— they want Minucius to go there and get credit for the win."

"Minucius is a soft-handed fool. He will amount to nothing," Scipio growls.

Cornelius arches his charcoal-blackened eyebrows. "Why him? Flamininus is a fine commander, but he is not you."

"But he will be me," Scipio retorts. "He has my troops, my Numidians, and my elephants. And he has my advice—which he follows. And Flamininus bested Philip at the Aous River."

Cornelius throws up his sausage-fingered hands and stalks away from Scipio, his plump neck reddening. "Why are you bothering me with all this? I can't just dictate an extension for Flamininus. It has to be approved by the Senate."

He's too scared to do it, Scipio decides. *I should have pushed for old Servilius instead of this worm.* He puts his arm around the diminutive patrician. "Gaius, all you have to do is approve a Senate motion to extend Flamininus' command. Can you do that much?"

Gaius stares up at Scipio. Scipio fixes him with his eyes, his hand tightening on his shoulder. Gaius nods mutely and looks away.

"Good. I will take care of the rest. Remember your promise, because I certainly will." He eyes Gaius. "You know, staying out of Macedonia may save your life. Philip is a true killer."

The next day, the Senate convenes at the Curia Hostilia. After the sacrifice of an ox to bring good fortune to the new consuls, Minucius and Gaius prepare to draw lots for Italy and Greece.

The Senate Elder hobbles out in front of the seated senators, clutching a marble bowl with two paper scraps inside. He faces the two new consuls. "Who will draw for their assignment?" he says.

"Neither!" comes a voice from the side of the Senate chambers. "I veto the proposal that they draw lots for Greece!"

A handsome young man steps out to the Senate floor, his black ringlets cascading down to his worn white tunic. He faces the astounded senators, his face flush with anger.

"You know me, patricians. I am Lucius Oppius, Tribune of the Plebs. I tell you now, this nonsense has gone on long enough! Each year a consul takes his army to far Macedonia and wastes months preparing to fight. By the time he has found Philip and is ready to conquer him, he has to return home! I hereby veto the proposal to send a new consul over there. We must allow Flamininus to stay there until he finishes the task."[civ]

An older man steps out from the side steps. He walks over and stands next to Lucius, his head held high. His back is bent but his scarred shoulders and arms bulge from his patched gray tunic. He extends two clenched fists in front of his chest.

"I, Quintus Fulvius, Tribune of the Plebs, veto this drawing of lots." He opens up his hands, revealing that his left is missing a forefinger, and the right has a stubbed middle finger.

"I am but a simple meat cutter, and you can see I have made several mistakes!"

"That you have, and this is another one!" barks a senator in the rear.

Fulvius scowls at them. Yes, I am an ignorant plebian. But I know one thing: recalling Flamininus would be a mistake! He has already defeated Philip's forces, and now he is closing in on him. When the spring thaws come, he can engage Philip, and end this war by summer."[cv]

"This is preposterous!" barks the Senate Elder. "We always draw lots. It goes back to the time of our kings!"

"Not always," retorts Oppius. "In times of peril, we have given our generals an imperium to stay until the war is finished." He points at Scipio, sitting in the front row. "Such a general sits with us today."

Fulvius exchanges a glance with Oppius, then crosses his arms over his chest. "We will not approve any proposal that does not keep Flamininus in Macedonia."

Scipio nods at Gaius Cornelius. The new consul balls up his pudgy fists. "I will support Flamininus remaining in Macedonia," he blurts, spit flying from his mouth.

"You would give up your chance to go to lead our army against Macedonia?" Minucius says, gaping at him. Gaius purses his lips and stares at the floor, looking like a stubborn child.

The Senate Elder examines the faces of his stunned colleagues. "We know you tribunes have the power to veto any Senate proposal. But this, this would break with our traditions!"

Traditions can take a boat to Hades, Scipio thinks. He rises from his place. "Circumstances change," he says, "and we must change to meet them." The senators stare at him, but no one speaks.

The Elder sighs wearily. "Apparently they do, Censor. Let us all discuss this. Perhaps we can come to an agreement."

Two hours later, a new proposal is finalized. Gaius Cornelius and Quintus Minucius are both assigned different parts of North Italia, to continue the war with the Gauls.[cvi] After finalizing the assignment of several praetorships, the exhausted senators file out from the chambers, wandering down the Curia steps to join the bustling masses inside the Forum square.

Fulvius and Oppius exit together, ignoring the angry looks of the senators that pass by them. Scipio trots down the Curia steps and joins them as they step into the Forum square.

"That was a wise and courageous move," he says loudly, attracting the ears of several senators. "Flamininus is clearly our best general!" When the other senators are out of earshot, Scipio steps closer to the two tribunes.

"I will abide by our agreement. Tell me again: what do you want?"

"Just what we mentioned before," Fulvius replies. "We want limits on the slaves owned by the wealthy landowners. Those slaves are taking jobs from our citizens."

"The small farmers cannot compete with the patricians' lower food prices," adds Oppius, "They have to sell their farms. Then they wander into the city, looking for work where none is to be found. Our citizens lie idle, and they have nothing but bread and circuses to fill their life." He shakes his head. "Or they join one of the Aventine gangs."

"They are fed and entertained for free," Scipio replies, his eyes searching the tribunes' faces. "Is that such a terrible life?"

"It denies them the thing most important to a man," Oppius says. "A sense of purpose. They have nothing to make, to grow; no one to fight. They are rudderless boats."

Scipio rubs the back of his neck. "I understand. But that will be a tough regulation to pass. Most of our patricians employ hundreds of slaves."

Fulvius shrugs, his face a stone. "You are the most powerful and respected man in Rome. You defeated the Three Generals—and Hannibal. You will figure it out."

So much for being the most respected man in Rome, Scipio thinks, smiling to himself.

Oppius spreads his mangled hands entreatingly. "Part of this problem is yours, Imperator. Italia is flooded with the slaves you sent back from your conquests in Iberia and Africa. They are taking our work!"

Scipio's face flushes. "My intent was to restore the farms that General Fabius burned to delay Hannibal's assault on Rome."

"Your intention may have been noble, but its effect is no less onerous," Fulvius growls. "You can repay us by solving the problem you generated." He spins about and strides from Scipio's presence. With a final, disapproving glance, Oppius trots after him.

Insolent peasants! How in Olympus can I get enough votes to remedy this? I'll have to get some of the Latins' support. Who among them truly cares about the farmers?

Scipio sighs. His right hand twitches with anxiety. *You know who. He is your only choice. If he comes over, the others will follow.*

Scipio trots back up the Curia steps. He approaches a knot of Latin senators who are conversing by the entryway. The senators are ringed around Gorgus, a Latin Party elder who is lauding Cato's plan to limit women's expenditures on jewelry and clothing.[cvii]

"Cato was just here a minute ago, Scipio says. "Where did he go?"

Gorgus smirks. "Are you sure you want to find him?" he says, with a wink at his colleagues, "Or do you want to make sure you go in the opposite direction?" The senators chuckle. They see Scipio's expression and cease.

"Must I ask you again, Gorgus?" Scipio says, taking a step nearer to him.

"You must have left your sense of humor in Carthage," he replies, avoiding Scipio's eyes. He points to a wide avenue to the north. "He went north, up the Via Piscarium."

"Gratitude," Scipio snaps. He hurries across the forum and enters the broad cobbled street, walking past the half-dozen fish markets that line its entrance. He does not have to go far to find Cato.

Cato is perched atop a toilet hole in the street's u-shaped public lavatory. His toga is draped around his hips, with his wool subligaculum gathered about his ankles. Cato is busy lecturing a young man who sits two holes down from him.

"All this newfound wealth from the wars is weakening us," Cato declares. "Where are the agrarian values of purity and strength that made us great? We are turning into a nation of soft-assed Greeks!"

At the mention of "soft-assed," the young man shifts about uncomfortably. "I am sure, Senator. That is what my grandfather says, too."

"He is right," Cato replies. "Get back to the land, and its simple virtues of hard work and honesty. A man has all he needs there."

Jupiter's cock, Scipio thinks, *he would have us all living in huts! Well, at least he can't escape me here.* He gathers the bottom of his toga in his left arm and steps over the low curb that fronts the open-air entryway.

Scipio pulls his cotton loincloth down and plops down next to Cato. He listens to the sound of the aqueduct water gurgling beneath him, flushing its way to the sewer canal of the Cloaca Maxima.

Cato turns from the youth and glances to his left. He draws back, surprised at the sight of Scipio next to him.

"Couldn't you wait until you made it back to your private toilet?" Cato rasps, his hands clenched in his lap. He gestures toward the busy street, where several passersby are staring at the two togaed senators. "Aren't you worried your effete friends will see you at a commoner's toilet? With me? You might lose your status as First Senator!"

"Cease your childish taunts, I need to speak with you." Scipio says. The youth next to Cato yanks up his leggings and hurriedly departs --he is well aware of the animosity between the two men.

"Did you come here to gloat about your Senate victory today, Scipio? Your lapdog Flamininus had best conquer Philip, or you will never see another Hellenic as consul."

Scipio shifts about uneasily. *Gods, the man does not waste words.* "I have no concern about him—he is a warrior born. My concern is for the small farmers. I need your support for them."

Cato barks out a laugh. "And when did you ever care about we who till the earth, patrician? When was the last time you had dirt under your fingernails?"

"When Laelius and I built Marcus Silenus' pyre on the battlefields of Zama," Scipio says levelly, "while you were sitting safely in Rome."

"So you did it once," Cato replies. "Hardly a working man's lot."

Don't let this sanctimonious little ass get to you. Scipio spreads his hands. "I ask you to put aside our differences for this one issue: to limit the number of slaves the large landowners can possess. Then our citizens can find land jobs, and the small farmers can compete with the big ones."

"Oh ho! So *that* is why the tribunes insisted Flamininus stay in Macedonia. You made a deal with them!" Cato smirks. "That was well played, I give you that."

"Give me your voice and vote instead." He cocks an eyebrow at Cato. "After all, you are a farmer. You and your old friend Flaccus."

Cato's bushy eyebrows arch up his forehead. He rises, then quickly sits down. "Flaccus! He is not a farmer, he is an estate manager! His slaves do all his work! Do not put him in the same sentence with me!"

There is dissension between them. Good. "Just so, Cato. Then you know your manager friend has bought the small farms around him, because the farmers cannot compete with his cheaper prices—because they cannot afford slaves."

"I do not follow his every move," Cato huffs. He gestures toward a waiting slave in the corner. "Bring me a sponge."

The bony young Iberian hurries over with a ceramic urn filled with water. Four long-handled sponges jut from its mouth. Cato takes one and rises halfway up, cleaning himself.

Scipio watches the street traffic. "Your father was a small farmer, was he not?" Cato is silent.

Scipio scrapes his sandaled toes across the floor slabs, waiting. "Well?" he finally says.

Cato still does not reply. Scipio smirks. "You are right, I do make mistakes. I thought better of you, and that was another one." He pulls up his loincloth and rises to leave.

"If I speak for your policy, what do I gain?" Cato blurts. He flips the sponge back into the urn and stands up, carefully rearranging his toga.

Scipio stares at him, as if seeing a new man. "What do you gain? I thought I would never hear you ask that kind of question. Very well, what do you want?"

Cato's face flushes. "There is a praetorship open for Sardinia. I would have it."[cviii]

It would give him power and prestige, but it would get him out of Rome for a year. "That is certainly possible. The new consuls would doubtless favor one with your 'unimpeachable character.' I will see what I can do."

"I want to make the slave limitation proposal myself, so that it will be credited to the Latin Party." Cato says, his chin set for a fight.

So that it will be credited to you. "I don't care who proposes it, I just want it done," Scipio says, waving his hand as if shooing a fly away. "Will you do it? Tell me now, I am anxious to leave this smelly place."

"Agreed," Cato mutters. "But there had best be no tricks!"

"Such suspicions are beneath you. You have been associating too long with Flaccus." Scipio treads out into the street.

"I will keep to my promise," Cato shouts to Scipio's back. "But do not think I have forgotten about the waste and theft I saw when I was your quaestor! There will be an accounting!"

Without turning around, Scipio jerks his right fist back toward Cato, his middle finger extended in the Roman stabbing gesture.

He hurries back past the fish markets, wrinkling his nose as he passes the open stands. *Gods, I have had enough bad smells today!*

Scipio pauses when he enters the Forum square, scanning the stalls that surround its perimeter. *I need something to wash the taste of politics from my mouth—and my nose. Where's a popina around here?*

He wanders down a Forum side street, nodding at the greetings from passing citizens. Several fellow patricians stop him, making complaints and asking for favors. Scipio spies a local boy from his neighborhood. "Flavus, come here!" Scipio says. The tow-headed ten-year-old trots over, his eyes big as saucers.

"Hold out your arms," Scipio orders. The boy nervously extends his thin limbs.

Scipio unwraps his purple bordered toga and lays it in Flavus' waiting arms, leaving himself wearing only a string-belted white tunic. He gives the boy a newly-minted bronze coin with Scipio's image imprinted on it. "Take that garment to my house. I will be there in a few hours." He pauses. "Three or four hours."

Feeling a weight drop off him, Scipio strolls down the side streets, pausing to buy a careworn hooded cloak from a clothier's stall. He pulls the olive-colored hood over his head and returns to the main market street, shuffling his way through the teeming crowds. No one gives him a second glance.

Scipio comes to a dusty corner wine bar, its stools and counters lined with tired looking men in raggedy tunics. Scipio edges his way to a stool in the back, facing a small table crafted from a battered round shield. Scipio plops down and leans his elbows on the table, staring down into it. A buxom older woman appears, her hamlike arms bulging from her sleeveless blue robe.

The serving woman places her hands on the edge of the table and leans forward, her breasts swaying against the worn fabric. "Hello, Sweetest! I'm Livia," she says, smiling invitingly. "What can I fetch you?"

Livia stares harder into Scipio's hooded face. Her smile vanishes.

"Fish stew," Scipio says quickly, staring down at the table. "And a small flagon of wine. Deep, red wine." The woman bows deeply. "As you will," she lilts, her smile returning. Livia whirls away, her ample hips swaying.

Scipio's eyes follow her. He smiles. *She's a saucy one. And sexy, for all her size!* He leans back, relaxing. He watches two men shaking dice out of a leather cup, alternately laughing and cursing at the results.

A curvaceous young woman edges toward his table, her carmine lips matching her gauzy robe. She smiles at Scipio as she runs her hand down her body, caressing her rounded hips. Scipio slumps down and stares at the table.

"Here now, you get away from him!"

Livia has reappeared, with a pewter serving platter cradled on her forearm. She shakes her thick fist at the prostitute. "He's not for the likes of you, money-butt!" The girl snakes through the tables and merges into the bustling street.

The serving woman crosses her ample arms. "Hmph! They're all over the place! But that's the only work for most of 'em. They can't join the army, like our men do, though they'd fight as well as most of 'em!"

Livia sets the platter on Scipio's table. She takes off a huge stone bowl of shellfish soup, a small loaf of spelt bread, a bronze wine flagon, and a stoppered jug of water.

"Gratitude," he says, reaching for his purse.

The woman's hoary fingers lightly touch his forearm. "No charge for this," she says softly. "You brought my Sertor back from the war safe and sound. He still sacrifices to your health."

She pats his wrist. "Now you just stay here as long as you want. No one will bother you, I can you promise that!" She weaves back through the tables, grabbing empty pitchers and platters.

Scipio blinks, surprised at the tears in his eyes. *There's one who doesn't want anything from me. I guess Virtus is where you find it.* He pours some water into his wine and sips it. His eyebrows arch with surprise. *Gods above, this is excellent! It must cost a fortune!*

He smiles and pours a dribble onto the ground. *To the gods and to you, my Livia.*

The hour passes into another, and still Scipio sits, savoring his solitude. Finally, reluctantly, he pushes himself from the table and wanders back out into the late afternoon sun. He makes his way back toward the main Forum street, heading for his house.

Woozy with drink, Scipio watches the angular light illuminate the stone temples and buildings on the far side of the Forum square. He can see that several senators still stand at the entryway to the Curia, their snow white togas glowing in the fading light. He squints to see if one of them is Cato, but he cannot tell.

Scipio passes under a twenty foot statue of Victoria, the winged goddess of victory. He cranes his neck upward, looking into her stern, noble face. *We need victory. You had best triumph, young Flamininus. Gods know, you have cost me dearly enough for it.*

War Elephant

IX. CYNOSCEPHALAE

SABINA HILLS, ROME, 197 BCE. Dawn light angles over the hills of the Sabina Valley, setting its fields aglow.

A stocky man in a purple-bordered praetor's toga treads down the hillside wheat fields, his white robe glowing in the bright morning sun.

The magistrate tromps into a freshly plowed field without breaking stride. He expertly picks his way through the droppings that line its furrows, planting his weather-beaten sandals onto the earth mounds above them. Minutes later, the man strides into a tiny clearing ringed by a perfect circle of elm trees.

A ancient stone hut stands in the center of the grove. The cottage is empty of any signs of life but it is immaculately clean, the circular clearing around it carefully swept and weeded. A red granite tablet rests next to the hut's slatted door, its surface bearing stone flecks from its newly-chiseled inscription.

Home of Manius Curius Dentatus

Savior of Rome

Man of the People

Praetor Marcus Porcius Cato bends over the plaque, examining it for cracks and imperfections. He runs his calloused finger inside each inscribed letter, feeling the freshly-chiseled edges grate against it. *The work is adequate.* Cato steps inside the hut he visited twenty years ago, when he vowed to resurrect the Porcius family name.[cix]

Cato sees Dentatus' iron sickle and hoe resting next to the empty hearth that dominates the tiny room. *Hm! They are in the same place as*

Cynoscephalae

last I visited. Good. No Roman of this age is worthy to touch them.

Cato recalls the story his father told him many years ago. When Rome was in danger of being overrun by the mighty Samnite king, the unassuming Dentatus dropped his hoe and picked up his sword, taking command of the budding republic's army. Fighting in the forefront of every battle, he led Rome's citizenry to victory over their Samnite oppressors. His mission accomplished, Dentatus returned to his small farm, spurning all offers of power and riches.

Cato slides his farmer's knife from his belt; a curved iron blade with a sweat-darkened oak handle. He extends his hand in a salute towards the hearth, his left arm rigid and unwavering. With a flick of his right hand, he slices into the side of his hoary palm, his eyes unblinking. A ribbon of blood blooms from the side of his hand. Its drops plop softly into the freshly-swept earth.

"Noble Dentatus, accept my sacrifice in your honor." Cato says. When the drops become a trickle, Cato wraps a linen scrap about his wound and clenches his fist, staunching the flow. He stares into the hearth, as if searching for something in it. Something or someone.

"I am now governor to Iberia, sent there to maintain the peace." Cato says to the fire-blackened hole. He grins sardonically. "And I was sent there to be far from Scipio's purview, too, I dare say."

Cato raises his chin, his eyes moist. "I renew my vow to you. I promise to act in accordance with our Latin virtues of strength, severity, courage and honesty in all that I do." And *I will restore the Porcius name*, he thinks. *No one will treat me like they did my father.*

Cato stands silent, as if waiting for a response. All he hears are the boisterous cacklings of the starlings that fill the elms. He shifts his feet uneasily. He bites his lower lip, recalling his tolerance of Flaccus' machinations.

"I am not being completely honest. There are a few things I must do— things that are contrary to our proud Latin traditions. I only do them to protect the genius—the spirit—of Rome."

Cynoscephalae

He shakes his head. "It is so very difficult to balance purity and power, Dentatus. Achieving one seems to detract from the other. But one thing I know: I will purge those who seek to make Greeks of us, including that thief Scipio!" Cato spins about and marches from the hut, heading back to his farm house.

That night, as the sun disappears behind the shouldered Sabina Hills, a small cloaked figure eases his horse down the dirt road to Cato's farm house. As he has done before, he ties his horse in the olive grove adjoining Cato's sprawling set of stone buildings. He sidles through the shadowed archway that leads to Cato's cottage, slinking back into the shadows when he hears someone coming,

The figure eases along the side of Cato's house until he comes to Cato's reading room at the back of the house. Peering into the window, he sees Cato is bent over his writing table, his broad back to him. The figure pads silently through the open doorway. His hand reaches into his satchel as he draws close.

Cato straightens up. He spins about and sees the man approaching him. His eyes flash.

"There you are!" he exclaims irritably. "Did anyone see you, Xerses?"

The man throws back his hood and steps into the light, revealing himself to be an elderly Greek, his curly gray beard sculpted into a spearpoint.

"I took pains to avoid everyone," Xerses replies. His sinewy hand darts from his satchel, holding a worn yellow scroll. "It's time for your lesson!"

Cato sighs. "If the Hellenics found out that I was learning Greek,[cx] I would never hear the end of it."

"It is the language of the great philosophers, of scholars from all parts of the world," Xerses replies. "And you are a scholarly man, friend Cato, in spite of all your hard-handed bluster."

"The language of a dying culture," Cato says. "I should be learning

Iberian, for my new appointment."

"What is it the great Scipio once said?" Xerses replies. "You must learn from your enemies to defeat them? The Hellenics all speak Greek. Now you will learn why they do."

"Do not use Scipio's name in my presence," Cato blurts. "I will ruin him and his degenerate party, with or without learning Greek!" He snatches Xerses' scroll. "Where were we?"

Xerses smiles. "Tell me, in Greek—how do you say 'I want another lesson'?"

Cato frowns petulantly, looking like a reluctant schoolboy. "*Thelo enna allo mathima.*"

"Very good," Xerses replies. "You are coming along nicely." His eyes twinkle mischievously. "Soon you'll be as educated as the patricians from the oldest families!"

"Wise men learn more from fools than fools from the wise,"[cxi] Cato says. "I will learn what these Greeks have to say. But if they are so smart, how come Flamininus is over there protecting them?"

CYNOSCEPHALAE, THESSALY, 197 BCE. "What! Where are they?" Philip demands, jumping up from the gilt oak throne inside his camp tent. "Flamininus has his men up here?"

"They are in the hills southwest of camp," Commander Philocles replies, strapping on his bronze cuirass. "There's thousands of Aetolian infantry with them, and five hundred cavalry." He tightens the cuirass' leather side straps. "Our men are sorely beleaguered. I'm going up there."

"No, I need you here," Philip replies. He turns to his cavalry captain. "Mitron, take a thousand of our cavalry over there. Now!"

"I hear and obey," the burly captain replies. He trots from the tent.

"That's just Flamininus' advance force, you know," Philocles says.

"His legions will soon be here. We have to strike first."

"How can we do that?" Philip sputters. "Half our men are out foraging!" "[cxii] He runs his manicured fingers through his dark ringlets, knocking his gold crown askew. "They're scattered all over the hills! We're not ready to fight the Romans."

"Ready or not, here they come," declares Philocles. "We can either take the fight to them or wait for them to come after us. But they are coming, my King. Our scouts saw them massing outside of their camp."

Philip is silent, rubbing his lightly bearded chin. His mouth wrinkles with distaste. "If we wait for them to assault our camp, we lose the advantage of our high ground," he says, more to himself than Philocles. "But if we attack, we can move downhill on them."

"We have a phalanx of eight thousand men in camp," [cxiii] Philocles says. "We can send them down the right side of the ridge. But the ground is rocky and uneven there, it will be difficult to maintain our spear wall."

"It's just not a good time to fight!" Philip huffs. "That fog is still lying down there—you can't see your hand in front of your face!"

"Good!" Philocles replies, his voice rising with excitement. "We'll pop out of the fog before they know what's happening! It'll give us the element of surprise." He grimaces. "Though it will be difficult to do that and hold formation."

Philip drums his fingers on the arm of his throne. *What would Alexander the Great do?* He sees Philocles staring expectantly at him, his mouth tight with impatience. *He wouldn't be sitting on his ass like you are, he'd take the offensive.*

Philip shoves himself up from his throne. "I still don't like fighting today, but we have no choice. I'll lead the phalanx attack down the right slope. Philocles, you take the left wing. Make sure you get the foragers assembled as soon as you can and bring them down next to me. Don't wait to get them all into a phalanx—send them down in columns as soon as you can get enough men to put one put together. I will need you to protect my flank."

"I'll be down there as soon as I can," Philocles says. He slides on his black-plumed dome and strides from the tent.

"Be there sooner than that!" Philip shouts to Philocles' back. He waves at his two male slaves. "Step to it, beasts! Prepare me for battle!"

The slaves help Philip into his polished, silver-plated armor. Shining like a god from heaven, he strides from his tent and clambers onto his armored black stallion. Philip wheels his horse about and faces his Companions, the hundred elite cavalry who comprise his royal guard.

"The Romans are coming, boys. It's the final battle today. Glory or death, for them or for us!"

Philip gallops up the slope to the ridgeline summit, his gold-hemmed black robe billowing behind him. The Companions ride beside him, their faces grim. The proud warriors are eager to avenge their army's loss at the Aous Gorge.

"Wait here," the king tells his lead officer. He trots to the front of his phalanx, a hedgehog of spears five hundred men wide and sixteen rows deep.

He calls over Jagoda, the phalanx's commander. "Follow me to the dropoff, we're going to plan our attack." he tells his lanky young captain. "We're going to come down upon them like an avalanche."

Philip trots toward the ridge line a half-mile away. As he nears the edge he notices several scattered mounds of Roman bodies. He turns to Jagoda. "These corpse piles are a good omen. Our men in the hills are winning!"

The words have no sooner left the king's mouth than a wide-eyed Mitron trots up to him, his gashed cheek streaming blood. "The Aetolians overwhelmed us,"[cxiv] he declares. "There are thousands of them in the crags below here." He places his hand on Philip's forearm. "We have to help them or we're lost."

Cynoscephalae

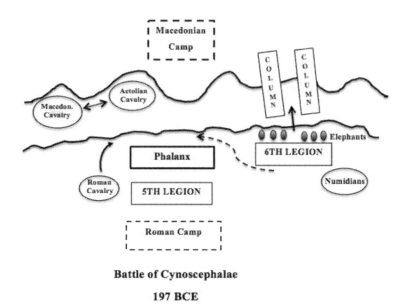

Battle of Cynoscephalae

197 BCE

That's it. There's no turning back. "Get your men over to the right flank of the phalanx. Join forces with them and retake the hills." He turns to his infantry captain. "Jagoda, I want to make sure the Romans don't breach our phalanx's center, like Scipio did at Zama. Double the depth and close ranks." [cxv]

"That will make it difficult for the men to hold their spears," Jagoda replies.

"Fuck their spears! They'll just get in the way marching down that slope. Tell them to leave their sarissas and bring their swords. We're cutting our way through the Romans!"

While Philip directs his cavalry and light infantry to the far side of the phalanx, the phalangites bunch up into a long, thick, rectangle thirty-two men deep and a quarter-mile wide, their bared swords at the ready.

Philip rides back to the front of the new formation and waves his sword over his head. "Quiet," his officers yell. "Your king is speaking!"

Cynoscephalae

"All right, men," Philip shouts "We're going to go over that ridge and come down upon the Romans like an avalanche! Remember, you are the finest warriors in the world; no Greek, no Egyptian, no Syrian has withstood your assault. The Romans shall be no different!"

The phalangites roar out their agreement, joined by the peltasts and cavalry on their right flank. Philip rides to the edge of the ridge and looks down. There, in the mist, he hears the distant clanks and shouts of an army on the move. *This is it—we win or lose Greece. Philocles, you'd better get here soon.*

He takes a deep breath. "Attack! Forwaaard!"

The command is relayed down the lines. The king eases his horse down the steep, rocky slope. His guard follows him, with the phalanx close on their heels. The reenergized light infantry and cavalry enter the adjoining hillside, driving back the Aetolians who preyed upon them. Slowly, implacably, the Macedonian army flows down the slope, readying themselves for a final rush into the Romans.

At the Roman camp, Flamininus is standing out in front of his command tent, surrounded by his Roman and Aetolian officers. The young commander's face is flush with excitement—his scouts have reported that Philip's army is massing on the ridge in front of his camp.

"The Aetolians are being routed, and Philip's army is coming after us." His fist bobs nervously as he paces in front of his officers. "We've got to help out the Aetolians and our light infantry, before Philip destroys them. And us."

"He's attacking on our left," the Aetolian scout reports. "Hard to tell how many men he has in this fog, but it's thousands."

"Then we shall send thousands against him!" young Flamininus replies, his voice rising. "I'm taking the Fifth Legion up on the left, with three hundred Roman cavalry."

"Good, let's settle this!" replies Vibius, Flamininus' barrel-chested senior commander. "I'm tired of chasing that weaseling bastard all over the mountains."

Flamininus nods. "No more chasing, Vibius. This is the day of resolution. I want to you take the Sixth Legion and come up alongside me on the right, to protect the Fifth Legion's flank."

Marcus Aemilius steps out from the knot of officers. "General, may I speak?"

Flamininus nods at the stocky little officer. "You have certainly earned that right, Marcus."

"I had the privilege of knowing the great Marcus Silenus. He was my, uh, mentor while I was growing up. He told me that strength and speed were critical at the outset of a battle. We have both with us: the elephants and the Numidian cavalry. We can employ them for maximum effect on the right flank, where the grade is not so steep."

"Elephants and Africans?" says Flamininus. "Those have not been used much in this region—these steep hills aren't the African plains, after all."

Marcus waves his hand airily and grins. "Not to worry. Vibius and I can handle them."

Flamininus quells a smile. *Did he say "Vibius and I?" The pup talks like he is a senior commander!* "What say you to that, Vibius?"

"Marcus has earned my trust time and again," Vibius replies. "We can use them to supplement our heavy infantry over there."

Flamininus rolls his eyes. "Very well. Put those elephants in front of our standards. They can be our shock troops. The Numidians will protect the right flank. Now get your men ready to attack, and wait for the horn."

The officers file out. Flamininus' face is calm, but his heart races with anxiety. *Your trained elephants had better work, Scipio, or we will both be the worse for using them.*

Minutes later, Flamininus is at the front of the Fifth Legion, mounted on a white stallion captured from his earlier conquest of the

Macedonians. He removes his black plumed helmet and looks out over the serried rows of his five thousand hastati, principes, and triarii.

"I am not one for windy speeches," he shouts. The soldiers erupt in mock cheers. Young Flamininus flushes, but he grins good-naturedly. He places his hand on the pommel of his sword, and his face becomes stern.

"I only want to remind you that the Macedonians you fight today, these are the same men we routed in a pitched battle at the Aous, the same foes that General Galba defeated before that.[cxvi] Victoria, she again awaits us. But we have to go up that hillside to meet her. Are you ready to kiss the goddess? Long will be the feast, and great will be the plunder she gives you!"

Amid enthusiastic roars, Flamininus dons his helmet and walks his horse up the fog-shrouded hillside. A scout scrambles down from the upper slope, his horse sliding under the loose rocks.

"The Macedonians are up there, General. They're coming straight down at us. The mist hides them, but it sounds like there are many, many of them."

Flamininus' heart flutters in his chest. *Gods, I wish I could see what we're getting into!* "Get back up there, Scout. Let me know when they are within four spear casts of us."

The scout whirls around and disappears back into the foggy slope. "Get Fontius!" Flamininus tells one of his guards. The guard returns with the grizzled First Tribune of the Fifth Legion.

"We are ready to take heads," Fontius rasps. His one eye twinkles merrily as he pulls out his dagger. "I may even take a few ears for my belt, just like the Gauls!"

Mars' cock, the man is half-barbarian! "Just get the men ready to march immediately. When the scout returns we attack."

"Most of us are General Scipio's veterans," Fontius says. "We know how to save our energy. We can fight to the night!"

Cynoscephalae

Soon, Flamininus hears the sound of galloping hooves. *Here he comes! Get ready to give the signal.*

The scout's horse emerges from the fog. Its headless rider is slumped over it, roped to the horse's neck. The scout's head dangles from a rope tied to his belt, its shocked face staring at Flamininus.

A deafening roar erupts from the fog behind the horse. Eight thousand Macedonians scream out their war cries. A wall of phalangites trots down the hillside, waving their iron swords high over their round bronze shields.

Flamininus' eyes start from his head. "Attack!" he shouts wildly. "At them, men. Attack!"

The cornu blare three times. The Romans tramp up the incline, each spaced three feet from his compatriots, their javelins pointing out in front of their scuta.

The Macedonians crash into the Fifth's shield wall, battering at the hastati from all angles. The thick press of enemy gradually pushes the legionnaires back down the hill, leaving scores of Roman bodies to mark the army's retreat.

Flamininus gallops back and forth behind the front lines, desperate to halt the retreat. "Don't give in to them! You are the pride of Rome! Beat them back!"

Fontius trots across the center of the battle line, shoving men into line with their fellows, calling for replacements to those who fall. "Don't back up to these pussies," the tribune bellows.

The sturdy old captain marches out from the front line. He steps sideways and jabs his sword into the thigh of an unwary Macedonian, who howls with pain. "Come on, get at them!" he screams.

"Bring up the velites!" General Flamininus yells. "Get their spears behind the hastati!" The Roman light infantry lope into the wide space between the front-line hastati and the backup ranks of the principes. "Loose!" Flamininus calls, a command echoed down the line by his

304

centurions.

The velites fling round after round of javelins into the advancing Macedonians. Without their spear wall to protect them, hundreds are pierced by the relentless rain of bronze, crawling among their fellows. The Macedonian horns sound. The phalangites draw back to regroup, leaving a thirty-foot space between themselves and the Romans.

Minutes later, King Philip rides into the space, followed by a score of his guards. "At them, men!" he shouts. "You almost had them! Follow me!" Philip spurs his horse into the front Roman line, renewing the fight.

Mad with the urge to conquer, Philip careens about like a madman, striking at the hastati with his gleaming silver sword. "Come on, boys! They'll be a fine feast tonight after we run these pigs away. Come on!"

Flamininus trots along behind the front rows of his hastati, exhorting his men to dig in and hold their place. He watches Philip boldly attacking the Roman front. *He may be a sly as a weasel, but he is as fierce as one, too.*

The reinvigorated Macedonians charge the Roman line. They batter at the legionnaires' helmets with their swords, and ram their bossed shields into the Romans' curved scuta. The force of their attack pushes the Fifth Legion farther down the scrabbly slope. Dozens of Romans lose their footing and fall. They are quickly stabbed by phalangites who storm into every break in the line, determined to destroy the Romans and feast all night.

I'm losing hundreds of men, Flamininus thinks. *They're going to break at any moment.* "Call the principes forward," he screams to his bugler. The horns echo across the din, sounding the call for a line replacement.

The principes step to the front, replacing the hastati. The veterans calmly deflect the Macedonians' mad sword blows, and turn their shields to deflect the ramming shields. Waiting for an opening, the veterans jab their spears into the Macedonian's arms and legs, knowing the cuts will eventually weaken them.

The Roman line holds, but battle-tested phalangites resist the Romans' efforts to push them up the hill. The Macedonians replace their first two rows from the thirty rows behind them. Both sides battle resolutely, and the fight becomes a stalemate.

They won't break! Philip fumes. He rides over to Jagoda, one of his infantry commanders. "Tell Mitron to get some of our cavalry into them," he says. "We'll destroy them from the side!"

The sun rises high over the surrounding hills, Mitron leads two hundred Macedonian and Thessalian cavalry into the legion's left flank, abandoning their hillside conflict with the Roman riders. Dozens of legionnaires fall to the rampaging cavalry. Mitron's riders rush into the breaches, and scores more Romans die.

Desperate to save their flank from disintegrating, the left side Romans break formation and swarm over the stampeding riders, pulling them from their horses. As soon as a rider hits the ground, a Roman stabs him down while another leaps onto the horse. Scores of improvised Roman cavalry lunge about Mitron's riders, chopping down at them with their swords. The Macedonian cavalry retreat and regroup, gathering themselves for another charge.

The Roman horns sound another call. The rear line triarii step out and march along the left flank in a three-deep column. They kneel in front of the oncoming Macedonian riders and dig their seven foot spears into the ground, forming an angled spear wall against the cavalry attack.

"Break that line!" Mitron shouts. He gallops out, leading his riders at the triarii. The Macedonian cavalry ride into the spear wall. Dozens of horses and riders impale themselves, crashing on top of the older legionnaires. Their spears broken, the old warriors calmly draw out their short swords and pull their shields off of their backs. They step over their fallen enemies and coolly thrust at any riders who dare approach them, determined that none will advance. The Macedonians continue the attack.

Cynoscephalae

The Fifth Legion is beset by enemies on two sides. The front ranks hold position, but they cannot advance. Scores of Romans fall under the relentless attacks from front and side. The legion edges ever backward.

Our men are trapped. Our only hope is the right wing.[cxvii] Flamininus races to his right, heading toward Vibius' legion. The sun breaks through the clouds, lighting up the misty battlefield. *The fog is lifting! Gods above, I hope that is an omen!*

When Flamininus reaches him, Vibius is leading his legion up the incline in a slow march, closing in on the massing Macedonian troops at the top of the ridge. Twenty mail-covered elephants march ahead of the Roman front, as perfectly aligned as the legionnaires.

"What's going on?" Flamininus asks. Vibius stabs a finger at the ridgeline. They're collecting up there, looks like there's two, maybe three thousand of them."

"Those Macedonians are late to the battle," Flamininus notes. "They're still in marching formation, arriving in columns."

"All the better," Vibius says. "They're nigh impossible to beat when they're in that cursed phalanx."

Remember what Marcus Aemilius said about strength and quickness. Flaminius thinks. *Strike while the iron is hot!* "We have to get at them now, before they organize." He stares at the mighty beasts in front of him. "Send the elephants at them. Where are the Numidians? Are they ready?"

"On the far right flank," Vibius replies. He smiles wryly. "They're certainly ready. They're chasing around like madmen, waiting for the attack signal."

"Let's use them and keep our cavalry in reserve," Flamininus says. "When the elephants hit the Macedonian front, send the Numidians into the Macedonians' left side. Those Africans were raised with elephants."

"It is done," Vibius replies. The old commander waves over one of his messengers and sends him away with the order.

Cynoscephalae

Flamininus and Vibius ride out to the front of the Sixth Legion and rein up behind the center of the elephant line. "There's Hamilax, he's the lead mahout." Vibius says.

He shouts over to a lean man standing next to the largest elephant. The mahout wears a leopard skin robe and sharply pointed helmet, a fourteen-foot goad resting against his shoulder. The lead mahout trots over to Vibius and prostrates himself upon the earth.

"I am yours to command," Hamilax declares in his pidgin Latin, his nose touching the ground.

"Get up and get ready," Flamininus barks, his voice edgy with nerves. "When you hear the horn sound twice, you will charge the elephants up to that ridge. I want them trampling through the front lines. If we drive them away, the rest will follow."

"The elephants, they mighty warriors," Hamilax declares. He bares his pointed white teeth. "They go wild there, kill many men. You keep Romans away from them."

"The Numidian cavalry will join you," Vibius says. "They will come in from the side."

Hamilax' grins widens. "Ah! Numidians know how fight with elephants. No problem." He repeatedly flashes the fingers on both of his light brown hands. "We all kill many-many, you see!" The mahout sprints over to his fellows, barking out orders in Carthaginian.

"Tell the tribunes and centurions to get ready for a rapid march," Flamininus says to Vibius. "The Sixth Legion will follow the elephants, once the beasts are two spear casts from us." He grips Vibius' wrist. "Tell them we are not coming back down, no matter what the cost." Vibius nods solemnly and gallops away.

Minutes later, Vibius returns with one of the legion's cornicines. "Prepare to sound two short blasts," Flamininus tells the bugler. The soldier lifts his large, g-shaped horn to his shoulder.

Flamininus stares up at the Macedonian columns massing along the

Cynoscephalae

ridge. He looks to his right and left and sees nothing but long rows of Roman soldiers, standing rigidly at attention as they await the command to charge.

Gods, they are such fine men. I hope I'm not killing us all! Flamininus stands rigidly, his fists clenched.

"General?" Vibius says, his tone as much an order as a question.

Flamininus raises his head, his eyes fixed on the rocky slope in front of him. "Sound the charge!" he orders. The cornicen blows two short notes.

The elephants lurch forward, goaded by the mahouts running next to them. Each elephant is flanked by a contubernium of twenty velites, agile infantrymen trained to defend the elephants from attackers while eluding the beasts' random charges.

Trumpeting with excitement, the huge beasts trample up the rocky slope. The legions' maniples march behind them at safe distance, the men anxiously watching the attack of these strange beasts.

The Numidian cavalry trot alongside the legion's right flank. Carrying a brace of javelins and a small round shield, the lightly armored Africans flow over the terrain in a loose square of two thousand men. They watch the elephants' charge, waiting for their chance.

The elephants rumble quickly up the ridge. When the beasts approach the edge the Macedonian horns erupt from everywhere across the ridgeline, as Philip's buglers frantically call the arriving troops to mass into a phalanx. But the signal comes too late—the elephants are upon them.

The ten-ton beasts crash into the two columns arrayed along the ridgeline, bashing the heavily armored phalangites aside as if they were children. Spurred on by the mahouts, the elephants stampede across the front of the Macedonian army, trampling down scores of hapless warriors. The pachyderms swing their tusks into the spearmen that charge them, flinging them high into the air. Screams flow through the Macedonian front, following the path of Flamininus' juggernauts.

Dozens more Macedonians charge forward with long spears, intent on goading the elephants from the battle. The Roman contubernia swarm at them. The legionnaires deflect the spears with their broad shields and dodge past them, leaving them free to stab their javelins and swords into the shieldless Macedonians. All the while, the elephants rage on.

High upon the backside of the ridge, Commander Philocles watches in helpless fury as the proud phalangites retreat back into their own men, trying frantically to escape the rampaging elephants.[cxviii]

"Get the cavalry to follow me down there!" he shouts to one of his captains. "We're going at those Romans who are protecting the elephants!"

Philocles gallops out from the back of the left column, heading toward the elephants. Five hundred cavalry follow him, intent on driving the Roman vanguard down the hillside.

The Macedonian commander draws his sword and leans over his horse's neck, guiding his stallion toward a knot of velites near the closest elephant. He hears the yells of his men behind him, screams of alarm and warning. Looking over his shoulder, he observes a dense cloud of dusky-skinned riders arrowing across the top of the ridge, heading straight into the side of his oncoming cavalry.

"Fucking Africans!" he mutters. He turns his horse toward the oncoming horde.

The lead Numidians whirl through the Macedonians as if they were trees scattered along the hillside, pausing only to fling javelins into their slower-moving foes. Yipping and crying, the Africans delve into the phalangites milling along the front columns. The Numidians lean low aside their mounts, bending over to stab their lances into the bodies of the foot soldiers, striking into a new enemy before the old one has fallen to the ground.

Hundreds of Macedonians ram into the lines in the center, desperate to escape the maelstrom of beasts and men. Hundreds more run out into the open spaces, flinging away shields and weapons as they dash madly for the safety of their camp. Bleeding from dozens of spear cuts, the maddened elephants wreak destruction in every direction, their mahouts goading them on.

Philocles pushes his horse into the center of the milling phalangites. "Back to formation, you cowards!" he rages. "You are the greatest warriors on earth! Get back there!" The crazed soldiers continue to swarm past him, ignoring Philocles' curses and sword blows.

"Cowards! Cowards!" he shouts.

A sword stabs into the side of his horse. The beast rears sideways and topples, pitching Philocles to the ground. He shoves himself upright, dodging the terrified infantrymen that flee from the rampaging Numidians.

"Guards! Where in Hades are you?" he shouts. "Bring me a horse!'

A young African notices the glint of gold on Philocles' sword pommel. He waves over six of his companions, signaling that they are to follow him. Lancing down the Macedonian foot soldiers in front of them, the Numidians close in and encircle Philocles. The Africans halt, studying the black bearded man who glowers at them, naked sword in hand.

"I will fetch much ransom," Philocles says, sheathing his weapon. The uncomprehending Numidians stare back at him. They talk to one another, glancing at the Macedonian commander. They point at his silver armor and jeweled scabbard. Several trot slowly toward him, their lances aimed at his chest.

So that's the way it's going to be. The Macedonian commander reaches inside the top of his cuirass. He pulls out a long gold chain and lets it fall across his breastplate. A hammered gold likeness of Eros, god of love, dangles against his armored chest. He pulls it to his lips and kisses it. *Sorry, Veronika. We had a good life, though. Take care of the children.* The Numidians edge closer.

Philocles whips out his sword. "All glory to mighty Macedonia!" he screams. He runs at the closest Numidian, dodging under his outthrust spear With a skill born of a hundred combats, he slashes open the African's thigh and spins about, his sword thrusting at the man he knows must be behind him. His sword catches the Numidian's horse in the throat. The animal rears back, flinging the rider to the ground.

The smiles disappear from the Africans' faces. As one, Numidians lunge in at defiant commander. One strikes Philocles in the side, wedging his spear between the front and back plates of his cuirass. Another catches him in his upper arm, lancing open an artery. Gushing blood, Philocles stumbles about the battleground, blindly swinging his sword. The Numidians lunge in. Their spears thrust home.

Flamininus leads the Sixth Legion over the ridgeline in time to see the Numidians gathered in a circle. Curious, he trots his horse forward. He sees the glint of silver armor, shining below a black-plumed helmet.

"Halt!" he screams. Heedless, the Numidians lunge forward.

Flamininus spurs his horse toward the Africans. "Stop, stop!" he shouts. "We want him!" He barges through the gathered Africans, just as Philocles crumbles to his knees.

Flamininus leaps from his horse and races to the fallen commander. He glances at Philocles' wounds, and his mouth tightens. Flamininus kneels into the bloodied earth. He shoves his right arm under the fallen general, and lifts his head up.

"Apologies, Commander. I tried to stop them."

Philocles' face twists into the rictus of a bloodied grin. "Ah, who wants to live forever, anyway?" He coughs up a clot of blood. "Especially if Romans will be running things!"

Philocles clutches his simulacra of Eros. He holds it in front of Flamininus. "Her name is Veronika. She lives in Pella. Give this to her."

Flamininus wipes his wrist across his eyes. "On my honor, It will be done." He lays Philocles back to the earth and waits, watching him die.

Marching shield to shield, the Sixth steps into the infantry mob in front of them, felling hundreds with their carefully placed sword thrusts. The Macedonians press together and plunge toward the rear. Seeing their compatriots swarming at them, the rearmost Macedonians turn and run. Thousands flee, and the battle turns into a rout.[cxix]

On the right flank, the Numidian captain raises his small brass trumpet and blows one long, plaintive note. The Numidians reverse course and swarm back into the fleeing Macedonian cavalry, flinging spears into their backs as they chase them into the hills.

Marcus Aemilius is directing the back rows of the Sixth Legion's principes. He watches the rout unfold in front of him, and he grimaces with disappointment. *They're running away—I won't even get a chance to fight!* The young tribune looks to back down the hill to his left. There, in the distance, he watches the Macedonian phalanx battering the Fifth Legion down the rocky slope, stepping over the corpses of the fallen legionnaires.

Marcus looks at the rows of principes alongside of him, veteran warriors who are watching the hastati cut through the remnants of the fleeing Macedonian columns. *We're just standing here, while our men are being massacred!*

Marcus runs to the front lines, searching desperately for his commander. He spies Flamininus on the right side of the second hastati line, conferring with Vibius.

"General! General!" Marcus shouts, shouldering his way through the spaces between the soldiers. Marcus halts in front of his commander and snaps out a salute, his lungs heaving.

Vibius stares curiously at Marcus, a wry smile on his face. "Why so anxious, Tribune? Our work is almost done here." The commander looks around. "Have you found a vulnerability somewhere?"

"Philip's men, over there!" Marcus shouts, pointing down the hill. "They've pushed the Fifth down toward the bottom of the hill. Now their rear lines are exposed to us! We have the high ground on them!"[cxx]

Flamininus' eyes widen. "He's right, Vibius. Jupiter's cock, those Macedonians aren't even looking this way!"

Vibius nods. "I should have seen that myself."

"Do it, Marcus," Flamininus says. "Take the hastati and principes with you. We have the velites and triarii to finish here." He sees Marcus staring at him, dazed. "Go on, Tribune—you thought of this! Take the men and get down there, before we lose any more!"

"I'll inform the rest of the officers," Vibius says, galloping off to the left flank.

Minutes later, the battle horns sound. Twenty maniples of hastati and principes wheel to the left and march quickly down the hill.[cxxi] Marcus trots out in front of them, holding his sword straight up over his head as if it were a legionary standard, with dozens of standards bobbing behind it.

"Double-time," he shouts excitedly. "Quickly, now, before they can turn around on us!"

The maniples angle down the hill, spreading out as they near the Macedonian rear. Without breaking stride, they march toward the backside phalangites.

The Macedonian commanders scream orders for the rear lines to turn about. The confused soldiers slowly turn and rearrange themselves to face the Romans, colliding with comrades who are pressing toward the front.

Marcus sees a muscular older man wearing a helmet sculpted into a lion's head. *That's got to be one of their commanders.* He runs across the narrowing gap between the Romans and the Macedonians, his sword in his fist.

Commander Jagoda spies the stocky tribune running at him. He sneers. *You want a fight, little man?*

"Leave him to me," he tells his men. Jagoda steps out from the shelter of his guards, pulling his double-edged xiphos from its leather scabbard. He crouches down and holds his large round shield in front of him. Only his face and shins are visible.

Marcus sprints toward Jagoda. *His men are behind him. I've got to make it quick, before they can get to me.* Marcus lowers his head. He plants his rock-hard shoulder inside the recess of his curved shield and stoops over as he closes in.

Marcus rams his scutum into the lower half of Jagoda's shield. He knocks the Macedonian backwards, turning his shield sideways. Marcus stabs his gladius into the arch of Jagoda's foot, delving through bronze scales that cover it until his sword blade is buried in the ground.

Jagoda arcs his head back, screaming in agony as he clutches at his pinioned foot. *Now!* Marcus tells himself. He darts his hand into his belt and flicks it outward.

A knife hilt juts from Jagoda's eye. The Macedonian commander collapses to the ground, twitching out the last moments of his life.

Marcus grabs his throwing knife and throws his shield over his back. He dashes back to his lines, just as the first Macedonian javelin thuds into his shield. Jagoda's guards chase after him, flinging spears and rocks. A rain of javelins drives them back.

"Jagoda has fallen!" cries a Macedonian. "The Romans killed Jagoda!" wails another. Their laments are cut short by the Roman attack.

The legionnaires shove their pila into their enemies' milling back lines, wounding and killing hundreds. Shouts of confusion erupt from Macedonian ranks, soldiers crying that Romans are attacking from the front, the rear, the flanks.

Along the front line of the Fifth Legion, Tiberius Servilius hears the enemies' cries of consternation. The centurion sees scores of Roman standards bobbing about behind the Macedonian rear.[cxxii] *Fortuna be praised, our men are behind them! We have a chance!* He grabs a nearby velite. "Get Rufus and Julius over here," he commands. "They are on the right flank."

The two centurions trot over from their centuries. Tiberius grabs them by the neck and bends their heads to his, that they may be heard over the metallic clangor of the battle.

"The Sixth Legion is behind those bastards! Now we have a chance to break them! When the horn sounds, push forward. Tell the men to shout with joy, as if Jupiter himself has come to fight with us! Go now, and alert the others!"

The two centurions jostle their way into the back lines, yelling for their fellow officers. Tiberius glances back toward the infantry center, where Philip and his Companions are raging against his front-line principes. He watches the king madly hacking at the retreating Roman shield wall, waving forward his royal guard. The Companions cut down several legionnaires near Philip, forcing the Roman line to retreat and reform.

Mars, god of war, give us time to make one more charge. I swear to sacrifice a white ox to you if you will but give us a little more time.

"Give me that," Tiberius shouts to his cornicen, grabbing his horn. The lanky centurion sidles between the first and second rows of the battling principes, edging toward Philip. The principes and hastati watch his every step, waiting for the horn to sound.

Tiberius pauses several yards from Philip. "Hold them just a little longer, men," he shouts to the principes battling in front of him. "We're going to counterattack!"

Tiberius spies the body of a fallen triarii lying behind the second row of hastati. He trots back and grabs the long spear lying under the corpse's stomach. Hurrying back to the front, Tiberius lays the long spear at his feet. With a final prayer, he slips the G-shaped cornu over his head and blows an ear-splitting blast, repeating the call until he gasps for breath. Dozens of cornu echo the call across the legionary lines.

Cynoscephalae

From front to rear, the legion erupts in a deafening, exultant roar. The hastati march to the front, screaming out their challenge, and ram into oncoming Macedonians. Philip's men stare at one another, confused by the Romans' shouts of victory.

"What in Hades is going on?" Philip demands. The captain of his guard cranes his neck into the back lines. "I see Roman standards!" he shouts to his king. "The Romans are attacking from the rear!"

"Silence, fool, you'll panic the men!" Philip shouts. But the damage is already done.

"Romans, the Romans are behind us!" shouts a nearby infantryman. The warning is shouted throughout the lines. Hundreds of Macedonians drop their weapons and run toward the exposed flanks, their eyes fixed on the forested hillsides.

"You idiot!" Philip spits. "He rams his sword into the guard's eyes, spitting on him as he collapses from his saddle. The Companions watch their captain fall, their eyes wide with shock.

"Attack, curse you, attack!" Philip yells to his men. He pushes his horse forward, battering at a hastati's shield. The Companions desultorily follow.

As his legion's horns sound, Tiberius casts down his cornu and picks up the triarii spear. "Let me through!" he shouts to the hastati. The senior centurion shoulders his way to the front of the battle line and runs toward Philip.

Philip notices the centurion coming toward him. *Another glory seeker!* He turns his horse from the hastati and faces Tiberius. He waves his sword at the charging centurion, beckoning him forward.

Tiberius draws his spear back, his eyes fixed on the large stallion's unarmored chest. *If I can bring him down from his high horse, I can kill him.*

A Companion's horse rams into Tiberius, knocking him sprawling. The Companion turns his horse about and tramples over the fallen

317

centurion. Tiberius cries out in pain; his spear tumbles from his crushed right hand.

In a flash, the Macedonian cavalryman jabs his lance into the base of Tiberius' throat, penetrating the unprotected area above his breastplate. Tiberius rolls onto his side, spitting blood.

Philip watches Tiberius fall, smirking as the spear cuts into the centurion. "Thought you had me, eh?" he exults. He looks over his shoulder. "Muster the infantry for a counterattack," he tells his officers. "Kill anyone who shows their back to you!"

Philip's stallion rears back, whinnying in agony. A spear dangles from its heaving chest. Philip catapults backward, crashing to the ground. He lays still, his hands twitching feebly.

Tiberius watches Philip's fall, grinning through his bloodstained teeth. "Some of us can throw spears with either hand, Macedonian cur." He feels a bronze spearpoint break into his spine. His eyes close.

"Philip's down!" a Companion shouts. "Help him!" His royal guard jump from their horses and swarm over their fallen king. Two riders lift him up onto the back of another's horse and lash him against its rider. The Companion gallops from the fray, with Philip drooped across his back. The infantrymen watch their mighty king's exit, horrified.

"The king has fallen!" redounds through the Macedonians, a blow more telling than any Roman assault. The disheartened infantrymen take flight,[cxxiii] dashing from the hillside in every direction.

The Numidians abandon their assault on the rear ranks and gallop after the hordes of fleeing, unarmed Macedonians. Trained since childhood to pursue and kill, the Africans expertly lance down the fleeing foot soldiers, delving into their backs and necks without breaking stride.

The Macedonians who are battling Flamininus' men see thousands of their comrades running from the battle. Their commanders see the futility of fighting any further. They instruct their men to point their spears straight up—the traditional Macedonian sign of surrender.

Cynoscephalae

Watching from the rear lines, Flamininus summons one of his senior tribunes. "What are they doing out there with their spears?"

The tribune shrugs. "Perhaps it is some new maneuver. Some surprise attack."

Flamininus rubs the back of his neck. "Really? I do not see the purpose."

The tribune calls over one of his centurions. "Cassius, you were in Greece. What are those fools doing?"

Cassius looks at them as if they are insane. "They are surrendering."

"Hera help us," Flamininus cries. "Do our men know that?"

Flamininus' men have never seen such a sign. They only know they have an opportunity to finally breach the Macedonians' bristling spear wall. When the Macedonians in front of them raise their spears, the legionnaires cut into the unprotected front lines,[cxxiv] slaying hundreds before the rest drop their spears and draw their swords, determined to die fighting.

"Call them off!" Flamininus shouts, "Call them off! Take nothing but prisoners!" *You fool. You let those warriors get killed like sheep!* The tribunes bark out Flamininus' order, and the Romans step back from their slaughter. The Macedonians drop their swords and clasp their hands behind their backs, awaiting capture.

The deafening din quiets to the sporadic screams of its final victims. The Romans bring out their ropes and chains and begin the tedious task of gathering five thousand prisoners. Eight thousand Macedonians and Thracians lie dead among the boulders and scree, their mounds of dead punctuated with the bodies of seven hundred Romans.[cxxv]

Up in the hills, Philip's Companions huddle about an unsteady Philip. The king sits on a tree stump, sipping from his wineskin, watching the campfire his men built for him. Minutes pass into half an hour. The Companions shift about unsteadily, their ears craned to the faint sounds from the battlefield below them.

"What now?" ventures one of his guard. Philip stares up at him. "Where's Philocles?" he murmurs, dazed. "Where's my commander?"

"Dead," one of his riders tells him. "I saw his body carried away by the Romans."

"Ah, shit!" Philip moans. He peers into the darkness "Mitron! Are you out there?"

"I am here, but not for long." The cavalry commander staggers into the light. His torso is wrapped from chest to stomach in a linen bandage splotched with bloodstains. As Philip watches, the stains widen—and drip.

"Your pardon, my King." He crumples to the ground. Grimacing with pain, he forces himself to a sitting position. "It was a bad day, but we will recover. I can see—"

Mitron falls sideways his breath rasping heavily. He shudders, gasps, and breathes no more.

Philip cradles his face into his hands. His shoulders shake, then shake again. He takes a deep breath and raises his head. His blue eyes burn with determination.

"We march back to Tempe, our last garrison in Thessaly. Then on to Macedonia. Send scouts out to gather our survivors. Tell them to meet me there."

"What about the Romans down there?" says his senior guard. "They might get our scouts." He looks over his shoulder. "Or they could be coming after us."

Philip shakes his head. Several bloodied twigs fall from his dressed ringlets. He picks up one and rolls it in his fingers. "No, we are safe for now. Night is coming, and the Romans will return to their camp. Then they'll be busy selling their prisoners and plunder."[cxxvi] Philip peels the twig and cleans his teeth with it. "Prisoners that were once my men."

"I need a drink." He blurts. Philip grabs a wineskin and tilts it high.

The dark red wine dribbles down his chin. He wipes his wrist across his mouth and looks up at his men.

"Perhaps it is time to send envoys to the Romans," he says to no one in particular. "I am not sure we can extend our empire, but I am sure we can lose it."

His men say nothing.

Night falls upon the Roman camp. Tonight, the sounds of celebration are muted. The exhausted soldiers crawl into their beds, grateful for another day of life.

As the camp torches are lit, Flamininus pulls out a sheaf of finest papyrus from his tent's storage chest. Fighting to keep his eyes open, he dips his quill into a pot of octopus ink and begins his message.

To Publius Cornelius Scipio: Consul, Imperator, and Princeps Senatus of Rome:

Honored Mentor:

> *Philip is broken. The war is won.*

> *Now begins our fight for peace.*

Consul Titus Quinctius Flamininus

By the Way: Gratitude for the elephants and Numidians.

Flamininus rolls up the papyrus and stamps it with his boars' head seal. He summons a messenger.

"Get this to Scipio Africanus in Rome, as soon as possible."

When the messenger leaves. Flamininus unstraps his blood-specked cuirass and slips out of his tunic. Naked and weary, the young consul slips into his sleeping furs. He looks up to make sure no one is in the tent, and the flap is completely closed.

The consul buries his face in the bedding and sobs out his relief.

Gallic Chieftains

X. Surface Glory

MODENA, NORTH ITALIA. 196 BCE. Cassius Severius bends over and groans, rubbing his naked lower back. "Hera's cunt, if I have to swing a pick one more day, I'm going to join the Gauls!"

"And I'll go with you," Agrippa replies. The wiry soldier unties his wool bandana and shakes the sweat from it. "How in Hades can I sweat so much in such a cool clime? If this is what summer's like, I don't want to be here for autumn!"

"Then we'd better get to killing Gauls pretty soon, because autumn is almost here. The architecti say we're going to dig this road all the way to Placentia!"

"Ah, then we're stuck here with this Consul Marcellus, just like we were with that little Cornelius last year," growls Agrippa. "All we did was build roads and forage fields. What a sponge! He would have shit his subligaculum if a Gaul came at him!"

"Well, at least this Marcellus had us built a sturdy camp before we started this slave's work. We're not likely to be taken over by any attacking Gauls."

"Gauls? Hah!" Agrippa spits onto the eight-foot wide trench. "They are the least of our problems! I haven't seen a Boii since we raided those farms up north. I think they've ran away to join the Ligurians. I'm more worried about breaking my fucking back than the Gauls!"

Cassius glances down the mile-long line of half-naked soldiers. He points to a large contingent of hairy, square-boded men. "Look at the Marsi. They've been hauling gravel all day, and still they roll those wheelbarrows as fast at they did in the morning! I wouldn't want to pick a fight with that lot."

Agrippa chuckles. "Me neither. They're a bunch of crazy men, living in those dark forests above Lake Fucinus.[cxxvii] I hear they're too stupid to even know when they're beaten. You cut their legs off and they'll crawl after you on the stumps!"

"Lot of good their prowess will do them here," Cassius retorts. "They'll be digging trenches with us until a new consul comes here!"

A quarter mile east of the two legionnaires, Corolamus peers out from the sheltering scrub of the Modena hillside. His dark brown eyes scan the thousands of half-naked Umbrians and Etruscans working along that section of the road.

The Boii chieftain notices that his enemy's weapons and armor are piled up in the fields next to the new road, a spear's cast from their work. He smiles. *It will take them a while to strap on all their stuff. Especially if we surprise them. Our patience is going to pay off.*

Corolamus hears a soft rustling in the brush behind him. The Boii chieftain spies a bright red plume flashing between the tangled branches, growing closer. He grabs his hand ax and slithers into the brush, determined to kill the Roman before he can cry out.

"It is me!" a man harshly whispers, raising his grimy hands in front of his face.

Corolamus lowers his ax. "By Belenus' cock, what are you doing in that helmet?" the chieftain hoarsely whispers. "I almost split your head!"

The young scout's gap-toothed grin splits his face. "This is my new prize! I took it from a Roman scout this morning. The little bastard was looking to see if any Boii were around." He holds up a bloody ear. "I guess he found one, eh?"

"Good. We don't want anyone warning them. Now get down and be quiet. We're going to charge them."

"Everyone is ready to fight. What are we waiting for?" says the scout.

"We're waiting for them to get tired from working on their road,"[cxxviii] mutters Corolamus.

The afternoon lengthens. The weary Romans stop more frequently now, taking long draughts from the water buckets the velites bring them. Ten thousand Boii line up along the edges of the hillside. They wait silently, watching the legionnaires.

Claudius Marcellus rides along the outside of the excavated roadway, urging the men to finish their trench section before sunset. The consul is a thin and angular man with skin as white as ivory. As a scholarly and refined Hellenic, he was favored by Scipio, who picked him to succeed the feckless previous consul, Gaius Cornelius.

Marcellus has joined coconsul Lucius Purpurio up in the Po Valley. The two are tasked with controlling the Gallic nations while Flamininus completes his operations against Philip in Macedonia.

"C'mon, men, one more hour," Marcellus shouts as he rides along. "Dig it out proper and you'll have an extra ration of wine tonight."

Looking at the miles-long excavation, Marcellus smiles with satisfaction; he has always preferred to build things instead of tearing them down. *Tomorrow we'll put in the gravel and fill it with concrete. Then we'll have a road for five hundred years.*

"I'm going back to camp," he tells Manius, his First Tribune. The squat old warrior nods. "I'll get those lazy Umbrians to put their backs into it."

Marcellus turns his dappled stallion and trots towards camp. *The Senate will be quite pleased if I finish this road. I won't have to get into any battles. I've got twenty thousand infantry and twelve hundred cavalry, the Gauls won't dare attack.*

The consul admires the snow-capped Apennines clawing against the azure sky. *Everything's working out fine. A few raids, a few skirmishes, and I can go back home in honor—and in one piece!*

Surface Glory

Marcellus hears his men shouting. The shouts turn to screams. *What in Jupiter's name is going on down there?* He sees a mile-wide wave of Boii racing across the narrow plain, heading for the trench workers. *Gods save us, the Gauls are attacking!*

The consul stares dazedly at the waves of brown-haired giants. He looks back at the open gates of his sheltering camp, his heart pounding. *You would be shamed forever if you ran in there.* He kicks his heels into his horse and gallops down toward his men.

The Italians fling away their tools and dash for their weapons, but the Gallic cavalry arrives before they reach them. Screaming with delight, hundreds of riders trample their thick-chested mounts through the Romans' piles of weaponry and armor, scattering it across the fields.

The Boii stab their long swords into scores of soldiers who scramble for the weapons and shields, killing dozens more as they frantically strap on their helmets and cuirasses. Many legionnaires wisely grab their shields first to fend off the attacking riders, using them as a defense and weapon.

The allied centurions run in to defend their men, having kept their swords and shields. Chopping at the riders as they hurl past, the line officers yell for the men to group into their maniples.

The Gallic infantry thunders into the milling Italians, chopping down hundreds of unarmored men. The legionnaires, stab their gladii into scores of overly eager Gauls that rush into them alone. They form roughshod maniples and step slowly backward, grabbing shields and swords from whatever corpses lie near them. Only the Marsi stand fast, chopping furiously with hoes, shovels and swords, outraged that anyone would dare attack them.

"Retreat!" Consul Marcellus screams as he rides into the line. "Get back to camp!" The Roman lines slowly withdraw, stepping back in unison with their shields held in front of them.

Marcellus spies a thick square of allies standing fast in the middle of the battle line, refusing to retreat. *Those fucking Marsi! They won't listen to reason!* He rides over and grabs the allied commander, a barrel-bodied man with a bear's head draped over his helmet.

"Return to camp!" Marcellus bawls, knowing better than to use the word 'retreat' with the Marsi.

"We kill right here," the Marsi bellows. "Die fighting; not scared of fat men." As if for emphasis, he hurtles a spear into the neck of a Gaul fighting with one of his tribesmen.

"Come back now," Marcellus urges. "We'll fight them another day."

"Fight now. Kill these bastards."

"Gods damn you, if you don't come back, I'll tell everyone they killed you as you ran away. And there won't be anyone left to deny it!"

The Marsi glares at him. "You lucky you the general." He screams for his men to withdraw.

Battling every step of the way, the Roman army retreats back up the hill toward their camp. The Roman cavalry stream out from the camp gates and hurtle into the flanks of the Gauls, throwing their javelins with deadly accuracy. Five thousand legionnaires march out after them, armored and ready.

The chieftain Corolamus is fighting on foot, wielding his hand ax with murderous delight. His son pushes his way through the pressing hordes about his father, and leans into his ear.

"The Romans are sending down a fresh legion, with lots of cavalry."

"Just a minute." The chieftain drives his ax into the shield of an Umbrian, knocking him sprawling. Three of his men swarm over the fallen warrior. A keening scream erupts from their midst.

Corolanus glances up at the setting sun. "Sound the withdrawal," he says. "Our day's work is done."

The Gallic horns sound the recall. The fierce Gauls turn about and stalk from the battlefield, leaving a field strewn with plundered and dismembered corpses. Corolanus leads them up into the back hills, regrouping his men in their mountain valley camp.

The Romans lower their swords and tools, staring mutely at the receding horde. Some sob with relief, their arms shaking with exhaustion. Others begin the grim task of identifying their compatriots from the three thousand who were slain,[cxxix] rolling over bodies and searching for heads.

Marcellus leads the survivors into camp, his men marching past the cohorts of legionnaires who came to their rescue. He rides to his command tent and slides awkwardly from his horse, handing the reins to one of his tribunes.

"Double the sentries and send out the scouts. I want no disturbances until tomorrow." The consul marches into his tent and goes directly to his writing table. Still clad in his gore-spattered armor, he pulls out several scrolls and begins to write.

Publius Cornelius Scipio Africanus:

The Boii have ambushed my army and killed thousands of them. Now they lie in wait outside my camp, waiting to attack us again. I am trapped here, and don't know how to escape.

When you made me promise to run for consul, I told you I was not well versed in the ways of warfare. You assured me that the Gauls in my area would be no trouble. Now I am faced with defeat and disgrace.

I beg you to come here immediately, and provide me with counsel.

Consul M. Claudius Marcellus

Marcellus pens an identical note, then writes two consular orders on small squares of papyrus. He seals each missive with his horse-head signatory and calls in his two best messengers.

"Take this message to Scipio Africanus," he tells them. "You are each to take different routes, that one of you may make it there safely."

328

He hands each of them one of the small squares. "These orders allow you to command whatever horse you find at each of the way stations to Rome. You are to deliver your message before midnight tomorrow."

The messengers rush for the stables. Marcellus sheds his armor and flops onto his sleeping pallet, his hand over his face. *You'd better come, you bastard. And you'd better get me out of this.*

At dawn, Corolanus leads out his men to collect the dead. Thousands of Romans and allies stand guard, while hundreds more heap bodies and onto large pyres. That night, the battlefield is bright as day from the field of funerary fires that burn long into the night.

The next morning, Corolanus' Boii army marches out from the forest and camps at the base of the camp's hill, clearly challenging Marcellus to fight. For days, no one emerges from the camp. Bored with waiting, the Boii return to their towns.[cxxx]

Four days later, Scipio, Laelius, and Lucius ride through the camp gates with their guards, their faces grimy with road dust. A large wagon trundles in behind them, its contents covered by wool blankets.

"Where is the consul?" Scipio barks at the gate sentry.

"In his tent, like he always is," the guard replies, with thinly veiled contempt. Scipio trots through the camp's orderly dirt streets, halting in front of Marcellus's large command tent. He pauses there, taking several deep breaths to calm himself.

"Wait for me," he says to Lucius and Laelius. "This will be quick. We'll either get what we want or leave."

"Fine," Laelius says. "But the way you look, perhaps you should leave your sword with us."

"He is a Hellenic," Lucius adds. "Remember, he is one of us."

Scipio snorts. "He will never be 'one of us!'" He slides off his horse and faces the two guards flanking the entry flaps. "Marcellus!" he shouts. "Are you in there?"

Marcellus pokes his tousled head out of his tent. A relieved grin crosses his face. "Imperator! You are indeed a welcome sight."

Scipio does not reply. He pushes past Marcellus and plops onto a tall stool at the general's map table. He studies the war figurines scattered across a map of the Po Valley.

"Can I fetch you wine? Bread?" Marcellus asks anxiously. "Do you want Laelius and Lucius to come in?"

"They can wait out there for now. What you say will determine whether they come in—or whether we all go back to Rome."

Marcellus' face flushes. "You were famous for your manners, General," he stammers, "but I confess I do not see it. You treat me like a common soldier."

"That's because you are leading like a common soldier!" Scipio blazes. "Your two scouts told me what happened. How could you let thousands of Gauls mass in the hills above that roadway? You should have had scouts combing those cursed woodlands, reporting to you every hour!"

"I had men out there," Marcellus says. "They did not return to warn me."

"And you did not grow suspicious? You did not send more to find them?" Scipio shakes his head in amazement.

Marcellus starts to reply, Scipio shoves his palm at his face. "No. No more discussion. That die has been cast. Now we must work on rescuing your consulship, for the sake of the party—and Rome."

Scipio turns toward the map table and jabs his finger onto the thick line designating the Po River. Three clay warriors stand along the river's edge, figurines with winged helmets and long beards.

"Is this true? The Insubres are gathered here across the river from you? Below Comum?"[cxxxi]

"That is what my scouts reported yesterday," Marcellus replies sullenly. "And the scouts are natives," he adds. Scipio nods.

"Where are the Boii?"

"They have left the area. They returned to their settlements."[cxxxii]

Scipio grips the round table with both hands and leans forward, staring into the map. "And why have you not attacked the Insubres?" he says, not deigning to look back at Marcellus.

"I—I didn't know if it was safe to go out yet. I just received the scouting reports about the Boii and Insubres."

"Safe? The Insubres are massing to attack you, and you are worried about being *safe* from them? Romans don't hide behind walls—our enemies worry about being safe from us!"

Marcellus' shoulders slump. Seeing it, Scipio pauses. *Easy, boy. He needs confidence to lead his men to battle. They will know if he is afraid.*

"Do not think me untoward. I only mean to help you win. If you can defeat the Insubres, and take some of their towns, Rome will celebrate your victory for days." He smirks. "Our people have a knack for celebrating victories and forgetting losses."

"I told you I didn't want to get into battles when you pushed me into this consulship," Marcellus snips. "I am a builder, not a fighter."

"I truly see that now," Scipio says. "But here you are. Do you want me to help get you out of this mess or not?"

"You're the best of our generals, I know that. I would welcome your help. If you think it is time to fight, we will go fight."

"Fine. Together we will beat them. And who knows, Rome may even give you a triumph for it."

At the mention of the word 'triumph,' Marcellus' eyes gleam.

Now, Scipio tells himself. *Get what you want.* He raises his forefinger. "I have one condition."

Marcellus eyes Scipio suspiciously. "What?"

"Laelius will guide your Roman cavalry and Lucius leads the allied infantry. They have both won battles in that capacity."

"Impossible!" Marcellus blurts. "I'm not dismissing the commanders of my equites and socii. They have done nothing to deserve it."

Other than listening to you, Scipio thinks. "You will not have to replace your commanders. I would not embarrass them that way. Laelius and Lucius will be at their sides. They will give no orders to your men, but your commanders are to do whatever they say."

He steps nearer to Marcellus. "And me, I will be next to you—acting in that same capacity."

"My men know who you are," Marcus says petulantly. "They will think you are leading me."

I had better be, if we are to survive. "Just tell them that I am here on a camp visit. Old generals frequently do that. I promise you will get the credit for our victory."

Scipio jumps off the stool and stands in front of Marcus. "So, what will it be? Do I stay or go?"

"I would welcome your *advice*, General," Marcellus sullenly replies. Scipio continues to stare at him. "And the *advice* of Laelius and Lucius."

Let him have his little victory. "Excellent." Scipio says. He pokes open the tent flap. "Laelius! Lucius! Come in." He turns back to Marcellus. "You should march on the Insubres as soon as possible. If the Boii join them, they could number over fifty thousand."

"My men can be ready in three days. But what about finishing the road?"

Scipio scowls. "Forget the road. Your prisoners can build the thing for you. You have to get at the Gauls now, before they grow too large."

Four nights later the Roman army is camped on the east side of the Po River, preparing to enter Insubre territory. Lucius, Laelius and Scipio enter Scipio's tent in the tribune's section, having concluded combat preparations with Marcellus and his officers. Laelius grabs a wine pitcher and hastily pours himself a cup.

"Whoo! What a meeting!" Laelius says. "Those men worry more about how they can lose than how they will win!"

"That young Umbrian Adrianus, he seems to have a thick spine," Scipio says. "He could lead the allied riders."

"The Marsi commander wasn't like the rest of them, either," Lucius says, "He was very angry that they had to retreat from the Boii. He acts like he's ready to kill them all himself!" A worried look crosses Lucius' face. "I hope I can get him to listen to me."

"Oh, I'm sure Larth will listen to you, Lucius. Marcellus and he have an understanding. Just don't give him orders in front of his men." He looks over at Laelius. "You have any qualms about going out with the cavalry?"

Laelius looks at Scipio as if he were mad. "Why should I? I taught half of them back in Rome, and that includes young Adrianus, their commander!" Laelius chuckles. "Why, those men idolize me!"

"Just don't embarrass Adrianus. Let him lead his men's charge. You tell him when and how."

"You know me. I am the essence of diplomacy," Laelius replies.

Scipio rolls his eyes.

Late that night, Scipio strolls through the somnolent camp, chatting with the few soldiers that are still prowling the streets. He strolls over to the allied section, and stops in front of a small tent with a wolf's head standard shoved into the ground.

Surface Glory

"Larth, are you in there?" Scipio says.

A bushy-bearded head juts out of the tent entry, a pair of brown eyes peering from the curly black bramble about it. "General Scipio!" he says in his rude Latin. "What you want this late? You drunk?"

Scipio chuckles. "No, unfortunately. I just wanted to talk to you about something. Something good."

Larth crawls out from his tent, his hairy, muscled body completely naked. "You worried about fight? No worry. We Marsi, we drive them back into forest. No running away this time, don't care what pussy consul say."

Scipio smiles. "No, I never worry about the Marsi. I just have a request. My brother Lucius will be joining you." He takes a deep breath. "When your men go in to battle, let him lead the charge."

Marsi's bushy eyebrows close above his flaring eyes. "I know you big hero, General, but you crazy. I the man; I lead my men. I earn that; kill many enemies."

"Just let him run out in front of your men, you can go alongside him. Rome needs to know he led the charge. If you do, I promise you this: your men will be back at home for the early spring plantings."

Larth's eyebrows arch up. "Back home before spring? You promise?"

"On my honor," Scipio says. "Consul Marcellus will listen to me about this."

Larth nods, his face doubtful. "I see your brother. He nice, but he not you. But he can do no harm out there, eh?"

Yes, he is harmless. That's the problem. "That's right, Larth. When you fight, he leads the charge. You fight however you want. That's all."

"I do it." His face grows anxious. "Hope we get chance to fight. Gauls kill forty my men."

Scipio's mouth tightens. "Oh, I would not worry too much about that.

334

Your chance will come, I am sure."

The next morning, Marcellus' army files out from its temporary camp, sixteen thousand Roman and allied foot soldiers flanked by a thousand Roman and Latin cavalry. Marcellus and Scipio ride in the vanguard, the light infantry striding along behind them, six abreast.

Hours later, the army steps across the timbered river bridges built by earlier legions. Regrouping on the other side, their columns enter the wide plains of Insubre territory. Three of Marcellus' scouts gallop in from the northern hills. Scipio has only to see their faces to know what they will say.

"The Insubres are coming!" one scouts says to Marcellus. "They are marching out from their camp, straight toward us."

"How many?" Marcellus asks, a quaver in his voice.

"Twenty-five, maybe thirty thousand," another scout says.

"Any cavalry?" Scipio says. A scout shakes his head. "Not many. A few hundred."

"Get back out there," Marcellus says. When the scouts have left, he leans toward Scipio. "What do you think?"

"If they're coming out of camp, they are looking to fight us before the end of the day. If I were you, I'd get into battle formation and let them come at us." Scipio pulls out a scroll from his saddle pouch. "My map shows the plain narrows by some low hills in front of us. We can set up there. Send your cavalry into the hills. Send them now, before we get there."

"You want me to send cavalry into the hills?" Marcellus says.

Scipio nods. "Half the force; both Romans and Latins. We need the rest with us so the Gauls don't wonder why we don't have any. Let Laelius take the men up there, he's very good at hiding."

Marcellus summons Laelius and Adrianus from the rear, where half

335

his cavalry are guarding the baggage train. "Adrianus, I want to send half our force into the Comum Hills. They will attack the Gallic flank." He faces Laelius. "Would you lead them?"

Laelius nods. "The Gauls will have scouts patrolling it, so we will take to the highest passes. Scouts rarely go up there. I'll lead the Romans. When the Latins see us come down, Adrianus can come from the other side."

"Why don't you take half the Latin socii and half the equites?" Marcellus says.

Laelius shakes his head. "I'll tell you who I want," Laelius says. "I'd like to take the cavalry I trained back in Rome." He smiles. "I brought some special weapons for them—they're in the wagon. We will give those Gauls a little surprise."

Marcellus shrugs. "Why not? Take who you want."

Laelius and Adrianus gallop back to their men. Minutes later, Marcellus and Scipio watch the riders race ahead of them, the equites heading to the left and the Latins to the right.

An hour later the Roman army columns enter the narrowed plain, flanked with darkly forested hills. The scouts race back with news that the Insubres are only a few miles away.

Marcellus summons his tribunes. "Prepare for battle," he tells them. Scipio stands several paces away, letting Marcellus have the moment.

The army spends the next half hour setting up in combat formation. The two Roman legions man the half-mile front. Following Scipio's advice, Marcellus has divided the legions into cohorts of five hundred instead of maniples of a hundred and twenty, to better withstand the shock of the Gallic charge.

The Marsi are arrayed in two cohorts behind the Romans, backed by cohorts of allies. The rear horses and baggage are rounded up into a circle at the rear, guarded by a contingent of light infantry.

The remaining Latin cavalry set on the right of the legions, and the equites on the left. Camp slaves run through the ranks with bulging waterskins, fetching men a last drink before they fight—or die.

Two miles away, a tall chieftain marches in front of the Insubres, his face as grim as death. His bare chest is carpeted with steel gray hair, but it cannot hide the blue boar's head tattooed on his iron-muscled chest.

There is no mistaking that Guidgen is the leader of the Insubres. The chieftain's gold neck torque gleams brightly, a carnelian-eyed skull glowering in the midst of it. A large red plume wafts over his demon's-head helmet, making him appear to be seven feet tall.

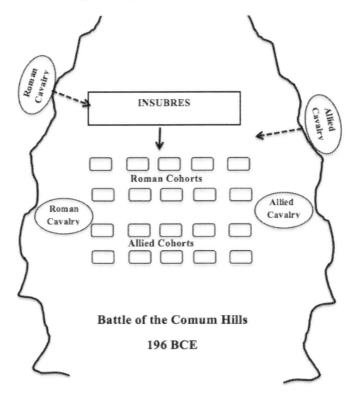

Guidgen's two sons flank him, one carrying the chief's aqua-colored shield, the other his yard-long ironsword. Almost as tall as their father, the auburn-haired giants sport their father's demonic crest on their battered bronze helmets.

Guidgen is in a good mood today. The soft-handed Roman general has emerged from the safety of his camp, and has had the temerity to march upon him—Guidgen, the mightiest leader of the mightiest Gallic nation. Now he can avenge the hundreds who died at Cremona, and wipe out the Romans before the Boii gain the honor. Now he will have plunder, and rich prisoners to ransom. Already he dreams of a new parcel of land, a new chariot. Perhaps a second wife—or a fourth concubine.

The Roman front comes into sight. Guidgen notices they arranged in an unexpected formation, in larger squares than the ones he is accustomed to fighting. He snorts derisively. *We'll break them, no matter what they do.*

He checks the amount of cavalry on their flanks. *Not too many. I'll send mine out to keep them busy.*

"What did the hill scouts report, Owin?" he says to his son on the right.

"They only found a few scouts in the foothills. They ran when they saw us coming."

Guidgen nods, satisfied. "We're going to march straight into those runts.[cxxxiii] I want to break them on the first charge."

Marcellus and Scipio ride their horses to the Roman front, halting their stallions in front of the center maniples. They watch the line of Gauls approach, straining their eyes to see an end to the rows of auburn-haired warriors. Waves of voices soon wash over them, the shouts and curses of thirty thousand men.

Watching the oncoming horde, Scipio feels the all-too-familiar flutter of nervousness in his stomach. His right hand begins to shake. *Oh no. Not now! Jupiter, I beg you, keep me from an attack.* He grabs his right hand and pushes it to his side, hoping Marcellus has not noticed.

Scipio sees Guidgen's gold neck plates shimmering in the early afternoon sun, his plume nodding above the tall men that surround him. *If we can just stop their first waves of attack, they might break. But if they get through us, they won't quit until we're dead.*

Still marching, the Gallic chieftain grabs his sword and shield from his sons. He raises the sword high. "Remember Cremona!" he screams. Thousands of voices echo his cry. The Romans stand unwavering, but many eyes are wide with fear.

Marcellus' velites dash out between the front-line hastati. When they are halfway to the Gauls, their centurion orders them to halt. "Loose!" he cries. The velites fling three rounds of javelins into the oncoming mob. Scores of Insubres fall, yelling with pain. The Gauls slow their charge, looking to see if more javelins are coming.

"You cowards!" Guidgen bellows at his men. "Do I have to kill them all myself?" He shoves his two sons. "Come on!"

Guidgen stalks forward, flanked by his sons. The Gauls in the center hurry after him, desperate to avoid the disgrace of their chief being slain in front of them. The Insubre attack forms into a roughshod wedge, its edges aimed at the legions' wings. As they close upon the steadfast velites, the barbarians fling spears, rocks, and clods— anything they can lay their hands upon.

The velites retreat from the hail of missiles, dashing for the front lines. Dozens of them fall, pierced by spears or clubbed by rocks. Their comrades grab them by each arm and drag them across the battle plain, crouching to avoid the onslaught of missiles. The light infantry edge through the hastati and principes and reform behind the triarii, waiting for their next attack.

"You see?" Guidgen bellows, smiling at his men. "The little men are little women!" He waves his sword over his head, and dashes forward.

Shouting with triumph, the Insubres stampede at front-line hastati. The stolid Romans raise their shields, their javelins clenched in their fists. They dig their sandals into the grasses beneath them, and lean their left shoulders into their shields. Then the Gauls are upon them.

The Insubres bash into the Roman shield wall. Howling and kicking, the barbarians pound against the steadfast legionnaires, frantic to get inside their lines. Mad with the urge for revenge, many forsake their safety and grab the Romans' shields, trying to yank them away. The hastati jab their spears into the invading hands and shove their shields into the Gauls' bodies, repelling the assault.

Dozens, then scores of barbarian corpses litter the front, but the Insubres do not relent. Guidgen rages in the center of battle, his two sons fighting by his side. He cuts down a hastati in front of him and pounces on the soldier marching up to replace him, battering him senseless with the butt of his axe. His sons battle on each side of him, beating back the hastati. The Insubres flow into the gap. The Roman front begins to break.

"Call for a line change," Scipio shouts to Marcellus. "They're going to break through!" Marcellus waves two fingers at his ever-watchful bugler, and he signals the change.

The principes march in between the retiring hastati. With fresh arms and legs, the experienced fighters attack the barbarians with renewed vigor, killing hundreds with their careful swordplay. Still the vengeful Gauls come on, heedless of the deaths around them. The Roman front is again driven back, with mounds of legionnaires in its wake. [cxxxiv]

Scipio and Marcellus ride across the gap between the front and rear lines, shouting encouragement. Scipio watches the veteran principes losing position. *They are our best men, and they're going to break.* He grabs the reins of Marcellus' horse and draws him near.

"They can't hold them," Scipio shouts. "Call up the Marsi."

"We don't need the allies—our men can beat them!" Marcellus shouts, his face reddening with embarrassment. "I'll bring up the triarii and the cavalry."

"Scipio grabs the shoulder of Marcellus' cuirass and shakes him. "There aren't enough of them, do you hear me!" Marcellus stares at him, his eyes glazed with indecision.

Scipio shoves Marcellus away. "Here, I'll bring them up myself!" He rides over to the lead cornicen. "Come with me," Scipio says, his tone brooking no disagreement. He trots his horse toward the waiting allies.

Lucius waits there, perched atop his white stallion, nervously watching the fray. Larth stands next to him, eschewing a horse so that he can fight on foot with his men. The lean chieftain grips his short thick fighting spear, his studded round shield resting against his shin. A naked short sword dangles from his rawhide belt.

The Marsi mill about restlessly, cursing and shouting, eager to fight the men that have ransacked their towns.

"Larth! Get the men ready," Scipio says. "We're going to the front!"

"Good!" Larth says. "Those big men, they get tired soon. We fight all day. They quit from us, you watch!" He grins and waggles a finger at Scipio. "You remember what you say. Home by spring!"

Scipio draws next to his brother. He forces a smile onto his face. "This is it, Lucius. Your chance for glory. Lead the Marsi to victory, and Rome will sing your name!"

Lucius looks at his brother, his eyes wide with fear. "Look at them up there—they fight like wild beasts!"

"Yes, and they have as just about as much discipline. If you get them moving backward, they won't stop." He notices the sweat trickling down the brow of Lucius' helmet. He grasps Lucius' forearm, and feels it quaking.

Scipio's voice softens. "Look, you and I will go in together, side by side. Just like when we were kids. We always whipped the other boys, remember?"

Lucius swallows. He nods mutely. "Get ready." Scipio raises two fingers to the cornicen. The bugler blows two long blasts. Scipio and Lucius trot out ahead of the Marsi.

"Time to kill!" Larth screams. The allied rams' horns sound the charge. Shouting at the tops of their voices, the Marsi tread quickly toward the battlefront.

Hearing the allies' call to attack, the Roman tribunes order their men to retreat. The front-line principes slowly retreat, always facing the Insubres.

The Marsi draw near to the rear lines of the legions. Scipio rides over to Larth. "When you see me charge, I want your men to come fast. Go between the Roman soldiers. You understand!"

Larth bares his gold-capped teeth. "No worry. We jump them quick."

Scipio rides back to Lucius. They ease into the open space between the two legions, moving slowly to keep pace with the Marsi. Scipio watches the Marsi turn their shields sideways and slide through the rear lines of the triarii, then the hastati. Only the double lines of the principes stand between them and the raging Gauls.

"Now!" Scipio shouts to Lucius. He spurs his horse forward, with Lucius following.

"Attack!" Larth bellows to his officers. He strides quickly forward as the Marsi horns sound a new command. The allies run through the three-foot gap between each principe, sprinting toward the battle line.

The Insubres hear a groundswell of screaming voices coming toward them, men bellowing as madly as themselves. They look at each other, confused and concerned.

The Marsi burst into the front, hewing to the right and left with their thick, double-edged blades. Larth surges sideways and buries his spear into the liver of an unwary Insubre, eliciting a satisfying scream of agony. "Kill all!" he shouts back to his men.

Fighting like whirlwinds, the rangy mountain men cut into the wearying Gauls, exultant in their superior energy and quickness. Hundreds of Insubres stagger back from the front lines, arms and bodies gashed by the whirling Marsi blades.

Surface Glory

Scipio charges into the front of the fight, his sword hacking at the Gauls in front of them. Lucius leans down and stabs at the foot soldiers with his cavalry spear, his fear forgotten.

Marcellus sees the Scipios fighting along the front. *I'm not going to let him take over my army.* He forces his horse to the front, joining Larth in the center.

"No retreat, no quarter!" Marcellus screams to the men around him. The Marsi cheer Marcellus' words, and fight with renewed vigor. The Gallic front becomes a jagged line, with the Marsi cutting deeply into their front.

Guidgen and his two sons rage in the center, refusing to take a single step backwards. Owin notices that there are two Roman officers fighting on horseback along the front, driving back the Insubres in front of them. He peers at the face of one of them, and his eyes dawn with recognition. *Is that really him?*

Owin steps back from the fray. He reaches into his purse and fumbles out a handful of plundered Roman coins. He picks out a newly minted denarius and studies the face upon it, glancing back at Scipio. His heart pounds. *It's Scipio Africanus! What a prize his head would make!* Owin strides toward Scipio.

"Get back here!" his father Guidgen cries. But Owin is already into the Romans, shoving away a soldier in front of Scipio.

Owin runs in behind Scipio and stabs his blade deep into his horse's haunch. The stallion rears, whinnying in pain. Scipio tumbles from the horse, crashing onto his side. He reflexively rolls away from his kicking mount and rises to one knee. Scipio picks up his gladius and holds his small round equites' shield in front of him, shaking his head to clear it.

Owin stalks forward. Scipio rises to his feet and extends his shield arm. He turns his body sideways, gladiator style, his feet splayed wide apart.

The Gaul swings his blade at Scipio's bare neck. Scipio blocks the

343

blow, angling the shield to deflect it. Nevertheless, the mighty stroke numbs his forearm, and his shield hangs limply from it. Owin levers another blow at Scipio's head. Scipio flips up his limp shield arm to stop it.

The Gallic sword splits the shield. Half of it falls to the ground, the other half hanging from Scipio's numbed arm.

Now or never. Scipio darts forward and stabs his gladius at Owin's middle. The young Gaul deftly blocks it with a swing of his oblong shield. His foot darts out and scoops Scipio's leg from under him, tumbling him onto his back. The barbarian steps in, cocking back his sword arm.

"Hold on, brother!"

Lucius' rams his horse into Owin's shield, knocking the Gaul sprawling. "Come on!" Lucius cries, tears running down his face. "He's getting to his feet!"

Scipio scrambles up, knowing his opportunity is brief. He runs over to the stunned barbarian and grabs his hair, yanking his head back.

"Here, prick!" he spits.

Scipio stabs his blade deep into the side of Owin's throat and yanks it out, stepping back with his blade at the ready. The young chieftain staggers to his feet and grabs his throat, trying futilely to staunch the blood that streams down his naked chest. His panicked eyes search Scipio's vengeful face, as if begging for help.

Scipio steps forward and plunges the blade into the Insubre's eye socket. With a final, anguished wail, the young man crumples to the bloodied ground, curling into a twitching ball.

Lucius watches in horrified fascination. He pulls up next to Scipio. "Are you all right?"

"Fine, Lucius. Just a minute." He pulls off Owin's demon-headed helmet and gives it to Lucius. "Hold that up and shout that you have it," he says. "Ride over near the front, but don't get too close. Go."

Lucius blinks at him. "Shout about this helmet? Why?"

"Just listen to me!" Scipio yells, still flush with excitement. "Show those barbarians that one of their leaders has fallen. Show it to the Marsi. Now go!"

Lucius raises the dripping helmet and rides behind the front-line Marsi, shouting triumphantly. The Marsi recognize the helmet as that of a chieftain. They scream with triumph.

"Owin is dead!" shout the Gauls, the cry echoing through the lines.

A distant cry is added to the Gaul's lament, the brassy wail of cavalry bugles. Laelius' equites stream in from the hills, hundreds of riders plunging toward the right flank of the Gallic horde.

The Insubre chieftains spot the oncoming equites. They direct their men to face their shields toward the oncoming horde, ready for the charge.

But Laelius and his men do not charge. They draw within a spear cast of the Gauls and begin to stream past them, looping around the flank and rear. As they gallop past, they pull short, curved bows from off their backs and nock arrows into them, watching Laelius for the signal.

"All right, sagittarii!" Laelius screams, using the Greek term for horse archers. "Do as I taught you. Shoot over the front men!"

Laelius sends an arrow whistling over the heads of the Gauls at the front-line shield wall. It crunches into the back of an Insubre in the middle.

Flocks of arrows land upon the Insubres in the inner lines. They yowl with pain and surprise, arrows jutting from their exposed backs and necks. The Insubres turn their shields to fend off the surprise onslaught, leaving them vulnerable to the charging Romans' spears and swords.

The front-line legionnaires see their opportunity. The centurions whistle for a line change, and fresh troops march forward. Wielding their spears and swords with deadly effect, the Romans cut through the first two lines of the Gauls, driving them back into their fellows.

Adrianus and his men flow into the plain from hills on the other side, galloping for the Insubres' left flank. The Gauls lower their shields into a wall, their swords at the ready.

When the fur-clad riders allies approach the shield wall they form an attack wedge, with Adrianus in the lead. The young commander lowers his head and shoulders next to the neck of his horse, his spear out in front of him.

The chieftain Sudrix notices the socii forming into an attack wedge. A veteran of a dozen Roman battles, the old chieftain nods knowingly. "Horse trap!" he yells to his warriors.

When Adrianus and his men plunge into the massed Gauls, the warriors dash to the side, leaving Adrianus and his men galloping into an open space in the Gallic lines. The Gauls run back together and swarm about Adrianus and a score of his riders, completely encircling them.

"Back out the way we came!" Adrianus screams, turning his horse around. His order comes too late.

"Get the horses!" Sudrix cries. He lumbers forward, with scores of his warriors following. They stab their swords and spears into the Romans' horses. The beasts rear and pivot, pitching their riders into the ground. While the horses gallop away through the lines, the Gauls pour over their fallen riders, chopping them to pieces.

Adrianus rises to one knee, scrabbling for his sword. Sudrix runs in behind him and swings his thick sword into Adrianus' neck. There is a sickening crunch. Adrianus partially severed head lolls upon his shoulder. His body crumples to the ground.

Grunting with delight, Sudrix grabs the young captain's helmet by its feathered crest and jerks his head upright. Another swing of the axe, and Sudrix holds Adrianus' head aloft on tip of his sword, roaring with triumph.

After the Gauls close their shield wall upon Adrianus and his lead riders, the other cavalry mill about in confusion, uncertain of what to do. The socii hear a great shout arise from the Gallic ranks. They see their commander's bloody head held up on a sword, his dead eyes staring out at them, as if entreating them for help. Moans of anguish erupt through their ranks.

"Revenge!" yells one of the riders. "For Adrianus!" screams another.

As one, hundreds of riders storm forward at full speed, heedless of the tall shields facing them. The Umbrians and Latins crash through the wall, trampling through the Gauls as if they were statues. Screaming with anger, they stab madly at any Insubre within reach, intent on hurting as many as possible.

Now beset from three sides, the Insubres mill about, not knowing which way to attack. Scores of them run from the battlefield, some riding the horses of the fallen Roman and allied cavalrymen. The Insubre chieftains shout vainly for them to reorganize.

Lucius returns to Scipio, his face flush with excitement. "You should have heard them cheer me!" he exclaims.

"I heard them," Scipio replies, glancing about for attackers. "Now do me a favor and get me a horse." *That will get you away from here before you get killed.* Lucius trots back toward the Roman baggage area, still carrying his trophy.

Scipio watches him go. *There. Now you're a hero. Mother would be happy.*

"My son!"

Scipio hears the cry coming from behind him, an anguished, furious roar. He whirls to face it and his heart leaps to his throat. Marsi warriors are stumbling sideways, as if a giant plow were pushing them aside. A bronze demon's head bobs above them, its grinning head closing upon Scipio.

Guidgen batters his way forward, his baleful eyes fixed on Scipio. A blade stabs into the chieftain's side. He swats the attacker away, his stride never wavering. The skull's carnelian eyes wink madly at Scipio, its gold teeth fixed in a malevolent grin.

Shit! Look at the size of him! Scipio jumps to the side of a dead legionnaire. He yanks off his large rectangular shield and slips his still-numbed forearm through it, snugging against his bicep. Scipio strides forward, peering out over the shield's iron edge.

Roaring with anger, Guidgen slams his sword against Scipio's scutum. Scipio retreats with the blow, but still the immense force almost knocks him off his feet. *I've got to wait this monster out*, he decides.

With every blow Scipio steps backward, desperate to maintain his balance. He repeatedly jabs his wasp-waisted gladius at Guidgen, searching for the slightest opening. Twice, the tip of his gladius cuts into Guidgen's chest, but the wounds only further infuriate him.

Scipio feels himself tiring. Listening to the ring of the two blades against each other, he makes a fateful decision. *His sword is made out of iron. Mine is steel. Good Iberian steel.* He remembers the time he pitted his Iberian steel gladius against Cato's iron sword in a friendly match—and its effect.[cxxxv]

Scipio drops his shield. He bends his knees and leans back, his legs tensed like a javelin thrower. Guidgen swoops his long sword toward Scipio's head, aiming to cleave his skull. Scipio grabs his gladius with both hands and swings it with all his strength.

There is a sharp clang. Two thirds of Guidgen's sword blade cartwheels into the air, leaving him clutching a jagged shard. The chieftain stares at the broken sword as if had betrayed him, giving Scipio the instant he needs.

With a short, quick chop, Scipio arcs his cleaver-like blade into Guidgen's wrist. The rest of his sword plops into the dust, his hand still clutching it.

Guidgen's face purples with rage. Ignoring his gouting stump, he charges in and batters his shield against Scipio's breastplate, knocking him flat. The chieftain leaps forward and straddles Scipio. He pitches away his shield and pulls out his dagger, squirting his stump into Scipio's face.

"You die first, pig!" Guidgen drops to his knees and stabs at Scipio's neck.

With a strength born of terror, Scipio jerks his head and shoulders away from the blade, blindly thrusting up his gladius. He gasps in agony as he feels Guidgen's serrated dagger saw through the top of his collarbone.

He hears the Gaul roar.

Guidgen stares into space, his mouth spasmodically opening and closing. A deep gash bleeds from his solar plexus, the spot where Scipio's razored blade has severed his abdomen. The Gaul slides sideways onto the ravaged earth, clutching at its bloody clods.

Scipio crawls out from the fallen chief and pushes himself upright, his sword poised. The enfeebled giant props an elbow on the ground and scrabbles to push himself upright. His eyes glare at Scipio, even as his life's blood drains from his stomach and wrist. Scipio steps back from him, fearing he might strike again. The Gaul rises to his knees, only to fall again.

"Gods, what is happening here? Are you all right?" Marcellus rides in with Lucius behind him, towing an empty horse. The consul's guards surround the officers, ready to repel any Insubres.

Lucius leaps from his horse and yanks off his red cape. He dabs blood off Scipio's face and bandages the cut on his neck. "Mars' balls, you look like a sacrificial cow!"

"I am fine," Scipio says, he picks up his scutum and leans on it, panting with fear and exhaustion. "Just a bit weak."

"That's Guidgen, the leader of the Insubres," Marcellus says, staring

349

at the twitching body.

Scipio spits a clot of blood on the ground. "Cut his head off, Marcellus," he mutters.

The consul blinks at him. "What?"

"You heard me. Cut his fucking head off!" Scipio hacks up more blood. He wipes his mouth with his wrist, glaring at Marcellus. "I've got to say you killed him and cut his head off. Do it while he's still alive, and it will be true."

"Go on, Marcellus," Lucius says encouragingly. "He's trying to give you the glory."

Marcellus slides off his horse and gingerly steps toward the dying Gaul. He stands over Guidgen and looks into his slitted, bleary eyes. Drawing his blade he looks back at Scipio. Scipio nods.

Marcellus stoops over Guidgen. He grabs his gladius with both hands and swings it down. There is a cracking, choking noise.

"It didn't come off," Marcellus wails.

"Gods curse you, finish it!" Scipio blazes. "Finish it, or I'll cut *your* head off!"

His sword chops again, and again. Lucius looks away, nauseated at the sight.

"That is enough," Scipio says. "Pick it up."

Marcellus reaches down and plucks the helmet up by its crest. Guidgen's head gapes from the helmet, fastened by a gory chin strap. Marcellus holds it at arm's length and looks back at the Scipios, a question in his eyes.

"Stick it on a spear and ride to the front," Scipio says. "Do that and you'll sow dismay in their ranks. They are already dispirited by Lucius' showing them that other chieftain's helmet. When they see their leader's head, they'll wilt."

Marcellus' eyes brighten. He grins with anticipation. "I see. Show it to the Gauls!" He wheels his horse about and gallops forward, his guards surrounding him.

Marcellus rides into a gap in front of the battling Marsi, brandishing the chieftain's head high above him. "Guidgen is dead!" he shouts in pidgin Gallic, shoving the spear up and down. "Dead!"

A javelin flies at Marcellus. He jerks up his shield just before the spear thuds into it. Alarmed, the consul races back behind the Marsi, savoring the cries of dismay that scatter throughout the Insubres.

Sensing victory, the Marsi charge forward. The dispirited Gauls are no match for the vengeful mountain men. Scores, then hundreds, run for the rear. Screaming with triumph, the Marsi cut into the remaining Insubres in the center, their tireless swords hewing down hundreds.

The Roman legions march into the wings and join the slaughter. Thousands of Gauls die in the surge, many trampled by their own men.

Finally, the Insubres' rear lines break for the empty plains. The rest of the Gauls follow them, chased into the hills by the cavalry.

Scipio and Lucius join Marcellus in the center of the erstwhile battle front, watching the soldiers tie up the Gauls who surrendered.

Scipio scans the layers of dead that carpet the field. "My gods, must be twenty thousand of them lying out there," he says sadly.

"But I doubt we lost a thousand," Lucius says excitedly.

"It is a great victory!" Marcellus crows.

Scipio glances sideways at the consul. "One that cost us a thousand good men." *Along with the three thousand you lost in that Boii ambush.*

Larth stalks in from the killing field, a bloodstained cloth wrapped about his middle. His teeth flash into a painful smile as he looks up at Scipio. "Big men dead. You keep promise, yes? We go home?"

Scipio turns to Marcellus. "Consul, I request that you send these men

351

home as soon as possible. I'll get you more allies."

Marcellus glowers at Scipio. "I need them here! They are good fighters."

Larch scowls at Scipio. "You keep promise, yes?"

Scipio draws his horse closer to Marcellus. "Do you want Rome to know you as the man who killed the Insubre chief? Or do you want them to know the whole story?" Scipio says. "I could tell the Senate that—"

"They'll go," Marcellus interjects, riding away. "I'm going back to camp. I have to prepare a victory celebration."

"Wait! You forgot this." Scipio trots toward Marcellus. He holds up Guidgen's bloody neck torque. "Take this back to Rome, Marcellus. Give it to the Senate as a symbol of your victory." [cxxxvi]

He smirks. "I will tell them I saw you cut the chief's head off—that much I can truthfully say."

Marcellus cocks his head. "And what of you, Imperator? What do you want?"

"Give my Lucius credit for leading the Marsi charge." *That will help him when he runs for office.*

"You want Lucius to be a hero?" Marcellus says, the hint of a sneer on his lips.

Scipio stares steadily at Marcellus. "Do that and you will have the glory for winning the battle. Otherwise, I will be more detailed in my report."

"Bring the torque," Marcellus says to a guard. He trots away, his back stiff with resentment.

Laelius rides in behind Scipio, his helmet cradled in his arm. "I don't think he likes you very much right now," he says, grinning.

"Wait until he hears that he's going to join forces with Consul Purpurio. That man may be a rock-headed Latin, but he is a born general. He'll keep Marcellus from killing any more of his own men."

"Marcellus is a consul. You may be the First Man of Rome, but you can't boss him about."

"No, but I can promise him honor if he does, and disgrace if he doesn't. I still have the power to do that." He turns his horse toward camp. "Come on, I need to get back to my tent. My wounds are taxing me."

Hours later, Laelius staggers into Scipio's tent, a half-empty wineskin in his hands. He proffers it to Scipio, who lies bandaged on his sleeping furs.

"Here, thought I'd bring you a drink," Laelius says. "You should come out and join the party, the men are asking about you." He grins. "They aren't stupid. They know who won that battle for them, and it wasn't Marcellus."

"Just what I need," Scipio replies, gulping from the wineskin, "a hangover on top of a headache and a neck wound."

"Take another drink—you deserve it. It was good of you to give Lucius the conquest," Laelius says. "It will help him move up the cursus honorum. Maybe he will make consul some day."

"I am not sure if I want to hope for that," Scipio mutters. "But I did promise mother I would help him make his way in life."

Laelius grins at Scipio. "Who knows? Maybe he can run for consul when I do. I'd be the plebian candidate, and he'd be the patrician. We'd be coconsuls!"

Scipio shakes his head. "I hope the wars are over by then. I can't imagine Lucius leading an army against Macedonia or Syria. I love him, but he reminds me of Marcellus!"

Weeks later, Marcellus' army joins Consul Lucius Furius Purpurio's in Boii territory. After taking over several of their citadels, the Romans surprise the Boii army returning from a plundering adventure.

Marcellus' men remember the Boii ambush that killed thousands of their brothers in arms. They attack the Boii with a relentless vengeance, leaving only a few messengers to relay news of the massacre back to their tribes.[cxxxvii]

Marcellus returns to Rome, leaving Furius Purpurio to conclude Rome's conquest of the Gallic tribes. He enters Rome as a hero, leading a mile long train of captured wagons filled with bronze and silver.[cxxxviii]

Even as he parades toward the Forum square, waving at the cheering throngs, Marcellus' mind is on Scipio, wondering what he has told the Senate.

But Scipio is not there to meet him. He lies abed in his house. Weak from his wounds, Scipio is taken with a fresh bout of fever. On the night of Marcellus' arrival, Febris' fever dreams fill his head.

Scipio is in a wide valley ringed with rippling hills. Thousands of legionnaires fill the dusty plain in front of him. The Romans stand rigidly at attention, their javelins clutched in their fists.

All around them, Syrians flow down the hills like a wave of insects, darkening every hill as far as the eye can see. Laelius and Lucius stand in front of the legions, both wearing the purple capes of Roman consuls. They argue animatedly with each other, their faces flush with anger.

The Syrians enter the plain and flow toward the immobile cohorts. Lucius and Laelius continue their feud, their eyes fixed on each other.

"Stop it!" Scipio shouts. "Get the men ready!"

The two look at him. "Which of us should give the order?" Laelius asks.

"I don't know," Scipio says. "Just attack them!"

Surface Glory

Lucius looks at him. "Should I do it, brother?"

"I don't know, it's not my decision!" Scipio rages. The two return to their bickering. The Syrians flood onto the plain, a massive dust cloud trailing in their wake.

The silver-armored Syrians plow into the unmoving Romans, their curved swords hewing down the legionnaires as if they were stalks of wheat. Antiochus rides in front of his murderous soldiers, grinning voraciously. He rumbles his sickle-wheeled chariot through the fallen warriors, its scythed wheels flinging heads and limbs.

"Get them!" Scipio wails.

"Who? Which one of us?" Laelius asks. "You have to decide." Laelius and Lucius look at Scipio, waiting for an answer.

Scipio vaults upright, his eyes staring at the walls of his bedroom.

"What is it, love?" Amelia sits up and cradles his sweaty back with her arms. "Another bad dream?"

"The Syrians. I saw them coming at our men," he babbles. "Hordes of them. Laelius and Lucius were generals, but they didn't do anything. They waited for me to pick one of them."

He stares at her. "But they can't be generals. They aren't consuls. They're not even running—yet."

"No, it will be Flaccus and Cato this year, the way things are going," Amelia replies bitterly. "Flaccus wooed a lot of senators to his side while you were gone. And to Cato's, too, even though he just got back from Iberia."

Amelia sits on the side of the bed, rubbing her neck. "I did all I could, but our candidates were too weak. I couldn't lie about them. If the citizens found out, they would never believe my propaganda."

"I should have stayed here to help stop Flaccus," Scipio says. "But Marcellus sounded lost—I should have never picked him to be consul!"

"You were right to go. Now the Gauls are no longer a threat, thanks to you. And Macedonia may soon follow. Then we can turn our eyes to Sicily."

"Antiochus will fill Philip's void, I am sure of it," Scipio says, plopping back onto his bed. "I only hope I am well enough to help stop him from taking Greece."

"Greece is not Italia," Amelia says softly, running her hand through Scipio's graying hair. "He would not be on our shores."

He closes his hand over Amelia's and brings it to his lips. "True enough. But if Greece falls, can Italia be far behind?"

Thracian Warrior

XI. Rising Powers

CARTHAGE, 195 BCE. Hannibal shuffles around his spacious trophy room, his bare feet poking out from the unadorned linen shift that drapes to his feet. Carthage's greatest general scans the souvenirs of thirty years of warfare, his eyes wandering across the statues, weapons, and skulls of many battles. He picks up a lion's head cape and fingers it, recalling the Numidian commander he killed to get it.

The graying mastermind lays the cape down and walks to a corner of the room. He picks up a rusting Roman helmet and strokes its rounded dome, running his forefinger across its tattered black crest. *Commander Paullus, you fought valiantly at Cannae. I would have saved you if I could. The gods truly favored me that day, didn't they? Forty thousand of your men strewn across those lovely fields. Half the armies of Rome, dead. Maybe it's best that you did not live to see the end.*

He taps the crown of the helmet. *What would have happened if I had marched on Rome after that, when its legions were depleted? What would have happened if I was not so horrified with all the killing? Would Italia then be paying tribute to us? Would our Elders be ruling your Senate?*

Hannibal rubs the back on his neck, rotating his head to loosen his muscles. *Maybe Maharbal was right. I knew how to win battles, but not how to use them.*[cxxxix] *And now look at us. Our empire has become a slave to Rome. I spend my days railing against flaccid politicians who care only for topping off their bulging purses. Curse it, Carthage has to recover its spirit, its power!*

He grins. *Is this what Scipio is doing now, reminiscing about past glories? I hope he has found more relevant pursuits.*

"General?" comes a voice from the doorway. "That man is here again."

Rising Powers

The envoy from Antiochus."

"Send him away, Gilgo," Hannibal growls. The elderly Libyan slave bows. "As you wish, Master." Gilgo pads out the door.

Hannibal looks back at the lion's cape. He hefts the Roman helmet in his hand. "Gilgo, come back here!" Hannibal shouts, his voice tinged with desperation.

The Libyan reappears. "Yes?"

"Tell him to wait in the garden. I will be there in a minute."

Hannibal sheds his robe and dons the purple toga that signifies his senatorial office. He walks into the rose-filled garden, his hand extended in welcome. A young man rises from a stone bench flanked by a spindly tree laden with soft pink almond buds. Hannibal stops short, gaping in admiration.

Hannibal faces the most beautiful man he has ever seen, a tall and stately youth with emerald eyes that gleam from his light brown skin. The youth's ash-blonde ringlets cascade down to his broad shoulders, his gold hoop earrings glimmering inside his thick hair. A smile splits his face as he strides toward Hannibal.

"General Hannibal. It is the honor of my life to meet you," he says. He genuflects in front of the commander, his right hand resting on his thigh. Hannibal notices a thin circlet of gold rests atop his head.

"Rise, friend. Who are you?"

"Seleucus, first son of King Antiochus of Syria," he says proudly. "I volunteered to come here as my father's envoy." Seleucus blushes and looks at the floor. "You are something of a hero to me, General."

At least someone remembers me. "What is your purpose in coming here?"

"My father invites you to visit him and give him counsel. He expects a war with Rome is coming." His dazzling smile reappears. "He knows that no one has been better at defeating them."

Hannibal's mind races. *A chance to lead an army again! But I could jeopardize our peace with Rome. If Antiochus conquered Italia, would he let us have our ships and army back? I could insist on that as a condition.*

Hannibal reaches out and takes the young man's muscular forearm. He grasps it firmly. "Tell your father, your king, that I will carefully consider his offer. Such a course of action has many ramifications. But the thought does fill me with pleasure—and renewed enthusiasm."

Seleucus' smile vanishes. He steps back and bows his head. "I will relay your message immediately," he says tonelessly, turning toward the entryway.

He thinks I've rejected him. "Do not rush off, son of Antiochus. If you have a day or two, be my guest here. Carthage may be under the Roman thumb for now, but it still has many wonders to see."

The smile returns. "It would be a pleasure. I am yours to command."

Well, they're the kind of words I like to hear. "Come, then, let's sample some of our local cuisine. Have you ever had camel's hump soup?" Hannibal and the envoy head down the spacious hallway, chatting as if they were old friends.

As they stroll past Hannibal's many statues and paintings, Hannibal glances up at one of his most recent acquisitions: a wall fresco depicting the Battle of Zama, Hannibal rides atop his elephant Surus, trampling down a handful of Roman soldiers. Scipio stands back behind his men, calmly directing them forward.

Hannibal winces at the scene—and the memory. He turns back to the envoy and walks on, smiling. *Who knows, Scipio? We may yet test ourselves against each other, one more time.*

ROME, 196 BCE. "All right, dip your foot into the bowl. It won't hurt. Just a little bite and then you will be fine!"

Rising Powers

The doctor scurries about the Scipio atrium, laying towels around the table-sized pottery bowl that rests on the floor. Scipio sits in a chair next to it, his bare right foot resting near its edge. Something stirs inside the bowl, splashing water onto Scipio's bare toes.

Seven-year-old Publius walks over to the bowl, attracted by the splashing noises. He bends over and reaches inside it.

"Publius, get away from there!" Scipio barks. Amelia rushes in and pulls her son from the bowl. "Bad! That's dangerous!"

"Yes, but apparently not too dangerous for me, the sick one," Scipio remarks. "I don't know why I let you talk me into this!"

While Amelia watches nervously as the Greek medicus guides Scipio's bare foot into the deep, wide dish. Inside, a two-foot ray darts about, its wide flat body flapping against the bottom. Surus sneaks over and sniffs at the swirling water.

"Get out, Surus!" Scipio blurts nervously. The hundred-pound dog slinks away. Scipio looks skeptically at the doctor. "You are sure this will help cure my fevers? Get rid of the night visions?"

"Oh yes," the aged doctor replies. "We use the torpedo fish all the time—it's a wonderful cure.[cxl] Nothing like a good shock to shake up the brain. And the spirit!"

Scipio squints down at the spade-shaped brown fish. "Well, I am desperate."

Amelia wrings her hands. "I may have made a mistake. Perhaps you should try some more herbal potions."

"Herbs! Plants!" the medicus sniffs. "Those are some foolish old woman's remedies. *This* is science!"

Scipio rolls his eyes. "It's worth a try, anyway."

"Go ahead, Imperator," the doctor coos, easing Scipio's toes into the water. "Step on the fish. It won't hurt him, just irritate him enough to bite you."

As if I don't have enough people biting at me already. Scipio takes a deep breath and plunges his foot down, pushing it on top of the torpedo fish. It slithers to the side of the bowl, its wavy body flapping angrily.

"Once more. He's really getting mad now," the doctor chirps. "You'll get a nice big bite!"

Scipio envisions pushing the scrawny doctor's face into the bowl, but he nods his compliance. He shoves his toes onto the back of the fish, aiming at the two blue spots on top of its back.

The fish contorts upward, baring serried rows of small daggered teeth. It chomps into Scipio's sole.

Scipio feels a sharp pain, then a jolting shock. His body convulses, his arms and legs flapping as if he were a puppet yanked by its strings. He slides from his elmwood chair and tumbles onto the tiled floor. Surus barks madly, pacing the room in circles.

Amelia screams, rushing to his side. The doctor clambers after her. The two and ease a groggy Scipio back into his chair.

"You old fool," Amelia blazes. "If he's hurt I will cut you balls off!"

"Oh no, oh no," the medicus stammers. "This is all quite ordinary. It shows he received a good dose."

Scipio leans back in the chair, breathing heavily. He flaps his limp hand at his wife and grins weakly. "I'm all right, truly. It's just that it was...such a surprise."

"Yes, yes, a good hard jolt," the doctor exults. "We should try another just to be sure." He grabs Scipio's other foot. "Here, let's try this one now."

Amelia's eyes flare. She steps toward the medicus, her hand reaching inside her robe. *Oh gods, she's going to go after him!* Scipio thinks.

"No, that will be quite enough for today, Medicus." Scipio says. "I have to prepare for a Senate meeting this afternoon. We will decide the fate of Macedonia." He joins eyes with Amelia. "And I can't have any more distractions."

Amelia steps over and strokes Scipio's head. She stares flintily at the doctor. "Time for you to go."

"Um, hm, " the medicus replies. "Yes, perhaps it is best I leave, so you can rest."

"That is a remarkably good idea," Scipio replies, his hand restraining Amelia's right wrist. The medicus scurries away.

Amelia helps Scipio up. The two walk to a couch by the fish pond and ease themselves onto it. She looks at the bloody dots lining the bottom of Scipio's right foot.

"I don't care what that old pig thinks, I'm going to make a poultice of gentian and aloe for that."[cxli] She hurries from the room, the hem of her green silk robe whispering along the polished marble tiles.

"Rufus!" Scipio shouts into the empty room. The old slave appears in the archway. "Wine," Scipio says. The family attendant soon hobbles back with a pottery cup of watered white wine. Scipio sips it gratefully, pondering what he will say at the Senate meet. Minutes later, Laelius appears in the doorway, leaning against its side.

"Look at you, lying on the couch and drinking wine in the middle of the morning. Ah, to have the hero's life, taking my comfort all day!"

Scipio grins wryly. "How is Rome's newest aedile doing?"

Laelius frowns in mock disgust. "Being a city magistrate is as repulsive as it sounds. Do you know, I had to take a work team out and inspect the public lavatories this week. And I had to listen to a whiny couple demanding that men and women have separate toilet sponges! What's next, the patricians wanting papyrus to wipe their asses? Gods above, how fussy can you be?"

"Knowing you, pretty fussy," Scipio replies. "Want a sip?" He proffers his cup to his friend. Laelius grabs it and drains it in a gulp. Scipio rolls his eyes. "Rufus! More wine!"

"I am glad you are moving up the cursus honorum," Scipio says. "In a few years, you will be able to run for consul, as you have dreamed." Scipio grabs Laelius' forearm and shakes it. "But you have to get married—and have children!"

"I know, I know," Laelius replies. "Perhaps I could shave a couple of those Thracian dwarves and call them my kids."

"They're not ugly enough to be yours," Scipio replies. He purses his lips and smiles. "I noticed you have been frequently associating with Prima. Is something growing between you two?"

"She is quite fine—for a woman," Laelius sniffs. "A bit brash and braggedy, though." He bugs out his eyes. "She thought she could beat me in a wrestling match. Me! Can you imagine?"

"I have seen her fight in the arena, so yes, I can imagine," Scipio replies as he drinks, his wine cup hiding his smile. "There's only one way to settle that, isn't there? Or do you have qualms about that?"

"Qualms? I just don't want to hurt her," Laelius huffs. His face grows serious. "And I don't want to lose her friendship. She is so full of energy and life—for an overpriviliged patrician!"

"And she is lithe and beautiful to look upon, whatever your proclivities." He eyes Laelius. "You could do infinitely worse, you know."

"I know, I know. I just want to let things take their own course for now," he replies. Amelia returns, carrying a dripping cotton sack. She sits next to Scipio and lays his damaged foot across her thighs.

"I don't think I need that," Scipio begins, reaching for his foot.

"Quiet!" she snaps, slapping the top of his hand. "This is exactly what you need!"

Amelia pulls a band of gauzy narrow linen from her robe. She wraps the poultice tightly about his foot. "There. Leave that on for an hour."

"What happened to you?" Laelius says, staring at Scipio's foot.

"Amelia became overly amorous this morning," Scipio replies, fetching another wrist slap for his troubles.

"It's the fevers, isn't it?" says Laelius. "It's gotten worse since Africa."

"I could live with the fever if it didn't bring the dreams," Scipio says. "All the images of the battles—all the bodies." He shakes his head as if trying to clear it. "Last night I dreamt I was in Syria, fighting against Antiochus. Can you imagine?"

"I can," says Amelia. "You are still Rome's finest general."

"Ah, I'm getting too old for fighting," Scipio says. "After I help settle down the Gauls, I'm going to stick to being a Senator. The fighting's more vicious there, but the wounds are less deadly. Which reminds me—I had best get ready for the meeting."

"You are still going to the Senate?" Amelia says, incredulous.

"What choice do I have? Today, we decide the fate of Macedonia. And Greece. And I know what the Latins want to do." He sighs. "With Flaccus in Sicily and Cato in Iberia, I thought they might be quiet. But old Senator Titus, he is almost as bad as they are. He wants us to conquer everything!"

Scipio pushes himself up from the couch. He walks slowly to his room, as Rufus scuttles along behind him.

Two hours later, Scipio is at the Senate. As befits his rank, he sits in the center of the circular bench that comprises the first row. Tiberius Gracchus, Rome's chief haruspex, affirms that the omens indicate the gods favor the Senate meeting today. The Senate Elder pounds on his staff of office and the Senate opens discussion of the major item that occupies its agenda: the fate of Macedonia.

"You have all heard Philip's envoys. He wants to make peace, and is amenable to our demands. All he asks is that he retain control of Macedonia and its ancestral dominions."

Senator Titus Fabius rises from his front row seat near Scipio. The old general's hair is silver with age, but his body still bears the broad shoulders and thick arms of a lifetime soldier. "That is unacceptable. We must destroy Macedonia, and put Philip to the cross. The only way to eliminate Macedonia's threat is to make it part of Rome's dominion!"

Amid scattered shouts of agreement, Titus slowly resumes his seat. Scipio strides to the speaking platform, his face still wan from the morning's travails.

"If we destroy Macedonia, we will loose numerous threats to Rome. Philip's ambitions have gotten the better of him, but his iron hand has kept Thessaly, Gaul, the Illyrians, and others from invading Greece.[cxlii] If he were not there, we would have to battle them all."

"Then we shall defeat them all," Titus bellows, rising from his seat. "Rome's destiny is to become the greatest empire in the world. Now that Flamininus has beaten Philip, Macedonia will be part of it. And so will Greece."

Scipio wearily rubs his brow. "Greece is not a single country to be conquered, it is a nation of city-states that will become our allies, our *amici*. If we deliver them from Philip's predations, their gratitude will be boundless."

"They treat us as if we were a bunch of witless farmers," declares Titus. "They give us no respect."

We are *a bunch of farmers*, Scipio thinks. *And if you had it your way, we'd stay like that.*

"Rome is a city, not an empire," Scipio replies. "We do not have the men to spread ourselves across the continent."

"And if you have your way, that's where we will stay," Titus says. He grins slyly. "I would remind the Senate you once said we were going to become an empire. I heard you myself, three years ago."

"I did say that, and I was wrong," Scipio says. "If becoming an empire means we take control all our neighbors, then I was wrong. What we need are allies. Allies against the growing threat from the East. From King Antiochus." He chuckles. "As the old saying goes, 'second thoughts are ever wiser.'" Scattered laughs greet his words.

"I have my own saying," Titus growls. "'Beware a snake in the grass. We who own farms know it is best to kill a snake. For soon it will bite you."

You own farms, but you are not a farmer, Scipio thinks. *Your slaves do your work, and our young men would do your fighting—and dying.* He steps forward and faces the back rows of junior Senators. "Philip will swear obeisance to us, I guarantee it. Then Macedonia will become a powerful ally, not a burdensome chattel."

"An ally?" blurts a young senator. "The man is as devious as Hannibal. He cannot be trusted."

Scipio nods. "King Philip is tricky, but he is no fool. Rome has beaten him twice. His army is in tatters. He knows we can take Macedonia at any time. He dare not betray us."

He stares at the young senator. "Might I remind you: Hannibal and Carthage were our bitter enemies, once in league with Philip. Now they send us elephants, grain, and money to fight him."

"And that is another mistake," Titus blurts. "If honorable Cato were not in Iberia he would tell you: Carthage must be destroyed!"

"You talk of naught but war, Titus. I speak of peace, peace with Macedonia so that we may focus our forces upon Sicily. We must give Flamininus permission to sign a peace treaty with Philip, following the conditions we set for it. And we will set conditions that ensure he cannot threaten us or Greece again. It is that simple."

The Senate Elder pounds his staff onto the tiled floor, its explosions ringing off the high stone walls. "Enough, the both of you! You have clarified your positions. I propose we call a vote. Those in favor of a vote?"

The senators in favor stand up. "The motion to vote has passed. Those in favor of preserving Philip as ruler, gather on the right side of the floor. Those who propose we depose him and take over Macedonia, gather on the left. If you are undecided, remain where you are."

The senators step down the rows and form into two groups, with a dozen of the younger senators remaining where they are. The Elder surveys the two groups and nods his head.

"You see the results for yourself, senators. Our next task is to draw up the final treaty conditions for King Philip. He must swear allegiance to Rome, or face the consequences."

Scipio returns to his seat, smiling to himself. *Now you have your chance, Flamininus. I hope you make peace as well as you make war.*

LARISA, MACEDONIA. "You are making your bed with a scorpion!" the Aetolian commander sputters. "We should put Philip's head on a spear by nightfall!"

Aristus stands up from the twenty-foot-long banquet table. The brown-bearded giant spreads his thick arms imploringly, his face entreating the other Grecian delegates. "Do you hear this Roman? He wants to keep this brutal murderer in power. The very man who burned our cities and towns!"

Flamininus rises from his chair at the head of the table. "Calm yourself, General Aristus. Philip is no longer a threat. We have destroyed his army. Rome wants to make peace with him. We will make him an ally against future threats from other nations."

"Future threats?" Aristus splutters. "*He* is the future threat! And we Aetolians should know! Let us not forget that we were the first in battle at Cynoscephalae. My peerless warriors were happy to fight—and die—to save Greece. But we are not happy to see Philip still walking the earth!"

"You were not alone in your fight," Commander Vibius says dryly. He leans into Flamininus' ear. "I think this one wants to be the next King Philip." The young consul gives the barest of nods.

Aristus shakes his head. "My fellow Greeks, members of the Achean and Aetolian Leagues, help me turn back the threat of Macedonia. We must make Consul Flamininus change his mind. Why does he persist in this misguided effort to save Philip? Why weren't we Aetolians involved in Rome's decision to seek peace—we who fought side by side with them?"

Flamininus wills himself to remain calm. *I know of your speeches, Aetolian. I heard about you taking all the credit for the victory. And all of the plunder from Philip's camp. You are bent on your own conquest of Greece, so I will continue to minimize your involvement. I will make sure your importance in diminished in the eyes of our allies."* [cxliii]

Aristus looks straight at Flamininus. His eyes grow sly. "I ask you, is there perhaps some motivation that Philip has given our consul to make this agreement? Some inducement to pursue his gutless folly?"

"Philip's fate is not my decision to change," Flamininus says. "Rome made that decision, just as Rome is the one who came here and saved Greece from conquest." He glares at Aristus. "And we have done that with the *help* of Aetolia. And Rhodes, and Athens, and the rest of you."

"I would speak," announces a lean, elderly man near the head of the table, on Flamininus' right. The allies all fall silent.

"What say you, King Amynander?" says Flamininus. *Good. Even that fool Aristus has to listen to Amynander.*

The king of the Athamanians rises up from the his seat. He leans forward and looks into each man's eyes before he speaks. "I have no quarrel with honored Flamininus' proposal to keep Philip in power."

Aristus flushes and starts to stand up. Amynander glares him back down. He shakes his index finger at the rest of the men. "*But,* I have one non-negotiable condition, and it is truly non-negotiable. The peace must be arranged so that Greece will be strong enough to defend itself from future attack, in the absence of Roman intervention."[cxliv]

Flamininus nods his head, his face solemn. "If it must be as you say, my King, then Rome will promise not to occupy Greece, only to act in defense of it, should you request it." He faces the allies. "What say you to that?"

The Grecian allies mumble and argue among themselves, debating the merits of the three men's statements. Flamininus' face is solemn, but inwardly, he smiles. *Well played, King. You have ensured we can keep Philip as an ally, but you have quashed those in Rome who would seek to occupy Greece. Scipio will be most pleased.*

"I suggest we put this to a vote," Amynander replies. "Let us see where we all stand on making peace with Macedonia. All those who favor my proposal, please stand..."

Three days later, King Philip enters the banquet room at nightfall, clad in his best silver battle armor. Flamininus and the allies are all seated about the table. The allies search the defeated king's face for signs of resistance or acquiescence, but they only see a wall. A goatskin scroll lies in the center of the table, next to a bronze stylus and ink pot.

Flamininus rises and walks to the entrance. He extends his arm and Philip grips it. "Welcome, King Philip. Thank you for making the journey from Tempe."

Philip's lips twist into a wry smile. "Gratitude, Consul. But I did not have much of a choice in the matter, now did I?"

Flamininus shrugs, not knowing what to say. He nods toward the goatskin scroll. "You have read the peace terms?"

Philip sighs. "I am to withdraw from all the garrisons and cities I have controlled," he recites, staring at the ceiling. "I will surrender all prisoners and deserters. I will pay Rome one thousand talents of silver."

His voice catches in his throat. "Macedonia will maintain an army of no more than five thousand men—and no elephants." [cxlv]

"Gratitude, my King." Flamininus says softly. "I can only imagine the difficulty in saying that."

Aristus rises, his face flushed. "What about some talents for us?" Aristus shouts at Flamininus. "The Aetolians fought and died with you, we merit recompense!"

"You fought and died for your homeland—we did not," replies Flamininus. "I will hear no more on the matter."

"Shut up, Aristus," Amynander mutters. The rulers of Sparta and Bithynia cover their mouths with their hands, their eyes twinkling.

"You have brought hostages to bind the agreement?" Flamininus asks.

"Bring them in," Philip says. His two guards exit. Minutes later they return with a dozen men, all dressed in Macedonia's black tunics. "These are all men of noble birth, their parents are the scions of Macedonia."

He walks over to a handsome, curly-haired youth and puts his arm about his shoulders. "This is my son Demetrius. He goes with you to Rome."

The allies mutter in surprise. Flamininus stares coldly at Aristus. "Do you still doubt the sincerity of his word, Aetolian?"

"Phah! Just make sure it is truly his son!" Aristus barks.

Flamininus rolls his eyes. "Ignore him. Just sign the agreement."

Philip steps over to table and unrolls the scroll. He dips the stylus into the ink pot.

"Do you want to read it first?" Flamininus says. "To make sure it's the same as the one we sent you?"

"I know you well enough by now," Philip replies. He sniffs, rubs a knuckle against the corner of his eye, and quickly scribbles his name.

The King of Macedonia stands up and straightens his back. His imperious gaze scans the faces around the table. "Now, if there is nothing else, I will return to my kingdom—such as it is."

Flamininus' head bows. "Thank you, King Philip, new Friend to Rome. I look forward to visiting you in Macedonia."

Philip whirls about and strides from the room, his black cape billowing behind him. His guards boom the doors closed, the finality echoing throughout the hall.

The Grecian rulers erupt into claps and cheers. "It's over," the king of Pharsalus declares. "After four years of blood, it's finally over."

"We have much rebuilding to do," Amynander says, rising. "And we had best get to it."

"Not quite yet," Flamininus replies. "He claps his hands. A cadre of kitchen slaves marches out, lugging enormous platters filled with pheasant, boar, squid, goat cheese, and beans. They are followed by a half-dozen more lugging child-sized jugs of wine. The Greeks grin with delight.

"What is a victory without a celebration?" Flamininus says. "And we start with wine!" The slaves scurry to give each ruler a silver goblet and to fill it with watered white wine.

Flamininus raises his goblet and pours a dollop onto the hall's stone slab floor. "To the gods," he says. He extends his goblet toward the allied rulers. "To an enduring alliance between Greece and Rome!" The rulers raise their goblets.

Aristus raises his cup. He pauses, staring fixedly at it. The Aetolian commander clacks it onto the table. The Greeks drain their cups and pitch them onto the floor, grinning at one another.

Aegeus, the rotund magistrate of Athens, grabs the pheasant platter and tears a huge piece of breast from the roast bird. He stuffs it into his mouth as the others watch, amused. "What?" he says. "Someone has to go first."

Flamininus laughs. "Ah Aegeus. First in war, first in peace, and first at the table!" The consul tears off a chunk of spelt bread and bites into its leathery crust, still chuckling. Dozens of hands grab platters, and the peace feast begins in earnest.

Hours later, Vibius and Flamininus totter toward the general's quarters in a stone block granary. Flamininus nods at the guards in front of the thick oak doors. They push his door open and stand aside, waiting.

Flamininus pounds his fist on his chest and emits a mighty belch. "Good food!" he slurs.

Vibius grins. "The lion of Rome roars before he sleeps!"

Flamininus chuckles. "Old Scipio—he is the lion. I am more the young leopard—who looks forward to crawling into his den!"

"Be careful in there," Vibius says. "Those Thessaly rats can get as big as cats, and they're everywhere."

Flamininus nods. "Good. Then I won't sleep alone tonight." He enters and sits upon a tall oak stool in the middle of his room. He eases out of his belt and sandals, then sheds his tunic, leaving him in only a snow-white subligaculum. The young general stretches languorously.

Now I can go home with my duty fulfilled. He looks longingly at his bed, then at his writing table. He shakes his head and smiles. *Duty— there is always another duty. But not much longer.*

Flamininus heaves himself up from his stool. He pours himself a pottery cup of dark red wine and summons a guard to taste it. When the guard shows no ill effects, the consul sends him from the room.

Flamininus rolls out a sheet of ivory-colored papyrus and picks up a stylus. He slumps over the sheet and slowly writes.

To Publius Cornelius Scipio: Consul, Imperator, and Princeps Senatus of Rome:

373

Rising Powers

Honored Mentor:

Today Philip agreed to the Senate's peace terms. He has ceded all his conquered lands and will return to Macedonia. Soon, if Fortuna smiles upon me, I shall return to my homeland. Gratitude to you, Imperator, for giving me the time to honorably conclude my mission.

Peace is not on the horizon, though, much as I regret to say it. You were right—we need to make Philip an ally against Syria.

Amynander's spies have returned from Pergamum. They report that Antiochus is planning to invade Thrace.

I fear the Syrians will not stop until they conquer Greece. And then Italia. And then Rome. Rome will need its ablest leaders for the dark task ahead. I hope we will be together for it.

Your dutiful pupil,

Proconsul Titus Quinctius Flamininus

Flamininus rolls up the scroll and seals it. He staggers from the writing table and plops onto his sleeping pallet, staring at the ceiling.

Gauls, Macedonians, Carthaginians, and now Syrians. Do we walk from one war just to enter another? He falls into sleep, leaving his question unanswered.

ISLE OF SARDINIA, 196 BCE. "Come on, Italus. Do I have to carry you on my back?"

"Yes, Praetor. Uh, I mean no, Praetor."

Cato's lanky assistant hastens to catch up to him, swiping the sweat from his sun-browned brow. "Do we have to keep walking all over this island? You have hundreds of chariots and men at your disposal." He eyes Cato's sweat-stained back. "Then you could save your energy for your meetings."

Cato does not reply. Italus shakes his head. "You know, the previous three magistrates I worked with all took chariots." *Carriages with soft, padded seats.*

"The previous magistrates were weaklings. The state had to bear the wasteful costs of their indulgences."[cxlvi] He raises his right foot, showing Italus a tattered brown sandal. "I have two good feet and I plan to use them. Now come on!"

Marcus Porcius Cato, chief magistrate of Iberia, stalks down the packed earth roadway to the costal town of Feronia. He fixes his eyes on the dusty road, oblivious to the snow-capped peaks that rise above him; ignoring the herds of sheep peacefully grazing in the grassy hillocks. Italus trots next to him, lugging Cato's sacrificial bowl and book of accounts.

"Are we going to walk to *every* city in Sardinia, master? It's almost as large as Sicily, you know."

"We are going to every town that has a record of usury. Their exorbitant rates are a plague upon our people. I'm going to run those criminals off the mainland!"[cxlvii]

Italus eyes the encircling peaks. "Some of cities are way up in the mountains. But they'd be just a day's ride on horseback."

"I don't care if they are way up in the mountains of Barbaria, where the savage Barbarians dwell. We will go there on foot."

Italus rolls his eyes. "As you say. But you know, everything is fine here in Iberia. It's been peaceful for a long time. No revolts or invasions." He looks sideways at Cato. "No reason to disturb it."

Cato snorts. "There is work to be done, though you cannot see it. Rome's consular elections are coming soon, and I must sail back for them. When I do, I want my accomplishments to follow me. No one will be able to say Marcus Porcius Cato wasted Rome's time and money in lavish parties and foolish trips, as my Hellenic predecessors have done."

Cato looks sideways and glowers at Italus. "You should have seen the money that puff Scipio wasted on his fancy feasts, and his gifts to his men. Disgusting!"

"Scipio defeated the Three Generals. He conquered Iberia. Surely his methods were not all so—"

"Don't talk to me about him 'conquering' Iberia!" Cato blurts. "Fortuna favored him in a few conflicts against a weaker opponent. Any general could have done the same."

But no general had the courage to take them on, Italus thinks. He glances at Cato's angry face. *How can such a sensible man be so irrational about Scipio?*

"Well, I am sure your record will be one of austerity and accomplishment," Italus tactfully responds. *Even if it kills the both of us.*

"I will need it to be," Cato says. "I am going to run for consul in a few months."

Italus gasps. "Consul of Rome? You are indeed ambitious, Governor. Won't that cost a lot of money?"

"I have a powerful friend who will run alongside me. He will help promote me." Cato says. *Flaccus needs someone with a conscience to keep an eye on him, anyway.*

"You would make a good ruler," Italus replies. "Your ethics are unimpeachable." *And a pain in the ass.*

"That is good of you to say," Cato says, his mouth a tight line. "I will need all the power and reputation I can muster. I am going to impeach someone who has too much of the both of them."

LYSIMACHIA, THRACE[cxlviii], 196 BCE. "Those pestilent little bastards," Antiochus says to his commander. "I want you to throw everything we have at them."

Antiochus is watching his treasured cataphractii attack the Thracian resistors, and he is not pleased. The heavily armored Syrians have ridden straight at the center of the tribesmen, seeking to break the Thracian lines before their infantry attacked. They have failed.

When the cataphractii closed upon the unarmored foot soldiers, the agile Thracians dashed to the side, creating a wide, empty lane in front of them. As the cataphractii thundered into the opening, the swift peltasts attacked the riders from every angle, flinging clouds of javelins and hacking at them with axes and swords.[cxlix]

Hundreds of Thracians discarded their shields and boldly leapt onto the backs of their mailed enemies, pulling them from their horses. Within minutes the fearsome cataphractii wedge has turned into a milling swarm of panicky warriors, men fighting to escape before they are swarmed under. Antiochus watches the remnants of his favored cavalry run from the field.

"The Thracians are embarrassing us," the king growls. "I want them destroyed!"

Commander Zeuxis touches the top of his forehead. "As you say, my King. We have forty thousand infantry to their ten. I'll send them all."

"Send the Parthians too," Antiochus commands. "And get the chariots out there. I want them crushed before nightfall!"

The Syrian army marches onto the plains in front of the captured city of Lysimachia, heading toward the battling Thracians. Five thousand Galatians lead the charge, the giant Gauls tramping along in loosely ordered groups, eager for kills and plunder. The Syrian phalanxes follow, bristling with twelve foot spears.

Seeing their enemies approach, the Thracians rearrange themselves into squares of 144 men. Scores of them wear the mailed armor of their recent cataphractii victims, a trophy of their battle prowess.

Three hundred Thracian cavalry wait behind their footmen, the finest horse warriors in Greece. The riders patiently study the gates of Lysimachia, waiting to repel any new cavalry attacks.

The Galatians halt within a stone's throw of the Thracian lines. A

dozen Gallic chieftains march out in front of their men, facing the
Thracians. The eldest chief raises his tribe's ram's-head standard over
his head. The Gallic horns blare the call to attack. The chiefs stride
forward, waving their swords and axes.

The Galatians run past their leaders, roaring with excitement, and
burst into the Thracian spear wall. As soon as the Gauls collide with the
Thracians, the agile peltasts strike out with their short spears, ducking
under the Gaul's heavy swords. Scores of bold Thracians ram their
bodies against their brawny enemy, wielding their dagger-swords with
deadly effect.

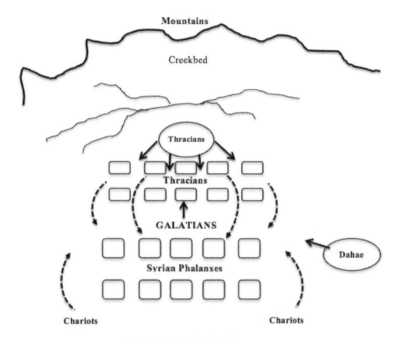

Battle of Lysimachia

196 BCE

The Gauls batter down hundreds of the front-line soldiers, but the
fierce Thracians refuse to retreat. Each fallen man is replaced by
another eager to avenge the pillage of Lysimachia, their prized city.
The Thracians rip the necklaces and torques from the necks of their

fallen opponents, pausing in the midst of battle to gain the plunder they covet as much as their kills.

After an hour of relentless combat, the Syrian horns sound a troop recall. Step by step, the weary Galatians retreat, dragging their wounded with them. The Syrian phalanxes move forward, each square moving as one, an impenetrable wall of spears.

The Thracian tribesmen are wise in the ways of phalanx warfare. They do not resist the advance. They retreat, step by step, maintaining their square formations, keeping themselves distanced from the fearsome spear wall that presses upon them. As their infantry retreats, the Thracian cavalry breaks into four squadrons. They arrange themselves behind the gaps between the Thracian squares in the center and on the flanks.

The Thracian soldiers back into the nearby creekbeds, stepping carefully through its brush and broken ground. The Syrian phalanxes follow. Their spears wobble as the Syrians lurch over the lowland's clumps and furrows. Scores of men fall on their face, dropping their spears.

Thrax notices the gaps that appear in the daunting spear wall. The Thracian chieftain sees the Syrians slip and stumble as they press forward, cursing the ground they walk upon. He knows the time has come.

"At them!" he yells to his chieftains. "Hit the right side of every phalanx." The chieftains dash off to relay the orders to their men.

Minutes later, the attack command echoes across the battlefield. The Thracians push into the advancing phalanxes, pitching their javelins into the middle of the formations. Four rounds of throws elicit hundreds of painful screams from the Syrians.

Their spear supply exhausted, the Thracians draw their swords and attack, chopping at the spear wall in front of them. With the Syrians engaged with the front-line infantry, the rear ranks of Thracians dash out and cut into the phalanxes' right flanks, the places where the sword arms of the right-handed Syrians are exposed to the open space. The Syrians on the right and center try to shift their lengthy spears toward the onrushing Thracians, but the tribesmen are already upon them.

The Thracians duck between the scattered spears, their swords bared and ready. They ram their shields into the shieldless Syrians, jabbing their short swords into Syrian bodies. Hundreds of terrified Syrians drop their spears and grapple for their daggers, vainly trying to defend themselves.

"Loose!" Thrax commands. More javelins hurtle into the phalanx's center and right, plunging into their exposed enemies. Hundreds of Syrians fall. Thrax smiles, savoring the cries of agony that erupt from his enemy's lines.

"Bring up the riders," he says.

The cavalry's four squads stampede in from the gaps between the infantry formations. They swerve into the rear of the front-line phalanxes, using their lances to stab down the vulnerable spearmen.

The front phalanxes begin to break apart. The remorseless Thracians cut deep into their ranks, their swords quieting the Syrians' surrenders and cries for mercy.

Antiochus watches in horror. "Get the Demon Riders in there," he screams at Zeuxis. "Bring the rear infantry to the front. Send everyone—*everyone*, damn it!"

Five hundred Dahae horsemen ride out from Lysimachia: short, lean, brown-skinned Asians who are adept at shooting arrows on horseback. The Dahae swoop down upon the Thracian cavalry, heading into the rear of the disorganized phalanxes. They cock their short horn bows and release hundreds of arrows into the Thracians, mowing down scores of them before the Thracians can reverse themselves and attack.

The Thracian riders gallop into the Dahae, spearing them down before they can loose more arrows. Many of the nimble Asians escape the attacks, giving them time to release arrows at point blank range. Soon, hundreds of the proud Thracian cavalry are upon the ground, arrows jutting from their heads and bodies. More Thracians fall but they still press the fight, chasing their tormentors around the plains.

With the Thracian cavalry occupied, fresh Syrian phalanxes move to the fore, driving away the infantrymen who were attacking the phalanxes' right flanks. The Thracians find themselves in a fresh battle, vastly outnumbered by reinvigorated troops.

"Stand! Thrax bellows to his men. "No one moves his feet!"

Thrax's men plant their right feet behind them and lean forward, putting their shoulders to their shields. They refuse to give ground, using the uneven terrain to attack gaps in the Syrian spear walls. For every dozen Thracians that fall, thrice as many die beneath their blades—yet their numbers continue to shrink.

Thrax fights on foot with his front-line infantry, directing charges into the weak spots in the Syrians' formation. *They'll break soon*, Thrax tells himself, slashing the thigh of an unwary Syrian. *If they break ranks, we can wipe them out. Just a little longer.*

Thrax see two enormous dust clouds coming at them from the plain, one on each flank. He hears a distant rumble, growing louder. Thrax sees scores of bright metallic flashes within the dust clouds, and he realizes what approaches.

Ares' balls, why did they have to come now! We almost had them!

Hundreds of bright bronze chariots rumble out of the dust, their iron hubs flashing with their scythed whirling blades. The chariots loop around their phalanxes and cut into the unarmored Thracian infantry, battering them aside while their wheels butcher the unfortunates who fall before them. The chariot drivers careen through the field of battle, sowing chaos wherever they go.

Scores of fearless Thracians throw off their shields and helmets and run at the chariots. They leap onto the backs of chariots and chop their swords and axes into their occupants.

The Thracians pitch the Syrians from the chariots and grasp the reins.

Rising Powers

They bash their chariots into the sides of the Syrians' carts, knocking them sideways to the earth. The Thracian infantry swarm over the fallen charioteers, rejoicing in their vengeance.

Watching their chariots cut apart the Thracians, the Syrian phalanxes smell blood. They stride forward with renewed vigor, shoving their long spears into the sides and backs of the milling Thracians. Hundreds fall to the relentless bronze, their bodies in rows where the spear wall has cut into them. Hundreds in the rear break and run, heading for the foothills behind the creekbed.

Thrax still rages in the center of the front line, surrounded by the thousands who refuse to retreat. Heedless of the danger, he dives between gaps in the spear wall. The Thracian commander slashes into the stomachs and chests of the shieldless phalangites, running back to his men before they can draw their swords on him.

One of his chieftains grabs him by the shoulder. "The flanks are caving in, Commander," he yells. "The greasy bastards are all about us!"

Thrax moves behind his front line, heading to the left flank. He sees that the flank is caving in, the chariots rumbling through his men while the Dahae horse archers shoot down dozens in the rear. He grimaces with regret. *There's too many of them. Too many weapons. We have to live to fight another day.*

Tears of shame well in his eyes. He waves over one of his attending captains. "Tell the horn men to sound the retreat. We will gather at the mountain camp. They won't dare follow us up there."

The horns soon sound the recall. The Thracians step backward, facing their enemies, battling every step of the way. The Syrians are only too glad to see their fierce enemy depart. They are content to skirmish with the retreating warriors, flinging rocks and spears at them.

A glint of silver catches Thrax's eye. In the distance, he sees a silver-masked Syrian stabbing into the chest of one of Thrax's men, adding to the pile at his feet. *The shiny one must be their champion. Killing him would be fitting revenge.* Thrax hands his attendant his sword.

"Give me Nightfall," he says. The attendant brings Thrax's favorite dueling weapon. Grasping Nightfall's handle, Thrax stalks toward the silver Syrian. *Who is this freak?* he wonders.

Thrax has never met Nicator.

"Ah, pig Thracian. You die slowly today, yes?" says Nicator, champion of the Syrian army. He leans over his supine opponent and raises his hand to his ear, as if he is listening to him.

"What, you no talk?" he says to the groveling Thracian. "I speak for you. I say 'yes!' Come on up and fight!" Nicator steps back, waiting for his man to rise.

The Thracian totters to his feet, his curved sword dangling from his numbed fist. His eyes roam the Syrian's body, looking for a weak spot. *There by the groin. One stab into his veins.* He raises his sword arm and stumbles forward.

"Oh, now we dance some more?" Nicator says, his eyes twinkling.

Antiochus' premier warrior is enjoying himself. He has made the twenty kills he sets as his goal in every battle, cutting down a score of front-line Thracians while the battle was still undecided. Now, as the Syrian hordes beat back their outnumbered opponents, the silver-masked assassin rewards himself with a lingering kill.

Nicator has toyed with the warrior as a cat would with a bird. He has parried his enemy's slashes and feints just before the blade cuts his flesh, whooping with mock fear. When the Thracian deftly slashed his sword arm with a counterthrust, it only made Nicator more eager to draw out the game, enjoying a fight with a worthy opponent. That the young Thracian is handsome has only added to the disfigured Syrian's relish in besting him, particularly when he sliced into his opponent's attractive face.

Nicator is becoming bored, however. He has cut the man in a dozen places, and the blood loss is telling on the Thracian's reflexes. *Finish it,* he tells himself. *There are more waiting.*

With a deft sweep of his right foot, the Syrian knocks the wounded soldier's feet out from under him. The Thracian crashes onto his back. Nicator leaps in and cuts into the Thracian's limbs before he can rise, disabling him.

The Syrian flicks the point of his sword across the throat of the Thracian. A ribbon of blood blooms across the man's neck.

"Oh, look! You wear a bright red scarf!" Nicator chuckles. "Perhaps you like to dress like a woman, Pretty One?" Nicator nicks another cut into the Thracian's cheek. "You not so pretty now!"

The Thracian rolls onto one shoulder and glares into the Syrian's face mask. "Fuck you, pot face."

The Thracian takes a deep breath. He jerks his head forward and spits a clot of blood onto the Syrian's silvered breastplate. The Thracian bares his carmined teeth into the rictus of a grin. "Now you're even uglier."

The Syrian laughs tinnily, his voice echoing inside his metal mask. "You have balls, don't you, Scarface? That is bad for you, what you say—no one call me ugly."

Nicator steps between the warrior's outstretched legs and angles his blade underneath the Thracian's tunic, resting its point against his testicles.

"Now we see how much you laugh."

"Get away from him, camel shit," comes a voice behind him. "Get back, or I'll cut your legs off." Nicator spins around, his blade arrowed out in front of him.

A rangy Thracian crouches in front of Nicator. His gray hair cascades down beneath his dark green helmet, draping around the blue snake tattoos that cover his shoulders and chest. The warrior holds a rhomphaia in his sinewy hands, a five-foot polearm that is half sword and half ax handle, its scythed blade perfect for slashing and battering. The Thracian's light gray eyes study Nicator's armor and stance, looking for the best killing spot.

Nicator bobs his head, delighted. "Ah, you are big chief Thrax!" Nicator chortles, eyeing the eagle crest on top of the Thrax's helmet. "You come to save your man? Too late; he dying."

"Then you will accompany him on his journey to the underworld," Thrax replies, his voice quaking with anger. He stalks toward the Syrian, his polearm cocked back for a butchering cut.

"I think not, old man." Nicator springs lightly from his dying foe, eager to kill the tribe's leader. *The fool has no shield*, the Syrian thinks as he closes upon the older man. *I'll cut his thigh open and watch him bleed out; I'll put their faces together so they can watch each other die!*

Nicator dips low, aiming for the thigh cut. With a speed that belies his years, Thrax whirls the polearm handle at Nicator's head. The Syrian jerks up his shield to ward off the blow, but he is an instant too late.

The handle clangs into the side of Nicator's silvered helmet. The dazed Syrian falls to one knee. Thrax leaps at him, aiming a murderous blow at his face.

Instinctively, Nicator ducks inside his upraised shield. The polearm's heavy blade cleaves through the shield, jamming against its center boss. The blow knocks Nicator flat. His head bounces off the ground, his legs splayed out in front of him. He shakes his head to clear it.

Thrax jerks at his rhomphaia, but the blade is wedged in the shield's brass boss. Cursing vehemently, he plants his left foot on the shield and jerks. "Gods curse you, come out!"

Nicator yanks his shield sideways, and slashes his sword across the Thracian's calf. Thrax yells. Nicator cocks his sword arm back, his eyes fixed on Thrax's leg artery.

Thrax realizes he is seconds away from death. Desperate, he lunges backward with his entire body. The polearm screeches free from the shattered shield, sending Thrax stumbling backward. He regains his footing just as Nicator springs at him, his sword poised for a killing stroke.

Thrax reverses his polearm and rams the butt end of the handle into the Syrian's shield. He hammers at it, again and again, driving Nicator backwards. Undismayed, Nicator aims a lighting quick thrust at Thrax's midsection. The former gladiator turns sideways, and the blade cuts air.

As the sword stabs past him, Thrax pivots on his right leg and kicks into the side of Nicator's knee, knocking sideways. Thrax leaps in and swings his curved blade at Nicator's sword arm. Nicator whisks his arm back, an instant before the polearm cuts off his hand.

This one moves like a striking snake, Nicator says to himself. *Best end him quickly.*

Nicator retreats from Thrax, feigning discomfiture. When the Syrian draws next to the Thracian's corpse, Nicator stumbles over the dead man's legs, tumbling to the earth.

Thrax runs in, his polearm raised. When the Thracian leans over him, Nicator wraps his legs around Thrax's ankle and jerks his leg into the air. The Thracian crashes to the ground, his sword-ax flying from his hands. Nicator springs up and bends over him, darting his blade at the Thracian's bare throat.

But Thrax has fallen before many a man in the gladiatorial ring, only to rise the victor. He reflexively spins sideways. The sword crunches into the scrabbly ground, burying itself to the middle. The Syrian yanks out his weapon and lunges toward Thrax. The Thracian rises to one knee and grabs a fistful of gravelly earth. He flings it into Nicator's face mask.

The Syrian halts, choking out the dirt in his mouth while he grapples at his clouded eyes. Instinctively, Nicator steps back from his opponent, but he does not step far enough.

Thrax bounces up. He swoops his polearm's curved blade behind

Nicator's knee guard and yanks it forward. The keen blade bites deep into the Syrian's upper calf, cutting into his tendons. Cursing with pain, the Syrian drops to one knee. He blindly swipes his sword about in front of him, blinking to clear his eyes.

Now to end this Syrian bastard. Thrax kicks the Syrian in the face, knocking him flat. Nicator's mask flies off. Thrax gapes at the scarred, pustulent visage that glares up at him. He grins.

"You are one ugly motherfucker, aren't you?" Thrax says. He bends over to make his killing strike. Nicator grapples for his sword.

A javelin thuds in front of Thrax, then another to his side. Angry shouts erupt behind him. He looks over his shoulder and sees two enemy chariots rumbling toward him, their occupants grabbing more javelins from their spear tubes.

"Another day, freak," Thrax says. He dashes toward the dissolving battle line, jumping onto the horse of a passing Thracian cavalryman.

Nicator dashes to his face plate and ties it into place. He straightens his armor and raiment, shaking his head to clear out the last of the pebbles. The two chariots pull up in front of him.

"You are all right, Captain?" says one of the drivers, wrapping a linen bandage about Nicator's bleeding calf.

"I will not be all right until I finish that one," Nicator blurts. "Come on, take me to the remains of the battle. I want to kill a few more Thracians, to make up for the one that got away."

The chariot rumbles toward the islands of Thracians that are surrounded by Antiochus' men. The unyielding warriors stand back to back, trying to kill as many invaders as possible before they die.

Nicator spies Thrax's horse riding toward the mountains. He pounds his hoary fist upon the edge of the chariot. *Gods help me, I will get that one,* Nicator fumes. *I will shit upon him as he dies under me, after I make his face look worse than mine.*

387

Rising Powers

Nicator points to a knot of surrounded Thracians. He sheathes his sword and withdraws his slim dagger. "Take me over to them. I've got to get some practice in."

As Nicator heads toward the surrounded Thracians, Antiochus rides through the battlefield, watching the remnants of the Thracian army meld into the thick trees at the base of the foothills. Screams of agony and triumph reach his ears, as his soldiers overwhelm the last of their surrounded enemies. *You'd think they'd have the sense to know when they're beaten*, he thinks. *They are strong warriors, though. I wonder if I can talk them into joining me against Rome.*

He watches a young Thracian leap up from the ground and jump onto a passing Galatian, brandishing a shattered sword. "Death to the invaders!" he screams. He jabs his sword shard into the barbarian's chest. *No, probably not,* Antiochus decides.

The king scans the plains and creekbeds, tallying up the blue-tattooed bodies that speckle the landscape. He frowns at the mounds of Syrian dead that seem to surround each Thracian corpse. *What did the immortal Pyrrhus say? "A few more victories such as this and I will lose the war." Am I truly ready for Rome?*

Zeuxis rides up to join him, a red tunic scrap tied around his head. "We've got the last of them," he tells his king. "They must have lost half their force." He is silent for a moment. "No prisoners, though. None would surrender."

"Get the townspeople out here tomorrow," Antiochus says. "I want those bodies burned before the stink rises. They can have whatever they find on them."

"They'll be lucky to find a decent loincloth after the Galatians are done picking over them" Zeuxis says. "We'd better get into the city soon. Those Thracians are crazy enough to counterattack."

Antiochus looks back toward the hills. *I've got to figure out a way to get the Thracians on my side. What if they joined Rome?"*

He shudders.

Rising Powers

ROME. *Ching, ching, ching.* The gold coins tinkle merrily in Flaccus' uncalloused palm. He shakes them seductively, eyeing the barrel-shaped man who stands before him, his horse-stable fragrance wrinkling Flaccus' pointed nose.

"You know our arrangement, Ursus. I want all those Hellenic pennants down by Saturn-day. Paint the walls with the slogans on them. I don't care if it's the Julii mansion itself—I don't want to see any more of those damning *Flaccus wants to be king* slogans, or drawings of me having congress with a mule. If I see even one out there, you won't become aedile when I'm elected, I promise you."

Ursus vigorously bobs his head, his stubbled jowls quaking. He looks anxiously at Flaccus. "I will do my best, Senator. But the last time we tried, Amelia and her attendant came after us with knives. They slashed up three of my men!"

Flaccus rolls his eyes toward Olympus. *I should have killed her before she got that bitch Prima to help her.* "Do I have to think of everything? Do it at night, after the eighth hour. They won't be out on the streets then."

"Can I do all that with just six men? How do we get around in the dark?"

Flaccus sighs. *Freedmen! This man grows more stupid by the day.* Bored, he opens his palm and stares at the bright gold aurei he was jingling. Scipio's face stares back from two newly-minted coins.

That annoying little prick is everywhere! Flaccus flings the coins at Ursus feet. "Here, hire five torchbearers. And I want a score of disruptors to shout down the Hellenic candidates when they make their speeches in the marketplace. We've got to take the advantage before Scipio returns."

Flaccus pushes his face into his palms and rubs his eyes. *I'll get that bastard for sending me to Sicily.*

"That will cost more," Ursus replies. "Another two purses, at least."

389

"I can manage it," Flaccus airily replies. "I was quite successful while I was praetor at Sicily." *Their treasury will never notice the missing money until later. And what if they do? I'll be consul by then.*

"Do you want the disruptors to come to your speech tomorrow, Praetor?"

"Of course I do," Flaccus snaps. "I will make some indictments of Scipio and his party. And bring some club men from the Aventine. We may have to bash a few dissenter's heads."

Ursus bows, his iron chain necklace scraping the floor. "It will be done. What of Cato? Should I find out what he wants?" Ursus says.

"Cato is to know nothing about any of this," Flaccus replies testily. "He would only pout about it violating his precious little sense of honor."

"He is a strange duck," Ursus adds.

Flaccus flips another aureus at Ursus. "Send a score of shouters to Cato's speech in the marketplace, he'll need all the support he can get." He eyes Ursus. "I'll be there to make sure they do their job."

An hour later, Flaccus leaves his spacious town house with his four guards, heading for the speaker's zone at the intersection of Market Street and the Forum square. Cato is there, standing next to a tall, table-sized platform built of elm wood. He wears a dark gray tunic as severe as the look on his face. Hundreds jam the space about him, most of them retired soldiers and working men. They have come to hear the Latin Party's plebian candidate for consul.

Cato steps onto the platform. In his customary manner, he commences without introduction or welcome, his right arm upraised with forefinger pointing toward Olympus.

"What have the Hellenics wrought in the years since Scipio became consul? Degradation of the Roman spirit, that's what! And how did they do that? By wasting public monies on statues, art, and plays. Look at them! They squander coin on foods that have more taste than substance." He pounds the rostra. "I tell you, our city is well on its way to ruin, when a fish costs more than an ox!"[cl]

Twenty grim men edge in from various places in the back of the crowd, jostling their way toward the middle. Once there, they cast their eyes toward the nearby temple of Jupiter. Ursus stands on the temple's upper steps. He shakes his head. *Not yet.*

Sensing he has the crowd with him, Cato's voice rises. "Why, some Hellenics—with Scipio as their leader—they have talked of building what they call a 'library' to house readings and stories of no value beyond sheer entertainment. An honest working man has no need for such fripperies—only the overpriviliged patricians have the time to waste on stories!"

Easy there, boy, Flaccus thinks. *Don't turn them against all of us, or I may have to dispose of you.*

"Why do you keep electing Hellenics to run Rome, year after year?" Cato continues, warming to his crowd. "They have done nothing for it." He mournfully shakes his head. "You will make people think that in your opinion, either high office is virtually worthless, or there are virtually no people who are worthy of high office!"[cli]

Flaccus chuckles. *The self-righteous little prick can speak, I give him that. He just needs someone to do the dirty work for him.* Amid the laughter, Flaccus' waves at Ursus. He nods at his men.

"Flaccus and Cato, Flaccus and Cato!" the shouters bellow, their right fists upraised. "Make Rome great again!" Slowly, sporadically, the crowd picks up the chant, overcoming the scattered jeers.

Cato returns the salute. "Gratitude. You know me. I am a man of the people; a man of the land. I will restore Rome to the days when we were men of simple, powerful, values—men of the enduring, values of home, field, and family. We will purge ourselves of Greek decadence, and return to glory!"

Cato speaks on for half an hour. He pledges to lower taxes, to distribute more land to veterans, and to bring Flamininus' troops home from Greece. All are popular topics among his audience. Frequently, the hired thugs interrupt with shouts for Flaccus and Cato as consuls, much to Cato's confusion.

Flaccus watches with arms folded, smiling predatorily. *Cato and I as consuls! That would show almighty Scipio who has the power in Rome.*

Flaccus eyes the statues of Roman generals that ring the square. *Hm. Maybe a treaty with Antiochus would be profitable. We give him Thrace and we take the rest of Greece. I'd be the ruler of a Roman Empire! Then we'd see who's face is on our coins.*

Amelia Tertia

XII. Cato's Wars

LYSIMACHIA, THRACE. Thrax the Thracian is very angry. The former slave soldier has fought long and hard to establish himself as the leader of the south Thracian tribes. Many challengers have fallen to the polearm he so adeptly wields, using the skills he learned as a gladiator and legionnaire.

Now, at the height of Thrax's powers, the cursed Syrian king has invaded his eastern realm, capturing Lysimachia and asserting his ancestral right to its environs.[clii] Thinking of what he has gained and what he may lose, it is almost too much to bear. Someone will suffer for his pain.

Thrax is camped in the jagged mountains above his domain, collecting the remnants of his army. Half his men lie dead on the plains of Lysimachia, but still he plans a counterattack. To do otherwise would be to capitulate—unthinkable to a Thracian.

That Syrian must have half the world in that army of his, Thrax muses, chewing on a roast boar haunch. *Parthians, Dahae, cataphractii, chariots—and thousands of those lunatic Galatians—how can we defeat them all?*

You know how, says the voice inside him. Thrax grimaces—he hates the voice; it never tells him what he wants to hear. *You know who would be willing to fight with you and for you.*

"Fucking Romans," he mutters to the flickering flames. "They made me a house servant and then threw me into their slave legion! They're empire builders—they'd take over Thrace!"

You know they won't, the voice says. *They are amici, declared friends of Greece. They have the strength to oppose Antiochus.*

Cato's Wars

"Shit!" He flings the boar leg into the fire, showering sparks onto his dozing soldiers. Several leap up, cursing vehemently as they swat at their smoldering blankets. "What in Hades is wrong with you?" growls one of his axmen.

Thrax chuckles. *They take shit from no one, not even me.*

Thrax runs his forefinger along the side of his neck, tracing the outline of the slave collar that once encircled his neck. *We fought off Philip, but this Syrian may be too much for us. Maybe this Flamininus would welcome us as equals.*

He smirks. *After all, Antiochus is coming for them, too.*

Back at Lysimachia, Antiochus is busy overseeing the restoration of a temple dedicated to Apollo, his favorite god. Standing in front of the decayed building, he watches his slaves draw in the ropes from two enormous pulleys, easing up two limestone columns.

"Mitry, I want Apollo's statue standing between them by sunset," he tells his chief architect.

The tall young Egyptian bends so low his head touches the ground. "It will be done, Peerless One," he babbles nervously. The architect is a proud man, descended from the pharaohs themselves, but he knows the penalty for those who disappoint Antiochus—as his skinless predecessor did.

It will be a beautiful temple, Antiochus thinks, feeling quite pleased with himself. *This was the fairest city in Thrace when my ancestor Seleucus claimed it. I will make it the jewel of my new kingdom. Along with Athens—I can't forget Athens.*

He smiles. *Who knows? Maybe Rome, too.*

"We should be reinforcing our walls instead of building temples," declares Zeuxis, the king's army commander. "If I know anything about Thracians, it's that they don't give up. I'd bet Thrax and his men are hiding up there in the mountains, plotting retaliation."

Antiochus frowns, irritated that his reverie was interrupted. "Then Thrax will be waiting for what he will never have. We've already destroyed half his little army. He has no chance."

"I don't know," says Zeuxis, rubbing his right ear stub. "There are several large cities to the north of him. If they join up, he could have a formidable force."

"Which we would then destroy, just as we did last week," Antiochus says, airily waving his hand. "Our real threat is Rome. If we go into Greece, they will rise up to stop us."

"Speaking of Rome, Lucius Cornelius and the other three envoys are back to see you, my King."

Antiochus flings up his hands. "What do they want this time?"

"They want to talk to you about your invasion of Thrace," [cliii] Zeuxis replies. He grins. "I had them wait in the freshly painted anteroom. The egg yolk fumes ought to drive them crazy. That, and staring at the murals of you conquering Egypt and Thrace!"

The king of Syria stares into the distance. "Rome is poking into my business again? Well, I'll just have to settle them down. Come on."

The hawk-faced king swirls his tan cape around his tunic and treads back to his waiting chariot. The chariot trundles back into the heart of the large walled city, stopping at a large marble building that looms above the town square.

"Send the four envoys into my meeting chambers," Antiochus tells Zeuxis. "I'll be there after I relieve myself. Otherwise, I might be tempted to piss on them!"

Minutes later, Antiochus enters the large meeting room, dressed in a flowing linen toga. Four middle-aged Romans sit at oblong plank table built for a hundred diners, their voices echoing off the lofty ceiling. The carved heads of satyrs and nymphs grin down upon them, as if mocking their presence.

"Lucius Cornelius," the king says tonelessly, "What a pleasure to see you again."

A small, lean man rises from his seat, his back straight as an arrow. He walks around the table and grasps Antiochus' forearm. "Would this were a pleasure trip," he says dryly, "but I have come to voice my Senate's concerns." He sweeps his wiry arm toward his three colleagues. "You know the other three commissioners."

Antiochus seats himself at the head of the table. "Of course, we met about Rome's concern that I was taking over Egypt." He gives them a puzzled look. "I must confess, I think Rome has no more right to inquire about what I'm doing in Asia than I have about what they are doing in Italia."[cliv]

"You have now moved into Thrace," a commissioner growls. "It is a neighbor to Greece, not Asia."

Antiochus spreads his hands. "I am merely reclaiming the lands that Syria acquired long ago. The Thracians have not kept it up, just look at the mess this city is in! As for Egypt, Ptolemy has willingly given me those lands. Why, he is even going to marry my daughter!" He grins at Lucius Cornelius. "Does that sound like an enemy to you?"

Lucius' face is a stone. "How do we know Greece is not your next target? Or Macedonia?"

"I am completely occupied with Lysimachia's reconstruction," he retorts, grinning sarcastically. "Besides, I would not deign to threaten the allies of the mighty Romans."

"Well, we would talk more with you about these matters," Lucius replies. "We would like a written declaration of your intentions."

"And you shall have it!" the king replies brightly. "I would not want you to leave here empty-handed!"

Hours later, after several prolonged bouts of haggling and disputation, a declaration of nonaggression is signed and sealed. The Romans are led to a sumptuous feast in the palace's house-sized feasting room.

Antiochus soon abandons the feast and repairs to his spacious bedroom. He grabs a wine goblet from an attendant and plops on top of his sleeping silks.

"Romans!" he mutters, downing his cup in a single gulp. "Always worrying about laws and agreements! As if those ever stopped anyone." A hand knocks at his brass doors.

"Go away or I'll burn you alive!" he growls, jiggling his cup for a refill.

"You do that and you'll miss some important news," comes Zeuxis' voice. Antiochus nods, and his guards pull open the doors. Zeuxis strides in, his eyes wide with eagerness.

"Ptolemy has died!"[clv] he exclaims. "With Philip's defeat, Egypt is yours for the taking!"

The king vaults from his bed. "The old cow is dead? When did you find out? Who told you?"

"One of our palace spies just returned."

"That gives us a golden opportunity!" the king says, his voice rising with excitement. "We'll go back to Syria and get our troops in Seleucia. When spring comes, we'll take northern Egypt. Then we march on Greece." He smirks. "The Romans can stick those declarations up their asses!"

"That will be the end of our peace with Rome," Zeuxis says. "If we enter Greece, their armies will rush to defend it. Scipio himself may come after us."

"Ah yes, the golden general of Rome! I'm not worried about him—or them. We just have to make sure we are ready for an extended war against them."

Zeuxis eyes his king. "The question is, should it be sooner, or later?"

"There is a man that can answer that for us," Antiochus says. "And this time, we will brook no delay in getting him." He points to his chamber door.

"Send our men to Carthage. I want Hannibal to meet me in Seleucia."

ROME, 195 BCE. Scipio is in agony, and he cannot see a remedy for it.

He twists around on the front row Senate bench, his body stiff with resentment. In front of him, the Senate Elder introduces Rome's two new consuls, Lucius Valerius Flaccus and Marcus Porcius Cato.[clvi]

Cato and Flaccus, Scipio wails to himself. *How could this happen? Is the world truly coming to an end?*

Flaccus' eyes roam about the Senate chambers. He winks at several Latin Party members, thoroughly savoring his moment of triumph. He notices Scipio looking at him. His smile turns into a smug grin. Scipio mournfully shakes his head.

Cato stares straight at the Senate Elder, intent on properly completing his oath of office. When he has declared his intention to conduct himself honestly and ethically, he faces the Senate and slightly bows his head. His eyes fix on Scipio, with the look a predator gives his prey.

"Our first task is the sortition of consular assignments," the Elder says. "One consul will take a full consular army to northern Iberia, where rebellion has flared up—again."

"The other will take an army to North Italia. It will be a smaller force. Since Marcellus and Purpurio's victories up there, the Gauls have posed no trouble.[clvii] Is that arrangement agreeable to both of you?"

Flaccus and Cato nod.

"Very well," the Elder continues. "You will draw lots to determine who gets each assignment." He holds up a battered pottery urn and shakes it, listening to its contents rattle.

"There are two dice in this urn. One has "Iberia" written on it, the other has "Italia." Who will choose?"

Flaccus shoulders his way in front of a surprised Cato. "If one of us must do it, let it be me."

Scipio's brows wrinkle. *Why didn't he let the Elder choose who draws?*

The Elder shrugs. "Very well." He sets his chin and pounds his heavy oak staff, booming it through the chambers. "Consul Flaccus will choose his consular assignment."

Flaccus closes his eyes and darts his hand inside the urn. His hand scrabbles about, his face reddening. *What is he doing?* Scipio wonders.

Flaccus' fingers touch a small bump on the side of one die. He yanks it out, slapping it into the Elder's palm.

The old man pulls out a shard of magnifying glass[clviii] and squints at the die. "Flaccus has Italia. Cato is assigned Iberia."

"Excellent," Cato replies. "I will leave for Iberia in six weeks, when May approaches. I will set things aright before winter sets in."

"I am sure you will," Flaccus replies heartily. *Thank Fortuna it worked! Let Cato go fight those savages.*

There is something amiss here, Scipio thinks. *At least Cato is the one going to war. Flaccus would be a disaster over there.*

"Our next order of business is to hear a report from the commissioners that visited Greece and Thrace," declares the Elder. He peers up at several new Senators who are chatting with each other. He points a vein-corded finger at them. "Pay attention. Lucius Cornelius has some very important news."

The commissioners march in to the Senate floor. Lucius Cornelius steps to the podium and relates a chronological chain of the commission's meetings and travels. He pauses before he describes the four men's visit with Antiochus, gathering his thoughts.

"It is my opinion that Antiochus presents the most serious threat to a lasting peace in Greece—and the most serious threat to Rome's security."

Cato rises from his place on the front bench, three senators to the right of Scipio. He throws up his hands. "Syria, Syria! I think Syria is only half the problem. We overlook the threat of Carthage. If we war with Antiochus, would Hannibal and Carthage join him? We would be fools not to think so."

Scipio rises from his place. He starts to speak when a violent coughing fit seizes him. He muffles his red face in the shoulder of his toga, holding up a forefinger in a request for patience. The senators wait; no one speaks or stirs.

Scipio clears his throat and continues, his voice hoarse. "Carthage has given us no reason to think it wants to renew hostilities. The Carthaginian army and navy are but a memory of their former force, and what remains is occupied in a border war with King Masinissa of Numidia. They pose no threat to us." He slowly resumes his seat, giving the senators time to mull his words.

"As long as Hannibal is alive, Carthage is a threat," Cato says. "We know he has befriended Philip, and now he bends to Antiochus. I have received letters from the Senate in Carthage, telling us that Hannibal has sent messengers to Seleucia, Antiochus' stronghold!"

Cato pauses, letting the weight of his words sink in. "They said Hannibal is like a wild beast who cannot be tamed. He sleeps now, but he will be wakened by the clash of arms, should war arise."[clix]

The Senate erupts with murmurs of agreement and dissent. Scipio pushes himself up and faces them.

"You know I have more experience with Carthage than anyone." He glances at Cato. "Anyone. I tell you now, those 'messengers' carry the words of Hannibal's enemies. I have met him, and fought him. Hannibal is a man of honor, a man who only seeks to help his people. It is beneath the dignity of Rome for us to associate with these vile accusers." [clx]

"I will tell you what is vile," Cato replies. "His murder of forty thousand of our men at Cannae!"

"He fulfilled his mission as a soldier for his country," Scipio says. "Were we to hate everyone who has done that, we should tear up our peace agreement with Philip, too. And the Numidians and Ligurians."

Flaccus stands up. "If I may have the floor, General?" he says unctuously. Scipio glares at him, but he resumes his seat.

"We can talk all day about the merits and demerits of sending a commission to Carthage. My suspicion, though, is that many of us already have our minds made up about his commission. I call for a vote on this."

You must have bought enough votes to win, Scipio thinks. He dolefully shakes his head. *I should have chosen stronger candidates to oppose them. If we don't win next year, we'll be back at war with Carthage.*

The senators rise and move to the floor, standing in one of two groups: those in favor of sending a deputation to accuse Hannibal of siding with Antiochus, and those opposed. Scipio stands in the opposed group, watching the senators step down from the upper rows and move into one of the groups. *We are almost even in votes.*

Gnaeus Servilius and Quintus Terentius are two of the last to come down, new senators from Rome's most respected families. Scipio watches them carefully, trying to judge which way they will walk. *Come on, fellows, you fought against Hannibal. I know you respect him.*

"Come down and join us, Gnaeus and Quintus," Scipio shouts. "Your votes are going to decide this!"

As they step onto the floor, the two senators look at Scipio. They look down at the floor, their eyes hooded. Scipio feels his heart sink.

Gnaeus and Quintus step into the group favoring the delegates. "The vote is decided," the Elder says. "We will send a deputation to

Carthage to investigate Hannibal."

"Do not forget the most important part," Flaccus says to the Elder. "The deputation is to declare they are coming to adjudicate the dispute between Hannibal and Masinissa, so that Hannibal is not alerted to their true purpose."[clxi]

"I like not this deception," Cato states. "We should be plain about our intentions."

"Too late. That is what we voted upon, Consul," the Elder says. "Now, who should we send? Consuls Cato and Flaccus, do you have any recommendations?"

"I nominate Gnaeus Servilius and Quintus Terentius," Flaccus declares. "They are both veterans of our war against Carthage, and have been to Carthage's court."

Scipio pushes out to the front of his voting group. His eyes search the two senators' faces. They look away from him. Scipio glares at them, watching their necks redden. *Is that what he promised you for your vote? Is that what your soul is worth?*

Marcus Claudius, a staunch Latin party member, is appointed as the third member of the deputation. The senators return to their seats.

"Now to the final order of business," the Elder declares. "We have a proposal that we repeal the Lex Oppia, the law that limits the wealth and jewelry that women may possess."

Cato pops up from his seat. "What!" he interjects. "Who proposed that?"

The Elder wrinkles his bushy grey eyebrows at the livid young consul. "It was proposed by Marcus Fundianus and Lucius Valerius, our esteemed Tribunes of the Plebs."

"It is nonsense," Cato sputters. "You want to reinstitute women wasting good money on needless decorations! And why do women need their own money? What's next, giving them a vote?"

A broad-shouldered young man stands up from the side of the middle row. The Elder sees him and raises his palm at Cato. "Please Consul, let young Marcus Fundianus explain."

Fundianus sweeps his right hand across the rows of senators. "My friends, we instituted the Lex Oppia so that Rome had money to fight the Carthaginians. It was a law instituted to serve our wars. Now it is time to serve our peace, and give back to women what they freely gave away."[clxii]

"I will hear none of it," Cato replies, his arms crossed over his chest. "If you repeal that law you will find daughters, wives, even sisters, less under our control."[clxiii]

Scipio winces at the angry consul's words. *Ah, Cato. Wait until the women find out what you said. I almost feel sorry for you.*

Fundianus whips his cloak over his shoulders. "This is a fundamental injustice. If the Senate will not rectify it, I will take my argument to the people!" He stomps out from the Senate chambers, with Lucius Valerius following him.

The Elder gapes at the tribune's empty seats. "Well, then! The people's representatives are gone! I guess that concludes today's session." The Elder pounds his staff, and the senators rise to leave.

For once, Scipio does not tarry to chat with his fellows. He summons his guard and hurries to the Scipio manse. Once inside, he rushes to his writing table and pens out a note.

General Hannibal Barca

Beware. Your enemies at Carthage have set three Roman dogs upon you. Soon they come bring you to bay.

S

Scipio seals the roll with a daub of hot wax, but he does not imprint it with his owl's-head seal. He summons his most trusted messenger and pushes a bag of coins into his palm.

"Terentius, you are to have this in Hannibal's hands as soon as possible. I have a bireme in Ostia, on the southern docks. It has a blue griffin painted on the bow."

"I will be at their court three days from now," Terentius says.

When the messenger departs, Scipio walks into the atrium. Amelia squats on the floor there, playing knuckle bones with Cornelia and Publius. She looks up and smiles at him. "Did the Senate meet proceed well?" she asks. "Did Cato and Flaccus get sworn in?"

"Well yes, they did," Scipio says cautiously.

"Did they cause any damage yet?" Amelia asks.

Scipio summons his courage. "Well, Cato did veto one proposal..."

"What was it?" Amelia says, growing irritable. "Why are you temporizing?"

Scipio smiles anxiously. "Beloved, perhaps you should sit down before I tell you..."

SELEUCIA, MESOPOTAMIA.[clxiv] The white bull falls to its knees, groaning out the last moments of its life. The high priest steps back from the mighty beast, clutching a bloody scimitar in his white-robed hand.

"There, my King, the gods are placated. Just one more thing." The priest sticks a shallow silver bowl under the dying beast's pulsing neck, filling it with the bull's blood. The young man walks slowly from the beast, carefully balancing the brimming bowl. He holds it out to Antiochus.

"Drink."

The Syrian king extends his arms and grasps the bowl. The priest chants his supplications to the goddess Nemesis. "Forgive our king if he gave offense, goddess of retribution. His hubris was unintentional. He humbles himself before you."

Antiochus draws the warm blood into his mouth, drinking deeply. Wiping his carmined lips on his wrist, he holds the bowl over his head and dumps the contents onto his head. The viscous liquid pours down his gold-wreathed forehead and dribbles onto his white linen robe. His staring brown eyes peer out from his red mask.

"Pray to him," the priest says. The conqueror of nations falls to his knees, his hands clutched in front of him. Bobbing his dripping head, he murmurs his prayer.

"I humble myself before you, oh mighty Nemesis. Forgive me if I have offended you." He hands the bowl back to the priest, who sprinkles the remaining droplets about the temple floor.

"You have the goddess' blessing," the priest intones.

Antiochus shakes his head. "I still don't know what I did to deserve the havoc she wreaked upon me," he says, half to himself. "I just lost half my fleet near Cyprus. The storm came out of nowhere—it was a sunny day! Now I have to spend all winter rebuilding my fleet."[clxv] He pounds his fist on his leg. "I was going to take Egypt, and Greece. It's all gone to shit!"

The priest holds out a thick cotton towel. "Sometimes the gods forestall your destiny until it is propitious to claim it," he says, watching Antiochus swab his face. "They might have known you would fail if you moved on this nation, where you would succeed if you waited. Or perhaps they are telling you not to go at all."

"That is very helpful," the king says sarcastically. "I think I will consult my oracle about it."

"The one at Delphi?" the priest asks, confused.

"No, this one is at Carthage. And it is going to come to me." The king tosses a handful of coins onto the floor and stalks out, his mood foul.

Nicator is outside waiting for him, his right hand resting on his chain mail sword belt. He stands as rigidly as if he were an armored statue—only his searching eyes betray the human inside. He turns his head toward this king, the sun flashing off his polished silver mask.

"Are you ready to return to your chambers?" Nicator asks, his voice tinny through the mask.

"Yes, for now. But I am sick of asking the gods to solve my problems. We are going to my naval base near Antioch, and supervise the rebuilding of the fleet. Two new ships a week, or someone dies!"

"As you say," Nicator replies. "I would be happy to deal with those who do not meet your quota."

Antiochus barks out a laugh. "I am sure you would. You can serve me better by just showing up at the docks. They will work all the harder for seeing you there."

Six days later, Antiochus is sitting on his gold throne at his palace in Antioch, meeting with Zeuxis and the rest of his generals. The chamber door cracks open. A comely young woman's head pokes in, her onyx eyes apprehensive.

"Forgive me, Peerless. The envoys to Carthage have returned."

Antiochus' eyes shine. "Excellent! Send them in!"

The two envoys march into the chamber, their robes and helmets filmed with road dust. The elder Syrian stumps forward, his bronze-covered wooden leg[clxvi] ringing off the marble floor slabs.

"I bring bad news. Hannibal refused to come with us."

Antiochus shoves himself upright. "What! Why?"

The former captain twists his dusty cape in his hands. "He is amenable to joining you, my King, but he says he is waiting for a sign before he decides."

"A sign from whom? The gods?" Antiochus says. "Does he need some portent or omen?"

The messenger shrugs, puzzled. "No. He said he was waiting for a sign from the Romans." He shrugs, staring in amazement at his king. "The Romans!"

CARTHAGE, 195 BCE. "People of Carthage, we have lost our power to rule our own country," Hannibal says. "The Council of a Hundred and Four make all our decisions. They serve for life, without recall, so they do what they want. Their lifetime appointments have made many of them indolent, and still more corrupt."

Hannibal stands in the center of the most beautiful forum in the world, surrounded by gleaming white temples and government buildings fronted with majestic swaying palms. Spotless stone townhouses line the avenues as far as the eye can see, each bordered with carefully tended trees and foliage.

As one of the two chief magistrates of Carthage, Hannibal has exercised his right to call a people's assembly. A hundred thousand citizens have gathered in the Carthaginian forum. They came to hear their hero, but none expected one of Carthage's privileged class to give such ringing indictment of his fellows. Listening to Hannibal's proposal, their surprise turns to dissatisfaction, then anger, and then hope.

"Citizens of Carthage, I propose that we end the Council's lifetime appointments. The judges will be voted into office by the people, not their own kind."

When the cheers subside, he raises his arms above his head. "And, those who are elected will serve a one-year term, subject to reelection. And no one, I say no one, can serve more than two years in a row."[clxvii]

This time the cheers are deafening. A hundred thousand fists punch into the air. A hundred thousand voices chant, "Han-ni-bal, Han-ni-bal, Han-ni-bal."

Inside the Senate chambers, the judges listen dourly to the people's accolades, their faces twisted with disgust—and fear. A large, fleshy man rises from his seat on the Senate bench, a man nicknamed "Fish" for his bulbous eyes and pouting lips. He gathers the hem of his ample toga and quickly pads into an anteroom. A gaunt older man follows him. The Fish plops onto a thickly padded couch and dabs his sweaty brow, his wattled face flush with anger.

"I tell you Hiram, he has gone too far. "We propose a tax increase to pay for our tribute to the Romans, and he audits the Council's expenditures and says we embezzled the funds![clxviii] Now he wants to have us elected like common politicians! And him a Barca; the oldest family in Carthage!"

"Why don't we just kill him?" says the thin man. "I know of a very good assassin. He would make it look like the Libyans did it."

"No, no, he's too popular right now. The people wouldn't listen to reason if he died—they'd come after us!" His eyes gleam. "It looks like we will have to let the Romans do it for us, just as we planned." His face grows stern. "But we have to prepare our fellows to follow our lead—when the Romans accuse him of conspiring with Antiochus we will make a token protest. Then we accede to their demands and let them take him back to Rome."

Hiram nods. "Most of our colleagues have secretly agreed to that. We have two days left to convince the others."

"Good," says the Fish. He grins. "And if any disagree to join us, we might employ your 'Libyan friend' after all."

Dusk casts its angular shadows through Carthage's towered landscape. A weary Hannibal marches back to his town house, happy with the day's results. The citizens of Carthage approved term limits and public elections for the judges. *Now we will become a true democracy, like Athens.*

He steps inside his vestibule and drapes his purple toga over a wall hook. Wearing only a gray tunic and sandals, the old general strolls into his atrium, rubbing the back of his neck. *Baal be praised, I'm getting too old for this!*

Hannibal finds an armored Carthaginian soldier waiting for him, flanked by two of his house guards. The man rises and puts his right fist over his heart.

"Greetings, Hannibal Barca. My name is Terentius, Centurion of Rome's First Legion. Forgive the disguise—I had to escape notice to make it this far." Terentius hands Scipio's message to Hannibal. "This is from a friend."

Hannibal unrolls the papyrus. He scans the note and looks up.

"Who sent you?" Hannibal asks. He crumples the message and pitches it into a burning fire pit.

"Apologies, General," Terentius replies. "I am not to mention his name. But I think you know who it is." The messenger shifts his feet, feeling awkward. "He is a man you met at Zama."

Hannibal fixes his eye on the muscular old centurion. "Sit, please. I will bring refreshment." The centurion nods curtly. He sits upright on the heavily padded couch, his Carthaginian helmet cradled in his arm.

Hannibal claps his hands twice. Two slaves appear as if by magic, lugging trays laden with wine and food. For a while, the old soldiers dine in silence. Terentius raises his goblet.

"To those who defend their country, whatever that country may be," Terentius says. Hannibal raises his cup, nods, and drinks deeply.

"Zama, that was quite a battle," Hannibal says. "Were you there?"

"I was on the right flank." Terentius takes another sip. "You and your Libyans had us beaten, for a while."

"But in the end, I did not," Hannibal says, his eyes distant. "Your goddess Fortuna, she was a Roman that day."

Terentius nods. "I was at Cannae, too. I barely escaped alive." He gulps from his chalice. "So many fine men gone. What would the world be like if they had lived?"

Hannibal looks up. "What else can you tell me, Terentius? Surely there is more."

Terentius is silent, choosing his words. "They are coming for you," he replies. "Three delegates from Rome will meet with your Council. They will accuse you of plotting against the Republic."

The centurion sighs. "I think the Council's judges will give you up. Your Roman 'friend' thinks they are the ones who paid to get them here. With some help from the Latin Party."

Hannibal smirks. "I am not unaware of the machinations in Rome. Your Senator Flaccus would make a fine Carthaginian judge. He has their touch for treachery."

Terentius lays his cup down. "Apologies. I must be going. I have to sail under cover of night."

That is a wise idea, Hannibal thinks. He grips Terentius' forearm. "We were on opposite sides, but we have a similar heart."

"Fare well, Hannibal Barca." Terentius spins on his heel and marches out.

Hannibal listens to the clacking footsteps fading down the hall. *Is he right? Am I to be led in chains back to Rome? I'll test his words tomorrow, before the Romans arrive.* Hannibal claps his hands twice. His trusted aide appears from a side room.

"You heard everything, Jarubo?" Hannibal says. The gaunt old man nods. "They mean you ill," he quavers. "You have to prepare."

"Just so," Hannibal replies. "Fetch our horses, we are going for a little ride into the country."

The next day Hannibal meets with the Senate's taxation committee, staffed by six senior judges.[clxix] Once again, he tells them that the people do not need to be taxed more to pay for the yearly tribute, that it can be paid by purging the corruption within the Council of a Hundred and Four.

For once, the committee does not recoil in anger, calmly receiving Hannibal's accusations. Hannibal watches each judge's face as he speaks. He notices that the judge known as Fish leans over and says something to his compatriot. The two chuckle, malevolently eyeing him. *Now I know,* Hannibal decides.

Hannibal lingers in the Senate for the rest of the day, fulfilling his duties as one of Carthage's two ruling magistrates. The Senate meeting concludes in the late afternoon. Hannibal strolls to a nearby wine bar with two Senators who live near him. They wine and dine until dusk, laughing and chatting.

Hannibal enters his manse and hurries to his bedroom. He pitches off his ceremonial toga and slips on a plain gray tunic. He throws a thick satchel over his shoulder and belts on a nondescript sword, his movements quick and decisive.

Hannibal knots a leather purse onto his belt. He reaches into the purse and pulls out an ivory figurine of his father Hamilcar. *I am glad you did not live to see what Carthage has become.* He strokes the figure's head with his thumb, staring into its stern bearded face. *I fret for Carthage more than for me.*[clxx]

Jarubo appears in the doorway. He watches Hannibal change. "This is it? You are leaving?"

"There is nothing for me here but chains and a cross," Hannibal replies. He embraces the gaunt old man, kissing him on both cheeks. "I have left some signed papers in the study. Give them to Sirom Barca. You and the rest of the household will not have to worry about anything for the rest of your life."

Hannibal trots through the mansion's rear kitchen and out into the walled back garden. Pushing open the garden door, he vaults onto the horse he had placed there earlier in the day.

Hannibal backs the horse into the middle of the broad alleyway and trots out onto the main avenue. He pauses for a minute, taking in Carthage's gleaming towers. His eyes fill with tears. *Forgive me. I have to leave you to save you.*

"Yeaah!" he yells, digging his heels into his horse's side. Like a thief in the night, Carthage's greatest man flees Carthage, heading for his unmarked ship.

ROME. "That little pig," Amelia fumes. "I'll kill him myself!"

"You kill Cato, you'll just make a hero of him," Scipio says. "We've just lost one election to the Latin Party. Do you want to make it a decade's worth?"

She smacks her fist onto her palm. "He's not going to get away with this. Women sacrificed their wealth to fund the war. We want our privileges restored."

Scipio bites his lower lip. "I will advocate its repeal in the next Senate meeting, but I fear it will make no difference. Too many of them are afraid of offending Cato and Flaccus. They *are* the consuls now, carissima."

"Well, *we* are not afraid," Amelia replies. "I'll talk to some of my friends. They are tired of being told what they can't wear, and what they can't own."

"And then what?" Scipio asks. His face contorts in mock horror. "You aren't going to deny men sex, as the Grecian women did in the Lysistrata?"[clxxi]

Amelia makes a face at him. "Your brains are in your subligaculum. No, we'll march on the Senate!" She glances at Scipio. "That's what your mother Pomponia would do."

"How can I help?" Scipio asks.

"Recruit those two tribunes who proposed its repeal. We can get them to speak out against Cato and his ilk. While you do that, I'll get my propaganda crew together."

"I will see Marcus Fundianus and Marcus Valerius today," Scipio replies. "They will be agreeable to your proposition. But the other two Tribunes of the Plebs are in the Latin Party's pockets."

"That is disappointing," Amelia states, "But I can deal with them."

Three days later, pennants fly from a multitude of apartments and town houses throughout Rome, nailed there under cover of night. Some say *Repeal the Lex Oppia*! Others declare the people should *Honor Women's Sacrifices.* The pennants fly from every street near the Forum.

Cato trots into Rome, journeying from his Sabina farm. He scowls at the brightly colored pennants flapping over his head. *This is the work of Amelia and her lot: women whose husbands can't control them.* He trots over to the city militia's blockhouse.

Cato jumps off his horse before the beast stops moving, barging into the headquarters. "Take down all those scurrilous banners," the consul bellows to the captain of the guard. "Get every man out there, now!"

While the city militia tear down the pennants, Amelia meets with forty women from Rome's most powerful patrician and plebian clans. The Scipio atrium is filled with members of the Julii, Fabii, and dozens of others, all determined to repeal the Lex Oppia.

Prima temporarily forsakes her role as Amelia's bodyguard. She attends as a member of the Julii, one of Rome's oldest families. Clad in a luxurious green robe that masks her combat scars, she looks every inch the patrician matron—a matron with two daggers cinched about her naked stomach.

After hours of debate, a vote is taken. Prima counts the black and white marbles thrown into the voting urn. "It is agreed. When the Senate meets three days from now, we make our voices known."

She smiles brightly. "Or perhaps we should do as the women of Lemnos did—just kill all the men." [clxxii] Some women laugh nervously. A few cheer.

As the women conclude their meeting, Cato convenes with Flaccus in a side chamber of the Senate. "I have heard the Scipio bitch is gathering a crowd of women," Cato growls. "A dozen or two are going to march on the Forum, and squawk about that Lex Oppia."

Flaccus takes the news calmly, but inside he rejoices. *She'll be in a big crowd. I'll use the one who did Pomponia. The Sicilian never fails.*

On the morning of the third day, they come. They come from the patrician manses, and they come from the rickety mud insulae that fill Rome's back streets. They come from outlying towns and distant farms.[clxxiii] They come wearing sweat-stained farm tunics and snow white togas. They come with babies in their arms and canes in their hands.

Many wear the many-colored clothing forbidden by the Lex Oppia, their illegal gold necklaces dangling beneath their uplifted chins. They walk, march, and limp in together, holding hands and singing songs to Victoria, goddess of victory. Resolute and willing, the women of Rome press on together.

The protesters mass near the Campus Martius, the starting point of Rome's triumphant parades. Amelia takes out a battered war trumpet and blows one lingering blast, initiating the march to the Forum. Hundreds tread forward, filling the streets of Rome.

Amelia and Prima walk in the vanguard, their calloused fists clenched in determination. With every side street and alleyway the group passes, their numbers swell with those joining them. By the time they approach the Forum's outlying temples, Cato's 'dozens' are a thousand, and still they grow.

"Onward!" Amelia shouts. "Get to them before they get inside!" Filling the avenues and side streets, the women of Rome stream into the Forum square. Scores of women march up the steps to the Senate chambers, intent on accomplishing the assignment Amelia gave them.

The senators soon enter the Forum square, heading for their morning meeting in the Curia Hostilia. They gape at the sea of women around them, women who watch them ascend the Senate steps.

When the senators arrive at the Curia's top step they find their entry blocked by a wall of protesters, their arms crossed and their faces set. Confused, the senators herd together at the landing on top of the steps, looking down at the crowd massing below them.

"Repeal the Lex Oppia!" a woman shouts.

"We want our dignity back!" shouts another.

"You are a consul—do something!" a senator bawls at Flaccus.

Cato and Flaccus walk to the speaking rostra that overlooks the crowd, glowering down at the protesters.

"The women of Rome are against us," a portly old senator wails next to them. "The city is in revolt!"

"Hmph!" Cato says. "It is because we have not kept them under control individually that we are now threatened by them collectively."[clxxiv]

He clambers up the rostra steps and looks back at his colleagues. "These women need to get back into their houses!"

Cato leans over the rostra, glowering at the thousand of matrons as if they were poorly-behaved children. "What sort of behavior is this?" he says, frowning down at the angry women. "Couldn't you have made the very same request of your husbands and stayed at home? Or are you more alluring in the streets than at the home, more attractive to other women's husbands?"[clxxv]

The jeers that erupt shock the pigeons from their Forum roosts. A turnip flies by Cato's head, smacking into the chest of a young senator behind him. An overripe pomegranate flies into the front of the rostra and splatters chunks into Cato's squinting face, bringing peals of laughter.

Cato wipes off his face, flicking the seeds at the crowd. He leans down and waggles a forefinger at the women. "Cease this infantile demonstration!"

"You know where to put that finger," one shouts, bringing more laughter.

Livid, Cato turns to his fellow senators. "If we allow women to carry this point, what will they next attempt?" He frowns at three Hellenic senators near him. "The very moment they begin to be your equals, they will be your superiors!" [clxxvi]

Cato faces the crowd. "Return to your homes! Your behavior is not only unseemly, it is unprecedented!"

The women's shouts wash over his next words. They jab their thumbs down at him. "He's had it!" they shout, mimicking the call for a gladiator to kill his opponent.

Lucius Valerius steps in front of Cato. The Tribune of the Plebs rises his arms for silence.

"Get out of my way," Cato barks, "I am not done here!" He shoves Valerius away, prompting more catcalls from the crowd.

"Let Lucius Valerius speak!" shouts Amelia, holding her arms up to encourage the crowd. Prima echoes her call, and hundreds of women join in.

"I have the floor!" Cato shouts, but his words are drowned in a sea of voices. "Valerius, Valerius," they call.

Flaccus sidles up to Cato and leans next to his ear. "For the gods' sake, let him speak. Trust me, we will settle this issue another way."

Lucius Valerius eases in front of a scowling Cato. He spreads his hands entreatingly. The crowd quiets.

"Cato thinks your actions unprecedented, women of Rome. As if that were cause enough for you not to do it." He looks back at Cato, a smile on his leathery face. "But are they unprecedented? Let's look at the history of Rome."

Fundianus hands a thick scroll to Valerius. Holding it up for the crowd to see, he unrolls it and runs his finger along the words. "Let's see, what does our history say?" He unrolls more of the scroll. "Ah, here it is!"

Valerius theatrically clears his throat. "At the very beginning of our history, when our capitol had been taken by the Sabines, the fighting was halted by the matrons. They rushed between the two battle lines and implored the combatants to cease." Hundreds of women shout their agreement.

"Then again, after the expulsion of the kings, Rome's women turned back the Gauls when they would have destroyed this city." Thousands of women thrust up their fists, shouting.

"And when Rome had actually been captured by the Gauls, where did the money come from to ransom the city? From the women of Rome!" He rolls up the scroll and brandishes it as if it were a sword. "And now, in this most recent war, when money was scarce, the women supplied our bankrupt treasury with their own stores of money." [clxxvii]

Valerius pitches the scroll away. "The Lex Oppia was passed in times of war, when money was low to support our troops. Now it is peacetime, and our coffers swell with plunder from Gaul and Macedonia."

Valerius looks back at Cato, who stonily returns his stare. "I beg you, women of Rome. Let the senators inside and conduct their business. They cannot stop the will of the people. I will call the People's Assembly tomorrow, to vote upon the repeal of the Lex Oppia. Together, we will restore what is rightfully yours, and repeal this odious law!"

Lucius Valerius steps from the rostra amid thunderous applause. He clasps hands with Fundianus and the two raise them high above their heads. Amelia waves to the women on top of the steps. They move from the Senate doors.

The Senators file gloomily into the chambers. Cato is the last to leave the landing, staring malevolently at the dissolving crowd. *They need a stick taken to them,*

Flaccus tugs at Cato's forearm. "Come on, we have more pressing matters than this."

"What could be more pressing than the moral decay of Rome?" Cato says. "Women politicking in the streets, disobeying their husbands, flouting their lawlessness. This stops now!"

"Do not be overwrought," Flaccus replies cheerily. "If the Assembly votes to repeal the law, the Bruti brothers will veto them. As Tribunes of the Plebs, they have that right."

"That is welcome news, but how can you be sure they will do that?"

"Oh, I convinced them," Flaccus replies, as if sharing some private joke. "I may not be the orator you are, but I can be very persuasive."

As the rally dissipates, Amelia and Prima march back toward the Scipio manse, arguing about what to do next. They push their way through the jammed side streets, sliding past the many women who have paused to conduct their day's shopping.

Amelia rambles on excitedly about the size of the crowd and the chance to marshal them to elect Scipio as consul next year. Prima grasps her hand and smiles, sharing her enthusiasm.

A gray hooded figure approaches them, a stooped figure that has followed them at a distance since they entered the Avenue of Merchants. The man limps along, shuffling and obeisant, but his tattered cloak cannot disguise his wide shoulders and muscular calves. Nor can the hood dim the predatory blue eyes that blaze from inside it, eyes fixed upon Amelia's back.

The Sicilian pushes between two portly matrons, edging nearer to Amelia. He slides a wooden-handled bone needle from his right sleeve, being careful not to shake the cork from its tip.

He sees what he has been waiting for. Amelia's companion drops her coin purse, scattering a half-dozen denarii onto the paving slabs. "Ah, curse me!" he hears her exclaim, as she bends over to collect her monies.

The assassin flicks the cork off his needle and steps past the bent-over woman. *Once, deeply, where no one will see the prick,* he reminds himself. *They'll blame it on the gods.* He stabs at the back of Amelia's shoulder.

A slender, sinewy hand clamps upon his forearm, shoving the needle skyward. A slim dagger jabs into his wrist. The Sicilian yelps and drops the needle.

In one quick motion, a hand snatches the needle in midair and jabs it into the assassin's forearm. The man gapes in horror at the pinprick, knowing its consequences. His mouth moves, but no words come out.

The Sicilian falls onto the street, bashing the side of his head against the stones. His body convulses, his arms flapping futilely. Screams erupt about him.

Prima spits on the twitching assassin. "Pig! I wish I could kill you again!" She hurries back to rejoin Amelia.

Amelia turns toward the screams. "What's going on, Prima? Did that man fall ill?"

"Oh, he's ill all right," she replies. "Deadly ill. The bastard was trying to kill you."

"What?" Amelia pulls out a small dagger from inside her robe, glancing warily about her.

"A poisoned needle," Prima replies. "And it was very effective. Come on, let's get home before we have to kill someone else."

Returning to the Scipio manse, the two women plunk themselves onto the atrium couches. Amelia's children swarm about her. She hugs them tight, her eyes shiny with tears. Laelius stands next to her, his hands balled into fists.

"Who did it?" Laelius blurts. "I want to know who ordered it!"

"We don't know," Prima snaps. "Probably the same one who sent that female assassin Spider. You were supposed to find out, remember?"

Laelius' face flushes. "My informants have found nothing. But it must be Flaccus. He is treacherous, and he hates the Scipios."

"Then why don't you kill him?" Prima says. "Must I do it myself?"

"I don't know if it was him," Laelius replies irritably. "I have nothing definite."

Amelia looks up from her children. "Beloved friend, how many of us must die before you find something 'definite?'"

"He is a consul, a ruler of Rome!" Laelius blurts. "Would you have me kill one of our leaders, even if I could get near him?"

"Based on the direction he is leading us, yes," retorts Prima. She puts her hand on his forearm. You are an honest and just man, carissimus. But he is neither. If he did it, he has lies and bribes to conceal his actions. Consider it."

"I will return the gutters from which I came," Laelius says. "If a killer was hired there, I will find out."

"Well, I have to go out again tomorrow, before the Assembly meets. My husband's informers told him that the Bruti brothers will veto the Senate's repeal." She wrings her hands. "I can't ask other women to get out there while I hide at home, but I don't want to put you at risk, Prima. And I don't want any men there helping us."

"I appreciate your concern for my safety," Prima says, with the barest hint of sarcasm. "But I would like to see one of them threaten me. Next time I'll wound the bastard and find out who sent him."

The gladiatrix rises from her seat and marches toward the door. "And don't worry about protection for tomorrow. I will take care of that."

The next morning dawns sunny and warm. The young Bruti brothers hurry from their dining room toward their front door, their barrel-shaped bodies clad in the white togas they bought for today's People's Assembly.

"Do you think we'll have to veto the repeal?" asks Lucius, flicking bread crumbs off his tunic.

"Who cares?" replies Sextus. "We've been paid to do that if they vote for the Lex Oppia's repeal, but if they don't, we still get to keep the money. Either way, we win." He grabs his brother's forearm. "Come on, we're going to be late. Open that door, slave!"

The brothers step out from their doorway. They halt in mid stride.

The Brutii brothers find the street completely filled with women, every one of them staring somberly at them.[clxxviii] Amelia and Prima stand directly in front of them, surrounded by six lean muscular women in black tunics, their short swords dangling from their belts.

Lucius stares at the wall of women, his mouth agape. "Let us through," he blusters, flapping his pale, meaty arms. "The Assembly is going to start!"

"You're not going anywhere," Amelia states matter-of-factly. "We're keeping you here until it's over."

Sextus' face darkens. He looks back over his shoulder. "Cassius! Caldo!" he shouts. "We have intruders!"

Two hulking Gauls fill the doorway, their naked swords dangling from their hands. Sextus glowers at Amelia. "Am I going to have to cut my way through here?"

Lucius stares at his brother, flapping his hands. "Please, brother! No bloodshed."

Prima steps out in front of Amelia, flanked by the women in black tunics. "Try it," Prima growls. The women slide out their swords and point them at the Gauls.

Prima shrugs her arms. A needle-thin dagger slides out from her robe sleeve.

Amelia steps in next to her, a throwing knife in each hand. "These women witness that you threatened us," Amelia says. "They will attest that we had no choice but to defend ourselves."

The Gauls take a step forward. Amelia stares into Sextus' eyes. "These young women are all gladiators in training. They are more than capable of holding your large friends at bay until I kill you."

"Or until I do," says Prima, sliding toward Lucius.

"Please, Sextus," wails Lucius. "It is not worth it. Please."

Sextus sets his chin. "We have to be there. It is our duty. I gave my word." He takes a step forward. The black-clad women tense, waiting to spring.

"I believe you did," Amelia says. "And I would not have you dishonor it. Will you give us your word that you will not veto a repeal of the Lex Oppia?"

"I can't promise that," Sextus growls.

"What choice do you have?" Prima exclaims, jabbing her dagger at Lucius. "You can resist and die, or you can stay here and live. Either way, the repeal will be voted in."

"We don't need money that badly," Lucius says to his brother. "We can give it back."

The seconds drag by as Sextus stands silently, trembling with rage and frustration. He glances at his two guards, then back at the women surrounding him.

"We will not exercise our veto," he mutters.

Amelia nods. "That is a wise decision. Now we will be about our business."

Amelia turns toward the street. "We can go home now!" she shouts triumphantly. The women cheer, hugging one another, and walk off into the side streets.

While they depart, Prima steps up to Sextus, ignoring his angry guards. "We will be by the Assembly Hall today. I promise you, if we find out you lied, I will eviscerate the both of you." She stalks back to join Amelia, leaving the two brothers to stare at one another.

Sextus wrinkles his nose. "What's that smell?"

"A minute, brother," Lucius says, his voice trembling. "I have to change my clothing."

The next day finds the women of Rome drinking wine early, celebrating the Assembly's repeal of the Lex Oppia.

Furious about the result, Consul Marcus Porcius Cato leaves Rome for the port of Ostia, determined to regain his honor by commencing his campaign in Iberia.

Feeling no less frustrated, Consul Flaccus begins to pack for his trip to northern Italia. He plans a time-consuming, circuitous route with many visits to gaming rooms and wine bars, entertainments to help him forget the loathsome Scipios.

While Flaccus prepares his exit, Amelia and Prima lounge in the Scipio atrium, savoring their victory. "What next, then?" asks Prima, picking an olive from a nearby tray.

"The ten-year rule has expired. My husband can run for consul next year," Amelia replies. "Cato and Flaccus will soon be gone from the city, so that will minimize their interference. I will devote my energies to helping him get elected."

Amelia's mouth tightens. "He is not in the best of health, but he is determined to do it. He says he must capitalize on his fame while he still has it."

"I would be happy to help you," Prima says, "but soon my days as your bodyguard will be over."

Amelia nods. "I can see why. Even the hardiest warriors become tired of danger."

"Danger I crave, but only for myself," Prima says. "Will you keep a secret for me, sister?" Amelia nods. "Do you swear to Jana, the goddess of secrets?"

Amelia glowers at her. "Yes, curse you. What is it?"

Prima lifts her wine goblet in a toast. "I'm pregnant."

Amelia drops her cup. "You? Who is the father?"

"You know who," Prima snaps. "Who else would it be?"

"But, how could that be? Laelius is—"

"A man of many tastes," Prima interjects. "And loving me is one of them."

Amelia nods. "I an happy for you, and I truly understand your leaving. A baby changes everything."

"Almost everything," Prima responds, a feral gleam coming into her eyes. "There is one more thing I must do, something Scipio promised me at Capua. Doing it will help him, too."

Amelia stares at her. "You're going back into the ring, aren't you?"

Prima grins. "One more time. Rome must see what a woman can do."

"Laelius will not allow it."

"Laelius will not know," Prima says. "You promised to keep it a secret, remember?"

Amelia crosses her arms. "If I had known that, I would have never promised! Laelius will skin me alive if he ever finds out!"

Prima chuckles. "No he won't. He's too ashamed that he hasn't found out who hired those assassins." She shakes her head. "Poor boy, he won't rest until he takes care of it."

AVENTINE HILL, ROME. Laelius creeps in behind the man

squatting in front of him, watching his every move. The man hauls back his right fist and shakes it furiously, angling it behind his head.

Now or never, Laelius decides. *Make your move.* He reaches for his swordbelt.

"Ten denarii on the throw!" Laelius yells.

"Taken!" replies a portly man in a sweat-stained gray tunic, his dust-covered arms identifying him as a stonemason.

The thrower pitches his dice. They clack across the paving stones and bounce off the bricks that ring the throwing area, a six showing on each of them.

"The throw of Aphrodite!" the referee exclaims, invoking the Greek name for the perfect throw.[clxxix] The stonemason glumly drops a pile of denarii into Laelius' waiting palm.

Laelius is delighted with the win but he has not come here, under the arch of Rome's southernmost aqueduct, to indulge in illegal gambling. He has come to find a man known as the Bear, a man who rules its teeming thousands with an iron fist. Nothing happens on the hill without him knowing about it.

Laelius eases his way through the crowd, clasping forearms with the occasional bettor who recognizes him from his wrestling days here. He finally sees the man he wants, a man as wide as he is tall, his thick arms matted with glossy black hair. The man wears worn sandals and a simple white tunic, as plainly dressed as the commoners around him. Only his four Nubian guards attest that he is a man of station and power—a man wealthier than half the patricians in Rome.

"Laelius, you old shitpot!" The Bear levers himself up from his pillow and hugs Laelius so tight the breath whooshes from him. "Good to see you! You have risen so high in the world, out playing soldier with the Imperator himself! What brings you down to my humble kingdom?"

"A name, Bear. I seek a name." Laelius says. "A single name means much to me."

The Bear's eyes grow crafty. "This name, is it of someone who has wronged you?"

"This person has hired assassins to kill those I love," Laelius says. "One of them was the woman known as Spider. The other was someone called the Sicilian. Do you know who hired them?"

"No. Nor have I heard of such a person," the Bear states. "I am sorry I cannot help you. But let me buy you a cup of mulsum. Come on."

"I'm really not in the mood for a—" Laelius begins.

"You should come," the Bear repeats, his voice heavy with implication.

The man shambles toward the wine vendor's cart outside the arch. "You stay here," he says to his guards. Laelius follows him, puzzled. When they are past the crowd, the Bear faces Laelius.

"There was a man who came to the stables at night. He spoke with Spider, that much I know. He remained in the shadows, but his words were those of an educated, older man. He gave her much money."

"Gratitude, Bear." Laelius says. "I think I know who it was. I only wish I knew for sure."

Bear laughs. "If I didn't act until I was sure of something, I'd still be a baker's apprentice!" He winks. "I will tell you this. Of the men who hire assassins, many are senators."

Laelius is silent for several long moments, staring his feet. He looks up, his face set. "I need to hire one of your men. A subtle, skilled man."

Bear slaps him on the back. "Good! I have just the man! Now let's get some honeyed wine!"

Two hours later, Laelius teeters into the Scipio manse, his head heavy with drink. He pads into the atrium and flops onto a couch next to the fish pond, covering his eyes with his arm. Scipio pads in from his bedroom.

"Where have you been?" Scipio says. "You smell like a cheap brothel."

Laelius props himself up on one elbow. "I was gambling over at the Aventine."

"Hm! I didn't know you were a gambler," Scipio says. "Be careful— gambling can get you thrown in jail. That won't help your career."

"Oh, I'll be gambling with my career, too. And a maybe with a man's life—a vile man, though he may be innocent of this." Laelius mutters. He blinks at Scipio. "I made a deal with someone. Can you loan me some money?"

"What? Of course. But what's this about gambling with careers and lives?"

"Ignore me, I have had too much to drink. You have other worries."

"That is certainly true. I just learned that Hannibal fled Carthage. He is going to join Antiochus." He shakes his head. "Antiochus can give him what Carthage wouldn't—unlimited men and resources."

Laelius burps wetly. "I tell you what: you take care of our affairs abroad, and I'll take care of those at home. I can best help you that way." He lays back and covers his eyes. "Gods help me."

"What affairs at home?" Scipio asks. But Laelius is fast asleep.

EPHESUS, SELEUCID EMPIRE, 195 BCE.[clxxx] *This boy has more ambition than wisdom*, Hannibal thinks, drawing deeply from his goblet of Lesbos red. *He will bear close watching.*

Hannibal and Antiochus are taking wine inside Antiochus' house-sized throne room. Cups in hand, the two study a twenty-foot wall map of Greece.

A waspish young man stands alongside them, his eyes as black as his cascading raven hair. He runs a wooden pointer from the city marker for Ephesus, straight across the blue area for the Aegean Sea, and taps it on Athens.

"There. You see? We can cross from here to Athens in a day, two at the most. We can take Thebes and Athens before they even know what's happening to them. With those cities secured as our garrisons, we march west to take all of Achea!"

Hannibal frowns, but he says nothing. Antiochus slowly shakes his head. "You would have us fighting Greece and Rome within the month, son."

"And what of it? Our armies are ready," he says. "We have taken what we want from Thrace and Egypt. Why not move on Greece?"

"Rome is the reason, son." Antiochus says. "An invasion of Greece would precipitate a war with the Romans. And they are too strong for us, until our fleet is restored."

"Too overrated, you mean," Seleucus replies sarcastically. "They can be beaten. Hannibal knows: he defeated them many times."

"I would not call them overrated," Hannibal says evenly. "But the Romans can be defeated with guile and planning—and with much persistence, because they will not quit until every one of them is dead."

"I don't think we should press on," Antiochus says, frowning into his cup. "We lost too many men when our fleet sunk. And that Quinctius Flamininus, the man who defeated Philip? He is out near Thrace with twenty thousand veterans." The king shrugs. "We have gained back much of my ancestor's kingdom—perhaps I will end our campaign."

"What!" Seleucus blurts. "We have the world in our hands!"

"I understand," Hannibal says. "You have a hundred thousand men, but most of them have not tasted blood. You need my Carthaginians. If I could sway Carthage to join you, Antiochus, Rome wouldn't have a chance."

"We can't depend on Carthage," Seleucus snaps. "You should know that better than anyone."

Insolent pup! Hannibal thinks. "Perhaps it is a time for peace, but only to prepare for war," he says. "Time may bring the Aetolians to our side. They asked Rome to restore some of the ancestral lands that Philip took from them. But Rome told them to talk to Proconsul Flamininus,[clxxxi] the same man who declaimed them as greedy plunder-takers." He chuckles. "The Aetolians did not welcome Rome's decision. Now they are looking to ally themselves with someone who can give them more power in Greece." He looks at Seleucus. "But the Aetolians are not ready to turn on Rome—yet."

"How long, then?" Seleucus asks, clearly irritated.

"A few years," Hannibal responds. He faces Antiochus. "Recruit and train more troops, build more garrisons, fortify the cities you have taken. Prepare for a world war, my King—a war to own the world."

Antiochus' eyes brighten with greed. *Now,* Hannibal tells himself. "If you desire it, I will fight by your side. If things go aright, Carthage may join your efforts." He spreads his hands. "Just think of it—Syria, Carthage, and Aetolia united against Rome! The gods themselves would quail to fight us!"

The room is silent. Finally Antiochus nods. "Very well. Peace for now. In the meantime we take our armies north, toward Thrace. There are lands there that belong to us, and men who may help us fight Rome."

"That is wise. Your recruits can be trained on the way," Hannibal says. "There is only one way to learn how to fight, and that's to actually fight. Send your troops to take every city and garrison on the way. Their kills will be their lessons."

Antiochus nods. "That is sage advice. Still, I would like some insurance that Scipio himself does not march on us. Something that would keep him at bay."

He grins. "I think I know just how to do that."

CREMONA, ITALIA. "Come on, dolts. I want to be at Placentia by lunchtime. I heard they serve the best roast dormouse in the region."

Consul Lucius Valerius Flaccus waves over his elite guard, taking care that they completely surround him before he rides out. As a man of treachery and murder, he lives with the fear that one of his victims may seek recourse upon him, even at this remote garrison in north Italia.

Flaccus and his men trot out from the front of his command tent, heading for the open gates. The riders push through the city workers milling about the entrance, lugging timbers and stones to repair the front guard tower. The workers ignore the retinue, intent on finishing their tasks before the summer day heats up. One youth, however, intently watches Flaccus' party, his black eyes following as they ride past.

"Ow!" Flaccus exclaims. slapping at a sting in the back of his neck. He retrieves his hand and stares at the fat green fly that bit him, feeling a twitch of satisfaction at having killed it.

"Fucking horse flies are everywhere," he mutters.

Flaccus flicks the bug onto the ground and rides on. Had he looked closer, he might have noticed that the fly's bottle green eyes were enameled paint; its body a clump of horsehair.

Two hours later, Flaccus' entourage approaches Placentia. The consul watches the army wagons trundle in with stone blocks for the wall.

I heard the Gauls totally destroyed the place, but the rebuilding seems to be going well. Good, I won't have to harangue the town's praetor about working harder. We can spend the night feasting and drinking. If that bastard Scipio hadn't cut off my balls,[clxxxii] *I could have had a nice young boy tonight. I'm sure it was him—I'll get them all when I get back to Rome.*

Flaccus dabs at his nose, feeling it begin to drip. He stares at the clots of blood on his fingers. He feels a warm trickle down his lips, and presses his linen handkerchief to his mouth.

Flaccus pivots sideways and vomits down the side of his horse, his guts convulsing spasmodically. His guards wheel about and rush to help him, but Flaccus is already sliding off the side of his horse. He thuds into the rocky soil, his body shaking violently.

"General! What's happening?" blurts the captain of his guard. Flaccus' mouth moves, but no words come out. His eyes stare pleadingly at the captain, tears running from their corners.

Flaccus feels himself grow cold, terribly cold, and his shaking grows more violent. He feels himself being lifted up, wrapped in blankets, and eased into an empty wagon.

The wagon trundles toward town, pitching him back and forth. His last thought before he loses consciousness is a single word.

Who?

For months, Flaccus lies abed in Placentia, flirting with death. As his failed consulship draws to a close, Flaccus prepares to return to Rome for the annual elections.

That afternoon, he joins praetor Lucius Camillus for a final tour of his rebuilt garrison. Still weak from the poison, Flaccus soon excuses himself and returns to his blockhouse by the town gates.

Stumbling his way into his bedroom, he finds a small goatskin scroll resting on top of his sleeping platform. He picks it up and examines the wax seal for a sign of the sender. It is unmarked. Flaccus breaks the seal and reads the terse message.

You will refrain from any more attempts at assassination. You will not participate in the upcoming elections in any way.

Heed this message, or the next time you will suffer a death ten times worse than what you just endured.

The message is signed with a perfectly drawn duplicate of the fly dart that bit into Flaccus' neck.

Flaccus pitches the scroll away as if it were a serpent. "Guards, guards!" he yells. His four sentries barge in with drawn swords.

"Who brought this message?" Flaccus blurts. The guards look at one another. "No one has been in here since you left," one of them replies.

Flaccus feels a shiver run up his spine. *They can get me anywhere, anytime, whoever they are.* "Never mind. You are dismissed."

The consul sits on the side of his bed, cradling his face in his hands. *I am undone. I can't endure anything like that again.* He looks at the scroll. *I don't need to involve myself in this election, anyway. That bastard Scipio won't get elected. He's lost the people's attention.*

ROME. Scipio puts his shoulder to the iron door and digs in his sandaled feet. It screeches open. *You gourd-head, you should have oiled this thing—every thug in the Porta Collina can hear you.*

Scipio steps into the darkness. He lifts his torch above his head and touches the flame against the unlit torches on each side of the doorway. The room dances with firelight, the flames flickering across piles of jewelry, coins, and armor.

"Get in here before someone sees us," Scipio says testily.

Celsus stoops through the doorway, his brown robe dragging over the dusty floor. The money changer gapes at the scattered mounds of treasure, paying particular attention to the four gold bars that rest near his feet. He rubs his hands together, his expression that of a child in a baker's shop.

"It's nowhere near as much as I had, but it is still a sizeable fortune," Scipio says. "And I want every sestertius of what it's worth. Actor, come in here."

A Greek dwarf steps into the room, his brown eyes surveying its contents. His bowed legs are covered in leggings of finest goatskin, his leather-clad torso half-covered by a silver studded belt. A foot-long sword dangles from his hip, its gold pommel glinting in the firelight.

"This is Actor, a former accountant for the Spartan army. He is quite experienced in converting valuables to money. He will conduct our exchange on my behalf."

"Accountant? I thought he was your slave," Celsus remarks.

The dwarf glowers at Celsus. "That will cost you dearly in the exchange." He wrinkles his nose. "You stink of kannabis."

"Come now, I want this to be a friendly transaction," Scipio says, pulling up a stool from the corner. "Actor here, he gets a twentieth of all he can negotiate. I will keep the tally to ensure everyone is treated fairly."

"You want me to buy all of this?" Celsus says. "Right now?"

"You *will* buy all of this," Scipio replies. Celsus starts to raise his hands. "Do not protest, I know you have the means. The money will be delivered here by tomorrow morning, the same time that you remove all this."

Celsus flaps his hands. "Too soon, too soon! I need time to get wagons, and guards, and to—"

"I am certain you can accomplish it. Just do it under cover of night," Scipio says. "I will insure that the city guards do not interfere."

Celsus nods mutely. His eyes roam over the treasure piles.

"Of course, if anyone should break into here between now and then, I won't bother finding out who did it. I will simply burn you alive," Scipio adds.

"That was unnecessary," Celsus mutters.

Scipio smirks. "I certainly hope so."

"Come on, let's get to it," Actor interjects. " I have an appointment with a patrician widow." He winks. "The gods might have made me short, but they compensated me elsewhere."

Hours later, the three men step into the evening streets. Scipio carries a wax tablet inscribed with a tally of what he is to be paid.

"My guards and I will be back at the second hour for the transfer,"

Scipio says. "Do not be late."

Celsus pulls his hood over his head and slinks into a side street, heading for his favorite opium house. Scipio and Actor walk toward the stable that holds their horses.

Actor scrambles onto his black mare. He grins at Scipio. "That was a good night's work. I'll double my fishing fleet with my share."

"Well done, Actor." Scipio says. "Trust me, the proceeds will be used for the good of Rome."

"I know, because I know you!" the dwarf replies, his eyes twinkling. He slaps his horse on the neck and trots into the night.

Scipio rides down the cobbled streets of the Vicus Africus, a street renamed to celebrate his victory over Carthage. He dismounts in front of the three-story insulae that Laelius owns.[clxxxiii]

He tramps up the oak plank stairs to the second floor and knocks on a red door with a saggitarius painted upon it. Laelius opens it, his eyes puffy with sleep.

"Hera's cunt, what are you doing here at his hour?" His eyes open with alarm. "What happened? Is Amelia all right? The children?"

"All are fine," Scipio says. "But I have to talk to you."

Laelius beckons Scipio inside. He eases himself into a woven wicker chair. "I guess you won't leave, so you might as well make yourself comfortable."

Scipio plops onto a gilt red couch with wood feet shaped as penises. "I want you to do me a favor."

"You mean I must return the favor you did for me, don't you?" Laelius says.

"Where you and I are concerned, favors are given, but they need not be repaid," Scipio says. "This is important—I need you to go shopping."

Laelius stares at him. "It's a little late for jokes, isn't it?"

"This isn't marketplace shopping. I need you to take a quick ship to Numidia and Carthage. Bring back foods and entertainments, the like of which Rome has never seen."

Laelius rubs his eyes. He cocks his head at Scipio. "This is about you running for consul, isn't it?"

"Rome's future hangs on the consular elections. I have to win."

"And eating elephant's balls will help you do that?"

Scipio shakes his head. "It's not just the eating, tin-head. We are going to put on show—a show such as Rome has never seen."

EMPORIAE,^{clxxxiv} NORTHEAST IBERIA. "Where in Pluto are we?" Paulus says to Tiberius, a ladder man of the First Legion.

As he marches along, Paulus stares at the dark silhouettes of the pine forest that flanks the wide dirt road. "Some place as black as the River Styx, that's all I know."

Tiberius stares up into the moonless night, reading the ceiling of stars. "As near as I can tell, we are heading west. Maybe northwest a bit. I think we've passed the Indigetes' fort." He grimaces. "Leave it to that dictator to drag us out in the middle of the night."

"What manner of man is this General Cato?" He's got us marching at midnight across unknown terrain. Who knows what we'll encounter?"

Tiberius chuckles. "At this hour? Not another army! Maybe that's his reason."

"I don't know, he seems crazy to me," Paulus says. "He made us build our walls and trenches twice as wide as they should be. Three days later, we pack up and leave in the middle of the night! That's crazy."

"Maybe so, but he is no soft-assed patrician like the last one. He sleeps on the ground, and eats the same food we do. He reminds me of Hannibal."

Paulus laughs. "Hannibal the Carthaginian? Cato had better not hear you say that! He hates Carthage. I heard he's always telling the Senate that they must destroy it."

"Carthage had better not hear him saying that," Tiberius replies. "We'll be fighting another war with them!"

"You men, be quiet over there!" their centurion rasps. "We are almost there."

The two men walk on in silence, listening to the creaking wheels of the wagons and siege engines. When the centurion moves away from them, the escaladers resume their conversation.

"Whatever we're doing here, there'd better be plunder in it," whispers Paulus. "I've got to send some money to the family, to get someone to take in the harvest. Got to pay the land taxes so some patrician doesn't grab the farm."

"Know what you mean," Tiberius replies. "That Senator Flaccus bought up two of my neighbor's properties. Those rich bastards start a war just so they can get richer at our expense."

"That is not a revelation," Paulus replies dryly.

Within the hour, Cato's army begins a wide, slow turn to the left. Twenty thousand men tramp through the inky darkness, the army wagons trundling behind them. The legionnaires watch the lights winking far to their left, realizing they come from the torches of an Iberian city.

Dawn washes across the landscape. The men see that the lights came from an enormous garrison with thickly timbered walls.

"That's a mighty big fort," says Tiberius.

"I wonder if our ladders are tall enough to get us over those walls?" Paulus says. He squints at them. "Oh, piss! The tops are lined with sharpened stakes!"

"It would be a tough climb, but we'd get extra pay for it."

Paulus smirks. "Yes, but would we live to spend it? This Cato had better know what he's doing."

The legions' horns sound a halt. The men fall into formation, facing the fort. The First Legion's ten cohorts line up nearest to the fort, five cohorts backing up the five in the front. The Second Legion array themselves behind them, up the incline that descends toward the fort.

Paulus and Tiberius shed their armor. They stretch out upon the thick spring grass, grateful for the respite from marching. The two men chew on the dried cheese and fruit they packed in their sarcinas, wondering what the morning will bring. Staring at the fort, they can see hundreds of Indigetes lining the staked ramparts, their iron spears resting against their leather-clad shoulders.

"Well, we certainly aren't going to surprise them," Tiberius says. He lies back down and covers his eyes with his hands. "Ah, shit on me!"

While Cato's soldiers take their rest, he huddles with the two legates who command his legions. "That is a sturdy fort, and it has thousands of warriors inside. We cannot storm it, so we'll have to draw them out. Get me two cohorts of men who are practiced at the turtle shell maneuver. Have them at the front within the hour."

An hour later, the Indigete garrison watches a thousand Romans tramp toward them, two enormous rectangles divided into centuries of eighty men. The legionnaires march straight toward the thick timbers of the garrison's front wall. Forty escaladers stride behind each of the cohorts, each pair lugging a tree-branch ladder.

The Romans halt within a stone's throw of the garrison's double gates. Cato rides out and faces the fort, glowering at the Indigetes lining the walls. The Iberians silently watch him.

"In the name of Rome, surrender this garrison!" Cato shouts in pidgin Iberian. He paces about on his horse, waiting. There is no reply.

Cato rides closer. "Did you hear me? Open the gates!"

An Iberian leans over the wall, his helmet's long red feathers nodding at Cato. He barks out a single, brief, order. Clouds of stones fly at the Romans, followed by flights of flaming darts.

"Testudo!" the centurions yell. The centuries cover their heads with their shields, forming a shield shell. The rocks bonk harmlessly off the Romans' scuta, but many of the burning darts stick into them. Several younger soldiers lower their shields to pull them out. The stones bash into their helmets, knocking them senseless. Their compatriots quickly drag them under the shield roof.

Cato holds his shield above his head, as calm as if he were sheltering himself from a summer rain. A stone thuds into his horse's flank. The beast rears, but Cato grabs his mane and pulls him in.

"You had your chance!" Cato shouts to the fort. He trots behind the front lines and dismounts, walking over to his two legion commanders and their lead tribunes.

"All right, get the men out of here," he orders. "We'll see if those barbarians take the bait." The lead tribunes trot back to the two cohorts. A minute later, their whistles sound two shrill notes. The cohorts turn around and march away from the fort, rejoining their legions.

The Indigetes cheer the Roman retreat, hooting out their defiance. As the Romans retreat, the fort's front gates fly open. The Indigetes stream out onto the plain, thousands of brown-skinned men in domed bronze helmets. The sinewy warriors carry oblong shields and six-foot spears, their dread falcatas dangling from their tunic belts. The barbarians fill the plain, screaming their eagerness to destroy the hated Romans.

Cato watches the horde of barbarians stampede toward him. *They're coming to destroy us. Good.* "Regroup," he commands. "Five and five."

The First Legion arrays itself in front of the massing Indigetes, five cohorts in the front with five behind. The Second Legion mimics the formation. Riding between the two legions, Cato directs three hundred cavalry to each flank. He rides out to the center of the First Legion's front line, the legion's lead commander at his side.

"Men, there is no turning back," Cato says. "Between us and our camp is the enemy, and behind us is enemy territory. There is no hope to be found anywhere save in your courage."[clxxxv]

"Now, while they are still collecting themselves, we attack! Victory or death, the choice is yours!" With a flourish of his sword, Cato trots his horse toward the Indigete horde. The First Legion tramps after him, soon followed by the Second. The cavalry race out on each side.

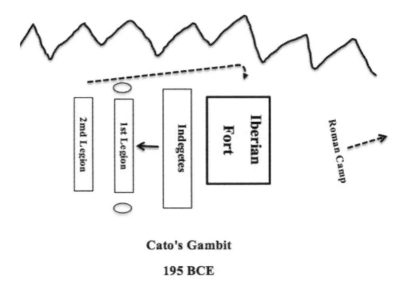

Cato's Gambit

195 BCE

The Indigete horns sound, and the charging barbarians pause to assemble, their army a long, uneven line of men tightly packed together. Hundreds of Iberian cavalry push their way out between the foot soldiers, unarmored warriors riding sturdy mountain ponies, using only a curved sword and small round shield. The Iberians race across the plain and slash into the heavily armored equites. A swirling cavalry battle erupts along the Roman flanks.

With ear-splitting yells, the Iberian infantry dashes at the Romans, flinging their spears as they run. The Romans raise their shields and return fire with their javelins, releasing three quick spear bursts. Scores of Iberians fall in mid stride, their bodies pierced by the iron-tipped spears. But still the Indigetes come on.

The barbarians crash into the Roman shield wall. The conflict becomes a collection of front-line sword fights, the Romans' disciplined resistance combatting the swarming fury of the determined Indigetes.

The Iberians hammer their swords against the hastati on the front line, their falcatas hewing away chunks of shield and armor. Scores of Romans fall, but they are swiftly replaced by the men behind them.

Cato rages along the space between the First Legion's front lines, threatening to kill any man that steps back from the conflict. After a half hour of furious fighting, he sees that many Indigetes are holding their shields low, that their sword blows are slower. He turns to his cornicen. "Line replacement!" he barks.

The horns sound three times. The cohort's first line withdraws, step by step, as the second line slides forward between them. The battle rages anew, with the Romans steadfastly holding against the waves of Iberian attackers. Cato barks another order, and the rear lines step forward to freshen the fight.

A half hour later, Cato notices that many of the Iberians are staggering from exhaustion. *Time for the next ploy.*

"Take the men back a spear's cast," he orders.

The front cohorts retreat and halt, standing their shields on the ground. Grateful for the respite, the Indigetes stay where they are, drinking water from their wineskins while they attend to their wounded.

Cato hastens to the Second Legion's legate. "Send two cohorts around our left flank, double-time."

Within minutes, two cohorts of reserves march quickly around the left flank of Roman's front line, looping toward the Indigete rear. [clxxxvi] The Iberian warriors anxiously watch them but they remain in place, more concerned about the Romans in front of them.

Cato watches the cohorts trot briskly around the flank, edging into the space between the legions and the cavalry. He waves a signal to Cassius, the First Legion's commander.

The cornu sound again. The First Legion's five reserve cohorts hasten to the front. The centuries in the center advance ahead of the side centuries, creating an attack wedge. [clxxxvii]

"No retreat," Cato bellows to this officers. "Kill any who turn their backs."

The wedge delves into the Iberian center, splitting their front lines. Scores of Indigetes fall beneath the disciplined Roman blades, then hundreds.

The Iberian chieftains shove their men at the Roman wedge, pounding on their backs to drive them forward. The Iberians' counterattack halts the First Legion's advance. Then the Second Legion's two cohorts crash into the Iberians' rear lines, driving them into the men ahead of them.

Beset from the front and back, the Indegetes run for the safety of their garrison. The Iberian cavalry abandon their fight with the equites and race for the open gates, leaving the Roman cavalry free to cut down hundreds of fleeing foot soldiers. Thousands of barbarians scramble for the open portal, with thousands more strewn along the plain.

Cato watches the tide of battle turn to his favor. He summons the First Legion's lead commander. "We need to finish this, Cassius. Bring on the escaladers. Roll in the ram."

The First Legion's men attack the front of the fort. The escaladers pitch their ladders against the walls as the infantry rams an iron-headed tree trunk against the sturdy gates. The desperate Indigetes fling down everything they can lay their hands on: spears, stones, furniture, even statues. The Romans huddle under the their shields, and gradually retreat out of range.

Cato's face flushes with anger. *Gods curse them, they act like a bunch of women! I have to find a weak spot.* He races around the outside of the walls, scanning the ramparts. He notices that a side gate has few sentries posted above it. *Here. If we move quickly, before they can get reinforcements.*

He races to the First Legion's legate and grabs him by the shoulder. "Attack the front with everything you have, Cassius. Use your rams and ladders, anything to keep them occupied. Now wait for my command." The legate nods, his eyes wide.

Cato spins his horse around and trots to the oncoming Second Legion. He pulls up in its center, next to the legion's legate.

"Hostus, give me two thousand hastati and principes," Cato says. "And forty ladder men and a battering ram."

Cato rides to the edge of the Second Legion's left flank and waits. The Second's hastati and principes soon march out to join him. The escaladers and the ram's men follow.

Paulus and Tiberius trot along with the rest of the escaladers, lugging their ladder on their shoulders.

"Where are we going?" Paulus asks nervously, eyeing the men pushing the eight-wheeled battering ram.

Tiberius forces a grin. "You know where we're going. Up!"

After the hastati and principles line up behind him, Cato calls over Cassius, the First Legion's legate. "Now! Attack the front and keep them occupied. And woe to you if your men retreat!"

The First Legion tramps back toward the fort's front, their light infantry leading the charge. The Indegetes crowd the front wall, hurling the last of their spears and stones. As they First Legion approaches the walls, the velites fling their spears at the ramparts, quelling the Iberians' assault.

The First Legion's battering ram rolls back to the front gates, its operators sheltered by a bronze-covered roof. The ram booms against the gate, prompting more missile assaults from the Iberians.

Seeing the Iberians are occupied along the front wall, Cato hurries his men toward the side gate. "Up with the ladders!" he shouts. "First man over the top gets a silver corona muralis!"

"You hear that, Tiberius?" Paulus exclaims. "I go over the top first, I get a silver crown! I can pay off everything!" He grabs the front of the ladder and dashes forward, pulling his friend with him.

The ladder men race to the wall and fling up their ladders, holding their shields above their heads. The two thousand hastati and principes fling their spears at the wall defenders, their covering fire buying time for the laddermen.

The Second Legion soldiers trundle their ram to the side gate. They pull back on the tree-trunk shaft suspended from ropes and shove it forward, bashing it into the timbered portal. The barred doors bow inward.

"Block those gates!" an Iberian captain yells. Dozens of wall defenders race from the wall, pushing themselves against the splintering side gates.

"Look," says Paulus. "They're running from the wall. Let's get up there first!" Paulus flings his ladder onto an unattended portion of the wall and scrambles up, his shield dangling from his back.

"Wait for me, fool!" Tiberius barks, crawling up the tree-branch rungs as fast as he can.

Paulus nears the top, glancing sideways to see if anyone has preceded him. He hears a scream and looks to his right. A ladder man plunges down, his neck gouting blood from a spear thrust. *Don't rush,* Paulus chides himself. *The crown won't do you any good if you don't have a head.* He slowly lifts his head over the top.

An Iberian pops up in front of him, a boy barely taller than the falcata he grasps with both fists. Trembling with fright, the boy chops at Paulus' wrist. Paulus screams as the blade bites into his forearm.

"You little bastard!"

The boy strikes again. Paulus falls from the ladder, his hand still clinging to the rampart stake.

Tiberius sees his friend plunge past him and crash to the earth. His eyes flame with rage. He scrambles up and vaults over the rampart, heedless of whoever may be waiting for him. He sees the young man standing there, clutching his bloody cleaver with both hands.

"You!" he snarls. He leaps at the boy and drives his sword blade through the boy's forehead, pushing until the hilt strikes his brows. The boy's eyes bulge from his head. Tiberius yanks out his sword and watches the boy topple onto his face. He rushes at the next Iberian on the wall, slashing at him until he tumbles from the rampart.

The rest of the escaladers join Tiberius on the wall, followed by scores of legionnaires. Fighting with measured ferocity, the Romans cut down the defenders and hurl their bodies off the wall. They rush down and thrust into the defenders bracing the side gate, forming a semicircle of death about it.

Minutes later, the gates open. Two thousand of Rome's veterans storm into the fort, with Cato walking in the forefront.

"On to the front gates," Cato orders. Sword in hand, he marches across the courtyard, his eyes fixed on Iberians protecting the front gates.

The hastati and principes stride toward the front gates, listening to the defenders scream out a warning. Hundreds of Indigetes rush to attack them. The veterans beat them back, pushing them into the Iberians massed by the gates. [clxxxviii]

Word spreads among the Iberians that the Romans are inside the fort, killing all that oppose them. Hundreds of Indigetes run out the rear gates, fearing that the legions have taken the town.

The front gates split open. The First Legion pours into the fort, beating back the Iberians that bravely rush to defend it. Jammed together by assaults from both legions, thousands of Iberians die where they stand, cut down by the Romans' relentless advance.

445

Seeing their death imminent, hundreds of Indegetes cast off their arms and fall to their knees, tears of shame streaming down their faces as they beg for mercy.

Soon, the din of battle settles into a series of sporadic screams, as the Romans begin the onerous task of rooting out those who hide in the fort's buildings. Cato stands in the center of the courtyard, calmly bandaging a deep gash on his sword arm.

"Let the men take what plunder they may find," he says. He glances at the sun. "Make the prisoners drag the bodies outside and burn them. We still have enough daylight to tidy up this mess."

The night finds the Romans inside the garrison, feasting on the wine and food they have taken from its stores. Outside the gates, a massive funeral pyre sends flames leaping into the blackened night, fueled by the burning flesh of twenty thousand Indigetes.

Tiberius sits on a log inside the fort, chewing on a large chunk of Iberian ham. "Here," he says, laying the ham on the ground, "let me freshen that."

Using a long strip of linen, he carefully wraps Paulus' stump with a fresh bandage. Paulus grimaces, but he nods his thanks.

"Ah, gods, it hurts. That little prick was barely weaned from his mother's teat, and he did this to me!"

"He was an Iberian. Be thankful he didn't take your head."

"Now how am I going to work the farm?" Paulus moans. "I don't have enough money for a slave." He stares at the ground. "Fortuna is a bitch goddess."

"Perhaps she isn't, soldier," comes a voice behind him. Cato steps in from behind them. His right hand slides out from his flowing red cloak. It holds a silver crown.

He bows slightly and gives the crown to Paulus. "You were first man over the wall," Cato says.

446

Paulus takes the crown in his good hand. He blinks at Cato, his eyes glassy with tears.

"You two were a key to our success today," Cato continues. "You will have first pick of the plunder."

Cato turns about and marches away, leaving the two friends staring at his back, dumbfounded.

"You will be rich," Tiberius says. Then, wonderingly: "*I* will be rich."

Paulus waves the silver crown at Tiberius. "But I will be richer. Maybe I'll hire *you* to do my work!"

Word spreads quickly of Cato's destruction of the Emporiae garrison. Soon, all of Iberia knows about the stern young man with the burning gray eyes. His army marches from one rebellious town to another, prepared for battle. At each town, Cato is met by a deputation of officials, magistrates who are only too willing to avoid a fight.[clxxxix]

Cato's response is always the same--unconditional and immediate surrender. He sends a cohort into each town and marches to conquer another, his mind fixed on elevating his family name to glory.

As he rides along, he muses about Rome and the upcoming consular elections. *Iberia will be under our control again, but Syria looms before us. I hope they elect someone who knows how to fight.*

SCIPIO MANSE, ROME. "More ostrich, Senator?" Scipio asks, proffering a platter with a ham-sized drumstick upon it.

"Gratitude, General, but I will explode if I take another bite," the fleshy young man replies, patting his ample midriff. "Where did you get such a delicious bird?"

"I brought it live from Carthage, Pontius," Scipio replies. "Near the site of my battle with Hannibal."

"Ah, Zama," Pontius says. "You saved Rome that day." He grins knowingly. "I will not forget that, Candidate Scipio."

"Good," Scipio says. "But save some room for the final dish—you will not be sorry." He hands the tray back to his slave attendant, a handsome young Gaul with straw blond pigtails.

Prima has loaned the slave to Scipio for his election banquets. The slave is an accomplished nomenclator.[cxc] He knows the name of every Roman senator, including the twenty-two who are attending tonight's festival.

The senators fill the domus' spacious atrium. Laughing and chatting, they recline on dining couches that surround a large table laden with meats and fruits from far-off Africa. Scipio bustles about with the Gaul following him, sharing jokes and gossip. He wears the unadorned, chalk-white toga of a consular candidate.

Amelia circulates among the senators, cradling a jug of dark red Numidian wine. She is a vision of loveliness, wearing a sapphire gown with a plunging neckline, her auburn hair piled atop a gleaming gold coronet. More than one senator gulps his wine so that he can ask her for a refill, enjoying the sight of her perfumed breasts swaying in front of him as she pours.

Laelius struts slowly between the couches, resplendent in his gold-embroidered black toga. He plucks at a lyre and sings the bawdy songs he learned at the docks of Ostia. Several tipsy senators join him as he walks, rising to bellow out half-remembered lyrics. Laelius rolls his eyes at their slurred words, but he never loses his smile. He knows he will need their support when he runs for consul.

The slaves clear out the main table's plates. Scipio moves to the center of the atrium. "Now for a special treat," he says. "Two foods from far Numidia, the delights of King Masinissa's court!"

Scipio claps his hands. Six slaves appear with shield-sized silver platters laden with small pewter plates. Each plate is ringed with slices of Numidian chicken, fragrant with the aromas of dates and coriander. The center of the dish is filled with a mound of savory cumin and beans.[cxci]

The senators take their forks and tentatively sample the exotic foods. Soon, the atrium fills with exclamations of pleasure and delight. Quintus Tertulius teeters to his feet. The senior senator raises his wine goblet and places his hand over his heart. He opens his mouth to speak but an enormous belch escapes him, leading to the loudest laughs of the evening. Nonplussed, Quintus raises his goblet higher.

"Well, you have just heard what I think of the food," he says, provoking more laughs. "Now let me tell you what I think of the man." He sips from his goblet and extends it toward the crowd.

"To Scipio Africanus, Rome's greatest general and finest man. And the next consul of Rome!" Amid a chorus of cheers and acclimations, Scipio rises to his feet.

"Gratitude for your attendance. We are truly honored by your presence. Do not forget to attend the games at the Circus Maximus this Saturn day. I am holding it in honor of Rome's triumph over Carthage!" The senators cheer.

"You mean your triumph over Carthage!" Quintus shouts. His comments provoke more cheers.

"I promise you will not be disappointed. The gladiatorial schools of Cassius Rufus and Aulius Certus will perform, with a very special guest leading them."

"I wouldn't miss it if Charon himself came to take me to Hades," Quintus says. "All of Rome will be there!"

Saturn day morning dawns bright and clear. Thousands of plebians and patricians file onto the wood benches that surround the Circus Maximus' oval racing track, ready for the day's entertainment. A dozen trumpets blare outside the stadium, signaling the entry of the game's participants.

Scipio rides into the stadium, flanked by Laelius and Lucius. All three wear silver-plated battle armor, their blood-red capes flowing down to the backs of their white stallions. Amelia and the two Scipio children follow in a white chariot, waving enthusiastically at the crowd. The

Cato's Wars

Scipio party rides to the center stands and sits under the white linen awning provided for them. Scipio stands and waves to the crowd, acknowledging their cheers.

A dozen flute players stride into the racing grounds, playing lively dancing tunes. A score of svelte young women follow them, spinning about in diaphanous white gowns, their moves coordinated with the flute players' notes.

The foot racers follow them, then the horse racers and the charioteers. All of them wave at the cheering crowds, bowing their heads toward those that call out their names. The crowds cheer the racers enthusiastically, but they are saving their loudest accolades for those that come next.

The gladiators march onto the race grounds, and the stadium erupts with deafening roars. Thirty pairs of gladiators parade in, each man marching with the one he will fight. A trident and net gladiator walks next to a hoplomachus bearing a sword and small shield. A heavily armored samnite fighter walks next to a scissor warrior garbed in quilted coverings, his right arm encased in an iron tube that ends in a half-moon blade.[cxcii] Each gladiator wears a red or blue ribbon about his arm, the red for those from the school of Rufus, the blue for those from the ludus of Certus.

Prima walks at the head of the procession, wearing only a black leather loincloth and breastband. For this game she fights as a dimachaerus, forsaking a shield to fight with twin swords. In honor of Scipio's victory at Zama, her opponent has the armor and weapons of a Carthaginian soldier.

The procession moves along the two-thousand-foot length of the circus, turning at the race post to march back the other way. The participants exit the stadium and mass outside their entry point, waiting for their turn in the competitions.

The games open with a foot race, one group racing the length of the track, the other three lengths. Scipio awards each winner with a laurel wreath, clasping forearms with him as the crowd cheers. He repeats the process for the winners of the horse and chariot races, holding their arms aloft until the cheers reach a crescendo.

Two hours later, the last of the charioteers trundle from the stadium, the slaves dragging away the wrecked chariots and bodies. The crowd quiets, waiting for the highlight of the games.

The trumpets blare. The gladiators march back into the stadium, accompanied by a dozen former gladiators who will act as referees. The thirty pairs of fighters face Scipio and salute him with their weapons.

Scipio rises and waves his hand in acknowledgement. "Commence!" he shouts.

The gladiators spread out and warily circle each other, measuring their opponents' stance and movements. The referees crouch down and watch the pairs nearest to them. The stadium trumpeters and organists blare out fast-paced tunes, the volume rising to increase the drama.

A gladiator clashes swords with another, and the melee' begins. The fighters dart in and out, feinting and jabbing, looking for the strike that will disable their opponent.

A retiarius ensnares a hoplomachus and yanks him off his feet. As the gladiator crashes to the ground the retiarius darts in and stabs his trident against the swordsman's chest, drawing a trickle of blood. A referee rushes in and raises the retiarius' arm, signifying his victory. As the crowd roars, the retiarius steps back and watches the other matches, waiting for his next opponent.

Fighting in the center of the combatants, Prima makes short work of her Carthaginian opponent. She blocks his thrust with her left sword and chops into his calf with her right blade, crashing him to the earth. She leaps upon him and plants her foot on his throat, her blade poised above his terror-stricken eyes. The Carthaginian raises his finger, signaling his surrender. A referee moves in and raises Prima's arm in victory.

Prima spins about and treads toward the waiting retiarius, whirling her blades like the scythed wheels of a chariot.

The retiarius jumps forward and sweeps his net toward her feet. Prima springs into the air, the net whooshing under her. She lands in front of the retiarius, grinning malevolently.

The gladiators stabs his trident at her face. Prima catches the fork in one blade and knocks it aside with the other. Spinning sideways, she sweeps her foot under the gladiator's left ankle and topples him, grabbing his net as he falls. She bends over and flings the net upon him, watching him ensnare himself in his effort to escape it. The referee reaches to grab her arm, but she is already striding toward her next opponent.

Laelius watches raptly. "Look at her, isn't she beautiful?" he says to Scipio.

"She moves so quickly without all that armor," Scipio replies. "I should try that on my velites."

"Oh gods, you are right! She doesn't have any protection!" Laelius wails. "If anyone hurts her, I will simply die. Then I'll kill whoever did it!"

The match pauses while the remaining fourteen fighters drink water and bandage their cuts. Scipio claps his hands and the matches resume. A half hour later, only two fighters remain.

The man who faces Prima is Rufus' best fighter, the victor of two dozen combats. The short and stocky man has a thick layer of fat about his belly, the better to protect his organs from cuts and slashes. He fights as a thraex, wielding a Thracian's short curved sword and small square shield, his bronze greaves rising above his knees. He raises the visor on his black plumed helmet and stares derisively at the gladiatrix.

"You have no business in this ring, woman," he growls.

"You should tell that to the six men I just defeated, pig-face."

"Hah! I'm not going to be watching your tits and ass like the rest of them," he says so low that only she can hear. "I'll be watching your throat. I'm going to cut it wide open."

"To the death then," she spits. "No mercy or quarter."

The thraex darts forward with dazzling speed. Prima spreads her arms out, her two swords ready to slash. The thraex steps in and swipes his thick shield to the left, blocking Prima's right hand cut.

Prima's left blade flashes down, but the man catches it with his thick leather arm protector. The gladius cuts through the thick covering and into his shoulder. The thraex howls in pain, but he does not pause in his attack.

The gladiator rams his body into Prima, knocking her backward. As she stumbles, the thraex reaches behind her and slices his dagger down her lower back. Prima screams. She trots backward, distancing herself from her opponent.

"Aah!" Laelius screams. He jumps from his seat and clambers down the seats, heading for the ring. Two stadium guards appear in front of him, their hands on their swords.

Laelius grapples for his dagger. He feels a steely hand on his shoulder.

"Leave her be," Scipio says. "She is twice the fighter he is. And she would never forgive you."

Panting with fury, Laelius resumes his seat. "I'll kill him if she doesn't, I swear to Mars."

Regaining her footing, Prima circles the thraex, drawing ever closer. She sees him beckoning her forward with his shield. She feels her warm blood trickling down between her buttocks, dribbling onto the sands between her feet.

The fat prick will soon tire with all that armor on him. But I am losing blood. It has to be quick.

Prima closes upon the thraex. She jabs at him with her two swords, taking advantage of her blades' longer reach over his dagger. The man deflects the blows with his shield and dagger, but Prima does not relent. She thrusts and slashes at him, her swords whirling in front of his face.

The gladiator slowly retreats, his eyes fixed on her weapons.

Prima edges to his right and continues her attack, moving him toward a fallen shield that lies behind him. *Now!* she decides.

The gladiatrix leaps forward, screaming so loud the plebians in the rear seats blink in surprise. Her swords become a swirling maelstrom. She batters one blade against his shield as she clangs another off his greaves, still screaming her attack. The thraex calmly retreats, knowing she will weaken soon.

His left foot steps upon the curved shield behind him. He stumbles sideways, raising his shield for balance. As quick as a striking snake, Prima's left blade knocks aside his dagger. Her other sword darts in and plunges into his underarm. The man gasps with pain. His shield falls from his grasp.

Prima ducks low and strikes again, Her razor-sharp blade severs the tendons in the back of the gladiator's knee, bringing him crashing to the earth. The thraex howls with pain, rolling about as he grabs his leg. The crowd cheers wildly, overcoming the scattered boos of those who bet on the thraex.

Prima stands over her fallen foe, gasping for breath. The referee rushes in to declare Prima the victor. Prima sees him coming. She shakes her head.

The gladiatrix plunges her blade into the fallen thraex's throat, pinning his head to the ground. The gladiator grasps feebly at the hilt of her blade, his lifeblood gurgling from his mouth. Prima bends over him.

"You wanted this to the death, prick. You have your wish."

The referee raises Prima's left hand, her gladius standing high above her head. The crowd claps and snaps their fingers as they cheer, the patricians flapping the ends of their toga.[cxciii] Many of the onlookers do not appreciate the sight of a woman defeating a man, but all recognize a ruthless fighter when they see one.

Prima stumbles toward the Scipio dais. She sees Rufus glaring at her from the front row, furious that she killed his prize gladiator.

"Send me a bill," she shouts to him.

Two slave attendants rush out and wrap a bandage around Prima's bleeding back. She raises her arms over her head, grateful for their ministrations.

Scipio steps into the ring, followed by an anxious Laelius. Prima drops her other sword and waves toward Laelius.

"I am fine, Love. Just let me finish this."

Scipio raises the laurel wreath high above his head, letting the crowd's roar reach a crescendo. Prima kneels before Scipio and kisses his hand.

"To the victor," Scipio shouts. "Long live Rome and the People's Republic!" He places the wreath upon Prima's sweaty brow.

Prima looks up at Scipio. A grin comes to her blood-spattered face.

"If this doesn't get you the people's vote, nothing will!"

An hour later, the last of the stadium crowd has left the Circus Maximus. The Scipio party has borrowed two of the chariot teams for their journey home, and they make their way toward the Scipio manse. They ride through the main streets of Rome, Scipio pausing to lean over and shake hands with the worshipful citizens that line the streets.

The chariots pass under dozens of Amelia's campaign banners. *The dyers request the election of Scipio Africanus,* read some. *Make Scipio consul of Rome. He is a good man,* say others. Some are aimed at Cassius Metellus, Scipio's Latin Party opponent. *The company of late drinkers all favor Cassius Metellus,* they declare.[cxciv]

Laelius and Prima direct their charioteer to take them to the Julii mansion, where Prima can receive further attention from her Greek medicus. Scipio and Amelia disembark at the front door of their domus, handing over the sleeping Publius and Cornelia to their nurses.

The two stretch out on the atrium couches. The house slaves bring them a small platter of bread and cheese, along with small jug of watered wine. Scipio pitches bread crumbs into the fish pond, watching the carp rise to feed upon them.

"Well, wife, that is the last of it. The last of our money and the last of our time. Tomorrow's elections will tell the tale."

"I wish I knew what would happen," Amelia says. "We have done everything we can. But the Latins mounted that rumor campaign about you being a thief."

"Hardly just a rumor," Scipio says, "although what I took, I spent for Rome." He rubs his eyes and chuckles. "At least Cato wasn't here to condemn me with his street speeches." He smiles as he raises his wine to his lips. "He's probably out in the mountains, lecturing the Iberians on the virtues of drinking vinegar and water!"

TARRACO, IBERIA. 194 BCE. Winter arrives early in northeastern Iberia. It finds a victorious Cato residing in the beautiful port city of Tarraco, preparing for his return to Rome.

With all of Northern Iberia under his control, Cato has relaxed his ascetic values. He allows himself some of the wine and food he has plundered from a dozen Iberian garrisons. Every day he visits the Roman baths and wrestles in its adjoining gymnasium. Every week, he sacrifices at the temple of Mars, grateful for his good fortune in war.

Cato sits in his headquarters, contemplating a venture against a distant Celtiberian garrison. His attendant ushers in a one-armed man clad in a red-bordered toga, one of the disabled veterans that Rome employs as official messengers.

"Come in, legionnaire," Cato says warmly. "He points to a table next to him. "Will you take wine with me? Perhaps a slice of boar? They are both quite tasty."

The veteran grins. "A bit of food would be nice. The seas were unfriendly; I found it difficult to take sustenance while we were under sail." He hands Cato a papyrus scroll. "This is for you, Consul."

The messenger grabs a slice of meat from Cato's laden food table. "The election results are in there," he says between chews.

Cato unrolls the scroll and begins reading, eager for news from home. He stops, staring at the papyrus. His hands grip the ends of the scroll. His mouth tightens into a line of bitterness.

"Leave me," he says, his voice toneless. The messenger takes one look at Cato's face and hurries from the room.

Cato crumples the papyrus and flings it into a corner. He pulls at his ear, his eyes glazed with bewilderment. *How could it be? Just when we took control again!*

There is a knock at the door. "Enter," Cato growls. His white-haired attendant peers inside.

"You are well?" he asks. "The messenger said you appeared ill."

"I am not ill, Caldus. It is bad news from home."

"Oh, I am sorry, Consul. A death in the family?"

Cato sighs. "More like the death of Rome. Scipio Africanus has been elected consul. Again! Gods damn him!" His attendant quietly withdraws.

Cato pounds the arm of his chair. *He'll undo all that we have done this year! Taxes will go back up. He'll befriend Carthage and that treacherous Hannibal.*

A feral gleam comes to his eyes. *Scipio's too powerful to defeat in the Senate. But Flaccus could take care of him. He knows the Aventine's Men of the Night, they could...*

Cato jerks his head up. What *am I contemplating?* He thinks of his hero, the incorruptible Dentatus. Fear creeps into his heart. *My gods, I am losing myself! I am becoming like them.*

The consul jumps from his command chair and stalks to his food table. With one sweep of his thickly calloused hand, he plows its jugs and platters to the floor. Muttering curses to himself, he grabs his plush bed mat and flings it on top of the food.

"Caldus!" he yells. His attendant scurries back in. "Get rid of this mess. Bring me a watered pitcher of vinegar, and a straw bed mat." Caldus summons four slaves. They quickly haul out the mess and bring Cato his requests.

Cato stands in the center of the room, lost in thought, the slaves bustling around him. He snaps his fingers.

"Fetch my copy of the Twelve Tables," Cato orders. Caldus returns with a thick scroll that contains the twelve rules of Roman law.[cxcv] "Leave me," he orders, unrolling the scroll.

Cato spends the next hour sitting cross-legged on the floor, pouring over Rome's lengthy sets of rules. He pauses when he comes to the Eighth Table. "There!" He reads the passage aloud, his voice rising with excitement.

A thief shall pay double damages for what he has stolen.[cxcvi]

Cato rolls up the scroll and leans back in his chair, tapping his forefinger on its arm. *With all the money Scipio stole from his conquests in Iberia and Carthage, he would be completely bankrupt! And completely disgraced. That would be worse than death.*

Cato's eyes blaze with excitement. "Caldus! Bring two silver goblets. No, wait—I forget myself. Bring me two pottery cups." When his attendant returns, Cato pours two cups of watered vinegar. He gives one to Caldus, who wrinkles his nose at it.

"Let us have a celebratory drink," Cato says, wearing one of his rare smiles.

"Wh-what are we drinking to?" Caldus asks.

"We drink to the Twelve Tables, from which no man is exempt. Under its laws, even a hero can meet his deserved fate."

Cato's Wars

PORT OF OSTIA, 194 BCE. Publius Scipio hauls in the sail on his tiny catboat. He leans over the railing, balancing the boat as it lurches over the choppy Mediterranean waves. Scipio's nine-year-old son grins widely, exuberant with the thrill of bobbing along the seacoast, the sun baking into his light brown skin.

In the distance, barely within his sight, a weathered fishing boat sits at anchor in the sea. The ship's two occupants lean over the boat, slowly pulling up their fishing net. The fishermen's heads are bent over the side, but their eyes do not leave the tiny catboat.

"That's him, Jammal," one fisherman says, his Latin heavily accented.

"Yes, it's the Scipio spawn," Sami replies.

"Publius! Poo-bliuuss," comes a cry from the shore. Laelius stands at the head of a sturdy pier that juts a quarter-mile into the water. "Come on in now. Your father and mother want to go back to Rome."

"One more turn around the dock, please Uncle Laelius?" Publius whines.

"'Now' is what I said," Laelius replies, his voice stern. "Don't make me swim out after you. It's unseemly for an admiral to be chasing a catboat."

"Oh very well." Publius says, pouting. He close-hauls the sail and slowly drifts back to the dock. Laelius waits for him with arms crossed.

Publius ties up the small boat and springs onto the pier. He and Laelius stroll toward their waiting horses. Out on the sea, the fishermen watch them go.

"We let him get away," Jammal hisses.

Sami sneers at him. "Dolt! Now we know he comes here to sail. We just have to bide our time. We still have two months."

"Two months before the boy leaves?" Jammal says.

"No. Two months before we deliver him to Antiochus."

459

TEMPLE OF BELLONA, ROME, 194 BCE. The nightingale trills out her honeyed song, celebrating the dusk's banquet of flying insects. She hops about the sacred oak trees that surround this beautiful little temple, oblivious to the somber men sitting on the steps below her.

Here, on the outskirts of Rome, Consul Scipio Africanus has gathered his inner circle of allies. Two months into his new consulship, he has realized that he has no time to spare. Rome's greatest threat gathers strength, at a time when he feels his own vitality fading. War looms— Scipio has plans to make and battles to fight.

Tiberius Sempronius sits next to Scipio. The new consul proudly wears the purple-bordered tunic that signifies his high office. Laelius and Lucius lounge next to him, chatting amiably about the upcoming religious games.

Tribune Marcus Amelius sits behind them. He has recently returned from Flamininus' army in Greece. He is eager to work with the man his father Marcus Silenus called the greatest man in the world. Two dozen Hellenic senators join the men, the same ones that met here seven years ago.

Amelia and Prima sit inside the temple landing, watching the men converse. Prima runs her hands over her bulging belly.

"Are you going train this one for the ring?" Amelia asks. "Or will that depend upon it being a boy or a girl?"

"No, Laelius and I have killed enough people for the entire family. If it's a boy, maybe he could become one of these new jurisconsults I keep hearing about—a person who studies the law. I think there's a future in that."

Amelia chuckles. "Good. My husband will need someone to defend him, if Cato brings him to trial."

The women see Scipio stand up and walk into the oak grove. He rustles about in the bushes and emerges with a shining silver javelin.

"Seven years ago I cast a spear from these steps, declaring war on the

460

Latin Party," Scipio says. "Now we have a new war to wage."

"Antiochus?" Marcus asks.

Scipio nods. "Hannibal has joined him, and the Aetolians may not be far behind. And King Philip—who knows what he will do? We only know that the Syrians are coming, and that Macedonia and Aetolia may not be far behind." He pitches the javelin toward the east.

"We will need all our allies. This isn't a war of nations, it's a war of empires. And I plan to win it."

Late that evening, Scipio pads into his sleeping chamber, weary with the day's activities. He picks Marcus Silenus' helmet off the shelf above his sleeping pallet and sits it on the side of his bed, caressing its battered helm.

"Well, old friend, we're getting near the end. I hope I can stay healthy long enough to fight one more battle, and get to the Syrians before the Latins get to me."

He feels his right arm twitch, his hand convulsing into a claw. "Maybe I should just retire to Liternum, while I still have some years left to me. Haven't I done enough?"

Scipio stares into the helmet's yawning darkness. He chuckles. "I know—that's the coward's way out. Your son would say the same thing." His voice chokes. "Gods, Marcus, he is so much like you, you would be so proud!"

Scipio bounces the helmet in his hands. "Very well, I will stay. It's the only honorable path. Would you be ashamed of me for hoarding plunder from my victories? I swear on my children, I saw no other way to do what we needed to do."

He taps the helmet's crown, his lips tight. "And I see no other way than what I am going to do to Lucius—and dear Laelius."

"Are you going to bed?" Amelia says, her voice echoing in from the atrium. "Wait for me, and I will make it worth your while."

"Then I will certainly wait," Scipio replies.

Scipio Africanus gently places the helmet back on the shelf. He stretches out on his pallet, his arms folded behind his head. He studies the ceiling's fresco of him battling Hannibal at Zama.

Will we meet one more time. old friend? Who will be the victor then?

About the Author

Martin Tessmer is a retired professor of instructional design and technology. He also worked as a training consultant to the US Navy, Coast Guard, and Air Force.

The author of twelve nonfiction and fiction books, his most current endeavor is the Scipio Africanus Saga, which includes *Scipio Rising*, *The Three Generals*, *Scipio's Dream*, and *Scipio Risen*.

He lives in Denver with Hector and Rita, his two Australian Cattle Dogs.

End Notes

[i] https://en.wikiquote.org/wiki/Scipio_Africanus

[ii] Gabriel, Richard. *Scipio Africanus: Rome's Greatest General.* Dulles, Virginia: Potomac Books, 2008. p. xxii.

[iii] Martin Tessmer. "Three Victories." *The Three Generals.* Denver, CO: Dancing in Chains Publications, 2015.

[iv] Livy. *Rome and the Mediterranean. Books XXXI-XLV of The History of Rome from its Foundation.* Translated by Henry Bettenson. London: Penguin Books, 1976. Book 31, Section 1, Page 24.

[v] Ibid.

[vi] Mutina was the archaic name for Modena, Italy.

[vii] Livy, 31, 2, 25.

[viii] Ibid.

[ix] Ibid.

[x] https://en.wikiquote.org/wiki/Virgil

[xi] *Scipio Rising*, by Martin Tessmer.

[xii] https://www.google.com/#q=first+macedonian+war

[xiii] Also called Abydo, this is now part of northern Turkey, in the Dardanelles.

[xiv] Livy, 31, 15, 34.

[xv] Livy, 31, 17, 36.

[xvi] Ibid.

xvii Ibid.

xviii The first Macedonian War formally ended in 205 BCE, with Macedonia and Rome making peace with each other.

xix Livy, 31, 18, 37.

xx Ibid.

xxi Gabriel, p. 205.

xxii https://en.wikipedia.org/wiki/Carthago_delenda_est

xxiii http://www.aesopfables.com/aesop1.html

xxiv Capitol of the Seleucid empire. Located near the site of present-day Antakya in southern Turkey.

xxv Antiochus' brother was murdered. https://en.wikipedia.org/wiki/Antiochus_III_the_Great#cite_note-11

xxvi Parthia was located in what is now a region of northeastern Iran.

xxvii These cavalry were also called the Companions, as well as the King's Friends or Royal Friends. To avoid confusion with the Macedonian Companions, I have used the "Friends" appellation. https://en.wikipedia.org/wiki/Philoi

xxviii http://www.womenintheancientworld.com/divorceinancientrome.htm

xxix "Real power lay with the nobiles, an inner circle of senators from a small number of the oldest families." Gabriel, p. 204.

xxx https://en.wikipedia.org/wiki/Temple_of_Bellona,_Rome

xxxi Gabriel, p. 204.

xxxii Gabriel, p. 208. Gabriel states that Flamininus was likely on the committee at Scipio's suggestion.

xxxiii Livy, 31, 6, 27.

xxxiv http://www.premierexhibitions.com/exhibitions/4/4/bodies-exhibition/blog/edentulous-brief-history-dentures

xxxv Ibid.

xxxvi Ibid.

xxxvii Ibid.

xxxviii Livy, 31, 7, 29.

xxxix Ibid, p. 28.

xl https://en.wikipedia.org/wiki/Publius_Sulpicius_Galba_Maximus

xli *Scipio Risen*, "The Raid," p. 133.

xlii https://en.wikipedia.org/wiki/Piacenza

xliii Livy, 31, 10, 31.

xliv Livy, 31, 19, 38.

xlv Livy, Ibid.

xlvi https://en.wikipedia.org/wiki/Hundred_and_Four

xlvii Livy, 31, 19, 38.

xlviii Ibid.

xlix Present day site of Euboea, Greece.

l Livy, 31, 14, 33.

li Ibid.

[lii] A.H. McDonald. Introduction to *Livy: Rome and the Mediterranean, p.12.*

[liii] Located near the southeast coast of modern-day Albania.

[liv] http://www.ancient.eu/Gladius_Hispaniensis/

[lv] Ibid, 31, 21, 39.

[lvi] Ibid.

[lvii] Ibid, 31, 21, 40.

[lviii] Ibid.

[lix] https://en.wikipedia.org/wiki/Battle_of_Cremona_(200_BC)

[lx] http://www.unrv.com/economy/roman-taxes.php

[lxi] Livy, 31, 30, 49.

[lxii] Livy, 31, 33, 53.

[lxiii] Ibid.

[lxiv] Ibid, 31, 34, 54.

[lxv] Ibid.

[lxvi] Ibid

[lxvii] http://www.crystalinks.com/rometheatre.html

[lxviii] Ibid, 31, 35, 54.

[lxix] https://en.wikipedia.org/wiki/Companion_cavalry

[lxx] https://en.wikipedia.org/wiki/Companion_cavalry

[lxxii] Ibid.

[lxxiii] Livy, 38, 57, 393.

[lxxiv] Livy, 31, 37, 56.

[lxxv] Ibid.

[lxxvi] Ibid.

[lxxvii] Livy, 31, 38, p. 58

[lxxviii] Ibid.

[lxxix] https://www.realmofhistory.com/2016/03/09/25-incredible-roman-quotes-you-should-know/

[lxxx] Brunner, Theodore. Marijuana in Ancient Greece and Rome? The Literary Evidence. *Journal of Psychedelic Drugs*, 9, 3, 221-225. http://dx.doi.org/10.1080/02791072.1977.10472052

[lxxxi] The Numidian king who Scipio defeated in *Scipio Rising*.

[lxxxii] https://en.wikipedia.org/wiki/Roman_litigation

[lxxxiii] https://en.wikipedia.org/wiki/Mamertine_Prison

[lxxxiv] Plutarch. *Roman Lives*. Trans. by Robin Waterfield. Oxford: The University Press, 1999, p. 14.

[lxxxv] In Harold Johnson's *Private Life of the Romans*, he notes that by the end of the Republic era, sixty-six days were devoted to public games. http://www.forumromanum.org/life/johnston_9.html

[lxxxvi] http://ancientolympics.arts.kuleuven.be/eng/TC007cEN.html

[lxxxvii] http://archive.archaeology.org/0811/abstracts/gladiator.html

[lxxxviii] Located near the Golan Heights of modern Israel and Syria. https://en.wikipedia.org/wiki/Battle_of_Panium

[lxxxix] https://en.wikipedia.org/wiki/Battle_of_Panium

[xc] Livy, 32, 9, 78.

[xci] https://en.wikipedia.org/wiki/Hannibal

[xcii] https://en.wikipedia.org/wiki/Carthago_delenda_est

[xciii] Livy, 32, 9, 76.

[xciv] Philip lent Hannibal a phalanx of his best men. Scipio's army defeated them at the battle of Zama (see *Scipio Risen*).

[xcv] Ibid, 32, 10, 77.

[xcvi] Rickard, J (5 November 2008), *Battle of the Aous, 24 June 198* , http://www.historyofwar.org/articles/battles_aous.html

[xcvii] Ibid.

[xcviii] Ibid.

[xcix] Livy, 32, 12, 79.

[c] Ibid.

[ci] Ibid.

[cii] Ibid, p. 79.

[ciii] Livy, 32, 13, 79.

[civ] Livy, 32, 28, 96.

[cv] Ibid.

[cvi] Ibid.

cvii https://en.wikipedia.org/wiki/Lex_Oppia

cviii Cato became praetor to Sardinia in 198 BCE, and it was likely through a consular appointment. https://en.wikipedia.org/wiki/Cato_the_Elder#Aedile_and_praetor

cix "Three Vows." In *Scipio Rising: Book One of the Scipio Africanus Saga.*

cx According to Plutarch (*Roman Lives*), Cato learned Greek later in life, although there are suspicions that he covertly learned Grecian language and literature much earlier. https://en.wikipedia.org/wiki/Cato_the_Elder#Later_years

cxi https://en.wikiquote.org/wiki/Cato_the_Elder

cxii Livy, 33, 7, 113.

cxiii https://en.wikipedia.org/wiki/Battle_of_Cynoscephalae

cxiv Ibid.

cxv Livy, 33, 8, 115.

cxvi Livy, 33, 9, 114.

cxvii Polybius. *The Histories.* Kindle ebook, p. 426.

cxviii Livy, 33, 10, 116.

cxix Ibid.

cxx Livy, 33, 9, 116.

cxxi Ibid.

cxxii The "Primus Pilus." https://en.wikipedia.org/wiki/Primus_pilus

[cxxiii] Livy, 33, 9, 116.

[cxxiv] Ibid, 117.

[cxxv] Polybius, p. 427.

[cxxvi] Livy, 33, 11, 117.

[cxxvii] https://en.m.wikisource.org/wiki/1911_Encyclop%C3%A6dia_Britannica/Marsi

[cxxviii] Livy, 33, 36, 129.

[cxxix] Ibid.

[cxxx] Ibid.

[cxxxi] Near present day Como, Italy.

[cxxxii] Livy, 33, 36, 129.

[cxxxiii] Ibid.

[cxxxiv] Ibid.

[cxxxv] Martin Tessmer, *The Three Generals: Book Two of the Scipio Africanus Saga*. Amazon.com

[cxxxvi] A large neck torque was taken from this battle and hung in the Capitol as a gift to Jupiter. Livy, 33, 37, 130.

[cxxxvii] Livy, 33, 37, 131.

[cxxxviii] Ibid.

cxxxix https://www.google.com/#q=battle+of+cannae+maharbal

cxl https://en.wikipedia.org/wiki/Atlantic_torpedo

cxli https://en.wikipedia.org/wiki/Medicine_in_ancient_Rome#Herbal_a
nd_other_medicines

cxlii This sentiment is echoed by Flamininus in Livy, 33, 13, 119.

cxliii Ibid.

cxliv Livy, 33, 12, 118.

cxlv Livy, 33, 30, 124.

cxlvi Plutarch. *Roman Lives*, p. 13.

cxlvii https://en.wikipedia.org/wiki/Cato_the_Elder

cxlviii Part of modern-day Turkey, near the Hellespont.

cxlix https://en.wikipedia.org/wiki/Peltast

cl Plutarch. *Roman Lives*. Trans. by Robin Waterfield. Oxford: The
University Press, 1999, p. 14.

cli Ibid, p. 15.

clii Livy, 33, 40, 133.

cliii Ibid.

cliv Ibid.

clv In fact, the rumor of Ptolemy's death was greatly exaggerated.
Antiochus did not learn this until later.

[clvi] Livy, 33, 43, 134.

[clvii] Livy, 33, 43, 135.

[clviii] Nero used an emerald for the same purpose.
http://www.museumofvision.org/exhibitions/?key=44&subkey=4&relk
ey=29

[clix] Livy, 33, 45, 136.

[clx] Livy, 33, 47, 138.

[clxi] Ibid.

[clxii] Livy, 34, 5, 147.

[clxiii] Livy, 34, 7, 150.

[clxiv] Located in present-day Iraq, on the banks of the Tigris River.
https://en.wikipedia.org/wiki/Seleucia

[clxv] Livy, 33, 41, 134.

[clxvi] http://www.amputee-coalition.org/resources/a-brief-history-of-
prosthetics/

[clxvii] Livy, 33, 46, 137.

[clxviii] Ibid.

[clxix] Similar to our Senate, Carthage's Senate would appoint special-
purpose committees from its ranks.
https://en.wikipedia.org/wiki/Ancient_Carthage#Government

[clxx] Livy, 33, 48, 138.

[clxxi] https://en.wikipedia.org/wiki/Lysistrata

clxxii http://www.maicar.com/GML/Lemnos.html

clxxiii Livy, 34, 1, 141.

clxxiv Livy, 34, 2, 142.

clxxv Ibid.

clxxvi Livy, 34, 3, 143.

clxxvii Livy, 34, 5, 147.

clxxviii Livy, 34, 8, 151.

clxxix http://www.ancient-origins.net/ancient-places-europe/gambling-ancient-civilizations-00931

clxxx Near modern day Selcuk, Turkey.

clxxxi Livy, 33, 49, 140.

clxxxii *Scipio Risen*, pp. 399-400.

clxxxiii Rome's patricians and equites would buy insulae as an investment. https://forums.spacebattles.com/threads/roman-insulae.523981/

clxxxiv Now known as Ampurias, Spain.

clxxxv Livy, 34, 14, 155.

clxxxvi Ibid.

clxxxvii Livy, 34, 15, 156.

clxxxviii Ibid.

clxxxix Livy, 34, 16, 157.

cxc https://en.wikipedia.org/wiki/Nomenclator_(nomenclature)

cxci https://followinghadrian.com/2015/03/16/a-taste-of-ancient-rome-pullum-numidicum-numidian-chicken-and-conchicla-cum-faba-beans-with-cumin/

cxcii https://en.m.wikipedia.org/wiki/List_of_Roman_gladiator_types

cxciii "The ancient Romans had a set rituals at public performances to express degrees of approval: snapping the finger and thumb, clapping with the flat or hollow palm, and waving the flap of the toga." https://en.wikipedia.org/wiki/Applause

cxciv These slogans are based on the ones found on the walls of Pompeii. https://sourcebooks.fordham.edu/ancient/pompeii-inscriptions.asp

cxcv https://en.wikipedia.org/wiki/Twelve_Tables

cxcvi Ibid, Article 18a.

Manufactured by Amazon.ca
Bolton, ON